**Rumors of War
By Peggy Tibbetts**
© 1999
Lunatic Fringe Publishing, all rights reserved

Rumors of War

Copyright 1999 by Peggy Tibbetts
Published by Lunatic Fringe Publishing
All rights reserved, including the right to reproduce this book or portions thereof in any form or by any means, electronic, mechanical, photcopying, recording or otherwise without written permission of the publisher.

For information regarding permissions, write to
Lunatic Fringe Publishing
PO Box 129
Silt, CO 81652

ISBN 0-9677868-0-0

Design by Ema Kwiatkowski

First printing February 2000
Printed in the USA

Part One

1

Bursts of lightning peeled across the sky. Bombs of thunder rolled along the autumn wind, feeding insomnia. A thunderstorm in November was a seldom, if ever, occurrence in northeastern Minnesota. So was the notion of war.

Holding his wife in his arms Philip Singleton pondered, "How many more nights will we have together like this?"

Overcome by his honest regret, Ilene's tears dripped onto his fuzzy naked chest like raindrops from the storm that intruded upon their dreary night. They made love over and over, as if passion could dilute the sadness. They barely slept.

The call came at dawn that Saturday morning, November 17, 1990. They'd been expecting it since Thursday when Philip's reserve unit went on alert status.

He grasped the phone as he sat up in bed, gazing forlornly through the windowpane at the leafless aspen treetops. Brooding, Ilene stared in the opposite direction at the sun rising like a red balloon over Lake Superior's drifting horizon.

Philip put the phone down and said, "We report to the base on Park Point this Wednesday at 0700. We leave for McCoy in one week."

Feeling the walls of time closing in around her, she asked, "Then what?"

He sighed and scratched his rumpled brown locks. "No word yet on our mission. But I still don't think they'll send us over to Saudi."

She flopped onto her stomach and pounded the bedding. "I can't believe the timing. We just moved in for chrissake. This house isn't even finished."

Five years ago, they'd decided to build a house. One of the resident interns at St. Mary's where Philip worked as a lab technician, had re-upped in the Army Reserve to supplement his income so he and his wife could afford to build. The whole idea had appealed to Philip, especially since he'd been a Naval officer in Vietnam, medical corps on an aircraft carrier. With his veteran's status, he joined the Reserve as a well-paid sergeant in a gentleman's career Army. No boot camp, just two weekends a month of training workshops plus summer camp. The 477th was a medical reserve unit. Ilene secretly believed that the training games afforded him the excitement of playing doctor without the pressures of a physician's life.

And Uncle Sam paid well, providing them with the extra cash they needed to get through the construction of what had become an incredible piece of architecture. They'd spared no expense, adorning the house with more than fifty-seven custom made windows, which ate up the budget, leaving them without the funds for finishing things like cabinets, moldings, frames, light fixtures, carpeting, window coverings—not to mention the basement.

"I'll get a hold of the contractor today," Philip offered.

"I can take care of that," Ilene argued. "You work on getting yourself out of this Desert Shield gig."

"That's not going to happen," he told her. "Right now I'm more concerned with getting a crew back in here."

"I thought we were going to wait on the finish work because of the money," she protested.

"We'll have the money sooner than I expected." He looked away, adding hastily, "I called my father. He's writing up sort of a loan."

"*Sort of?*" she drawled. "Donald Singleton is president of the National Bank of Chicago. Obviously it's a loan."

"Whatever. He's got the money," Philip said flatly.

"Can't we get through this without borrowing more money?" she complained.

Not that money was ever a problem. Throughout the past nine years, Philip had managed their financial affairs effortlessly. Even though he worked as a lab technician, he'd lived alone for more than a decade and had come into their marriage debt free. Unlike his bride, whose baggage contained a pile of past due bills.

Until three years ago Ilene held onto her job in the chancellor's office at the university. Finding the details connected with owning land and building a house more challenging, she left office politics behind. Of course the girls loved having her work at home. She kept her own bank account as a cash reserve for the project. But without her paycheck it was Philip who deposited funds these days.

Tossing his hands in the air, Philip fumed at her. "What do you expect me to do? You and the girls have to get by somehow, while I'm gone. Not to mention this house. I don't want to be stuck down at McCoy worried about what's going on up here."

Ilene tugged on her nightshirt. "You'll be a phone call away. Anyway I bet you guys'll be down there for a month. Two months tops. Once Bush scares the shit out of everybody and Saddam releases the hostages, it'll all be over."

Philip shrugged. "Rumor has it we might've been called up to fill in for personnel shortages at the bases out east."

She chewed her thumbnail. "That's all part of their military propaganda."

He shrugged. "Even if that's true, for now I have to play the game."

"What about your job?"

"According to hospital policy, the job will be waiting for me when I get back."

"There's got to be a way to get you out of this," she said. " Why can't your father use his political clout to get you a discharge?"

He shook his head woodenly. "Believe me, over the past couple days I've called everyone but the Pope. Hardship discharge is the only cause they'll even consider. Building a house doesn't exactly qualify. I'm in, till I'm out."

"But that's not till next June." The nauseating reality seeped through her.

Philip nodded in resignation. "That's why it's so important that we get this place finished as soon as possible."

"That seems so obsessive." Resenting the panic she sensed in him, she didn't doubt for a second she could supervise the finish construction. After all, if it wasn't for her persistence with the wholesaler back in July, they'd still be waiting for roof trusses. Anyway she didn't believe this military thing would amount to anything more than a temporary disruption in their lives. "If you ask me, the smart thing to do is put everything on hold until this Desert Shield thing blows over."

"Can't do that." Noticeably switching gears, Philip hopped out of bed and pulled on a long-sleeved T-shirt and blue jeans. "All we need is a few guys from Wilson Builders in here. They can handle what's left."

"Where are you going now?" she asked wistfully.

"Just remembered Terry Wilson has breakfast every Saturday at Perkins. Maybe I can catch him there."

"You just can't let go of the reins."

Philip searched for his wallet. "That's right." His kiss lasted longer than any other normal Saturday morning kiss. "I'm outa here."

After he left, she stretched across the bed for the phone and dialed her best friend, Cathy's number. A trademark military gag order had accompanied the initial alert papers. But Ilene hadn't paid much attention. She'd confided in Cathy as soon as Philip's unit went on alert status.

"Hullo." Cathy's voice sounded thick with sleep when she answered.
"Oops. Didn't mean to wake you." Ilene apologized.
"Ilene. That's okay. I was up with Arnie."

Arnie was Cathy and Stan Carrick's second baby. Their daughter, Sara, was almost two. After five years in and out of fertility clinics, Cathy eventually became pregnant when she was thirty-four. Compulsive by nature, she told Ilene they'd decided to go for it and get the child birthing out of the way in record time. Just in case her biological clock stopped ticking again. Two babies back-to-back like that had caused a tremendous upheaval in their lives, not to mention the unavoidable yet frustrating gaps in Ilene and Cathy's relationship.

"Philip's reserve unit was formally activated this morning."

"Ohmygod. This is just unbelievable."

"We're still in shock over here."

"Is he going to Saudi Arabia?"

"I doubt it. All we know for sure is that his unit leaves for Fort McCoy a week from today."

Cathy gasped. "One week. What's the rush?"

"Beats me. Everything's happening too fast."

"What have you told Hazy and Gladdy?"

"Little by little. They know he'll be going to McCoy for a few weeks because of Desert Shield. You know how kids are. Hazy thinks it'll make her a big shot in the fifth grade. And Gladdy wants to know how they build a shield in the desert."

Cathy laughed nervously. "Me too. This is getting really scary. Anyway, it's probably better that they're so oblivious."

"Basically, they won't know he's gone until they wake up one morning and miss their daddy real bad. Kids are funny that way."

"What about you. Are you okay?"

"He's gone off to McCoy for camp lots of times. We'll get by," Ilene reassured Cathy, and herself. "I've still got my hands full with this house."

"You're going to need help."

"You sound just like Philip. In fact he's gone out to line up a crew. Wish he'd let me handle things. He's obsessing on me."

"What do you mean?"

"He's back to full steam ahead with finishing this house. Even asked Donald for money, for God's sake."

"What else can he do? This is an emergency. That's what rich daddies are for."

"I just don't understand why he's in such a hurry to get it all done. The plan was to avoid a big loan."

"Everyone who builds a house eventually runs out of money and has to borrow. I know people with three mortgages."

"Ugh. Now *that's* scary."

"One little mortgage isn't going to kill you."

Arnie bawled in the background.

"You'd better go," Ilene warned.

"Just be glad for the help. Keep me posted."

They hung up. Ilene rolled over as her oldest daughter, Hazy bounced onto the bed.

"Wow! That storm last night was awesome," Hazy cried. Dressed in baggy jeans and a huge hyper color T-shirt, she looked ready for action.

Hugging her, Ilene smiled at the mock terror in her daughter's expression. She was named after Hazel Burton, Cathy's mom, who had been a surrogate mother to her during her tumultuous teens. Her own mom, Betty had been a major misfit in the school of raising adolescents. Hazy, as everyone knew her, died from breast cancer in 1978.

Hazel Lee Rosenthal Singleton was born two years later on March 17th. Her birth father was Bill Davies, whom Ilene had lived with for four years in the seventies. He'd left to work the gold mines north of Perth, Australia, before Hazy was born. Ilene hadn't found out she was pregnant until two months after they'd split up. She'd convinced Bill, and herself, that she could raise a kid on her own.

"Whatever you think is best. That's cool," he'd said through the phone from halfway around the world.

Child support was never an issue between the two of them. It wasn't as if they were married and planned to start a family. After she moved out on him in frustration, she'd stopped taking the pill. Her pregnancy was an unwelcome surprise at first. The night she conceived Hazy had been an impromptu parting gift when Bill came to say good-bye. Even though she wasn't in love with him anymore, the romantic notion of having his baby, to always remember his place in her life, grew on her in more ways than one. It had been *her* decision to go through with it.

Hazy reached across her mother's legs and grabbed the TV remote. The portable screen on the stand next to the bed filled with cartoon characters.

"Oo! Muppet Babies," she cooed as she stretched out on the quilt.

Back then Ilene had hoped for a boy. Sort of a *little Bill*. Maybe because their relationship had ended over his refusal to mature out of treating her like his mother. What she got was Hazy, a little girl with her daddy's spunk.

Every year Bill faithfully sent Hazy a thousand dollar money order on her birthday and Christmas. After Ilene married Philip, she tucked them in a savings account instead of cashing them in to live on. That he'd never possessed even an ounce of curiosity at meeting his daughter, squelched any flame that might have still flickered for him inside her.

She eventually moved to Duluth behind Cathy and Stan because they'd convinced her that it was a good place to raise a kid. When Hazy was only a year old, she was hospitalized with scarlet fever. Philip Singleton turned out to be the only lab technician who could draw her blood without invoking a tantrum like the other vampires did. Ilene had insisted that he alone do the deed daily. He'd already taken a special interest in Hazy's case, running interference with the bossy pediatric staff, supporting them both through a tough time. The three of them fell into love casually over six months. Much to his mother, Marie Singleton's dismay, Philip married Ilene and adopted Hazy. He was the only *Daddy* she'd ever known.

While Hazy watched cartoons, Ilene lay back against the pillows and surveyed the room. The huge master bedroom had more square footage than her first apartment. During the move in August, they used it as a living space until the walls were taped and painted downstairs. Philip had removed the headboard from their king size bed and positioned it in the far corner, surrounded on two sides by tall thermopane windows. He and Ilene grew attached to sleeping under the Big Dipper at night and waking over the north shore in the morning, so they kept it there.

She'd covered the hardwood floors with two blue and rose Oriental pattern rugs, brought up from the dining room and living room in their old split level in Lakeside. Two futons framed a low ash table at the other end of the room. Since it was the second floor and there were no neighbors in sight, she'd decided against shades or blinds, for the time being.

"Uh-oh." Hazy gasped. "Look Mom."

Ilene regarded the *Special Report* slogan as it intruded on the picture. Since Iraq invaded Kuwait, TV shows were peppered with them. Ever since Philip's unit went on alert status she dreaded them.

A local news anchorman began, "*KLKS-TV has just learned that the 477th Army Reserve Unit from Duluth has been called to active duty by the Pentagon. Information is not yet available regarding the specific mission of this medical unit. However it is clear this action is related to Operation Desert Shield. Earlier, I spoke with Commander Glenn Cusick at his headquarters on Park Point. Here are some of the highlights of that conversation.*"

Watching intently, it soon became obvious to Ilene that Cusick had revealed less information to the reporter than he told Philip.

Finally the reporter asked. "*At this time I understand that it's unclear what your mission will be. Based on past experience, what would you wager is in the cards for the 477th?*"

"*I'm not a gambling man,*" Cusick responded. "*I would simply like to point out one significant aspect of this military action.*"

"*What would that be?*" the reporter asked redundantly.

"*This particular unit, the 477th, was never activated during Vietnam, which may or may not point to Desert Shield as a significantly larger buildup.*"

Staring at the TV, Ilene felt her throat tighten. She and Philip had known Glenn Cusick for five years. An Army lifer, he'd been trained to speak in riddles. But she knew exactly what he meant. Vietnam was always labeled as a *military action*. Clearly Cusick had hinted that Desert Shield contained the potential to become something much larger in scale.

"Let's go find some breakfast." Ilene switched off the tube.

"Teen-age Mu-tant Nin-ja Tur-tles!" Hazy roared out of the master bedroom.

She pulled on a pair of sweats and pursued her daughter down the great spiral staircase. The sanded oak felt slippery under her bare feet. She considered whether the stairs needed a runner or if they should go ahead and carpet, for warmth. Her spirit sank as she realized that she would probably make that decision without Philip.

According to their specifications, the architect had designed the dining room as part of the kitchen and living room—not many interior walls, more like sections for better heat transference. The floors on this level were jade and sand-colored, square ceramic tiles laid in a diamond pattern. While Ilene made coffee, she could see Hazy standing with her nose and fingers pressed against the center window in the dining room.

"Look! There's Mr. Kitty." She tapped on the glass. "He just pounced on something."

Cringing at first, Ilene knew she'd have to get used to fingerprint smears. Windows spanned the entire southwest side of the house, from the kitchen through the dining room to the living room—floor to ceiling—almost like a greenhouse. The view from just below Hawk Ridge included Lake Superior and the city of Duluth. She was still amazed by the daylight, even without sunshine, as it danced through the windows onto this brand new environment. Like a mural in the background, the lake spread across the horizon.

Ilene surveyed the grounds below the windows. "Look what that lousy storm did. Our lawn's a mess."

"That's a lawn?" Hazy teased. "Not."

"How about lawn-in-progress."

Faced with her own reflection in the glass, Ilene caught a glimpse of weariness that eclipsed her green eyes. Turning her head from side to side, she noticed that summer's red highlights fading from her shoulder length, auburn hair. She knew that when her natural hair color dulled, winter breathed down their necks. At least the snowfall would cover up the barren yard. She frowned at the thought snow with so much left unfinished on the house. They hadn't even ordered storm doors yet.

"There he is again." Hazy pointed. "Don't you see him?"

Squinting at dried weed patches surrounded by muddy rivulets, Ilene finally spotted the long-haired silver cat crouching under a scrub oak with his back to them, obviously gnawing on his catch. "I see him now."

She'd encountered that cat once before, just after they moved over from the old house. She remembered balancing an armload of empty boxes in the middle of the living room. On TV, Dan Rather had announced, *"Two more US Naval Reserve units were called to active duty today. They will be serving in Saudi Arabia as part of Operation Desert Shield."* Back then she'd switched off the tube with her foot. She and Philip were so preoccupied with construction and moving, they hadn't paid much attention to the invasion of Kuwait. Except for the price of gas shooting up to a dollar fifty-nine a gallon, the military build-up had little impact on their chaotic lives.

After the Duluth-based Air National Guard unit was activated in September, Philip had predicted, "We're safe. They'll never call up two units from the same district."

Since the basement was unfinished, Ilene had decided that day to pile the boxes down there. Plumbing and electricity had been installed for a sauna, hot tub, bathroom and game room, but no laundry room. Instead Ilene had insisted the washer and dryer be installed in the insulated porch room, next to the kitchen. That way if the dryer ever caught fire, she could shove it out the back door.

When she was a girl in St. Paul, the dryer had been in the basement of her parents' house. It caught fire one day. The whole place was engulfed in flames when the firemen arrived. Ilene and her sister, Gail were in school. Their mom and dad, Betty and Wes Rosenthal were at work. They lost everything including Malibu, Ilene's fluffy red tabby. Within a year, Wes walked out. She figured he'd never gotten over the loss. She learned then that a little thing like a dryer fire could really blow the lid off ordinary life. The newspaper report of the fire had claimed, *"no one was hurt"*. But for Ilene and Gail and Betty, the hurt had just begun.

On that particular day back in September, when she'd hit the switch next to the basement door, nothing happened. Probably no bulb, and the light fixture was out of her reach. Attempting the stairs in partial light, her foot had tapped something soft and squishy.

"*Arr-eow.*"

As she'd shrunk back, the boxes clattered down the steps. A streak of silver darted across the debris, and toward the open doorway to the garage. Ilene didn't think she'd ever lay eyes on *him* again. Now he sat there beside the red pine over at the edge of the rocky hillside, preening himself.

"He's too pretty to be wild," Hazy purred.

"He doesn't belong here," Ilene said.

"But he came up to my loft one night," Hazy confided eagerly. "I couldn't think how he got inside."

"Apparently we left the garage doors open a lot while we were moving. I bumped into him downstairs myself once."

"I think I'll just go out there and catch him." She moved away from the window. "Do we have any tuna?"

Ilene followed her to the kitchen area. Pouring coffee into her favorite Far Side cartoon mug she shook her head. "No cats, Hazy. Daddy's allergic, remember."

"How bout we let him live in the basement. He already likes it down there." Hazy's dark brown eyebrows danced up and down, almost too cute to resist. *Almost.*

Smirking a little, Ilene pulled the box of Mueslix out of the cupboard. "Here. Eat some breakfast."

Hazy tossed her Buster Brown haircut back and forth, reaching around her mother to grab the Frankenberry cereal box.

Six year old Gladdy showed her face around the corner.

"Good morning," Ilene said.

Her birth name was Gladys Marie Singleton, after both their mothers. Betty's middle name was Gladys. Ilene shortened it to Gladdy.

When Ilene hugged her, she felt a little sweaty, probably from playing up in her room. "Whatcha been doing?"

She shrugged. "Playing school."

Gladdy didn't notice the cat outside. Ilene popped popcorn for her. She hated cereal. Hazy reached over her little sister's shoulder and grabbed a handful.

Gladdy pushed her arm away. "Mommy, Hazy's eating all my popcorn."

"You little goonie." Hazy slugged back. "It's not your popcorn."

"Mommy!" she cried. "Hazy punched me."

"Hazy, why don't you go outside and see if you can find that kitty?" Ilene suggested. "Grab your jacket off the porch."

Shuffling toward the back doorway, Hazy grumbled over her shoulder, "If I catch him, you better let me keep him."

Sitting on the oak bench at the dining room trestle table, Ilene and Gladdy crunched popcorn together in the front of the windows and spied on Hazy as she searched the rocky hillside for the silver cat.

Their land, adjacent to a public hawk migration sanctuary known as Hawk Ridge, had been in the Singleton family for three generations. When they first started clearing it four years ago, an environmental posse marched in with a court order to cease and desist. Unfortunately the legal process tied them up for three years. One day after a particularly grueling hearing over land rights, an Ojibwan woman clutched Ilene's arm as she exited the court house.

Her ruddy face weathered from the years, she confronted Ilene. "I must warn you about the territory of the hawk. You are prey, like the other creatures who inhabit the land. The course of nature cannot be changed. The land—your life—will never be the same."

Ilene shook off her words at the time. If she'd learned nothing else about life up north, it was that the people were quirky. However once the court battle ended, she did indeed witness their home transform that ridge forever, just as the Ojibwan's sage words predicted. And now, it was beginning to look like her life would never be the same.

"I followed that kitty once." Even Gladdy had her own version of the creature. She pointed toward the other side of the house where there was red pine forest across the road. "You guys were moving stuff. I got a little bit lost."

Ilene choked unexpectedly on a popcorn hull. Gladdy had a habit of narking on herself quite regularly. Sipping from her Far Side mug, she studied the cartoon image of two bears standing side-by-side in the cross hairs, one grinning and pointing to the other.

"I guess you didn't hear about the big old black bear that lives over in those woods," she fibbed.

Gladdy shrugged. "Didn't see him."

"Next time you'd better come and ask me first," her mother scolded.

Ignoring her, she peered out the window. "Hazy's not gonna find that kitty."

The phone rang. Ilene picked up the remote from the table. "Hello."

"This is Marie. Let me talk to Philip."

"He's not here."

"Then give him a message," Marie Singleton ordered. "We're scheduled to fly to Duluth Wednesday evening. We'll be staying at the Radisson. I've also made arrangements to have our Thanksgiving dinner catered."

Ilene simmered at her presumptuous mother-in-law. "What do you mean by *we*?"

None of Philip's family had ever approved of Ilene, Hazy's unwed mother. Especially Marie. When first introduced at their Lake Geneva estate, she had remarked, "*Elaine*, I believe Philip is more taken with that little baby of yours, than he is with you."

"My name's Ilene," she'd snapped.

Ilene felt eternally grateful that the entire Singleton clan lived in the Chicago area.

"I'm trying to gather as much of the family as possible on such short notice," Marie was saying. "As it is, we've had to cancel our plans for Grand Cayman."

"Philip's just going down to McCoy," Ilene told her. "Don't change your plans because of him. Go ahead with your trip."

"Not until we inspect that house he built."

"*Our house* isn't exactly finished yet. Philip's orders caught us off guard too."

"But Philip said you moved in months ago," Marie insisted.

"We sold the house in Lakeside and had to be out by August tenth. So we moved in here. It was a hassle living with a crew under foot so we let the contractor go. We've been doing a lot of the finish work ourselves. Until now, obviously."

An uncomfortable silence elapsed. "Tell Philip to call me," she bossed.

"I'll do that." Ilene set the phone down on the kitchen island. "Ugh."

2

"Look at this yard. It's an absolute mess. I'll call the landscaper in tomorrow," Marie complained as she marched up the redwood stairway to the deck. "Donald, you need to get someone out here to pave that driveway."

Like hell you will, Ilene thought. Hoisting a load of towels into the dryer, she took advantage of her in-laws lack of familiarity with the house to spy on them from the porch. The window nearest the dryer was open, so Ilene could see and hear everything. Ordinarily, Thanksgiving Day could be frigid and snowy up north. This year it dawned crisp and sunny, like Indian summer.

Wearing a red suit with black piping along the jacket lapels and pockets, in true Marie Singleton fashion she swooped in and started handing out orders. She rarely dressed her petite, five foot figure casually and kept her short hair dyed black and permed. Donald appeared less business-like in a black sweater, gray flannel slacks, and tweed sport jacket. Even though they'd flown up in their private jet, a driver in a black Mercedes had dropped them off and disappeared.

"Hi Grandma," Gladdy boldly greeted this woman she barely knew.

"And how is my little Gladys Marie?" Marie cooed, holding out her hand.

Gladdy shook it politely. "Good. I'm in first grade."

Ilene had never witnessed Marie Singleton hug or kiss her grandchildren. This day was no different.

Bounding the deck stairs, Hazy shouted, "Look at my dad! He's a soldier."

Back from an early check in at headquarters, Philip climbed the steps still wearing those goofy looking sand-colored camouflage fatigues he'd been issued.

"Why Philip Singleton! What is this uniform you're wearing? Don't tell me you have to be on some sort of duty today." Marie tugged on his shirt sleeve. "I should be relaxing on my verandah overlooking the Caribbean, you know."

"I'm yours for the day, Mother." With a quick hug, Philip thrust his hands into his pockets and discussed the yard and driveway with Donald. "I'm sure glad we got the stairway and boardwalks built. Been a wet fall. We'll do sod next spring."

"Absolutely not," Marie commanded. She linked her arm in Philip's. "Darling, think of the lawn and the driveway as our housewarming gift."

Sneezing from the dryer lint, Ilene prematurely announced her entrance. She stepped out the porch door and greeted them. "Happy Thanksgiving. Where's the rest of the gang—Donna and Joanie?"

At forty-two, Philip was the youngest of the Singleton clan. His sister, Joanie was married to Dave Saxon, a Chicago contractor. Their son, Matthew was a freshman at Harvard. Donna, the oldest, was married to Michael Pfeiffer, an attorney. They had two boys, Chase was in high school in Evanston and Don was at the University of Wisconsin. Ilene could count on one hand the number of times she'd seen his sisters socially over the past nine years. She wasn't surprised they didn't show up. They'd never even pretended to like her.

"*Elaine*, did Philip forget to tell you?" Marie unlocked her grip on his arm.

"I-*lene*," she enunciated.

"They weren't able to rearrange their schedules. It's parents weekend at Harvard. And Donna's on her way to London. They were both so disappointed."

"I'll bet," Ilene said quipped.

Hands on hips, Philip gazed up at the three stories of redwood and glass, towering above them. "So. What do you think of the place?"

"Impressive," Donald spoke up. "Who's your architect?"

"Vasey and Holland," he replied.

"Never heard of them." Marie turned up her nose. "There certainly is a great deal of work left to do. I never imagined!"

Donald slapped his son's shoulder. "Let's have a look around. I'm anxious to see what you've done with the place so far."

Her mother-in-law watched the two of them walk along the deck toward the lake view, then blurted, "I trust you have a more formal entrance than this porch. It looks absolutely *tacked on* to the rest of the house."

"Follow me. I'll take you through the *formal* entrance." Ilene stomped off.

Marie followed her up the boardwalk to the front of the house. Hazy and Gladdy marched along jabbering about school projects. Usually it drove Ilene nuts when she couldn't get a word in edgewise around those two. At that moment, she felt grateful for their aimless chatter. Years ago she would've snapped back at Marie for that snotty crack about the porch. But it wasn't worth the effort anymore. *Besides*, she wondered, *how much of a threat could a petulant, sixty-eight-year old woman be?*

Admiring the oak front door framed by full-length side bar windows as they entered, Marie observed, "Now this is more like it."

Hazy squinted. "Like what?"

"Listen to this!" Gladdy pressed the lighted button. Carillon door chimes echoed through the foyer. Bored to silliness by the tour, the giggling girls trotted into the bathroom and slammed the door.

"Obviously that's the bathroom. That door goes to the basement.

And there's the closet," Ilene droned on.

Marie twirled slowly on the jade and white ceramic tile, frowning. "This is such a cold, empty space. You need a settee against that wall. And two or three paintings at least."

Exasperated Ilene replied, "As you can see, we don't even have the light fixtures hung yet."

Stalking off to the kitchen, she noticed Philip and his dad still leaning against the deck railing. They hadn't gotten very far with their tour either. The longer she observed them, the more Donald appeared to be lecturing as Philip danced from one foot to the other.

The same age as Marie, Donald was a smooth, polished stone possessing a cool refinement. Over the years he had treated Philip more like an employee than his own flesh and blood. The quintessential banker, he stood only five ten with a square build and thin gray hair framing a face that betrayed no secrets. Ilene never fully understood the gulf that apparently existed between the two men. Though she never pried. Philip had as much right to his own private scars as she did.

"Let's just say that I never did what he wanted me to do," Philip had assessed their father-son relationship. "It's better if I keep my distance." A confirmed rebel, he had decidedly kept his *distance* over the years.

Donald and Marie cut such contrasting figures that it was hard for Ilene to see either of them in her Philip. Taller and more muscular than his father, he possessed his own kind, hazel eyes and curly brown hair, in spite of a sharply receding hairline.

Through the windows, she watched him studying a flat black notebook, like a portfolio. Then he handed it back to Donald. Bowing his head, he shook his father's hand, almost like a gesture of defeat.

"And this here's our living room." Gladdy was back giving her grandma a halfway decent tour of the main floor.

Scoping out the view, Marie chattered, "Open. Very nice. Spacious." She spotted Ilene. "That bathroom has so much wasted space. And there's two doors, one to the porch, or the laundry room—whatever you call it. You certainly did that *all* wrong."

Ignoring her Ilene asked, "Did you show Grandma your bedroom yet?"

"Come on," Gladdy tugged on Marie's sleeve.

As they headed up the steps, Ilene heard her asking impatiently, "So tell me. Is your bedroom actually finished?"

"Nope." Gladdy skipped ahead.

The glass door rattled open. Philip and Donald stepped into the dining area.

Ilene peered at her husband until his eyes met hers. "What's up?"

Eyebrows knit with concern, Philip shrugged. "What do you mean?"

"The notebook. That black thing you were holding. What is it?"

Cheeks flushed, he glanced at his father.

"It's an insurance policy," Donald explained.

"Insurance policy," Ilene repeated.

"In case we go overseas. And something happens," Philip added.

"That's ridiculous. You are not going overseas," she argued. "This will all be over in a couple months. You'll see."

Donald cleared his throat. "No matter what happens, the deed to this house will be safe."

"What's *that* supposed to mean?" Ilene asked with sarcasm.

Thanksgiving dinner arrived in the hands of a rotund chef and young blond waitress from the hotel delivering a fourteen pound roast turkey stuffed with wild rice dressing. Ilene helped them transfer the steaming bird from the catering case to her stoneware platter. The waitress handed Hazy and Gladdy tubs of mashed potatoes and gravy, along with a squash casserole, coleslaw, and buttered rolls.

Descending the staircase wearing dark green slacks and a caramel sweater, Philip remarked, "I gotta hand it to you Mother, you sure know how to throw a classy dinner together."

"I wanted it to be special. But this is the best I could do on short notice." Marie conferred with the chef, then dismissed them both. "I believe we can handle things from here on out."

After they left, Marie insisted on table linens and lit candles. With the afternoon sun streaming through the windows everyone gathered around the dining room table to share the feast.

"This is rather like a picnic with your long trestle table and these medieval benches for chairs in this unfinished house." Marie simpered.

"A turkey picnic!" Hazy exclaimed. Both girls giggled.

A surrealistic picnic, Ilene thought.

During dessert, Gladdy spoke up, "Are you going to the parade with us on Saturday?"

"Parade?" Marie asked.

"A local radio station is using our deployment as some sort of publicity stunt," Philip explained. "They're the ones calling it a *parade*."

"I don't really think you'd want to stand out in the cold that early in the morning," Ilene warned, wishing Gladdy'd kept her mouth shut.

"We pull out of Park Point at 0700," Philip told them.

"That's seven *a.m.*," Hazy informed them.

"Might not be a bad idea," Donald put in. "Go see what all the fuss is about."

"Goodie!" Gladdy shouted.

Ilene's face fell. "Then you'll be staying until Saturday."

Marie nodded. "That will give us more time to make arrangements for finishing some of these projects."

Stifling her aggravation, Ilene's fingers trembled as she smoothed the hem of the tablecloth. "That really isn't necessary."

"Oh, but it most certainly is," Marie said shrilly.

"There is a substantial amount of work that needs to be done on this place to satisfy the bank, so to speak," Donald declared.

Ilene looked blankly at Philip. She felt betrayed. Not just by him but by life and the stupid little tricks it played. "What have you done?"

A heavy sigh belied his flimsy words. "It's enough money for you and the girls to live on while the house is getting finished."

"You turned the deed over to them. Didn't you?" She leaned forward, glaring. "This can't be what you wanted."

"Oh, ple—ease," Marie begged sarcastically. "Stop the melodrama. You ought to be thankful we decided to get involved when we did. Left to your own devices, you could lose everything Philip has worked for all these years."

"That does it." Ilene threw down her napkin like a gauntlet. She jumped up, ready to tear into Marie but the table shook, toppling the candlestick and spilling hot burning wax. She fled up the staircase, while Philip quietly doused the flaming linen with ice water.

3

"He's the boogie woogie bugle boy of Company B."

That old Bette Midler tune cackled through the frosty air as Ilene, Hazy and Gladdy crawled out of the cozy Toyota Camry onto the chilly Canal Park pavement at 6:58 a.m. Saturday, November 24th. The wind had switched, turning blustery off the lake. Not a nice day for a parade. Running behind schedule, the three of them hustled toward Bette's voice. Block after block of parked cars indicated that several hundred people had arrived much earlier.

Philip had ridden down to the Park Point Armory with Commander Cusick at five-thirty. According to procedure, the hundred or more who made up the unit would be traveling the five hour trip south to Fort McCoy on two chartered buses. There they would link up with their ambulances and medical equipment. More than twenty other people in his unit were also his co-workers at St. Mary's. Gifford, the hospital administrator had encouraged participation in the Army Reserve because he believed it made them a better team on the job. Ilene wondered how he felt now, stranded with record-breaking personnel shortages. No one had dreamed they would ever be activated.

Boogie woogie Bette bugled for the second time around. From their booths in front of Burger King, TV personalities and radio jockeys handed out miniature American flags. A scary little man wearing a VFW hat hawked *Support Our Troops* buttons and bumper stickers. Red, white and blue banners had been draped across the intersections. Every tree in the boulevard was trimmed with yellow ribbons.

Unprepared for this patriotic fervor, Ilene grumbled. "Yikes. What a circus."

While the girls searched the crowd for their grandparents, Ilene trudged behind. She'd had her fill of Mom and Pop. By noon on Friday, landscapers and bulldozers had swarmed in to build a lawn and driveway over the weekend. Mowed down by the overwhelming power of Singleton money, she'd retreated to the computer in the den off the living room to work on construction inventory files.

"Over here, *Elaine*. Hurry. You're late. The buses are on the way. You almost missed it."

The damp air vibrated with one long horn blast, two short, from the Aerial Lift Bridge. Then again as Hazy and Gladdy covered their ears. As the echo of the blasts faded, a hush fell over the crowd. Two coach buses draped like coffins with American flags, lumbered under the span's spotlights.

Shuddering from the harsh wind, Ilene realized that Marie was right. She'd come perilously close to missing the procession. Captured by the moment, tears stung her eyelids. Up to that point, she had ignored the Army in their lives. All those weekends of reserve training, it was as if he'd been away at health care seminars. The people in the 477th were more medical than military. They'd never been exposed to that whole storm trooper mentality. Or the threat of war.

Cheers and applause exploded along with the high school band drummers' steady military cadence. Waving their flags, Hazy and Gladdy screamed as the buses approached the corner. Ilene neither clapped nor cheered, paralyzed by the tears streaming down her face. She clung to her daughters' hands like anchors. Only they were far too excited to stand still, much less keep their mom afloat.

As the lead bus rolled around the corner in front of them, the crowd noise deafened. Philip's head appeared at an open window. From behind his video camera, he waved ardently at his daughters, then blew a kiss to his wife. He didn't seem to notice his parents. In an instant the buses, followed by two army green equipment vehicles pulling box trailers, were swallowed by the crowd and the twinkling of flashbulbs. She had forgotten to bring their 35mm camera. Anyway, she did not *treasure the moment.*

Peering down the noisy, fog-shrouded street through misty eyes, Ilene wondered how a photo of the scene would have looked, when lifted out of context for future generations. In the half-light it seemed impossible to detect whether the hour was night or day, the season spring or fall. Instead it looked like a clip from a sad old black and white war movie.

"Here you are." That voice again. Ilene felt that the time had come for Marie to hit the road. "Donald and I have made a decision."

Having wiped away all traces of tears, she turned around. "What decision."

The five of them stood silently while the slow moving herd passed by. In an uncharacteristic grandfatherly gesture, Donald held Hazy and Gladdy each by the hand. Ilene wondered how deep he had to dig to feel the impact of Philip's leaving.

"Donald is taking the jet back to Chicago," Marie informed her. "I plan to move out of our suite at the Radisson, and into the guest room for a few days."

Choking from surprise, Ilene coughed and sneezed at the same time. As Marie rushed toward her she held up her hand. "No. Don't."

Halting impatiently, Marie snatched a fresh silk hankie from her alligator purse and thrust it at Ilene. "There is still so much to be done. It would be impossible to get a decent appraisal under these circumstances."

"We don't need an appraisal!" Ilene objected, mopping her nose.

"Besides the guest room—it's not finished. There's no furniture."

"Furniture will be delivered by this afternoon." Marie checked her diamond Rolex. "The workmen should be there by nine. Someone has to make certain the work we paid for gets done properly."

Ilene glanced over at Donald and the girls. The three of them had cornered a *Support Our Troops* vendor and were shamelessly contributing to the crass commercialization of her pain. Panicked at the thought of forty-eight hours on the ranch with "Leona Helmsley" Singleton, she persisted, "Look. I don't care what kind of deal you made with Philip. It's *my* house too. And I'll do things my own way. In my own time."

Marie sniffed. "Then it's best we clear the air right now. As of yesterday, that house became an asset of DMS & JDP Holding Company. *You have no ownership what-so-ever."*

"Okay. If that's the game you're playing." Stunned, Ilene's fingers trembled as she fished in her canvas bag for keys. Yanking the front door key off the ring, she shoved it into Marie's hand. "Then you'll be needing this." Brushing past the woman, she snatched Hazy and Gladdy by their wrists.

"Watch out for my balloon," Hazy griped.

Gladdy dug in her heels. "Stop. I can't find my yellow ribbon."

"I'll get you another one," Ilene bribed as she herded them through the maze of people. "Come on."

"Where we going." Hazy hesitated along the final block.

"Uh—Christmas shopping." Ilene baited them, then set the hook. "In Minneapolis."

"Oh boy," Hazy cried. "Can we go see Grandma Betty and Gail?"

"And Santa Claus?" Gladdy added.

Nodding, Ilene smiled with satisfaction. They'd latched onto the juicy bone like eager little puppies. Steering the car out of the St. Louis River valley, she wondered how long before Marie and Donald realized she'd split town. While escaping to her mother's in St. Paul wasn't exactly a radical step, she'd been feeling some quiet act of desperation coming on for days.

Hazy and Gladdy dropped off to sleep in the back seat. Short on cash, toting two kids out in the real world, Ilene needed some place safe to melt down. On the CD player, Johnny Hates Jazz sang, *"I don't want to be a hero, I don't want to die for you"* while she maneuvered through the freeway traffic.

4

The telephone echoed through the apartment kitchen.

Betty answered. "Yep. She's right here."

Philip finally caught up with Ilene at her mom's apartment late Saturday night. The two of them had been at the Silver Dollar restaurant and bar downstairs earlier but they'd since retired upstairs to the kitchen table drinking wine, smoking cigarettes. Ilene could always count on her mom to referee her binges, such as they were.

"I'm so sorry this whole Persian Gulf thing has turned you kids lives upside down the way it has and all. But I want you to know how proud I am," Betty gushed into the phone. "You're like my own son, you know."

There was that pride thing again. Ilene didn't get it. Hundreds of families had been forced to put their lives on hold for months while George Bush and Saddam Hussein bickered over an invisible line drawn in the sand. Where was the *pride* in that?

Betty listened then said, "Gail took the girls to the movies. Ninja Turtles or some dang thing."

She handed the receiver to Ilene.

"What's going on?" Philip queried. "Mother's having a cow."

"Then she can build it a goddamn barn in our backyard for all I care," Ilene deadpanned.

"She's just trying to help."

"Like hell she is!" Ilene exploded. "I'm curious. Did she mention the bomb she dropped on me this morning?"

"Look. I realize she's no fun to have around. But that woman can pull strings and get things done. We could use her help right now."

Ilene laughed bitterly. "That's not what I meant. She told me that as of Friday morning our house became an asset of the DM-what-the-hell-ever holding company. That I had no ownership. *What-so-ever.* I don't have to take that shit from her."

"Mother always sees things her own way. You know that."

"All I know is I've tried really hard to be patient with her," Ilene complained. "But she's a control freak. You see how she treats me."

Sounding exasperated, Philip replied, "Dammit Ilene. I've done little else these past two weeks but scramble to get work done on that house. Then when I bring in the two people who can literally make the earth move with one phone call, you pitch a fit."

"Did you hear what I said? Marie thinks she owns the place."

Philip sighed. "She'll be gone by tomorrow night. And probably forget all about that house."

"I wish," Ilene muttered. "Sure is a lot of shit piling up between us."

"What do you mean?"

"I don't know. Feels like we're trapped on some kind of runaway train."

"You're with Betty. And you've been drinking," he stated. "We're making the best of a bad situation."

"Doesn't feel like that to me."

"Ilene, I can't change the way things are. Believe me. I've tried."

She heard that twang of lament in his voice. "I know. It's not your fault. How's about I bring the girls down to see you tomorrow. It's only a couple hours from here."

"No don't," he protested. "It's chaos. There's another unit here. They were supposed to go over last week, but a sandstorm grounded the plane in Saudi. We'll be sleeping on the floor of the mess hall."

"Oh God. That sounds miserable." She groaned, then added, "Anyway I love you."

"I love you too."

Ilene hung up the phone and shuffled over to the table.

"Don't let it get you down, sister." Betty lit a cigarette. She always called Ilene *sister* when she drank. Ilene never asked why. She figured her mom needed that equalizer in order to open up. "Everything's gonna be all right. You'll see."

Ilene shook her head. "You don't know that. I don't know that. Nobody knows that anymore."

"What I do know, is I got so damned depressed after that fire, I let it ruin my marriage. I'm tellin ya."

"Wes walked out on all of us. You didn't do anything."

"That was my whole problem, right there. I should've done something. You know?"

"Don't start, Betty. It's ancient history."

"All I'm sayin is you got to stand by your Philip. Have faith. Don't let those rich sonsabitches get you down."

Ilene chugged her glass of wine. "What're you Tammy Wynette now? Gimme a break."

Betty tossed her hands in the air. "So what's the big deal?"

"You heard what I told Philip."

"So he's using a little family money to protect you and the kids while he's gone."

Ilene toyed with the back door key still attached to her ring. "Except it looks more and more like I got cut out of the deal."

"The way I see it, you're livin in one hell of a castle. Count your blessings." Betty shook her finger at her daughter. "Don't you go gettin in between Philip and his family. You'll wind up the loser. Every time."

Ilene jumped up and tugged on her mother's finger defiantly. "And what do you suppose will happen if the Singletons come between Philip and me?"

Betty pulled her finger away. "Calm down, sister. You know you don't have shit without that man."

"Forget it. You don't even know what you're talking about." Ilene waved her off—*the drunk*—and staggered off to the spare bedroom.

She lay on the daybed feeling woozy. The clock glowed 11:28 p.m. Betty inhabited this quaint two bedroom apartment by herself above the Silver Dollar. A classic old river front establishment, all the rooms had high embossed ceilings. The phone rang. She heard Betty answer.

Next thing she knew, her mom peeked in the doorway. "Gail took the girls over to her place for the night."

"Okay, thanks." Then she asked, "Betty? Why are you proud of Philip?"

Her mom raked her fingers through her dyed red curls. "What're you talking about now?"

"What you said to him on the phone," Ilene reminded her. "You said you were *proud* of him."

Betty waved her hand. "Oh that. Just something you say to men going off to war. Like good luck. Or break a leg."

Ilene shook her head. "Has everyone gone mad? There is no war. We're not even in any imminent danger. God. This whole Desert Shield thing boils down to a silly border dispute over oil rights."

Betty turned away. "It's too damn late for politics. Get some sleep."

Ilene curled up on the bed thinking what a pleasant distraction it was for the girls to be able to sleep over at Aunt Gail's new townhouse. Thirty-three and younger than her, Gail had yet to marry. Ilene thought she might be bi-sexual, even lesbian, but didn't cope with it well enough herself yet to come out. She'd dated men but it had never worked out. She had close women friends too, and they seemed to suffer the same consequences. She was unattached right then, living alone in expensive new digs in White Bear Lake. Someday Ilene planned to come right out and ask, *men or women—which do you prefer?*

For all practical purposes, Gail was boss at the Silver Dollar. Betty had bought into it with an old guy named Sid Fisher. She'd made him a happy man during his golden years. All that happened fourteen or fifteen years ago, around the time she met Bill Davies. The two of them were backpacking up and down the Pacific Coast back then. They'd barely kept in touch. Within three years Sid had died of liver disease, and Betty ended up with his honky tonk bar and grill.

At that time, Gail was in her early twenties and jumped into the opportunity head first, landing herself a career jackpot. She transformed the Silver Dollar from greasy spoons to mugs and sandwich boards, trendy but chic. Ilene had always been intensely proud, nearly envious at times, of what Gail and Betty had accomplished. Even though her mom still drank, Gail saw to it that she led a productive life. Ilene worked at the Dollar for a few years before moving to Duluth, but never felt the urge to buy into it. Old mother-daughter wounds, she guessed. The idea of a family partnership had never appealed to her.

"The Dollar's part of me, like a work of art," Gail confessed once.

Ilene didn't know what that meant until she and Philip built their house on Hawk Ridge.

The swiftness with which everything in their lives had changed nauseated her. How could Philip let his parents take over like this?

"You have no ownership what-so-ever."

Marie's bitter proclamation echoed in her brain. Philip was evidently too wrapped up in the events in the Persian Gulf and finishing the house to realize the impact of his family so entangled in their lives. Ilene knew in that moment it was up to her to go back home and stand vigilant over what was left of her territory, as Philip's wife, the mother of his child.

5

"Bye!" Hazy hollered over her shoulder as she hopped on the bus Monday morning, November 26th.

She wore jeans rolled at the ankles, her new black Ninja Turtles T-shirt, and a jean jacket, which was what most of the fifth grade girls at Lakeside Elementary would be wearing, or at least the ones that mattered. Hazy should know. Ilene figured she must have called every single one of them that morning, instead of getting dressed for school.

"Look, there's the kitty." Gladdy hesitated, pointing over her mother's shoulder.

"Keep it moving." Ilene ushered her up the bus steps. "Have fun today."

Waving at the bus as it bounced away, Ilene surveyed the patchwork of burlap on the lawn. Arriving home late Sunday night, she'd read over the paperwork left on the kitchen counter by the landscaper, indicating that it was too late in the season for sod to take hold. Instead, they had terraced the dirt slopes with green timbers and blanketed the ground with burlap strips. The idea was to prevent erosion before laying down new sod in the spring. She derived great satisfaction from knowing that in the north woods, Mother Nature had proven to be the ultimate match for Marie Singleton's ambitious landscaping project.

Noticing a maroon pickup pass by slowly, she had become sensitive to curious onlookers since the day they moved in, knowing the architecture of their home was unusual, jutting from the ridge like a tower. As she pulled the yellow construction banner aside she couldn't help feeling astounded, albeit begrudgingly, that the pavement had been put down on the weekend. Especially considering that she and Philip had waited six weeks for concrete last summer. One after another, she drove the Jeep and Toyota off the roadside and down the new driveway. That chore completed, she climbed the stairs and leaned against the deck railing. Light frost shone along the black asphalt. Next to the graveled city limits road, the new blacktop looked urbane, out of place.

"*Prr-eow.*"

She jumped half a foot. Out of the corner of her eye, she caught the streak of silver tail. Then she smelled tuna. Glancing down she saw the crumbs of white albacore left in a one of her china bowls.

"Those kids," she grumbled, bending down to pick it up.

Through the bare birches, Ilene saw the glint from the maroon pickup again, as it slowly ascended the hill toward the house. Heart thudding against her chest she stood up, slowly flattening her back against the redwood siding. On this desolate end of Skyline Parkway, any traffic was noticeable. And a double drive by was reason enough for her to feel the hairs rising up along the back of her neck. She had almost forgotten the perils of living alone. Maybe if she brought home a big old German shepherd from the shelter, the girls would forget about that cat.

Morning sun reflected off the tinted windshield as the pickup entered the driveway. Breathing shallow, she tugged on the neck of her fisherman knit sweater and watched. The driver's door opened, a tall attractive man stepped out. She didn't think he saw her at first. Removing his sunglasses he drank in the full visual effect of the windows rising from the wrap around deck like pillars. He wore a buffalo plaid wool shirt, black corduroy vest and jeans. Ilene stepped into view.

"Howdy," he yelled out to her, as if he'd seen her there all along and was simply waiting for her to make the first move.

Veering away from the stairs, Ilene leaned over the railing and called down to him. "Looking for something?"

"Heard you all were looking for a carpenter."

"Is that so." With his attention focused on her, she saw that he was quite young. She guessed twenty-six. "Who told you that?"

"Terry Wilson. Your contractor," he said.

"Do you work for him?"

"You don't remember me."

Detecting a hint of southern accent, she smiled slyly at him. He didn't look like a construction worker. With his shiny dark brown hair pulled straight back into a tight tail, he looked more like a candidate for smooth operator on *Miami Vice* re-runs. She wondered if he knew the first thing about finish carpentry.

"Where are you from?" Saying those words gave her a sense of power. This was after all, sort of a job interview.

"What difference does that make? I live in Duluth now."

Obviously *he* didn't see it the same way at all. She pressed on. "Do you have a business card? Some ID."

He reached for his wallet. "Yes, ma'am."

She sneered at his obscure reference to their age difference. He waved a white card at her. Pompously descending the stairs, she lifted the card from his hand and studied it.

"Wilson Master Builders," she read aloud. "That's the company. And what's your name."

"Kevin Wyland," he told her. "Look, I got plenty other jobs if you're not interested."

Ilene ignored his hard sell. "Did you talk to my husband?"

His brown eyes looked steadily back at her. "Didn't Wilson call him?"

"It's been pretty hectic around here," she informed him. "Philip's reserve unit was called up. We only had about a week to prepare."

"That's rough," he said. "Met him here last summer. Guess you don't remember."

She used the opportunity to study him. "A lot of men traipsed through this place back then. You don't look familiar." What she neglected to say was even though they all looked the same in their blue jeans and tool belts after while, she would've remembered this particular man.

He shrugged, gazing up at the house with what Ilene thought to be a look of admiration. "Mind if I look around? See what needs to be done."

Frowning, she told him, "I'll show you around. Follow me." She led him through the garage, into the basement level first. "Philip wants this basement finished."

His eyes surveyed the framework. "What's the plan?"

"Weight room, sauna, and hot tub on this end. Game room over there, closer to the stairway."

He ran his hands along the studs. "Hot tub's gonna be a real humidity problem. Shoulda put your laundry down here. That porch off the kitchen would be a perfect spa."

Ilene bristled that his blunt criticism reflected such an intimate awareness of her home. He was certainly *acting* like a typical carpenter, analyzing the way they'd done things. "Too late now, we'll just have to live with our mistakes."

He held up his hands, as if in surrender. "Trust me, this place is no mistake."

Ilene folded her arms across her chest in silence. She didn't know how to read this guy. The gas furnace hummed in the corner. "The other side of that wall will be mirrors all the way around."

Undaunted by her glare, he commented further, "Must be at least half a mil invested in this place by now."

"No way," Ilene said abruptly.

He laughed. "You're not done yet."

Caught off guard by his lofty assessment, Ilene turned and headed upstairs. "That reminds me, the light fixture for this stairwell needs to be moved. I can't reach it to change the bulb."

He didn't answer. She turned around. He wasn't even there. She cleared her throat. "Excuse me."

"On my way," he hollered.

Rolling her eyes she stomped upstairs. The awful reality of having someone—some *man*—*that* man invading her home every day was beginning to sink in. She stopped at the basement door to yell at him again.

He bounded up the steps. "Right here."

"What were you doing down there?" she asked brusquely, stepping into the foyer.

He gazed around and replied. "Guess I see things the average person doesn't."

"What's that sposed to mean?" Realizing that the question only invited more of his critical appraisals, she continued describing the first floor woodwork and light fixtures before he could respond.

"You order frames and moldings yet?" he asked.

"Three months ago," Ilene griped. "Everything takes so damn long."

Heading upstairs to the second floor, Ilene was faced with another reminder of Marie's weekend miracles. She'd had the steps and the upstairs hallway carpeted in natural wool Berber. Upon discovering it in a fit of rage the night before, Ilene had vowed to rip it out and choose her own carpeting.

"Nice carpet." Kevin sniffed. "Smells brand new."

"It is," was all she said.

In the calmer light of day, Ilene realized that no matter how cosmopolitan Marie's carpet choice had appeared at first, the natural fibers looked stunning against the polished oak banisters. She noticed that the carpet had been laid into the guest room doorway.

Throwing open the door, she announced, "And this is—the guest room."

The Berber had indeed been carried into the bedroom. Placing her fingertips over her lips, she tried to conceal her amazement as Marie's crowning glory was revealed. The walls were papered in berry and white stripe, with a floral border. A miniature crystal chandelier hung from the ceiling. A bleached oak, half moon headboard adorned the king size bed covered with a cranberry satin spread. Across the room, a pair of berry and gray striped fabric chairs surrounded a table, next to a dresser in the same Scandinavian motif. As she peeked around the corner into the closet, she could feel his eyes upon her.

"Something wrong?" he asked.

Caught in the middle of a bad act, she laughed self consciously. "My mother-in-law had this done while I was gone over the weekend."

He laughed. "Yeah right. Would've cost a bundle to get help like that on the weekend."

Gazing around, Ilene nodded. "No doubt."

He shook his head. "Unreal."

She decided to really blow his mind. "She also had the driveway paved and the yard landscaped. Not to mention this cushy, wool carpet you're standing on."

He studied her. "You don't exactly seem filled with gratitude."

She let out a sardonic laugh. "She didn't do any of this for my benefit."

Having seen an eyeful, she stalked out of the room. What really bugged her was that she kind of liked the room. But it was killing her to admit it, even if only to herself. Realizing that if Marie had touched their rooms, the girls would have thrown fits last night when they got home, she still felt a sense of relief when she opened the door to Gladdy's familiar mess.

"As you can see, some of the rooms still need to be finished." Before he could comment, the doorbell chimed. "Scuse me."

Ilene dashed downstairs. Breathless, she opened the door to a woman dressed in a navy blue suit. Her silver frosted short brown hair suggested late fifties. She carried a red leather briefcase.

"Good morning, you must be the maid," the woman chirped.

Kevin chuckled in back of Ilene, unnerving her. She hadn't heard him follow. "Not exactly. I own this house. Who are you?"

"Pardon me," she looked past Ilene and Kevin. "I was looking for Mrs. Singleton."

"I *am* Mrs. Singleton." Ilene fumed. "Like I said, who are *you*."

Clutching her briefcase with both hands, looking thoroughly aghast, the woman declared, "I don't understand this. *My* name is Dorothy Bradford of Bradford Interiors. I worked here—in this house, all weekend—with Mrs. Singleton."

"That was my mother-in-law," Ilene explained.

Mrs. Bradford frowned. "Mrs. Singleton gave me the distinct impression that she owned this home."

Ilene bit her lip furiously. "Oh, I'll just bet she did. Why are you here? She forget to pay you?"

Shaking her head she said, "Not at all. In fact, I still have work to do on our contract."

Ilene tossed her hands in the air and looked at Kevin. "I have to take care of this. You'd better leave."

"Doesn't matter to me. I got other jobs," he warned.

Nodding, she ushered him past Ms. Bradford. "I'll—um—call you."

Pushing herself away from the closed door, Ilene launched into the woman. "I don't care what Marie Singleton told you or how much she paid you, *I* don't need you."

Ms. Bradford raised her hand in a gesture of diplomacy. "Mrs. Singleton, I'm terribly sorry for any misunderstanding. You have a spectacular home here."

"Yes, I know," Ilene agreed.

"It will be my pleasure to continue advising you along the way. Your mother-in-law has already signed a generous contract with my company."

Managing to keep her fury in check, Ilene shook Ms. Bradford's hand. "I'll—uh—get back to you."

After shooing the woman out, Ilene leaned against the cool oak door. Two months ago she'd finally convinced Philip that it made sense to hire an interior decorator. Now she'd sent a good one packing without so much as a consultation. But it wasn't about rugs and wallpaper. It was about her mother-in-law taking control.

Ilene shook her fist at the ceiling and cried, "This is my home Marie!" As if she could hear her.

6

Snow fell by mid-morning mail delivery on Tuesday, November 27th. Ilene waved at the woman carrier while she swept the white flakes off the boardwalk.

"Looks like winter's here to stay," the woman called from her white postal service Jeep.

Ilene nodded and carried the mail inside. Holding her Far Side mug, she sat down at the table. Noticing an envelope bearing the familiar Wilson Master Builders' logo, she thought about the man who'd come by yesterday. He'd given her a business card bearing that same logo.

She had told Philip about him when he called Monday night. "Terry Wilson sent a carpenter over here this morning."

"Great. Get him started right away on frames and moldings."

"A strange man drives up in a fancy pickup and you expect me to hire him on the spot."

"What'd you do, scare him off?"

"I think we should at least check him out."

"Meanwhile the guy's got two other jobs that pay twice the money. Just put him to work. What's his name?"

"Kevin Wyland." Ilene was surprised at her own recollection.

"Can you still find him?"

"What if the guy's on parole from prison?"

"I'm sure some ex-con would be looking for carpenter work in a fancy pickup," Philip retorted.

Reminded of his impatience, Ilene grabbed the cordless from the edge of the counter and punched in the numbers.

"Wilson Master Builders. This is Wendy," a woman answered.

"Hi Wendy. Can I talk to Terry?" Ilene asked.

"Terry's not in," Wendy explained. "May I ask who's calling?"

"This is Ilene Singleton."

"Oh hi. Real bummer that your husband had to leave."

"I'm sure it's only temporary. I wondered if you could tell me anything about Kevin Wyland. He was here yesterday looking for work."

"Oh yeah. He's a good guy. Hasn't worked here long. You know, Terry usually handles these kind of referrals. I'll tell him you called."

"Okay. Thanks." She hung up.

Tearing open the envelope from Wilson Master Builders, Ilene found a bill for boardwalk and stairs. Materials and labor totaled over forty-seven hundred dollars. She understood that Philip meant for her to transfer money into her account to pay for bills like that, but she wished he'd been more explicit about their finances before he left.

When Philip called around seven that evening, Ilene had to wait in line behind Gladdy and Hazy for a chance to say "hello."

"Yes. We got three inches of snow." Hazy talked into the kitchen wall phone.

Gladdy, on the remote, added, "But they made us stay in school, anyway."

By the time Gladdy handed the phone to Ilene, the news had all been told. Feeling frustrated she asked, "So how's it going?"

"Today was lousy," Philip answered without hesitation. "Inventory and catalogue supplies. All day long. It's mind numbing."

"Look Philip," Ilene blurted. "We'd better get some of this financial stuff straightened out."

"I told you, all you have to do is pay the bills when they come in. Transfer the funds from our joint account into your account."

"Is that the money you got from your parents?"

"The idea is for you *not* to worry about that. There's enough to cover everything. Did you get a hold of that carpenter?"

His deflection did not escape her notice. "Not yet."

"Get on it. Don't lose this guy Ilene. We need all the help we can get right now," Philip reprimanded her. "Look, I'm tying up the line here. I'll call you tomorrow night. Love you."

"Me too."

As Ilene hung up the phone Hazy informed her, "Dad said I could sleep over at Jessie's house Friday night,"

Irritated, Ilene cast her a sidelong glance. "Is that so. How come you didn't ask me?"

"I asked you yesterday," Hazy argued.

"Yesterday, I told you to stop feeding that cat. But you kept right on doing it."

"Not," Hazy shot back. "Gladdy's feeding him."

"Not," her sister cried.

"Are too," Hazy retorted. "Daddy's gone now anyway. Why can't we just keep it?"

She cringed at her daughter's selfish comment. "Hazy you better go straight to your room, and think about what you just said."

In spite of Ilene's determination to eschew the topic of that stray cat, the very next morning both girls picked up the squabble where they left off.

Nursing a bowl of lukewarm soup for breakfast, Gladdy pestered, "Mommy, can I give Mr. Kitty some of my chicken and stars?"

"See what I mean. She's feeding him, too." Hazy stood at the counter spreading peanut butter on toasted English muffin bread. "Anyway, what are we sposed to do. Let him starve to death?"

Ilene leered at her. "Pretty cheeky, Hazel Lee Singleton."

"Wanda the bus driver said Jesus sent an angel kitty to watch over us while Daddy's gone," Gladdy informed her.

"Angel kitty. Hmm," Ilene responded. "That's very interesting."

Hazy picked up on it immediately. "I know exactly what she means. It feels like Mr. Kitty's always there watching me."

Gladdy looked soulfully at her mother. "Do *you* think our kitty's an angel?"

Annoyed by the girls' new twist in conversation, she knew full well they were manipulating her into a guilt trip in order to keep the stray. "No. That cat is not an angel. I don't believe an angel would expect you to sneak behind my back and feed him. Especially when I told you not to. Got that?"

Gladdy shrugged and bent over her soup bowl. A sullen Hazy kept an eye out for her kitty through the windows on the lakeside. Someone pounded at the porch door.

"Who could that be at this hour?" Ilene looked down at her green plaid flannel nightshirt and navy blue sweat pants. Whomever it was would have to settle for sloppy. The digital clock on the microwave flashed 8:05 a.m. as she rushed by. Turning the doorknob, she peeked out the porch window. Kevin Wyland shifted from one foot to the other on the deck.

Flinging open the door impatiently, she rebuked him. "Ever hear of a telephone? Works great for making appointments."

Wearing a red Wilson Master Builders baseball cap on his head backwards, he nodded. "And good morning to you too, Mrs. Singleton. Heard you called Wilson's. I'm here to work."

She clucked her tongue. "Shouldn't we clear this with Terry first?"

Dressed in torn blue jeans revealing long underwear, and a faded Redskins sweatshirt under a patched down vest, Kevin shivered as the wind whipped his ponytail around his neck. "Mind if I step inside while we hash this out?"

Ilene backed up and held the door open for him to enter. By that time, Hazy and Gladdy were playing peek-a-boo from the bathroom doorway.

"The deal is, if I don't start today, it'll be three weeks before I can get back here," he warned.

"We can't wait three weeks." Remembering Philip's phone calls, Ilene knew he'd have a seizure if she let this guy get away again. Raking her fingers through her messy hair, she scolded him, "You should've called me first. I'm not real keen on you dropping by like this."

Kevin looked past her as the two giggling girls took turns slamming the bathroom doors. "Figured you had your hands full."

"I don't even know where to start." Ilene glared at them and instructed, "Girls, your bus will be here in ten minutes. Get going."

"Thought I'd start with frames and moldings," Kevin suggested.

"We ordered them from Slawson Millworks," she informed him. "They should be ready by now. You'll have to pick them up or have them delivered. Just sign for them, and have the bill sent to me."

"Mind if I check around?" he asked. "See if I need to pick up anything else."

Ilene stepped aside to let him pass. "All right."

She scuttled Hazy and Gladdy out the door to meet the bus. Twirling around, she opened the bathroom door to gather towels for a wash load.

"*Arr-eow.*" A silver streak raced past her, flashed through the kitchen and up the stairs.

"Boy are those two in trouble now," she declared in hot pursuit. Kevin kept tabs on her from the living room as she bounded the steps two at a time. She cornered the terrified animal in Hazy's loft bedroom. The spiral staircase was the only way out and she'd blocked it. "I've got you now."

Appearing at the bottom of the steps, he asked. "What's going on?"

"There's a wild cat up here," Ilene explained breathlessly. "I'm trying to get rid of it."

He ascended the stairs halfway. Ilene stepped up into Hazy's room.

"*Arr-eow.*" The silver gray cat mourned fearfully.

"Doesn't look too wild to me," Kevin decreed.

Ilene folded her arms. "It doesn't belong here. I want it outside."

"Poor cat'll die out in the cold," he assured her.

"You sound like my ten-year old," she quipped. "I am so sick of dealing with this cat." She looked down at him, but he'd already disappeared. Gradually, Ilene coaxed the timid creature from under Hazy's bed, and painstakingly herded him down three flights of stairs to the basement. Peering out the patio doors, she didn't see the maroon truck. Smirking, she wondered if her tirade had scared him off. How would she ever explain that to Philip?

After shutting the cat in the basement, she marched upstairs to take a shower. She needed to get to the bank and transfer funds so she could pay bills. She planned to stop by Sportstalker, Cathy and Stan's ski and bicycle shop downtown, and steal Cathy away for a lunch date. They hadn't really talked in weeks. Baby Arnie and building the house had preoccupied each of them.

An hour later, dressed in black stretch pants and a black and ivory print sweater, Ilene pulled on her suede boots in the foyer. She heard rummaging in the basement. Strolling through the bathroom to the porch, she saw Kevin's pickup in the driveway again. Breathing a sigh of relief, she had to admit she needed his help. Whether it was his arrogant demeanor or simply the fact that he was invading her privacy, she couldn't put her finger on it. Something about the man annoyed her. Closing the bathroom door she remembered that the kitchen door was still in the box downstairs. She found Kevin sorting and stacking the frames and moldings along the basement floor. Perched on the windowsill, the silver cat turned its back on her.

Kevin looked up in time to catch her sticking out her tongue at it. He shook his head in bewilderment. "What's with you and the cat?"

"My husband's allergic," Ilene told him. "It'll have to go when he gets back."

"Kids are sposed to have pets," Kevin said.

"I don't know. We had a beautiful golden retriever for six years. Last spring the girls were walking him down on Glenwood. He bolted after some cat. Hazy dropped the leash at the same time a dump truck came barreling down the hill." Ilene hesitated at that painful memory of their beloved Fozzie Bear. She sighed. The rest was too gruesome and sad to think about, much less share with this stranger.

Kevin removed his work gloves and slapped them together. "Know what you mean. Lost my white shepherd a couple years ago. It's rough."

Unprepared for this brief comradeship, Ilene looked away. "That's hardly the word for it."

"Wasn't the cat's fault."

Showing him a wan smile, she sparred back, "If you like that cat so much, why don't *you* take it home."

"Can't have him in my apartment."

"Where do you live?"

"Down the hill. Lester Park Suites."

"That's not very far away." Checking her watch Ilene informed him, "I have to go out now. But I want to show you something in the kitchen before I leave."

Hands on hips he asked, "What's that?"

Ilene eyes searched the perimeters of the basement. "There's a kitchen door around here somewhere."

"Dutch door. Ash. Over here." Kevin strolled toward the stairway. Kneeling down he slid the door out of the box. "Nice wood."

She leaned back. "How did you know that was down here?"

"Like I said, I pay attention to details."

Letting his arrogance slide, Ilene pressed on with her original mission. When she arrived at Sportstalker the racks of new K-2 and Rossignol skis caught her eye. Both she and Philip had planned to buy new skis this year. In fact they all had season passes for Spirit Mountain. She decided she'd better have him call Stan and put together a ski package for her by Christmas. Waving to Stan who was busy with a customer, she scooted past the dressing rooms, down the basement stairs, then found Cathy plunking away at the computer in the office. She gazed through the picture window into the recreation room next door.

Sara was playing with another toddler, their secretary Sally's daughter. Arnie was asleep in the crib. The Carricks were courageously testing on-site day care for themselves and their employees.

"Hey Cath. Can I steal you away for lunch?" Ilene tempted her.

She waved in acknowledgment. "In a minute. Just let me finish this."

Ilene strolled over to peer at the monitor. "What are you so wrapped up in over here?"

"Payroll. Tomorrow's payday so I have to get it done."

"How do you do payroll checks on the computer?" Ilene asked.

"Easy. We do all our banking on computer. It's perfect for payroll. I just send over the info on modem and *voila*—the troops are paid."

"We have a modem on our PC at home. I could do my banking the same way. Philip set it up so I have to draw from a joint account into my personal account to pay the bills. It's a hassle transferring money."

Cathy nodded. "All you need is a program. We use Smart Bank. It's easy."

"Philip has all the construction records on the computer, I can just look up the file and use his codes. What a great idea."

For lunch they both chose the veggie melt sandwich with French onion soup and Beck's light at the New London deli and bar.

As soon as they sat down, Cathy started in about Desert Shield. "Ohmygod. It's all happening so fast. We didn't even get a chance to see Philip before he left."

"Don't worry. He'll be back in a couple months," Ilene affirmed. "This Desert Shield thing isn't going anywhere. We'll all be skiing together in a couple months. That is if you're not swamped with work."

"Tell me about it," Cathy raved. "Since our new Spirit Mountain shop opened last weekend, we've definitely shifted into high gear. I can't seem to get as much done with the two kids. Really feeling frazzled these days."

"At least your day care experiment seems to be working out all right."

"I hope so. It's expensive and there's so many obstacles. But we're keeping our employees longer, so we don't have to spend a lot of time training new people. Maybe it all evens out."

"Having a sitter right there with you is a good idea. I should do that more often at home. I have a hard time getting things done when the girls are around. We never should've let the contractor go in the first place," Ilene lamented.

"But you didn't know Philip would be called up. Anyway I thought you said you were bringing a crew back in."

Ilene made a face. "Can't seem to get a whole crew. Terry Wilson sent over this guy. Kevin Wyland. He's there now, working on the place. You know I have this thing about strange people around my house. So I'm thinking, yeah right he's probably watching TV and drinking beer. Or worse yet, looting the place."

Cathy laughed. "Let's go spy on him. Is he cute?"

Ilene wrinkled her nose. "Definitely not cute. I don't know how to describe him. He's got this long dark ponytail—so retro."

"Does Philip know him?"

"He doesn't remember. But then, I can't tell you what the plumber looked like who walked in on me in the bathroom last August."

"In a way it's kinda creepy," Cathy warned. "All those construction workers paraded through your house last summer. And now they all know your husband's gone. Maybe you need a watch dog."

"I was thinking about a big old German shepherd. But the girls are pushing for this cat that's been hanging around."

"Not much protection."

"Looks like I'm stuck with the cat. And that carpenter dude."

"So I get the feeling you don't like this guy."

Ilene shrugged. "I don't know. He rubs me the wrong way. Typical contractor. Can't resist putting in his two cents worth about how we coulda done things better. I mean, Philip asked for a crew of carpenters and we end up with Mr. Wiseguy."

"Sounds to me like the guy's doing you a favor."

She rolled her eyes. "Oh he's made that crystal clear. I don't know if I can cope with that attitude in my face all the time."

Cathy laughed. "Maybe you should let him go before it gets ugly."

"Philip would have a cow if I did that." She groaned. "Damn. I don't want to deal with any of this. I just want my life back."

7

Kevin hadn't shown up by the time Ilene left on Thursday, November 29th. Some of the light fixtures she'd ordered hadn't come in. She had to spend the morning down at the Northern Lights showroom picking out replacements and going over the rest of the order to make sure the fixtures that *did* come in were the right ones. Home by noon, she pulled the Jeep alongside his pickup in the driveway.

How did he get in the house? She didn't recall leaving any doors unlocked. Entering through the garage, she tried the basement door. It was locked. One of the newer keys on her ring opened it. She flung the door wide. The burst of natural light cast eerie silhouettes.

"*Prrr-eow.*" The silver cat startled her as he leaped from the window ledge.

"Where *are* you?" Her voice echoed in the empty basement.

The fear rising inside only angered her. Heart racing she stomped upstairs through the house. She found Kevin on his knees in the second floor hallway, gluing moldings along the baseboards wearing his backwards baseball cap. He had his back to her, and she noticed the cassette player sticking out of his tool belt, with the wires connected to his ears.

Just like a kid, she thought. "How did you get in here?"

He turned around, pulling the earphones away. "Howdy."

"I asked you how you got in here."

He stood up and faced her defensively. "Luckily the patio door was open."

"That's not true," Ilene accused. "All the doors were locked. You never told me what time you'd be here."

Hands on hips he fired back, "Look Mrs. Singleton. You want me to work here, either give me a key or leave the door unlocked. That's the last time I hunt for a way in."

"Hmm." Ilene sniffed. She thought about what Cathy had said yesterday about letting him go. "Maybe that's the problem."

"What's that."

"I'm not sure you're the right man for this job." She couldn't believe the words came out of her mouth.

"Fine." He tossed his hands in the air. "I'll finish up today. Then I'm outa here."

"Good." She turned to walk away.

"Wilson's doing you all a huge favor sending me up here on this piddly job. The rest of his crew is booked through January."

"Guess I'll have to call in another contractor," Ilene retorted.

"Suit yourself." He went back to work.

Ilene returned to the Jeep and backed it into the garage. She carried the boxes of light fixtures from the Jeep into the basement by herself. Full of resentment at Kevin's arrogance, she decided not to ask him for any more help.

When Hazy and Gladdy clamored through the front door after school, Ilene was holed up in the den, searching the computer files for a list of independent contractors, comprehending the price she'd have to pay for letting this guy go. She closed the file and wandered out to the living room to find him. The girls were watching *Darkwing Duck* on TV. The phone rang.

"Hi. You heard the news yet?" It was Philip. "Bush set a January fifteenth deadline."

Ilene decided not to mention her confrontation with Kevin. "Deadline. For what."

"If Saddam Hussein doesn't release the hostages and get out of Kuwait by January fifteenth, we're gonna start bombing Baghdad. And if that happens, we go too."

"Christ Philip." Ilene rubbed her entire face with her left hand and sat down. "January?"

"To Saudi Arabia."

"Wait. Maybe this is just another line in the sand. Everybody's got trigger fingers right now. They'll back down."

"I don't think so," Philip said solemnly. "We're being vaccinated next week."

She closed her eyes. "This is not happening. I'll bring the girls down next weekend."

"We'll see. Did you get a hold of that carpenter?"

Grasping the opportunity to erase the past couple days she lied, "No. He never called back. I checked the computer file for some other contractors."

"No way, Ilene. It has to be one of Wilson's crew. Those guys know the place. I don't want some rookie fucking things up."

She winced at the truth. "You're right. I'll keep trying."

Obviously needing to talk, Philip updated her about his unit's inventory battles. He complained that next week they'd probably start painting their vehicles the color of desert sand. "Anyway, enough about all that. What's going on around there?"

Ilene told him about her visit to Sportstalker hinting, "You should talk to Stan about my Christmas present."

"Can't imagine what that could be," he fibbed.

"By the way, Cathy showed me her banking program. I'm going to start banking by computer."

Philip cleared his throat. "We don't really have enough account activity for that. Remember, Stan and Cathy run a business. I'm sure computer banking's not available on personal accounts."

Ilene sighed with disappointment. "Oh. I never thought of that."

"Can I talk to the girls now?"

Hazy and Gladdy squealed and giggled on the phone to their dad while Ilene gazed out the window. Fog had filled in where the lake was supposed to be, creating the appearance of infinite layers of gray clouds into a darkening sky. The notion of Philip actually going off to war in the desert was incomprehensible. After they all said good-bye, she fixed grilled cheese sandwiches and alphabet soup for the girls. As she sat down to eat one herself, the evening news came on the portable TV. Switching through the stations she found the news shows bombarded with stories about the January 15th deadline. Her appetite gradually succumbed to the sickening parade of reactions from Margaret Thatcher's hard line politics to the bawling eighteen-year old wife of an enlisted man in North Carolina. They all seemed pretty gung-ho about bombing Baghdad.

The girls bolted their sandwiches. Scrambling from the table, they grabbed a box of mini Oreos on their way through the kitchen and disappeared upstairs. Alone with CNN, Ilene caught the reflection of a male figure in the window. Flinching at Kevin's appearance out of the dark hallway, she had forgotten he was still there.

"Stayed late and finished all the moldings upstairs," he explained in a husky voice. She could tell he was angry.

Staring at the TV screen, Ilene also knew she needed to find a way to work things out with him. "Look. I—um—I guess we should talk about this."

Kevin stepped over to the table where she sat and tossed his ponytail. "You could start by saying you're sorry."

Ilene groaned. "Sorry for what."

"You are one hard headed woman." Kevin turned to walk away.

"Wait. Please." Ilene stood up and ran her hands through her hair. "Must be all the pressure lately. I'm really not such a bitch. But I have to be careful. You can't expect me to trust you, just like that."

"I'm just here to do a job, ma'am," he declared.

"You see, I have this thing about privacy. I don't like other people in my face," Ilene warned.

"So. That was *in your face* when I asked for a key."

She nodded. "You can't come and go as you please around here."

"That's the way I operate. Take it or leave it."

Ilene shrugged and reached for her purse on the center island. Plucking a key off her ring she tossed it to Kevin. "That's for the porch door."

He caught it, then carefully rolled it across his hand, considering her gesture. Finally he set the key down on the counter. "I have this thing about bitchy women in my face."

He headed toward the Dutch door. Ilene was reminded that not only had he hung that door yesterday like she asked, but he'd hinged it on the proper side, without her supervision.

"Okay. I'm sorry," she said at last.

He stopped and tilted his head in her direction, his gaze still aloof. She tossed him the key once more. He caught it and strolled out.

8

Ilene grabbed the mail out of the box as she cooled down from a thirty minute jog on a frosty Thursday morning, December 6th. The envelope on top was from the hospital, Philip's final paycheck. Standing at the front doorstep, she peeled it open and stared at the amount—$1,146.11

"What the hell," she muttered.

As she pushed on the handle, the door seemed stuck. Tripping over Mr. Kitty as he circled her ankles, she fell against the door.

"Watch out!" Kevin hollered.

A commotion ensued on the other side. The door swung wide. Ilene sprawled headlong onto the tile. The cat clawed across her spandex legs.

Kevin stood over her with a wry grin. "By the way, I'm putting up fixtures in the foyer today."

Lacking a witty comeback, Ilene attacked instead. "Don't leave a big mess behind like you always do. The broom closet's in the kitchen."

Offering a hand, he pulled her off the floor. "You want me to clean your house."

Composing herself, she gathered up the scattered pieces of mail.

"Look. We have a rule in this house. You make a mess. You clean it up."

He cocked his head. "I got news for you. Better get a fucking maid."

The phone rang before she could strike back. Fuming she limped into the den to answer.

"Ilene. It's Gerry Cusick." Commander Cusick's wife, Captain Geraldine Baker Cusick retired from the 477th last December. Rumor had that she tried to get permission to go with the unit this time but was denied, which in Ilene's mind qualified her as a radical patriot. "Just calling to remind you of the family association we've organized at the Armory. And the Red Cross recently put in a direct phone line to McCoy. Calls are free on family night. Friday night we're having a pizza party, sponsored by Dominos. Will you come?"

"I don't know." Ilene stalled. She felt about as comfortable with Philip's Army family as she did the Singletons. "What time?"

"Eighteen hundred hours," Gerry answered in military time. "By then we should have more news about their mission."

"That would be nice for a change." Baited by the possibility of information, Ilene jotted herself a note at the computer desk after she hung up the phone.

Philip's paycheck stuck out from the rest of the mail—$1,146.11 Something was definitely wrong. The record on the stub declared his gross pay was $1,750 for a two-week pay period. Calling up the calculator on the computer screen, she figured his gross annual income at around $45,000. But she felt certain he earned more than that.

She called up their checkbook records. His Reserve paycheck netted him an additional $1200 a month. She thought he kept those funds in a separate account for the house. Between their joint account and her personal account, nearly $6,000 had been deposited each month. She had always assumed the money came from his paycheck at the hospital.

When he called after seven that night, she asked him about the discrepancy right away. "Your final paycheck came from St. Mary's today. Philip, how much do they pay you there?"

"How much was the check for?" he asked.

"A little over a thousand dollars," she told him. "For two weeks' pay."

He hesitated. "Go ahead and deposit that in your account."

"I'm confused. There's about six thousand going through our accounts every month. Where's that money come from?" Ilene asked.

"Why do you even worry about stuff like that? There's enough money in the bank to get through the next year. All you have to do is draw the funds out of our joint account and pay the bills with your personal account. What's so confusing about that?"

"That's not the point, Philip," she argued.

"I think it is," he stated. By then Hazy and Gladdy had figured out it was their dad on the phone and were clicking on and off the loft extension.

Ilene surrendered. "Okay. Okay. You girls can have him now."

9

The drive to Fort McCoy in southern Wisconsin was uneventful on Saturday, December 8th. Heavy gray skies hovered over the snow crusted landscape and frostbitten roads. Ilene made Minneapolis-St. Paul suburbs by 8:25 a.m. The girls slept in the back seat since she'd roused them at five-thirty. They awoke when she pulled into Hardee's drive-thru in White Bear Lake, not far from Gail's townhouse.

"Can't we go inside?" Hazy begged. "I *hate* eating in the car. It makes me sick."

"This way we get to see Daddy faster," Ilene coaxed.

Rubbing her eyes Gladdy whined, "I have to go potty."

"Okay. You win. Let's make it quick." Ilene parked the car.

Neither of them enjoyed traveling all that much. So when they haggled over the Disney Christmas ornaments they'd begged her to buy them with their breakfasts, Ilene was tempted to drop them off with Gail for the weekend and keep Daddy all to herself. She was hoping that time alone with Philip could bridge the gap that was slowly widening between them. She noticed that Hazy and Gladdy bickered more since he left.

Overwhelmed by her own struggle she was at a loss as to how to affect their behavior one way or another. Instead she counted on their dad coming home in January, ending this breach in their lives.

"Let me see your Mickey Mouse for just two seconds," Gladdy hassled her sister.

"You wanted Goofy, you got Goofy." Hazy laughed at her own joke.

"Mommy, she keeps making fun of my orm-a-nent."

Trying not to smile, Ilene handed her two dollars. "Here, go buy the one you want."

"That's not fair," Hazy protested. "Now she gets two."

Handing her a five Ilene caved in. "Go get another one. And stop tormenting her."

Because Camp McCoy was designated a restricted area Philip arranged to meet them at the Holiday Inn of Tomah. Ilene perched on the chaise by the pool and worked on her Christmas lists, finally. Consumed by the upheaval at home, she hadn't put much effort into the holiday season. Philip played with the girls in the pool. She was glad to have their attention focused on someone besides herself, every waking moment. Single parenting was definitely for the birds, as if she had any choice. Dripping wet, they scuttled over to Ilene. She handed out three towels.

While Philip dried his hair he mentioned, "Hazy said you let them keep that cat."

"Miss-ster Kitt-tee," Gladdy corrected him. "He's a angel."

Ilene glared at Hazy for stretching the truth. "All I did was buy some cat food because the girls were feeding him tuna. Then I put a litter box in the basement because he gets in down there and goes on the floor. He'll eventually leave with that carpenter. They like each other."

"So how's it going with what's-his-name?" Philip asked.

"His name is Kevin," Hazy informed him.

"He took over my room," Gladdy pouted.

Philip raised his eyebrows.

Shaking her head, Ilene explained, "We're still waiting for their carpeting. All her stuff's piled in the hallway. And she's sick of sleeping in the guest room."

"He doing a good job?" Philip prodded.

"Yes," Ilene admitted. "But he doesn't keep a schedule. Just comes and goes as he pleases. You know how that gets on my nerves."

"He's got this really cool cell phone," Hazy brought up. "Keeps it in the pocket of his vest."

"Oh, I've seen him talk on that before," Gladdy put in her two cents worth.

"See what I mean?" Ilene complained. "He never said anything to me about a phone. Yet I keep bugging him to call and tell me when he's coming to work."

"Maybe it's just a two-way phone to the office," Philip suggested.

Hazy spotted the video game arcade. "Can I have money for tokens?"

Philip handed each of them a twenty dollar bill out of his wallet on the table.

Their mom groaned. "Whoa. Take it easy."

While the girls scampered away gleefully, their father leaned forward and planted a delicious kiss on their mother's mouth. "I've got something else for you," he whispered nibbling her ear. "Let's sneak off to the room."

Ilene grinned and trotted eagerly behind him. Although once they climbed beneath the sheets their lovemaking turned into raw sex. She felt as if Philip had shut down his emotions and switched over to animal instinct. He was demanding, yet hard to satisfy. Eventually spent, he lay back on the bed and watched CNN. Kissing him, Ilene clutched the remote and turned off the TV. He pulled away, and switched it back on.

Ilene stared at the screen and sighed. "How can you stand that constant barrage? It's bad enough with those special reports every hour."

"Christ Ilene," Philip grumbled. "Don't you want to know what the fuck's going on? This is the real thing."

"Please don't let's go there right now. Anyway, there isn't going to be a war."

"War or no war, we *are* going over to Saudi Arabia." he confirmed.

Ilene shuddered. "But your unit hasn't even left Wisconsin yet. That last group was here how long?"

"Three months," he conceded. "But when we *do* leave—and the district brass have all but guaranteed there's a transport plane in Saudi with our number on it—I could be gone for six months."

"You heard what I said," she insisted. "That's not going to happen."

"Okay. How bout some good news for a change." He tousled her hair. "Rumor has it they're busing us home for Christmas."

She hugged him. "See what I mean? That's the first step toward sending you back."

"Listen to me Ilene. Our current orders put us right here at McCoy till January fifteenth. No matter what."

"By then United Nations' peace objectives will expand into negotiations. Bush'll trade some arms for hostages under the table to placate Saddam. And you'll be coming home for good. Maybe you'll even be granted early discharge for so radically disrupting your life."

Rolling his eyes he snickered. "Dream on, honey."

Leaning forward she guided his hands underneath her T-shirt. "When I dream, I dream of you."

They kissed long and luxuriously. She felt him finally letting down his guard.

"Knock, knock," Hazy called out. "Let us in, we're hungry."

"Me want pizza." Gladdy imitated Cookie Monster.

The clamor outside the door split them apart.

10

The doorbell chimed and the phone rang at the same instant shortly before noon the following Tuesday, December 11th. Grabbing the cordless in the front hallway Ilene ran into Kevin at the top of the basement stairs.

"Get the door for me," she ordered.

He flung open the heavy oak door as he strode past.

Frowning after him she answered the phone. "Hello."

"Ilene. It's Gerry Cusick. We missed you and the kids at the pizza party last week."

"We decided to drive down and see Philip instead." Ilene flattened herself against the stair wall while two burly men hauled in the carpeting for the girls' rooms. Practical Hazy had chosen a lush sponge back in earthy terra cotta. Gladdy had fallen for the flat pile, red and black checkerboard carpeting at the store. No doubt she fantasized playing games in her room for hours on end.

"Then you must've heard about Christmas," Gerry was saying. "Terrific news, isn't it?"

Mr. Kitty bolted in the door with the workmen and dashed downstairs.

Distracted by the commotion and how Kevin seemed to have disappeared, Ilene didn't answer right away.

"Ilene. Are you still there?"

"Yes. I'm sorry. The carpet layers just arrived. I'm a little distracted at the moment."

"Just wanted to let you know the family association has decided to meet every week. I hope you'll join us."

"I've just been so swamped with this house lately. But thanks for calling." As Ilene turned off the phone, the guys were bringing in Gladdy's carpet. The corner flopped over, exposing Disney characters printed on a cherry red background.

"Oh no." She groaned. "That's the wrong carpet."

The two men dropped the roll.

"And please don't tell me there's not a roll of red and black checkerboard in your truck."

They shrugged and said in unison, "Okay."

Ilene hunched forward as if struck by a blow. She rubbed her face with her hands. "I ordered that carpet a month ago."

"Tell you what, we'll install that other roll while you call the store and get this one straightened out," the taller, bearded one said.

As they headed upstairs, Kevin appeared and leaned against the bathroom door. "Another day. Another fuck up."

"Go on up there and make sure they install it right," she demanded, then marched off.

When the girls burst through the front door in the late afternoon Gladdy hollered, "Boy is it ever snowing!"

"Our bus almost crashed twice," Hazy added.

Ilene grimaced. "You're kidding. Right?"

"Not."

"The carpet layers were here today. I think Kevin's putting up the molding in your room as we speak."

"Really? Cool!" Hazy raced up the stairs.

63

"What about my carpet?" Gladdy whined.

"They sent the wrong stuff. It'll be here next week," Ilene told her.

"You mean Hazy gets her room back and I don't. I hate that guest room. I hate it!" she squealed and fled upstairs.

Ignoring her tantrum Ilene retreated to the kitchen to start supper. Rummaging through the cupboards and refrigerator she found enough ingredients to stir up a hamburger casserole. After putting it in the oven she stared out at the driving snowstorm in the premature darkness and thought about Gladdy. She'd definitely overreacted to the carpeting glitch. Something bad must've happened at school to set her off. Ilene decided to go have a talk with her.

Knocking on the guest room door she sang out, "Glad—dee." No answer. She turned the knob and peeked in. The lights were on and a TV news show blared another Desert Shield update. Obviously Gladdy wasn't around. Ilene turned off the tube and climbed the spiral staircase to the loft. Midway she paused to hear the conversation above.

"Do you have any kids?" Hazy was asking.

"Nope," was Kevin's reply.

"Do you like kids?"

"Guess so. They tell me I was a kid once."

Hazy giggled. "Doesn't your wife like kids?"

"Not married."

"So do you have a girlfriend?"

"Nope."

"Don't you like girls either?"

"Actually I prefer women."

"Oh yeah? What kind of women?"

With that inappropriate question Ilene made a sudden, noisy ascent. She found Hazy struggling with her bed sheets while Kevin reassembled her storage units on the other side of the room.

Grabbing the elastic corner of the Ninja Turtles sheet Ilene asked, "Where's your sister?"

Hazy shrugged. "Haven't seen the little goonie."

"Did you look in the basement?" Kevin spoke up "The cat's down there."

Ilene bounded down two flights of stairs and through the front hallway. Stepping in a dirty puddle on the floor next to Hazy's boots, she noticed Gladdy's hot pink jacket was missing from the pile.

"Shit." Opening the door she called out, "Gladdy!" A volley of snowflakes pelted her as she listened for an answer. Harsh wind swooped down from the pine treetops tearing her eyes. "Glad—dee," she cried, her stomach tightening. Switching on the outdoor lights, she saw dwarfish boot prints that disappeared off the edge of the snowy boardwalk.

Kevin's shadow filled the doorway. "What's up?"

Ilene sucked in the wind. "Gladdy's jacket's gone." She pointed. "Those're her tracks."

"Where at?" He ventured out into the blowing flakes and studied the snow. "Looks like she's with the cat. She hasn't been out here too long."

Ilene stared at the cat tracks next to Gladdy's prints. "Damn cat. I'm going out after them." Rushing past him, she hauled out layers of gloves and jackets from the closet.

Kevin closed the door after her. "I'll go with you."

"Hazy!" Ilene hollered, pulling on her pac boots.

Her oldest daughter stood at the second floor railing. "I'm coming too."

"No. It's too cold. You stay here," Ilene ordered.

"Should I call 911?" she asked.

"Not yet," Kevin answered. "Make sure all the doors are unlocked so she can get inside anywhere."

"Okay." Hazy ran down the stairs to her mother. Glancing with uncertainty toward Kevin she babbled, "Mom. Sometimes we go on that trail across the road."

"I know," Ilene said.

Hazy rolled her eyes. "Don't tell me. Gladdy tattled. Anyway, Mr. Kitty goes over there too."

"I'll get a flashlight," Kevin interrupted. "Meet you out front."

11

The great oak door closed behind her like an airlock. Brutal gusts off the lake set into motion driving ice pellets, feeding her panic. Ilene shivered. Kevin met her in the front yard which the snow had transformed into an alien planet surface.

Wearing a dark gray parka with the furry hood up, his thick wool gloves waved a flashlight beacon. "Follow me."

As they forged the four to six-inch drifts on the road, Kevin stopped abruptly as the beam of light revealed blood and gray tufts in a tire track.

"Oh sh—shit." She breathed. "The cat's hurt."

"Looks like it was hit. Not that long ago."

"Gladdy must've found it. There's a trail on the other side."

They picked up Gladdy's boot prints across the road. Numbed by an awful aching guilt about the cat, Ilene trudged silently behind Kevin. Luckily the old snow had packed down hard and the new layer was only ankle deep. At the crest of the small hill she stopped.

"Glad—dee!" she hollered.

An air horn blasted from his flashlight case. Ilene jumped and stumbled into him. He boosted her upright.

Nose dripping from the cold she sniffed. "That thing's obnoxious. Warn me next time."

Ignoring her complaint he said, "No response yet. Let's keep moving."

Even with his body shielding her, the wind whipped across her eyes forcing tears. Kevin hit the air horn again.

Irritated, Ilene punched his padded shoulder. "Knock it off."

"Quiet. Thought I heard something. Here goes."

Ilene pressed the backs of her mittened hands against the wool hat covering her ears. The air horn blasted a third time. She heard a muffled cry. They stomped toward it.

"Gladdy!"

"Mommy!" her child's voice wailed.

"Keep talking kiddo," Kevin hollered.

"Mommy! My kit—tee." She sobbed.

They were close. Ilene felt like she could reach out and touch her grief. They found her huddled against a great boulder, sheltered from the wind. Next to her on a nest of leaves lay poor Mr. Kitty, obviously dead.

Ilene fell to her knees in the snow and wrapped her arms around her daughter. "I'm so sorry baby."

"That's okay. Daddy's ler-jik. And you never liked him anyway."

"Oh honey! I never wanted him to die," Ilene bawled.

She sniffled. "Will you help me bury him?"

"Of course." The two of them piled leaves and snow over Mr. Kitty's broken body. Kevin stood over them, shining the light.

"Dear God," Gladdy prayed. "Now he's really truly a angel kitty."

"Let's move out, ladies," Kevin ordered. "The wind's not letting up."

He swooped in and hoisted the little one onto his shoulders.

Hazy met them at the front door. "Where've you guys been?"

Kevin set Gladdy down on the tile inside the door. Ilene closed it behind them.

She shuffled over to her big sister and whimpered, "Mr. Kitty's gone to heaven."

"What are you talking about?" Hazy cried. She glared tearfully at her mother. "What did you do to him?"

Ilene cringed. She hadn't realized how deeply her disdain for the cat had hurt them both. "It wasn't me. Honest."

"I took him out to see the snow," Gladdy confessed. "But the wind scared him. And he like blew away. Into the road. Then the car hit him."

"You stupid little moron. It's all your fault," Hazy accused.

Gladdy sobbed. "I know."

Ilene rushed in between them and hugged both girls. "That's not true. He was wild. It was an accident."

"I wanted that kitty so bad," Hazy cried.

"I know." Ilene comforted her. "I'm sorry."

Gladdy stepped back and shook away her sorrow. Wiping her nose, she bravely uttered her best Cookie Monster imitation. "Me hungry. Me want pizza."

"I better be going," Kevin declared in the midst of it.

Rising to a stand Ilene offered, "There's casserole in the oven. Nothing fancy. You're welcome to stay. It's the least I can do. You found Gladdy."

He sniffed. "Smells pretty good."

Plunking himself down at Philip's place at the table, Kevin ate hungrily. Hazy and Gladdy chattered about the new carpet and the wrong carpet. Eventually they grew somber.

Gladdy stared sadly at her plate. "There's no kitty to share my food."

"Like Mr. Kitty ever even ate with us," Hazy snapped.

"Did too."

"Not."

"I'm sure you both have homework," Ilene interrupted. "Time to head upstairs."

Gladdy slid off the bench, trotted over and hugged Kevin's forearm. "Thank you for rescuing me."

He patted her head. "Next time tell your mom what you're up to."

Thinking he was leaving, Ilene waved him off and coaxed the girls to their rooms.

Stopping first in Gladdy's room she asked, "Feeling better now?"

Reminded of the night's trauma once more, tears slipped down her cheeks. "I guess so. It's just that I miss my daddy so much."

"Just remember, Daddy's coming home for Christmas." Ilene hugged her. "Now do your spelling."

In the loft Hazy sat at her desk. "I love my new carpet. It's neat how Kevin fixed my room."

"That's his job." Ilene stood over her. "Still mad at me?"

Shaking her head, Hazy's eyes swelled with tears. "I miss my dad."

Ilene caressed her shoulders. "He'll be home soon."

"Mom," Hazy called out as she headed down the steps. "I want a puppy for Christmas."

Not about to touch that subject, Ilene replied, "Do your math homework."

Kevin was still sitting at the dining room table, drinking from a bottle of Molson. "I was thirsty. Found this in the fridge."

"I could do with one of those my own self." Ilene strolled over to the refrigerator and grabbed a beer. Searching her purse for the cigarettes she'd snitched from Betty's carton two weeks ago, she came up with an empty pack and crumpled it on the counter. "Damn. I could sure use a smoke. Got any cigarettes?"

Kevin glanced over. "Fresh out. Didn't know you smoked."

"Old habits die hard." Developing a thirst, Ilene sucked down the beer. The buzz of alcohol surged through her like a second wind. She wondered why Kevin stayed and said so. "Why are you still here?"

He rose to his feet. "You want me to leave."

"No. No. That's not what I meant." She sat down and motioned for him to do the same. "Help yourself to another beer. Fetch me one too while you're at it."

Twisting the tops off two more bottle he slid onto the bench next to her.

"I'm glad you stayed," she confessed. "I wanted to thank you."

After a long slow drink from the green bottle he replied, "Then why not just come right out and say it."

"Thank—you," she enunciated.

He laughed. "You'll get my bill."

Ilene cocked her head. "You're quite the mystery man. I don't know the first thing about you."

"Haven't we had this conversation once before?" He scratched his head innocently. "What do you need to know?"

Ilene lunged through the opening. "Okay. How old are you?"

Feigning surprise he quipped, "You go right for the tough questions Mrs. Singleton."

"Answer the question, Mr. Wyland."

"Twenty-nine."

"You seem younger than that."

Kevin smiled. "You don't believe me."

Shaking her head impishly she said, "If you say you're twenty-nine, then you're twenty-nine."

"How old are *you*?" He joined her game.

"Guess."

Leaning back, he covered her with his gaze. His eyes were violet. How strange she'd never noticed such unusual eyes before now. "You're younger than your husband. But Hazy's ten. I'll say thirty-two."

"I wish." She drank from the bottle and nodded. "Thirty-six."

"Hmm. Must be the jogging."

Noticing the square bulge inside his denim vest, Ilene brushed aside the offhanded compliment with a probing question. "Is that your cell phone?"

He clutched his vest, looking ambushed. Pulling out the small black phone, he flipped it open and shut. "Looks that way."

"Why don't you give me the number?"

Raising his eyebrows he tucked it away. "You mean so you can call up and give me shit any time you want."

Ilene smacked the table top. "You really think I'd do that. I'm not that bad. Am I?"

"Let's just keep things the way they are."

"What that sposed to mean?" Ilene grumbled. "Look. If you think I'm a bitch you should meet my mother-in-law. Marie Singleton. Her life's work is making others miserable."

"You don't like your mother-in-law."

Ilene frowned. "She started it. Calls me *Elaine*. She landed here at Thanksgiving like Columbus in the New World. Just marched in and took over the place."

Peering over his shoulder, Kevin teased, "Think she's still around here somewhere?"

"She left her mark in the guest room. Not to mention that stairway carpeting. I have no idea when she'll fly in on her broomstick. That family has mega bucks. God only knows what elaborate stunt she'll pull next time."

"Has she always been this overbearing?"

"Are you kidding?" Ilene scoffed. "That's the whole rub. Before Philip's unit got called up. Before we built this house we saw those people maybe once a year at Lake Geneva. Philip was never close to his parents."

Kevin stared outside at the snowdrifts swirling in the wind on the deck.

Ilene finished her beer. "Guess I'm boring you."

He stood up. "I'm sure the roads aren't in too good a shape. Better get moving."

"At least you've got four-wheel drive." She followed him through the kitchen to the porch. Putting on his parka he said, "Too bad about the cat."

"I really blew it. I had no idea how much they loved that kitty." A single tear slid down her cheek. "Can you believe this? I didn't even like the cat." Brushing it away, she unwittingly smeared dust from the windowsill off the back of her hand.

Tucking his ponytail into the hood with his left hand, Kevin reached out with his right and wiped the smudge off her cheek with his thumb. Ilene sneezed. He pulled his hand back and wiped it on his sleeve. Giddy from the beer, they both laughed until she had to sit down on the wicker couch.

Kevin leaned against the back door to catch his breath. "I'm outa here." He exited in a swirl of snowflakes.

12

Coffee mug in hand, Ilene sequestered herself in the den with the computer mid morning Monday, December 17th. She faced a showdown with a stack of construction invoices totaling over ten thousand dollars. That was before she added the girls' carpeting and Christmas shopping bills from the past weekend. At least Gladdy's carpet arrived and was installed last Friday, resolving one crisis. When the phone rang she was surprised to hear Philip's voice. Personal calls had restricted hours at the base.

"I waited until the girls left for school. I'll call them tomorrow. Wanted the chance to talk to you alone without interruption," he explained.

"Something wrong?" Ilene clenched her teeth.

"It's about Christmas."

Gripping the receiver she groaned. "Please don't tell me you can't come home."

"Not that. It's my parents. They're flying up for the day."

"Sh—shit," Ilene cursed. "This is so unfair."

"It's my fault. I never should've mentioned the forty-eight hour leave when I called them."

"That should be our time together as a family."

Philip sighed audibly. "At least you won't have to cook. Mother said Thanksgiving worked so well, she's going to have the Radisson come up with Christmas dinner, too."

"How dare she make plans without running them by me," Ilene fussed. "She treats me like a non-person."

"She's pissed at you for firing the decorator she hired."

"Hah!" She laughed. "Ask me if I care."

"Gotta admit it takes a load off you," he insisted. "What should we do about a tree?"

"Haven't even thought about it."

"How about a ten foot spruce with hundreds of those tiny white lights in front of the dining room windows. Wouldn't that look spectacular?"

"I can't handle a ten foot spruce by myself."

Someone was asking Philip a question in the background. "That's the wrong supplier," he replied. "Listen. I gotta go. You'll figure out something."

Ilene put down the phone. Looking up the number of their bank she muttered, "Christmas tree. Bah humbug." She dialed the phone and asked for an account executive.

"This is Esther Cray," a woman's voice came on line.

"This is Ilene Singleton. I want to check the balance on my account. I need to transfer about ten thousand from our joint account into my personal account to pay bills."

"May I have those account numbers, please?"

Having called up their bookkeeping program on the computer, Ilene read the numbers off the screen.

"Actually you already have seventeen thousand five hundred three and twenty-four cents in your personal account. And your joint account shows a balance of three hundred twenty-five thousand and forty-seven cents."

Stunned, Ilene repeated the amounts as she wrote down the figures.

"Mrs. Singleton, I am aware that your husband is at McCoy with the 477th. I want you to know that we value your family's business with this bank. If there's any way I can be of assistance in handling these accounts don't hesitate to call on me."

Staggered by the numbers in front of her, Ilene tapped her pen on the mouse pad.

"Mrs. Singleton? Are you still there?"

"Yes," she spoke up. "Actually it would be so much easier if I could transfer funds by computer from my home. Is that service available on personal accounts?"

"By all means. Let me set that up for you. I can train you on the software after the holidays. Will that be soon enough?"

"Sounds good to me." Ilene said. "And who knows. Maybe this whole Persian Gulf thing will be resolved by then."

After hanging up the phone, she mulled over their hefty bank accounts. No wonder Philip had been so evasive about their finances. He knew she'd have a fit over such a huge loan from his parents. That explained why Marie walked all over her at Thanksgiving, acting like she owned the place. Taking a deep breath she vowed that once Philip comes home in January, they would free themselves of that entanglement. Noticing the mail delivery through the windows, she headed for the door. She yanked on the knob, thinking it was shut, then stopped short nearly tripping over Kevin who was gluing moldings to the wall.

"Excuse me." She stepped around him, then glanced over her shoulder, wondering if he'd eavesdropped on her phone conversations. That was the whole problem with having hired help—no stinking privacy.

When she returned with the stack of Christmas cards and bills, Kevin was on his feet, leaning against the door frame of her den. "Got an extra set of blueprints laying around anywhere?"

Breezing past him she asked, "What for?"

"Need some way to keep track of all these projects." He followed her.

"Over here. On the computer." Gesturing for him to enter she nearly swatted him. Directly behind her he ducked. "We had the blueprints scanned. I'll print copies for you." She worked the keyboard while Kevin hovered over.

"Put the basement on screen," he directed. She pressed the "L" key twice for *"lower level"*. Reaching around her shoulder he pointed at the floor plan. "If you leave out this wall and combine the game room and family room, it'd make better use of the natural light down there. Otherwise it's gonna be real dark."

Leaning away from him, Ilene rolled her eyes. "I'll make a note of that." The printer hummed and spat out fresh copies. She handed them over.

"Thanks. I'll let you know if I need more."

"I'm sure you will."

Ilene fretted about the money through the rest of that day and long past midnight. Propped on pillows in bed, the old movie *Ordinary People* played in the background as she mulled over her dilemma. Philip kept referring to it as a loan. Compared to the financial woes of other Reservists' families, she had a hell of safety net in those accounts. But that was the thing about a safety net that bothered her, it was after all just a bunch of strings attached. Talking to him over the phone wasn't a good idea. He usually backed away from the subject. Knowing the military, she figured the phone conversations originating from McCoy were probably being monitored anyway. Outside the row of windows she glimpsed the spectacle of northern lights above the treetops. As the green and yellow hues rippled across the dark sky, she grieved for the way their lives used to be.

Ilene overslept the alarm in the morning. Instead a racket on the deck below her bedroom window startled her awake. Crawling across the bedclothes she pressed her face against the cold glass. Strands of rope hung off the railing. Peering in the opposite direction, she made out the tail end of Kevin's truck parked on the roadside. *What was he up to so early?*

Curious, she pulled her red plaid robe over her pastel striped nightshirt, slipped on a pair of navy sweats and shuffled out to the hallway. Since it was after 7:30 a.m., she felt relieved to find Hazy and Gladdy awake and noisy in their bathrooms. She padded downstairs on the soft wool carpet as Kevin emerged through the front door, huffing and puffing.

"Mornin'." He held up a box. "Can you put together a tree stand?"

"A tree stand."

Casting a long look at her morning layers he commented, "You overslept."

Barefoot and frowning, she crept after him through the south atrium door. She stopped short and shivered. "W-what's with these r-ropes?"

"Put some shoes on," he ordered. "Have a look."

"Stop with the suspense," Ilene grumbled. "Why don't you just *tell* me what you're doing."

With an injured look he said, "It's an eight foot blue spruce."

"A tree." Ilene leaned over the deck railing. "And it's huge!"

Hazy showed up in the doorway. "Mom, you forgot to wake us up."

Gladdy wasn't far behind. "What's going on?"

"It's our Christmas tree," she told them.

The three of them watched while Kevin yanked on the ropes, lifting the tall pine off the ground. Chattering their approval, the girls helped him hoist the green paper wrapped bundle onto the deck.

Ilene breathed in a whiff of pine sap. She looked gratefully at Kevin. "Wow. This is quite a surprise. How much do I owe you?"

Dusting needles off his gloves he shrugged. "Let's call it a Christmas present."

"Uh-oh. Does that mean I have to get you something?" she teased.

"Can we trim it tonight?" Hazy asked.

"Please," Gladdy begged.

"Okay. Sure. Right now you better get ready for the bus." Ilene turned to Kevin. "Want some coffee?"

"After I'm done here."

Since the bus was late, Ilene fed the girls bagels and juice boxes while they waited on the front step. She noticed that Hazy had begun wearing her Minnesota Twins baseball cap backward like Kevin. As she wiped butter smears from the other one's cheek, a black Mercedes rolled swiftly by along the gravel road.

Gladdy stared as if her eyes could pop right out of their sockets. "That's the car that hit Mr. Kitty!"

"Maybe it's the same color," Ilene declared. Although something about the car did seem familiar. "But I don't think it's the exact car."

"Is so!" Gladdy insisted. "We've seen it before."

"Probably someone who lives around here," her mom explained.

"With Illinois license plates?" Hazy asked.

Heart thumping Ilene's awareness snapped into focus. "Are you sure?"

"Positive. HMP 672," she recited confidently.

"You memorized the license number. Good girl," her mom praised, although she trembled inside.

"That's how we always know it's the same car," her youngest informed her.

"Did either of you see the driver?"

Hazy shook her head. "Tinted windows."

Repeating HMP 672 in her brain, Ilene put the girls on the bus and retreated indoors. In the living room she found Kevin heaving the awkward pine into the stand. She rushed over to help him steady it. Once they set it upright, the tree fit easily into the brackets. While he crawled underneath and adjusted the tension at the base, she peeled off the paper tape.

"God. This thing's a monster!"

Kevin rolled out from underneath and sat up. "You don't like it."

"Did I say that? I like it. See?" She forced a grin. "I'm smiling."

He stood up and put his hands on his hips. "Need help with the lights?"

"I'll have to buy more. We've never had a tree this big."

He looked past her toward the kitchen. "Any coffee left?"

"Pot's on the counter. Help yourself." She followed him. "Like you always do."

Grabbing her Far Side cup from the counter, he poured from the pot and sat down at the table.

Stifling a gasp she objected, "That's *my* mug."

He looked down at the black and white cartoon cup. "It was empty."

Standing across from him she declared, "It's mine. As in, no one else uses it."

Kevin deliberately sauntered over to the cupboard where he chose a blue pottery cup from the rack and dumped the coffee from the Far Side mug into it. Returning to the bench he set hers down with a thud. "There's your *damn mug*."

Ilene stared at the empty mug and laughed at herself. "What can I say? I'm touchy about my mug."

Replacement cup in hand, he started to walk away when Ilene blurted, "Wait! I need to ask you something."

He paused with his back to her. "Fire away."

"Have you ever seen a black Mercedes drive by here? Illinois license. HMP 672."

His eyes pursued her as she walked over to the counter and filled her mug. "Maybe. So what if I did?"

She frowned at his defensiveness. "We saw the car earlier. Waiting for the bus. Both girls said they'd seen it before. Hazy memorized the plate number. And Gladdy's sure it's the car that hit their kitty."

"What do you think?"

Ilene shrugged. "I guess it's possible that Philip's parents hired someone to keep an eye on things around here while he's gone."

"Why would they do something like that without telling you?" he pried.

Caught off guard by the question, she knew the answer but decided that it was none of his business. It was a mistake to call his attention to it. "You're right. I'm probably overreacting."

Kevin squinted at her. "Then why'd you bring it up?"

"Good question." She dismissed him with a wave of her hand. "Forget I said anything. Really. I'm just paranoid."

"In that case, I'll leave you alone with your paranoia." Turning on his heel he vacated their conversation.

13

On Christmas Eve, Hazy and Gladdy giggled and ran ahead of their dad into the living room, then hit the light switch. Hundreds of tiny blue lights glimmered on the tall lonesome pine.

"Blue lights." Philip turned to Ilene and squeezed her hand.

"Blue Christmas," she replied.

He kissed her forehead. They had just picked him up from the bus at the Armory, and a month's absence. While he reminisced over the shimmering ornaments, Gladdy babbled about the yellow ribbons that she and her first grade classmates had tied. "I got to take them home because I'm the only one whose daddy's in the war."

"Desert Shield," Ilene corrected. "It's not a war." The whole idea of yellow ribbons was depressing, but she kept her mouth shut for her daughter's sake. "Philip. Could you do me one big favor?"

"I know. Ditch the desert fatigues."

"Thanks." Plucking the round brimmed desert cap from his head, she handed it to him. He kissed her lips.

Approaching the stairway he commented, "I like the carpet. When did we decide to do that?"

Reminded that he was seeing it for the first time, Ilene sneered. "Marie made that decision for us."

"That's right. Looks great. I noticed the window frames and moldings are all done."

"Kevin should be starting on the basement soon."

"I'd like to talk to him about that before I go back."

"He hasn't been around for a couple days," Ilene told him. "I don't know what happened to him."

"It can wait." After flipping the switch he climbed the steps, admiring the new fixtures. "Nice lights."

In the kitchen, Ilene poured eggnog and brandy into cups and set out the vegetables and dip on the table. She'd put shrimp scampi and rice in the oven before they left to pick up Philip. The girls sat quietly in the living room while Dickens' *Christmas Carol* played on TV. It was the best version, with George C. Scott as Scrooge. The holiday shows offered a welcome relief from the relentless Desert Shield updates. She wandered upstairs. A dim light from the bathroom silhouetted the bedroom. Wearing his favorite gray sweats and Sportstalker T-shirt, Philip sat on the bed with his back to her, staring out the windows at the cloudy evening sky. Deck lights illuminated the light snowfall.

"Hi there," she spoke up from the doorway.

Bowing his head, he wiped his eyes.

She crawled across the bed and hugged his torso.

"I *really* miss this place," he whispered in her hair.

"This place misses you."

"They tell us to block out thoughts of home. Put them in another place. I didn't know that would make it so hard to come back here."

"Don't do this to yourself," she pleaded.

"I left in the fall. Now it's winter. Everything's changed."

"Things *have* changed." Ilene sat up and eyed him steadily. "You see what's happening. Saddam released the hostages. Bush has all those allies at the UN. There's even an anti-war movement already. The madness is coming to an end."

"They're sending our unit over to Saudi, Ilene. That hasn't changed."

"That's just propaganda," she scoffed. "They're preparing you for the worst."

"I hope you'll be able to handle it when the time comes," he warned.

"Of course I can handle it," she insisted. "It's your financial arrangements that make me uneasy." As soon as the words came out, she sensed the timing was all wrong.

And Philip said so. "Not that again."

"Sorry." She tossed her hair off her shoulder. "I'll deal with it on my own."

"Let's have it out. Once and for all," he insisted. "We gotta get past this."

"There's over three hundred thousand dollars in our accounts."

He raised his eyebrows. "Most other families aren't so lucky. Transferring from reserve to active duty can mean financial disaster."

"Okay. I'm one lucky duck." Ilene sighed. "That's not the point. It's where the money comes from that bothers me. And what it means."

"I keep telling you it's a loan. My name's still on the deed."

"What about my name?" His eyes averted her glare. "Dammit. Philip." She pounded the patchwork bedspread. "Admit it! You sold me out of the deal!"

"Calm down." His words were meant to soothe, yet he maintained his distance. "Nobody sold you out. My will leaves you with my share of the property."

"Listen to yourself!" Ilene railed at him. "God forbid something happens to you. Me and the kids'll be out on the street. You underestimate Donald and Marie's perception of this little *loan* arrangement. They could make my life miserable while you're gone."

"You have to make a choice," he said dispassionately. "Do you put up with them for a few months? Or risk losing the house."

"You already made that choice for me," she snapped.

"I'd say the reason why is pretty obvious."

"Meaning?"

"Now it's your turn to listen to yourself. You're so goddamn stubborn, we'd have spent the past six weeks arguing instead of doing something about it."

"Am I allowed to register my opinion?"

"You have. Many times." He rolled his eyes. "Bottom line is, you have to trust me on this."

Gladdy appeared in the doorway. "Mommy can't we *please* open our presents?"

"One each. Then we eat." Ilene jumped off the bed. "Time to go be a family."

In a gesture of retaliation, Ilene built herself a buffer zone on Christmas Day by inviting Betty, Gail, and the four Carricks. Marie and Donald arrived first. Wearing a high-collared white silk blouse and long burgundy and green plaid skirt with a hunter green sweater jacket, Marie laid into Ilene right off the bat.

"Philip was kind enough to let me know that you had invited more guests."

"Good." Ilene was ready for her. "He also warned me that you'd be coming."

Marie sniffed and sauntered off with her granddaughters, teasing them with gold and silver wrapped boxes. No doubt they contained expensive jewelry, Ilene thought.

Arms laden with presents Betty showed up with Gail around eleven. "Merry Christmas. Here comes Mrs. Santa. Where's my grand-babies?"

"Merry Christmas!" Ilene helped Gail with the packages, noticing her chic short haircut and red highlights. "Your hair looks great."

"Thanks." Dressed in worn jeans and cable knit sweater like her big sister, she asked, "How you holding up these days?"

Ilene bit her lip. "I'm a good little soldier."

"Where is that soldier anyway?" Gail glanced around. "And those kids. Hazy! Gladdy!"

Two hyperactive girls bounced into the kitchen, shadowed by Marie.

"Whadja bring me?" Hazy clapped her hands.

Giggling, Gladdy scampered off with a couple gifts in hand.

"Someone's been feeding you guys candy." Ilene looked at Marie. She simpered.

"Merry Christmas," Betty said to the woman.

"And to you," Marie responded. "Of course this isn't our real Christmas. We usually spend it in Aspen with family. We'll go for New Years."

Strolling in from the living room Philip greeted Betty and Gail with hugs and kisses. Accompanying him, Donald stopped at the center island and poured wine.

"The house looks fabulous!" Gail cried.

"I expected to see more done by this time. We were here for Thanksgiving, you know," Marie informed Betty. "Unfortunately that cut short our stay at Grand Cayman."

Handing out glasses of wine, Donald asked. "How much of a crew did you get in here?"

"It's a one man crew," Ilene told him.

Marie stared at her. "But there's far too much work for one person."

With a stern glance in his son's direction, Donald placed his hands in the pockets of his wool tweed pants. "Need to get some more manpower on the situation."

Philip shook his head. "All the contractors are shorthanded from the Guard and Reserve call-ups. With so little snow, they're scrambling to finish up bigger projects that got delayed last fall."

"One man can't handle this job," Donald dictated.

"I'm satisfied with his work so far." Philip turned to Ilene. "What about you?"

"What difference does it make?" she fumed at all of them. ""What's the big rush? Philip will be home in January. The work will get done."

They heard footsteps on the stairs outside. Cathy and Stan appeared outside the windows on the deck carrying two kid bundles. They squeezed through the north atrium door.

"Merry Christmas!" Stan called out, holding a rambunctious toddler clutching gift bags. "Sara wanted to try a different door today."

Patting her cranky baby, Cathy exclaimed, "Ohmygod. You've gotten so much done!"

Ilene laughed out loud at the irony of the moment. "Unfortunately not everyone agrees with you. But thanks anyway."

Stan grinned at the odd mixture of guests. "Looks like a house full. Hope we're not too late."

"Actually your timing is perfect," Philip conceded. "Merry Christmas."

14

The day after Christmas, Ilene planned a more intimate good-bye than that parade fiasco they had endured at Thanksgiving. This time she kept the girls at home with Betty, who volunteered to stay on in the guest room by special request. They shared their hugs and kisses with Daddy in private, the same as when Philip left for camp at McCoy in past summers.

"Did you tell him about the black car?" Hazy whispered to her mom as they were leaving.

"Not now," Ilene waved her off.

"What car?" Philip asked.

En route to the Armory, Ilene confided in him, "There's a black Mercedes that's been driving by the house a few times. Illinois license plates. The girls and I have seen it. In fact Gladdy insists it's the car that hit Mr. Kitty."

"New neighbors?" he responded.

Ilene groaned. "Come on, Philip. You know as well as I do. Donald and Marie probably hired some goons to spy on me.'"

"Or watch out for you."

"I don't like to be watched," she huffed.

"Don't be so paranoid."

"Dammit Philip. Tell your parents to call off the dogs. Or I will."

They lapsed into strained silence until he parked at the Armory, with the engine idling.

Ilene wrinkled up her nose. "I hate this."

He kissed it. "So do I."

Their mouths met and the windows fogged for several minutes. Due to the bitter wind chill, arriving personnel and family members scurried past. Eventually they relinquished their intimacy and joined the crowd. Inside the building the Red Cross booth offered coffee and Christmas cookies. And not to miss a golden opportunity, a grinning recruiter chatted with the young sons of officers.

Gerry Cusick marched up to them and tattled, "Philip Singleton. I have yet to coax Ilene here to one family night. We've got a terrific support group growing. Maybe you can convince her. Be good for the kids."

"I told you it's been hectic, Gerry," Ilene spoke up on her own behalf.

"Once things settle down at home she'll get the girls involved," Philip assured her.

"Great!" She clutched Ilene's shoulder. "We'd love to see you there." And she dashed off to hassle some other unsuspecting civilian.

"She's right about the kids," Philip said. "They might start to feel isolated."

Glancing around at the familiar faces of the Medical Reservists and their families in the milling crowd, Ilene sighed. "I don't feel comfortable with these people." She ducked out before the buses loaded with a quick hug. "See you soon."

The dwindling days of 1990 were filled with chauffering the girls to ski lessons. On New Year's Eve, Ilene took her new equipment out to Spirit Mountain and skied with them. They met up with the Carricks in their new shop, ate pizza, then watched the torch light parade and fireworks. Both girls fell asleep on the drive home. Ilene noticed a light on in the house as she climbed up the hill in the dark. Kevin's truck was parked in the driveway for the first time in ten days. As she climbed out of the Jeep and opened the back door to wake Hazy, the garage door shuddered open. Kevin stepped under the yard light.

"Welcome back, stranger," she said. "I see you let yourself in."

"And a Happy New Year to you too, Mrs. Singleton." He tossed his ponytail. "Need some help?"

"Sure. Unload the skis from the rack and put them in the garage."

She hustled the sleepy kids into the house and up to bed. By then the peppermint schnapps she drank earlier had worn off. Back downstairs in the kitchen she discovered a bottle of champagne in the ice bucket on the center island. She inspected the label—Mumm's—how presumptuous of him.

He walked in the door. "Where's the kids?"

"Passed out in bed. Too much fun today."

"How was skiing?"

"Windy. But the fireworks were great." Eyeing the champagne she quipped, "See you made yourself at home. Having a party?"

"That's an apology," he told her. "Figured you'd be all bent out of shape that I sorta disappeared."

Ilene pantomimed holding a receiver to her ear. "Forget to charge the battery in your cell phone? Philip wanted to talk to you about the basement."

Gritting his teeth, Kevin said, "Sorry. Something came up."

She backed off. "So where'd you go?"

"East." He hesitated. "Virginia."

"Really. What part?"

"North."

"I don't know much about the east. You have family there?"

"My folks are dead."

"Well." Ilene tossed up her hands. "This is going nowhere. Must've had something to do with a woman then."

"Something like that." He opened the refrigerator door. "Brought you all some Chinese."

"Go ahead. I already ate."

"Good. I'm starved." Kevin heated up a carton in the microwave.

"So what made you think we'd even be here. We could be off skiing in Aspen for all you know," she pursued the issue.

He flashed a sly grin. "Took a wild guess."

She stuck out her tongue at him.

Leaning against the center island, he handled mouthfuls of fried rice with chopsticks. "How was your Christmas anyway?"

"Pretty weird with Philip just dropping in for a brief visit."

"Did the in-laws show?"

"Oh yes. And Betty and Gail and the Carricks," Her voice trailed off.

"Sounds like fun."

She laughed. "Weird is more like it. Think I'm suffering from over exposure to the Singletons." Glancing at the clock she changed the subject. "Hey. It's after eleven. Wanna pop this cork or what?"

"Sure thing." Kevin set the carton on the counter and grabbed the bottle.

She opened the north atrium door for him. He stepped out and shot the cork over the railing. "Got a glass?" He caught the overflow in his mouth.

Ilene shivered. "Brr. It's cold. I'm going inside.

He closed the door behind her. She held out the champagne flutes as he poured. The last time she drank the bubbly with Philip out of those glasses was their ninth anniversary last September. Now, standing in the kitchen she clinked her glass with this stranger.

"Here's to peace on earth." The sparkling liquid slid down her throat until it was gone.

Kevin refilled her flute. "Pretty tall order these days."

"I almost forgot." She set the drink down. "I have a present for you." Dashing out to the porch she pulled the broom and dustpan out of the closet. Hazy and Gladdy had wrapped the bristles in Santa paper and the dustpan in candy cane wrap. Kevin turned on MTV.

Sinead O'Connor wailed, *"Anybody want a drink before the war."*

Ilene cleared her throat. "Merry Christmas."

When he turned around she shoved the broom and dustpan at him. He grasped them, smiling. "Very funny, Mrs. Singleton."

She grinned at the joke. The champagne was kicking in. "You're a pain in the ass. But you do nice work."

"Let me get this straight. You go ballistic over a cartoon mug, but you think I'm a pain in the ass."

"I'm a bitch. Remember?" She gulped more champagne.

Kevin fell silent. The clock on the microwave flashed 11:58 p.m.

She emptied the bottle into both flutes. "Almost midnight."

He looked down at his glass. "So it is."

Overwhelmed by his sullenness, Ilene touched the sleeve of his denim shirt. "Look. I'm sorry. I didn't mean to hurt your feelings. Deep down I think you really are a nice guy. And you'd probably rather be a thousand other places on New Year's Eve."

Kevin looked her in the eye. "Happy New Year."

Pink Floyd's *"Dogs of War"* played on the tube. Their glasses clinked again.

Caught up in the surrealism of the moment Ilene downed the last of her champagne. "Happy New Year then." The phone rang. She groped for the cordless on the kitchen counter. "Hello."

"Happy New Year, my love."

"Philip!" she cried too loudly. "Happy New Year!"

"You sound high," Philip commented. "Having a party?"

Taking his cue, Kevin set his glass on the kitchen counter.

"Not." She imitated Hazy. "Met up with the Carricks at Spirit Mountain. We had a little food and drink."

"Sounds like fun."

Kevin waved and let himself out the porch door. Ilene switched off the lights and TV, then stood before the windows in the dark, watching him drive off, listening to Philip talk out his frustrations.

"You're kinda quiet tonight," he said. "Anything wrong?"

"I miss you. I'm glad you called."

"Me too." He sighed. "That Kevin guy ever show up?"

Ilene thought over her reply. "Actually he was here earlier. Guess he's back on the job."

"Don't be too hard on him. I know it pisses you off having him around. But he does a good job."

"You're right. I know." Ilene assured him. At the same time she realized that she'd neglected to tell Philip that it was Kevin who bought the tree and put it up. Or about the time he found Gladdy in the snowstorm. Nor was she completely candid about this night, only that she didn't know the reason why.

15

"Found a plumber," Kevin announced on the morning of Wednesday, January 9, 1991.

Seated at the dining room table reading the paper, Ilene replied absently, "And you're telling me this because . . ."

"He didn't tell you." He poured himself a cup of coffee. "Your husband faxed a memo to me at Wilson's last week. You all need a certified plumber to install that bathroom and spa downstairs."

"Dammit," Ilene swore. "That'll cost a fortune. And more bookkeeping for me."

"Didn't mean to piss you off."

"Forget about it." She waved her hand. "Anyway that reminds me. I need to call the bank." On her way to the den to gather up statements, the phone rang. She grabbed for it at the desk.

"It's me. Sit down. I've got news," Philip declared. "Our plane leaves for Dhahran on Friday. 0900 hours."

"Oh God." Ilene's heart sank. "This is it, isn't it?"

"Yeah," was all he said.

"I'll drive down today. Can you get away?"

"Sometimes. I'll get us a couple rooms at the Holiday. It's gonna be a madhouse."

"I'll call you when we get in."

"Drive careful. They're predicting freezing rain for southern Wisconsin. Better take the Jeep."

"I will. Bye. I love you."

Kevin helped her toss the last of three overnight bags in the back of the Jeep. He closed the rear gate while Ilene piled sleeping bags and pillows in the back seat.

"Thanks." Not knowing what else to do, she shook his hand. "Go ahead and hire that plumber. And take care of the house while I'm gone."

"Yes ma'am." He winked at her.

"We'll probably be home Friday night." After picking up the girls at Lakeside School, she headed south.

Hanging out with her two kids at the Holiday Inn of Tomah was not exactly Ilene's idea of something to do. She felt trapped in the twilight zone. The first time in December was a novelty. Philip had been able to spend time with them. During these two tortuous days however, he was only able to sneak away from the cargo loading operation for a few hours. But they were not alone in this time warp. In fact, the motel was filled to capacity with family members and friends somberly waiting out the departure of the 477th. A hundred rooms full of strangers living through the same ordeal. Philip was one of the privileged few to be able to get off base for even a little while. Ilene called Cathy late Wednesday evening after he'd left.

"Here's your live reporter from the Army base at Fort McCoy." She filled her in on Philip's travel plans.

"Ohmygod. Poor Arnie's covered with chicken pox. And Sara has a fever. No spots yet. I wish I could be there for you."

"You're here for me on the telephone," Ilene conceded. "That's what matters."

During the morning on Thursday a hopeless pall descended over her. By noon a migraine throbbed at her temples. Wearing sunglasses she watched the girls turn to prune babies in the pool water.

Time trudged by. The four of them shared a pizza at pool side on Thursday night. Philip was signed out until 3:00 a.m. Later while Hazy and Gladdy slept in the adjacent room, Ilene celebrated the waning hours alone with her husband. Their lovemaking was the sober dance of two desperate souls torn apart by shifting sands. She drifted off to sleep in his arms. When the phone rang at 6:00 a.m., she awoke alone.

It was Philip. "Don't wake the girls yet. The plane hasn't even left Fort Dodge."

"What time?" Ilene asked groggily.

"We'll be out of here by noon," he said as if they were in someone's way.

By 9:00 a.m., Hazy and Gladdy were restless and bored. Ilene headed for the airstrip within the half hour, which proved to be none too early. With the unrestricted parking area already jam packed with vehicles, she had to park in an Army occupied cow pasture across from the main gate. She herded the girls through the biting sub-zero wind chill into the warm cafeteria mess hall overlooking the single runway. The place was bursting with Red Cross coffee and doughnuts, families, well wishers and media.

"How will we ever find Dad?" Hazy asked.

"Don't worry," Ilene reassured her. "He'll find us."

She'd no sooner said the words when Gladdy jumped up and down. "There he is!"

Ilene and Hazy looked out the plate glass windows just as Philip stepped off a loading cart. They snaked their way through the crowd toward him. Within the hour, the L1011 passenger plane drifted out of the gray sky and landed. With bone chilling somberness, personnel and loved ones eventually filed out to the loading ramp like rats caught in a maze. The four Singletons huddled against one another in the multitude. No band played John Philips Sousa. No grinning disc jockeys handed out slogans or yellow ribbons. Instead a cruel wind seemed to take everyone's breath away.

Ilene was fine until Gladdy sobbed, "Please Daddy. Don't go."

Before boarding the plane, he bent down and kissed her first. "I love you, Cookie Monster."

She shivered and hugged him tightly. "I love you, Daddy."

Next, like a ritual he kissed Hazy. "I love you baby."

She vigorously wiped her eyes and shuddered against the cold as he hugged her. "I love you too D-daddy."

The flood of tears chapped Ilene's cheeks in the bitter wind. Philip stood up with both daughters hanging onto his legs. He kissed her deeply, his lips trembling.

"I can't believe this is happening," she cried.

He held her face in his hands, shielding her damp skin from the cold. "We'll get through this all right. I made sure of that. Just remember, I love you."

She buried her face in the tuft of his flack jacket and whispered, "Oh God. How will we know you're safe?"

"Try not to worry. We'll stay out of danger. I'll call you from Dhahran."

"I love you Philip."

He nodded wearily and pulled away from them. Wiping his own tears, he walked up the steel ramp. Then he was gone. Back inside the heated building, they watched the plane take off from behind the windows. Ilene felt as if the winter wind had torn apart the last frayed strands from her web of happiness. She needed the safety net her mother and sister could provide Hazy and Gladdy right now, while she put the pieces of her own heart back together.

16

"I'll baby sit the kids. You gals go paint the town whatever the hell color you want," Betty announced that Friday evening, January 11th.

Ilene and Gail sat across from her in the booth at the Silver Dollar. For years Betty had set herself up with brandy and water, cigarettes and her pile of paperwork every day without fail in the same booth back by the kitchen door. Reserved for family, employees and customers were seated there by invitation only. Barking orders from her throne, she enjoyed intimidating newcomers until they got to know her softer side.

"You'll have to drive," Gail told her sister. "My MR2's in the shop."

"I don't know." Ilene toyed with the pack of cigarettes on the table. "When I left, Kevin was going to hire a plumber to do the basement. Feel like I need to get involved in that."

"What you need is a break from that albatross you call a home," Betty chided. "Can see by the look on your face how it's worn you down. Looking so pale and thin."

"Christ. I'm doing the best I can." Ilene snatched a cigarette out of the pack and lit it.

"Of course you are," Gail patted her shoulder. "Come on. Cheer up. There's a great little Mexican place over on Calhoun. Hacienda del Sol.

They shake up a mean margarita."

Ilene exhaled the smoke gradually. "Okay. I give up. We'll stay the night."

Hacienda del Sol was crowded when they arrived. Ilene squeezed into the restroom first, then met Gail in the lounge. Amidst the elbows and assholes, she'd managed to occupy two bar stools.

"How long do we have to wait for a table?" Ilene asked.

Her sister glanced around. "Half hour at least from the looks of this crowd. I ordered a couple margaritas."

They both grabbed cigarettes at the same instant, then lighted them for each other, laughing. When the drinks arrived Ilene peered up and down the bar.

"Can we get some chips?"

Pencil thin fingers slid a basket in front of them. The gray haired man seated on the other side of Gail leaned forward and winked at Ilene. Raising her eyebrows she avoided his eyes.

He leaned rudely across Gail's chest and slurred, "Can I buy you a drink?"

Pushing him away Gail said, "We're good here. Thanks anyway."

He threw his arm around her. "Nope. I insist. I'm gonna buy both you gorgeous women a drink. And I won't take no for an answer."

Plucking the sleeve of his green plaid sports jacket, Gail removed his arm. "Okay. How about scram. Does that work for you?"

He rocked backward, toppling off the bar stool. "Say now. You're quite the puss-shee cat. Bet you know how to have a good time."

"Hey mister! What do we look like to you. Prostitutes?" Ilene snapped. "We're just sisters out having a couple drinks. So leave us alone."

"What're you. Coupla dykes?" he shouted. "Hey! I'm game."

Gail reached out and grasped him by his white shirt collar. "Look you sonofabitch. I said scram!"

"Excuse me ladies." The bartender who was bigger than Philip showed up. "This guy bothering you?"

The plaid man shook free of Gail's fingernails and staggered.

"Not anymore," Ilene declared.

"Hows about two more 'ritas? On the house. Make up for the trouble here."

"Twist my arm," Gail challenged him.

Laughing he fetched more drinks.

"God. What a moron! I don't know how you can stand the singles scene," Ilene confided.

Gail stirred the ice in her glass. "Actually that's what I wanted to talk to you about. I've met someone."

"Congratulations!" Ilene clinked her sister's glass. "What's his name?"

"Sandy." Gail paused. "She moved in last week."

"She," Ilene repeated, lighting another cigarette. "I wondered that about you."

"What do you mean by that?"

The bartender served their free drinks.

"I only just admitted it to myself," Gail continued defensively. "I'm tired of being alone."

Ilene eagerly sipped her drink. "Does Betty know?"

Gail nodded. "She's cool. Except I had to sit through a creepy story about some woman she knew forty years ago."

Ilene shuddered. "Spare me the gory details."

"So what do you think?"

"Is this a survey?"

"You don't have to be sarcastic."

"Did you think I'd be shocked?"

"I don't know. Maybe I'm looking for approval. Or something," Gail confessed.

"Okay. I approve," Ilene offered. "But your sex life is really none of my business."

"I should've known you'd be selfish about this."

"Then why the fuck did you bring it up?"

"I wanted to tell you about Sandy."

"Don't let me stop you." Her sister raved over her latest infatuation. By the time more drinks arrived, Ilene accepted this Gail Rosenthal Show she'd been lured into. It kept her mind off her own troubles, which was just as well. Talking wouldn't change anything. Philip was on a plane bound for the Middle East. And Kevin and the Singletons had intruded on her life. She would have to find some way to cope.

"Did we miss our table call or what?" Gail asked finally.

Ilene cast a blank stare. "What name did you give the hostess?"

"Me! I thought you put your name on the list."

"Shit." They said in unison, then laughed hysterically.

Gail checked her watch. "God. It's almost midnight."

"And here we are." Ilene hiccuped. "Smashed. On an empty stomach."

"But I'm starved," Gail whined.

"Look. I've gotta face two kids and a long drive home in the morning. Let's hit the road," Ilene urged.

In the Jeep on the drive back to Betty's, Gail blurted, "I have to pee. Stop at that White Castle on Division Street."

"Remember how we used to hang out there after school? I loved their fries." When Ilene pulled into he parking lot, hers was the only vehicle. "Busy place."

"Hey. Let's split a dozen minis," Gail suggested as they walked into the bright glare of the burger palace.

"I thought you had to pee."

"Yeah. Like you would ever stop here for the food." Gail sniffed the air. "Besides, that smell is making me hungry."

"Well I do have to go. Just get me some fries." Ilene headed for the john while Gail ordered from the Vietnamese man behind the counter. She rejoined her sister in the first booth and they dug through the white sacks, sipping Diet Cokes. Five young boys exited, leaving them the only two customers in the place.

"My turn. Don't eat all the food." Gail grabbed a mini burger on her way.

Ilene gobbled the stray fries from the bottom of her bag. Facing the parking lot, she watched the gang members circling the Jeep. They didn't look much older than Hazy, maybe twelve or thirteen. A couple of them tried the locked doors.

"Sh-shit," she whispered. Their brazen behavior combined with her tequila buzz was enough to send her charging out the glass doors after them.

"Move along boys. Don't be touching my Jeep," she hollered in her bitchiest mom voice.

"Back off!" the leader with the big mouth shouted.

The other four closed in on the vehicle. Under the dim street lights she observed these five children dressed in oversize green camouflage, talking smart like little terrorists, poised to steal her car. Hands on hips she stomped her foot. "Shame on you kids. You should be home in bed."

"Shut up and gimme the keys," the Mouth demanded.

Hearing a snap she saw the gleam from a switchblade in his hand. "Put that away! Or I'll call the cops."

"Hey! You little bastards!" Gail shrieked at them as she sprinted out to her sister's aid. "I called 911. So scram."

"Fuck you cunt!" The Mouth screamed at her.

Jumping up, he kicked the lock button at the rear gate. It swung open. The boys swarmed the vehicle. While the Mouth monkeyed with the ignition, the others pushed. Rolling backwards, they practically ran down a dumbfounded Ilene. The driver popped the clutch and the engine roared as the four hopped in. Tires screeching, the Jeep swerved and disappeared down the adjacent alleyway.

Ilene sprinted after them screeching, "You little brats!"

Gail tossed her hands in the air. "Fucking sonofabitches should be spanked."

"Were you bluffing about the cops?" Ilene inquired walking past her.

"Hell yes."

Ilene retreated inside and dialed the phone. When the woman dispatcher answered she repeated her name and location. "Five gang members just stole my Jeep. Gang members. God. What am I saying. They were children."

"Ma'am, were these *children* armed?"

"One had a knife," Ilene replied.

"Ma'am, since you're not in any immediate personal danger, I'm going to have to ask you to sit tight."

"Sit tight!" Ilene cried.

"Ma'm, we've got a hostage sniper situation downtown. All available units are responding to an officer down in that vicinity."

"So. Take a number. What the hell is this?" Ilene demanded.

"Ma'am. Please try to stay calm."

"Hey! Ma'am yourself. I just put my husband on a plane to Saudi Arabia. It's the middle of the goddamn night. The little rascals from hell just snatched my Jeep. And you want me to calm down."

"Ma'am, we'll send an officer as soon as one's available. But like I said, it's going to be awhile." The woman's voice conveyed a dull, eerie dispassion.

Succumbing to the pressure building over the past two months Ilene came unglued. "Fuck you!" She slammed the receiver against the wall. Wide-eyed with frustration she yelled at her sister, "Can you believe it? Car theft is a real low priority these days."

Gail looked at the Vietnamese man. "So what's your story? What do you know about those goddamn kids?"

"Na sa good ing lish," he replied with a shrug.

"How the hell do you get a job when you can't even speak the language," Gail muttered.

Ilene moaned. "I feel like I'm in a really bad movie."

The quiet little man held up more fries and another bag of burgers.

Gail rolled her eyes. "Just like a Norwegian. When in crisis—eat." She seized the food off the counter. ""I'll take that. Besides, you short changed me before." She peered at her sister. "He owes me big time."

"I'll call a cab." Ilene surrendered.

17

Nursing a headache, Ilene nibbled a raisin bagel and sipped coffee in the restaurant late that next morning. Across from her in the booth, Hazy and Gladdy champed on juicy cheeseburgers.

"If I have to drink milk, then make it chocolate," Gladdy demanded, kicking her heels against the bench.

"If that little goonie gets chocolate milk I want a shake," Hazy decreed.

"Mom! Hazy kicked me," Gladdy cried.

"Stop it you two." Ilene ran her fingers through her hair. She'd slept poorly the night before. It seemed as though sirens had wailed all night long while she mourned the loss of Philip's Jeep. How much the interior smelled like him. And how they'd both been ripped from her. How much she felt like she'd screwed up.

Betty marched over and handed her the remote. "Phone's for you."

Squinting, Ilene accepted it gingerly. "Hello."

"Mrs. Philip Singleton?"

"Yes."

"This is Sergeant Brisco. St. Paul Police Department. That '89 Jeep stolen earlier this morning was involved in a high speed chase with my officers. The two occupants in the vehicle collided with a tree and were subsequently killed."

Ilene gasped. "My god! That's horrible. What a waste!"

"Ma'am. The Jeep was totaled," he restated the obvious. "Let me verify your address and phone. We can handle all the paperwork by mail."

She gave him the information and put down the phone. Massaging her temples, she fought back tears.

"What's wrong?" Hazy asked.

"The Jeep got smashed. I need to find us a ride home."

"What about our other car?" Gladdy piped up.

Ilene sighed. "The Camry's in Duluth, honey. We're in St. Paul."

Gladdy shrugged.

"Why not just call Kevin," Hazy suggested.

For lack of a better solution, Ilene called home and left a message on her own answering machine. "Kevin. Are you there? We're stranded in St. Paul. Call me at Betty's. 612-444-3300." She'd no sooner hung up when the phone rang.

"What's going on?" It was Kevin.

"Oh god. Some kids stole the Jeep last night," Ilene informed him. "Smashed it up and got themselves killed."

"Heavy duty."

"I need you to drive the Camry down here for me. The keys are hanging on that funky hanger by the back door."

"But that's a three hour drive," he protested.

Head pounding Ilene reprimanded, "It'd be so nice if just this once, you didn't give me a ration of shit."

"Have to charge you for my time," he warned.

"Fine!" she snapped. "What are you doing there anyway? It's Saturday."

"Working," he answered. "Besides you told me to take care of the place. Remember?"

"I didn't give you permission to move in," she griped.

"Want me to come get you all? Or not."

In no mood Ilene gritted her teeth. "Gimme a break."

"That's gimme a break *please*," he teased.

"Fuck it. We'll fly home." Ilene slammed the phone against the table top. Damn. He could ignite her fuse instantly.

Three hours later, she chain smoked in the booth. Pinned there by Betty as she guzzled brandy and described every single vehicle she'd ever owned and what became of it, Ilene was surprised to see Kevin waltz through the door. Although she couldn't remember giving him the name of the place, much less directions.

"Hey there." He strolled over, sniffing the air. "Place smells great. I'm starved."

"Best cheeseburgers in town," Betty bragged. "Siddown. I'll order one up."

"Kevin this is Betty. My mom." Ilene shoved her off the bench and stood up. "I have my own keys. I'll go get the girls and load up our stuff."

Kevin cleared his throat. "I didn't actually bring your car."

"What did you actually *bring*?" she asked snidely.

"My pickup."

She groaned. "I specifically asked you to bring the Camry."

He shrugged. "Couldn't find the keys."

"I told you the keys are by the back door."

He shook his head. "What can I say? They weren't there."

Ilene tossed up her hands. "How are we going to stuff all four of us into the cab of a truck?"

He grinned mischievously. "We could leave the grumpy one here."

"Don't be such a jerk." Ilene brushed past Betty, who stood by observing their animated exchange.

On the ride home, Hazy and Gladdy huddled against one another between Kevin and Ilene and drifted off. She felt grateful that their grandma let them stay up too late and road trips made them sleepy.

Ilene shifted their leaning bodies, lamenting, "I can't believe you brought this damn pickup."

"Loud and clear, Mrs. Singleton."

"Stop calling me that."

"What. Mrs. Singleton. That's your name isn't it?"

"My name is Ilene."

"Okay." He paused then tried it out. "I-lene."

"Did you hire that plumber?"

"I did. He starts Monday."

"I'll reserve final approval on that."

"Yes ma'am."

"All of a sudden everybody calls me ma'am. What is that all about?"

He coughed. "Ilene."

"Oh don't start."

"I have other news," he baited her.

"What news?"

"I tracked down that Illinois plate number."

Ilene swallowed. She'd forgotten about the black Mercedes. "And?"

"Registered to Donald Singleton."

Wild speculation was one thing, but this confirmation coming from Kevin renewed the throbbing in her skull. "Surprise. Surprise," she repeated with an acid tongue.

"You already knew?" Kevin asked defensively.

She shook her head. "Lucky guess."

"So it's no big deal then."

Ilene turned away. "Philip said I'm paranoid. They're probably just looking out for us."

"Without telling you?" he pursued the matter.

"Look. Donald Singleton's very rich. And very eccentric," she explained. "He's also a banker. Real into security. If you know what I mean."

"So it's some sorta drive by security guard?"

Ilene smiled at his clever observation. "Good point."

"Want me to dig a little deeper?"

Tempted to say yes, she bit her lip. Finally someone else who recognized the peculiarity of the situation. She glanced over at this irksome individual who'd been thrust into the lunacy that had become her life. "I don't think you should get involved in this."

"What are you talking about?"

"It's too personal. That's all."

"If that's the way you want to play it."

Taken aback she accused, "What are you insinuating?"

Staring at the road he shrugged. "You tell me."

"Look. I'm too wasted to get into this with you. Just let it go."

Kevin fell silent. Ilene surrendered to the fatigue as the hum of the big wheels lulled her to sleep.

"Where are you? It must be eight a.m. there by now."

Ilene collapsed into her desk chair as she discovered Philip's message on the answering machine when she got home later that evening.

"Made it to Dhahran. It's raining. So much for hot desert sun. Let's see. No room in the barracks. Have to set up camp. Wet. Won't be here long. Don't know when I can call again. Kiss the girls, I lov"—Beep.

The machine cut him off. She laid her weary head down on the desk and mourned. That Philip had managed to travel halfway around the world in less time than it took her to get back home from McCoy, two hundred fifty miles away, was a cruel absurdity.

18

Philip reached her at home finally Monday, January 14th. Their conversation was strained. "Don't have much time to talk. Curfew's in effect."

There's no point in telling you about the Jeep then, she reconciled to herself. That would take up precious time. Instead she asked, "Are you still in Dhahran?"

"Can't say. Wherever we are, we're moving out soon. Don't know where yet. Probably won't know till we get there." His voice sounded like an astronaut communicating with NASA from outer space. There were eerie gaps in the connection, but his words eventually came through after a delay.

"Why all the secrecy?"

"Security's tight here. Everyone's poised for war. You can breathe it in the air."

"Don't say that. Are you still camped out in the rain?"

"Stopped raining. We're still camped. On tarmac. How are the girls holding up?"

"School keeps them occupied. Report cards come out next week already. Of course I'm busy with the house."

"Everything okay around there?"

We already discussed the black Mercedes. Didn't seem to bother him, even if it was his father's doing, she thought again. "The plumber started work on the bathroom downstairs. Kevin's installing the cabinets." The strain of keeping things from him bore down on her. She cleared her throat.

"Sounds good. Listen. I can't tie up this line anymore," Philip said. "We're in the dark ages of telecommunications over here. I wish we could talk. I can hear you not saying things."

She held her breath. "Guess it's your turn to trust *me* now. Everything's under control."

"Okay. Gotta go. I'll call again. Love you."

"Love you too."

Exhausted, she put down the phone and lit a cigarette. The bond between them was almost psychic now. The way he talked about hearing the things she wasn't saying. Feeling frustrated she wasn't used to glossing over their lives that way. But she didn't want to worry him with the stolen Jeep story, or argue with him over family business. There wasn't anything he could do about it from the other side of the planet anyway.

The January 15th deadline came and went. Nothing happened. The Iraqi Army did not withdraw from Kuwait. Nor did the Allies launch any offensive action. Ilene slept soundly for the first night in months.

Flakes of snow fell steadily throughout Wednesday, the 16th. Gladdy had Brownies and Hazy had Girl Scouts after school. Conveniently both meetings were held at the Pilgrim Congregational Church, a block away from Cathy's house. Since neither of the girls had chicken pox before, Ilene stayed away from Carricks'. Although they'd kept in touch by phone. When she dropped off the girls, she saw the station wagon in the driveway. Assuming she'd suffered through chicken pox as a child, Ilene couldn't resist taking advantage of Cathy's captivity. She was usually working at the store.

"Meet me at Carricks' when you're done," Ilene instructed the girls.

Later she tiptoed through the living room of the Victorian home, past two poxy-faced babies napping on the couch in front of *Mr. Rogers*.

In the kitchen, Cathy coughed and waved Ilene's cigarette smoke away. "When did you start that nasty habit again?"

"Sorry." Ilene squashed it in the sink and washed it down the disposal.

"Look at you. Get a grip girl," Cathy chided.

"You're right. I'm still so flipped out about the Jeep."

"Ilene. It's just a jeep," Cathy declared. "What matters is that two kids are dead."

She groaned. "It just makes me sick. I asked the sergeant for the names and addresses of their families so I could send condolences. They had foster parents."

"Ohmygod." Cathy shook her head sadly.

"After a night like that it makes you wonder what the hell we're doing waiting on a war in some God forsaken desert. It's like war every night on those city streets."

"Speaking of war," Cathy began. "I'm sure you've noticed it's January sixteenth. No bombs were dropped. That's a good sign."

"At least something's going right," Ilene agreed. "I'll be so glad when Philip comes home. Then I can tell Donald and Marie to go fuck themselves. And the Gestapo in that black Mercedes."

"Why don't you just tell them to back off?"

"Afraid it's not that simple."

Cathy arranged fruit and cracker bowls for her toddlers. "Once they find out that you know they're spying on you—or whatever they're doing—the car might just disappear."

Ilene nibbled red grapes from the bag on the counter. "Come to think of it, I haven't seen it lately. Maybe Philip said something to them before he left."

"Stan had the strangest reaction when I told him about it," Cathy persisted. "Especially when I mentioned that Kevin was the one who told you the plates were registered to Donald Singleton. He wondered how he got that information."

"I never gave it any thought. He said he tracked it down."

"And Stan said that's quite a paper chase. He's done it before. It takes several weeks."

Heart thumping, Ilene calculated the time frame in her head. Less than a month with the holidays thrown into the middle of it. "Maybe Kevin knows a cop. Or something."

Cathy pressed her lips together. "I don't mean to stir up trouble. I know you don't get along with him. But I also know how much you need his help. Maybe you should just ask him how he found out. Then leave it at that."

"You're right," Ilene admitted. "By the way, I have an appointment at the bank on Friday for the computer banking thing."

"You can borrow my manual," Cathy offered. "It's in my office."

As they crept through the living room, Arnie awoke wheezing for air.

"Poor baby," Ilene cooed. "Let me get him."

Arnie whimpered while she mopped the sweat and mucous from his face with tissues from the box on the end table. She felt his forehead—still feverish. She kissed him and wiped his tears.

"This is pretty much self explanatory." Cathy walked into the room paging through the three-ring binder.

"Good. Thanks." Ilene looked down at the baby. "God. He's covered with pox and he has a fever. Is he still contagious?"

"I don't think so."

"I'm sure I've had them. But the girls haven't. I told them to meet me here." Ilene kissed the baby again. "He's such a good little boy."

They heard boots stomping on the front porch. Chimes rang out wildly as Hazy and Gladdy burst through the front door, startling Arnie and rousing Sara from her nap.

"Guess what," Hazy announced. "We made French toast today and fed it to the Brownies. For the cooking badge."

"Mm. That was *so* good." Gladdy licked her lips.

"Great. That takes care of supper," Ilene said.

"Wow! Polka dot baby." Hazy pressed her nose against Arnie's. He giggled happily.

Ilene handed the baby to his mother. "Time to go girls. I don't think this exposure is such a good idea," she said warily.

"Ohmygod. The last thing you need right now is chicken pox," Cathy warned.

Waving good-bye, she maneuvered Hazy and Gladdy out the door.

The pickup was still there when they got home. Over three inches of wet snow had accumulated slowly throughout the day. Someone had blown out the driveway and shoveled the decks and stairs. That someone she knew, was Kevin.

Hazy rolled snowballs in the fresh snow along the edge of the driveway. " This stuff packs good. I'm gonna make a snowman."

Ilene looked at her youngest, who seemed a little sullen. The lonesome toll of a church bell echoed across the hillside. "Doesn't that sound like fun, Gladdy? I'll go turn on the yard light."

"No You stay here and make a snowman with me," she whined.

"You two get started. I'll be right back," she assured her.

From the porch Ilene heard muffled media voices. Flipping the outdoor light switch, she wandered inside. Kevin sat at the table, glued to the TV.

"Thanks for moving all that snow," she spoke up.

He turned down the volume and stood up. A green hue emanated from the small screen. Deep frown lines covered his face.

"Oh shit." Her gaze shot to the CNN broadcast. "What happened?"

"They started bombing Baghdad. About twenty minutes ago."

Ilene's mouth fell open. Hot tears stung her eyes. Lunging for the remote, her knees buckled and she lost her footing. Kevin caught her as she collapsed. But she pulled away and sat down at the table. "I'm okay." Her mouth felt dry from the words.

The phone rang.

"I'll get that." Kevin picked it up on the second ring. "Singleton's . . . Who's calling?" He handed her the phone. "Cathy."

She took it. "Turn on the TV."

"I know. That's why I called." Her friend sounded out of breath.

Ilene stiffened at what looked like fireworks in green fog on the tube. "Can you come over?"

"I'll come get you."

"No. I have to be here in case Philip calls."

"That's right. Ohmygod. This is so hard. Stan's out at Spirit Mountain. I haven't been able to reach him yet. I'll try to find a sitter."

"Don't do that. You got sick kids.

"You shouldn't be alone."

"Kevin's here."

"Is that okay with you?"

Ilene smiled at her insinuation. "Yeah. I'll be fine." Promising to keep each other posted, they said good-bye.

Kevin channel surfed for more information. "CNN's got Peter Arnett inside Baghdad. That's the best coverage so far."

She stared at the live night vision silhouettes of onion shaped domes, as tracers illuminated the skyline like huge, green Roman candles. "My god. They even named it. Desert *Storm*. How insane. Like it's a fucking TV show or something."

His eyes locked onto the bombing footage he uttered, "Definitely surreal."

Ilene shook her head incredulously. "I can't believe this is happening."

He glanced sideways at her. "Then you haven't been paying attention."

Hazy and Gladdy clamored into the porch. Jumping to her feet, Ilene herded them away from the TV, deliberately delaying the news of war.

"Come and see our snowman," Hazy coaxed.

"You said you'd help," Gladdy scolded.

"I know. I'm sorry," Ilene apologized. "Let's go see."

Hugging her jacket sleeves she trailed them out to the yard. They'd built a short stocky snowman at the bottom of the driveway next to the garage. A lump rose in her throat when she noticed they'd dressed him in Philip's old green camouflage jacket and cap.

"We call him Daddy," Gladdy told her.

Ilene nodded, blinking back tears. "I can see why. Where did you find those clothes?"

"In that box in the garage," Hazy said.

"We need stuff to make his eyes and nose and mouth," Gladdy informed her.

Ilene grabbed her by the hand. "Let's look in the basement. There's all kinds of junk in there."

While the girls rummaged for suitable facial features, Ilene wandered through the framing walls behind the furnace to Kevin's workbench. She studied the printout of the floor plan for the main level. Lines and spurs were drawn in red pencil. She recognized the spurs as locations of phone jacks.

Kevin sneaked up behind her. "What're you snooping around here for?"

"Snooping." She sniffed. "This is my house." Holding out the copy of the floor plan she asked. "Why'd you mark all the phone jacks in red here?"

"You don't know."

"How should I know?" She glared at him. "Obviously you made these marks."

Exasperated he exhaled. "Shit. I don't believe this." He walked away.

Fuming she caught up to him and clutched his arm. "Goddammit. Answer me."

Staring down at her grip he whispered. "This place is full of bugs."

She dropped his arm and squinted. "Bugs." It was his turn to yank her by the arm as he pulled her out to the garage. "What the fuck is going on?"

"Listen to me," he said hoarsely. "The phones all have pieces in the receivers. The light switches are miked with hair thin wires connected to a transmitter on the roof. Real state of the art."

"What?!" Clearly flabbergasted, Ilene gasped. "How long have you known about this?"

"Awhile."

"Why didn't you tell me!" she demanded.

"Frankly until this moment, I figured you knew."

"Jesus Christ, Kevin. You're blowing my mind here."

He heaved a sigh. "I don't know what to say. Maybe your husband put it in."

"Philip would never do anything so sinister."

"That may be. But I can't believe he doesn't know about it. I found it. Some of the wires were obvious. Unless . . ."

"What."

"Unless it was done after he left."

"Wait a minute. You're the one who has it all mapped out on paper here. For all I know this was *your* doing. And you just got caught."

"Why would I bug your house?"

"Maybe Donald and Marie hired you to come in here. Keep an eye on me. Bug the place. That antenna probably transmits to your apartment in Lester Park. And the Mercedes is your contact."

"That doesn't make any sense."

"How did you know the plates were registered to Donald Singleton?"

"Called up Illinois Motor Vehicle."

"I happen to know for a fact that takes several weeks and lots of paperwork."

"Okay." He tossed up his hands. "Friend of mine's a cop."

"Which is it, Kevin."

"Look. He could get in trouble for that."

"You're lying."

"Why would I bug this place when I'm here every day?"

Ilene shrugged. "If the price is right—and believe me when it comes to the Singletons the price is always right—some people will do just about anything."

"I don't have to take this shit from you." He turned to leave.

"Don't bother coming back." She spat at him.

Grasping her shoulders he shook her. "I don't work for your father-in-law."

"Whatever." She pushed him away. "I'm so pissed off right now I can't even see straight."

"Mom—mee!" Gladdy hollered. "Come see the snowman's face."

She called out, "I'm coming sweetie."

"Can we talk about this tomorrow?" he asked wearily.

"Tomorrow there'll be nothing to talk about. Tonight I'll use your diagrams to rip them all out."

"Dammit Ilene. Don't do that," he pleaded.

"See what I mean? That's so—incriminating."

"Listen to me. Please." He cupped her face in his hands. "Obviously somebody installed these devices. And if you rip them out you won't find out a thing. Trust me."

"I'm not so sure I can," she said.

Without another word, Kevin stormed off. His pickup swerved out of the driveway.

"What's the matter with *him*?" Hazy drawled.

"He's just grumpy."

Ilene glimpsed the snowman's new face. Ten washers arranged in a grin, under a bolt nose, while two blocks of wood eyes watched her. She peered over her shoulder at the roof line of the house. A thin, foot high antenna balanced insidiously atop the highest peak.

Philip called around 1:00 a.m. Ilene was wide awake, propped up in bed mesmerized by CNN's continuous coverage of the war throughout the night.

"I take it you've heard about the bombing raids." He sounded agitated.

"Saw them," she corrected him. "Live via satellite. Weird green bomb vision. Or something. Without a doubt. This is scary."

"How'd the girls react?"

"They don't know yet. I'm planning to keep them home from school tomorrow. What should I tell them about you?"

"I'm okay. We're buggin outa here soon."

"Interesting choice of words."

"How so."

She hesitated. "No reason."

"What's going on, Ilene?"

"Nothing." She was so tempted to tell him. But the phone was tapped, so she'd only be advertising what she knows. "So where are you going next?"

"All I know is we'll be traveling in a convoy. They won't tell us till we're en route. Can't risk any breach in security. In this war everyone's a potential spy."

"So it seems," Ilene conceded.

Part Two

1

Kevin showed up shortly after eight Thursday, January 17th. Ilene slipped him a note across the center island. He read it silently.

"I'll leave the bugs in place. For now."

He grabbed a pencil and scribbled, *"Your car might be wired."*

"Check it out," Ilene said aloud. She tossed him the keys. He headed out the back door.

Hazy wandered downstairs rubbing her eyes, still wearing her pajamas. "You forgot to wake us up for school."

Ilene turned down the audio on the *Today Show*. "You're not going to school. We're having sort of a family day."

"Cool. How come?"

Wrapping her arms around her first born, Ilene replied, "Come over to the couch." They curled up together.

Hazy shivered at the snow flurries outside. "Is this about the bombs in Baghdad?"

Her mother peered at her. "You know?"

"Mom. The war is like all over the TV."

"I guess you're right." Ilene wondered how she ever thought she could control the onslaught of news. "Then do you have any questions?"

"What about Dad? Is he where the bombs are?"

"No. He's safe. He called during the night."

"Could you like hear the bombs in the background?"

"No. It was very quiet."

Gladdy arrived downstairs oblivious of Desert Storm and more emotional than her sister when Ilene broke the news.

Crawling onto her mother's lap, she burst into tears. "Are they bombing my daddy? Does he have his gas mask?"

"Daddy's okay sweetie. And I'm sure he has a gas mask." Seeing as how they'd never discussed the topic before, Ilene suspected that her teacher must be filling little first graders' heads with morbid war images.

The phone started ringing at 9:00 a.m. First Cathy called, though Ilene was forced to keep silent about the wiretaps, then Gail, Betty, and the Lakeside School counselor—*oops*—she'd forgotten to call in the girls' absences. Call waiting kept the cordless practically glued to her ear as she sucked down cups of coffee.

Gerry Cusick phoned to guilt trip her about the family support group again, though she did offer one tidbit of information. "The word from other units abroad is that mail is taking one to two months to get through. I'm not sure it's worth the trouble. It's your call."

"Sounds pointless," Ilene agreed.

Caffeine and CNN's relentless breaking news pumped up her adrenaline all day long. While keeping otherwise occupied with video games for Hazy, Barbie for Gladdy and school work for both, Ilene grew addicted to the allure of the war waging on live TV. On the one hand she loathed it. Yet time and again she had to force herself reluctantly from the coverage. At least the media blitz kept her mind off the listening devices.

The call from Marie came in while she dished plates of spaghetti for the girls at supper.

"Have you heard from Philip?" she started right in, without even a "hello-how-are-you". "And what about the children?"

"What do you mean?" Ilene replied, slyly baiting her for a slip up.

"I am concerned," she stated. "Gladys is my granddaughter after all."

"Curious," Ilene mused. "What are you concerned about?"

"Are you saying Gladys and her sister are fine? They aren't frightened by the news on TV. And everything went well at school."

With the vague clue she'd been fishing for still echoing in her ears, Ilene lied, "Yes."

"I see."

Feeling her mother-in-law sneer through the phone line, Ilene informed her briskly, "Philip called during the night. He's in Dhahran. But I guess they're moving out of there soon."

"How did he sound?"

"Far away," Ilene answered, then backed away from the sarcasm. "We didn't talk long." Thinking about him in that dangerous part of the world brought a lump to her throat. "Anyway that's all I know. So if you don't mind I'm in the middle of feeding the girls."

"Our best to the children then."

As Ilene set the phone on the center island Hazy warned, "Mom. You better see this. Missiles or something."

She flew across the kitchen to the portable. Big as saucers, Gladdy's eyes were peeled to the screen. The sight of CBS Israeli correspondent Bob Simon and his crew donning gas masks horrified them all.

"Weird. They look like space aliens or something," Hazy cried.

It was too late to turn it off, they were hooked. Kevin appeared in the kitchen and helped himself to a plate of spaghetti and a chunk of bread.

"Come and see the scary elephant people," Gladdy called out.

He strolled over and sat at the table to watch along with them as news of the US patriot missiles blowing scuds out of the sky over Israel broadcast across the globe on all networks. No fatalities.

Ilene clutched her chest to quell the quickening anxiety. "It's like they staged this whole thing for prime time."

The girls clapped and cheered for the patriot missiles.

"That's enough war for you guys for one night." She turned off the TV. "Time to head upstairs and finish that homework."

As they shuffled off to their rooms, Kevin smirked. "Can't exactly keep them from watching it when they've got TVs in their rooms."

Irked at his implied criticism she cleared the table in silence. Rising to his feet Kevin motioned for her to follow him out to the deck. Already wearing a black fleece cardigan over a green wool sweater, Ilene slipped on a pair of clogs and stepped into the frosty air. In the glow of the interior lights, he gazed out at the steam rising from the open lake water into the darkness. "Camry's clean."

Jolted from scuds in the air to bugs in the walls by his simple statement she shivered. "That's very interesting. I had the car in the Cities right after Thanksgiving. Marie was here by herself. She could've had the equipment installed then. Hell. You saw everything else she did."

He considered that theory. "Possible."

"What do you think?"

"As if you give a shit what I think."

Eyes wide she locked onto his icy stare. "Where'd that come from?"

Turning to face her he leaned against the railing, arms crossed. The January wind whipped the treetops and whistled through the gulf between them. "Last night. You accused me of a few things. One of which was working for your in-laws. Did something change your mind?"

"When Marie called tonight she asked if everything went well in school today." Even as she said it she felt uneasy confiding in him this way. "She seldom calls. And she never asks about school. I think she knew they were home today."

"What's important is not so much who's listening. It's why," he stated flatly.

"Donald and Marie don't need a reason to do anything. This is just their fucked up way of protecting me and the girls."

"Wiretaps. Audio surveillance," he restated evenly. "That's about information. Revealing it. Or concealing it."

With a blank look she maintained, "Why should I care? I have nothing to hide."

"But protection? Think about it. Your mother-in-law didn't install a burglar alarm system that weekend. Did she?"

Gleaning his inference she paced the deck. "Look. Philip borrowed a shit load of money from his father before he left. To finish the house. Provide income for me and the girls. That sort of thing. I was against it. But it happened anyway." She laughed bitterly. "I wasn't exactly consulted."

"So your father-in-law's keeping an eye on his investment."

"Your guess is as good as mine. But I'm afraid I've said too much already." She headed for the door.

Blocking her path Kevin asked, "What do mean?"

"It's a touchy subject."

He reached out and brushed a stray wisp of hair away from her face. "Been a rough day."

"Oh god." Gritting her teeth, she blinked back the tears. "Tell me about it."

His lips pressed her forehead in a tender kiss.

The coldness melted from his touch. At that moment kissing him seemed like the most natural response on earth. Yet as soon as their lips met she felt the strangeness of his skin and withdrew. Stumbling backwards she fingered her lips and exhaled. "What the hell? I can't believe I did that. I'm—uh—sorry." Avoiding his eyes she retreated indoors.

Her hands shaking she finished cleaning up the kitchen while on the other side of the glass Kevin's gaze lingered after her for what seemed an uncomfortably long time. Then he disappeared.

2

"I need to make a phone call." Ilene barged into Cathy's kitchen on Friday morning, January 18th, before her appointment at the bank. "Long distance. I'll use my calling card."

"Something wrong with your phone?" Cathy asked.

"You could say that." Ilene fixed herself a cup of tea. "Found out it's tapped."

"Tapped," her friend repeated.

"As in bugged. All the phones. The rooms are wired with tiny mikes. There's even a little antenna on the roof."

She gasped. "Ohmygod. How'd you figure that out?"

"Found a diagram Kevin made of the floor plan. When I asked him what it was he told me."

"Wait a minute. Kevin again?"

Ilene held up her hands in mock surrender. "Believe me. I know what you're thinking. Hell, I accused him of spying on me for Donald and Marie. We had a huge fight about it."

"What'd he say?" Cathy asked incredulously.

"He denied it of course."

"Do you believe him?"

Shrugging off the question she analyzed the situation aloud, "He did make the diagram. But it was out in plain sight in the basement. He certainly didn't hide it. Obviously he could've done it. He has access to the whole damn house. But you'd think I would've noticed him doing something that unusual. This equipment is really sophisticated."

Cathy peered at her. "Do you realize how bizarre this sounds?"

Nodding absently she confided, "To tell you the truth it's got Singleton written all over it. For that very reason. They're bizarre people. Even Kevin claimed that he figured we must've known about it."

"Did you tell Philip yet?"

"I can't talk to him about it. The phone's tapped."

Holding her head with her hands, Cathy moaned. "Ohmygod. You better call up some security service and have it all removed."

"I already threatened to take it out myself. Kevin begged me not to. Said I won't find out what's going on if I rip them out."

"Mommy?" They heard Sara talking on the nursery monitor.

"I don't think I like the sound of that." Cathy headed for the stairway. "I've gotta go check on her. Feel free to use the phone."

Using the wall phone in the kitchen, it took two tries before Ilene finally connected with a young male voice at the Illinois Secretary of State's office in Springfield. She explained that she needed to put a name with an Illinois license plate number.

"I can send you the forms," the man told her. "Return them with a check for four dollars."

"I'm in kind of a hurry. Can you overnight the forms to me?"

"The earliest I can get them to you is Monday. And there's an additional fee for that. I'll need a credit card number."

"No problem. I just need the information as soon as possible."

"That might be problem," he warned. "There's a ten day waiting period while the owner is notified that you are requesting the information."

Ilene gritted her teeth. "Do you give him my name?"

"That's the law."

She wondered how Donald and Marie would react to that. At least it would be out in the open. Like Cathy said, maybe they'll back off once they know she's on to them.

"Hello? Are you still there?" the male voice beckoned.

Cathy walked in the kitchen carrying Sara whose spots had almost disappeared. Little fingers waved at Ilene. "I'm here. Go on."

"The owner does have the right to object to the request. But the final determination is made in our office, based on the reason for your request. So make sure it's a good one," he coached.

"I have to give a reason." Ilene squirmed at the prospect.

"Do you want me to send you the forms or not?" He was starting to sound testy.

"Sure. Yeah. Why not?" Eyebrows raised in search of approval, she gave the man her name and credit card number but Cathy's address, who in turn gave the okay sign. Sara copied her.

"I'll send those out to you today."

"Tell me something," Ilene inquired. "Is there any faster way to ID a plate number?"

"Not unless you work in law enforcement. Then you could find out immediately. No notification required."

"You mean like a police officer."

"Or federal agent," he added.

After hanging up the phone, she looked at Cathy. "I hope you don't mind them sending the forms here. I don't want anyone else to know what I'm up to."

While settling Sara into her booster chair she pried, "So what are you up to?"

"I took your advice and confronted Kevin about the Mercedes license plate," Ilene explained. "First he said he called Illinois Motor Vehicle. When I challenged him, he said his friend's a cop and could get in trouble for doing him the favor."

Offering the toddler a cup of apple juice, she replied, "I suppose that's a logical explanation."

"But what if he was lying on both counts?" Ilene ventured. "He didn't call Illinois Motor Vehicle. I just made a few calls. Stan's right. That's not how you do it. He could also be lying about his friend. Maybe he doesn't really know who owns the Mercedes."

"You mean he just made it up?" Cathy unwrapped a package of graham crackers.

"Or he's guessing," she suggested. "Anyway I'll find out for myself who owns that car."

"I have a feeling whoever it is has something to do with the bugging devices," Cathy advised.

They heard Arnie fussing on the nursery monitor.

Ilene checked her watch. "I'm supposed to be at the bank right now."

Heading for the stairway again, Cathy walked her to the door. "I still think you should get a professional in there and have all that shit removed once and for all."

"Then again it might be a good idea to find out exactly who I'm dealing with first." She opened the door. "Thanks for the phone."

"Anytime." Cathy hugged her. "I'm worried about you. Call me."

At Northwest Bank, the secretary ushered Ilene into a private office immediately and poured her a cup of coffee. Account Executive Esther Cray reminded her of Della Reese as she strutted through the door, grasping Ilene's hand as she walked by. "Mrs. Singleton. It is a pleasure to meet you. I want you to know that Northwest Bank values your family's business."

Perched on the edge of the blue gray office chair, Ilene replied, "It's nice of you to be so supportive of the Reservists' families. These are hard times."

"It's true we do see quite a few military dependents who need help handling their accounts. Especially now with the payroll glitch."

With a blank look she asked, "Excuse me?"

"Has Mr. Singleton received a military paycheck?" Ms. Cray queried.

She thought about that. "Actually. I'm not sure. I think it goes directly to him."

Ms. Cray shook her head. "That seems to be the problem. None of the Reservists have received payment since their deployment. It's been quite a hardship for the younger families. You're very fortunate to have the financial stability to see you through this crisis."

Ilene bowed her head. "I didn't even know there was a hassle with the paychecks. Guess it's good timing for me to get more involved in money matters."

"I have your software all ready to go. Don't you just love computers?" Adjusting a pair of reading glasses, Esther Cray positioned herself at the keyboard and called up the program. "Even though you don't have access to all of your husband's accounts, I assumed you'd want to keep track of the activity. We put them all on one disk."

Stunned Ilene repeated, "All?"

Ms. Cray ceased tapping on the keys and looked over the rim of her glasses. "Mr. Singleton has several accounts with our bank. An account in his name, joint accounts with you and your daughters, and several numbered accounts. Your husband is one of our largest depositors."

Tucking her ice cold hands underneath her knees Ilene stared out the window so as to disguise her bewilderment. "Can you print a copy of those for me?"

"Certainly." She crunched more keys until the printer spit out a fresh sheet. She handed the figures to Ilene. "Right at your fingertips. That's the beauty of this program."

Dumbfounded, Ilene studied the information. Sure enough Philip held joint accounts with Gladdy and Hazy, plus herself. Along with his own personal named account, he also held nine additional numbered accounts. All ten account balances ranged from $325,000 to $340,000—totaling over four million.

"Is there anything wrong Mrs. Singleton?" Esther Cray inquired.

"Please. Call me Ilene." She deflected the question.

Tapping her pencil on the incredibly neat desk top Ms. Cray stated, "I have a feeling I know what's going on here."

Heart racing, Ilene glanced up from the numbers. "You do?"

Esther Cray looked squarely at her. "Honestly. Most women don't keep tabs on their husband's bank accounts. I can understand if this is somewhat overwhelming."

"Overwhelming." Ilene feigned calmness. "That's a good word for what I'm going through these days."

"Once you learn the program it'll get that much easier for you," Ms. Cray responded eagerly. "Slide your chair over here now. I'll show you the keystrokes."

Head pounding, she longed to flee those four walls for the anonymous downtown street where she could breathe in the crisp lake air and absorb this latest bombshell. Instead she forced herself to pay attention to Esther Cray while she went over the Smart Bank program, assigned her an access code and booted up to see if it worked. Knowing that in her frame of mind she would never recall most of it, Ilene took notes in the margins of the manual.

Scrolling through the accounts on screen Ms. Cray explained, "Now remember. You can deposit money into any of these accounts but you can only withdraw from those accounts bearing your name."

Scrutinizing the visible accounts, Ilene noticed that the activity on the numbered ones was deposits only. She wondered where the money came from. "Can I track account history?"

"Press alternate F1, go back to the main menu. Choose number one—cash management services. From there you can go into each account and learn more about it." She punched the keyboard. "See how easy this is?"

Staring numbly at the screen she murmured, "I get it."

Bogged down with too many details, Ilene clutched the Smart Bank package as she left the bank. She drove by the Sportstalker and saw Cathy's station wagon parked in the rear. Desperately needing someone to help her sort this out Ilene pulled in and parked. A sudden uneasiness swept over her like nausea. Perhaps it wasn't fair to burden Cathy with this new revelation. Shaking off the paranoia, she trotted across the lot and ran inside. She found Cathy at the computer downstairs. "We need to talk!"

"Can it wait?" She didn't turn around. "My back's against the wall here. I had to call in reinforcements back at the chicken pox coop so I can wrap up these accounts payable. I have until two o'clock to get the deposit ready."

"Damn." Ilene touched ground long enough to sense her bad timing. "How did it go at the bank?"

"That's what we need to talk about."

Cathy stopped punching keys and turned around. "What happened?"

Ilene grimaced at the back of Sally's blond head. "In private."

Rushing over, Cathy grabbed her arm. "Come with me. The day care's empty. Or should I say *quarantined*." She closed the door. "Okay. You've got five minutes."

Feeling hot and shaky, Ilene took a deep breath. "Today at the bank I found out that Philip has like ten accounts with balances over three hundred thousand each. Like four million. That's dollars, Cathy."

"Wow." She plopped down on a red plastic toy chair. "Then again it's not all that surprising. Actually Stan and I have always thought Philip must be worth a small fortune. Look at his family after all. Maybe it's a trust fund."

Ilene shook her head in frustration. "These are active accounts."

Her best friend stared at her. "Get a grip girl. You're blowing this way out of proportion."

Closing her eyes she breathed deeply. "Okay. Would you please explain it to me in a way that makes sense? Please. I'm listening."

Cathy looked at her watch. "Maybe he had some sort of investment stashed that you didn't know about and cashed it in to protect you and the girls. Why is that so hard for you to comprehend?"

Ilene frowned. "Philip had plenty of opportunities to tell me about those bank accounts before he left. Believe me. I even asked the right questions. He didn't say a word."

"Ilene. You've been with Philip for *nine years*. You know the man. Give him the benefit of doubt."

"You think I'm overreacting."

"Bingo." Cathy pointed her finger. "When you think about it this pretty much solves the other mysteries. The bugging. The black Mercedes. You talk about how wacky his parents are. Maybe they're freaked out about him leaving you so much money. So they feel like they have to keep an eye on you."

"But that's my point," she insisted. "He told me they loaned us three hundred thousand on the house. Why would he do that if he had access to millions?"

"Maybe he lied because he didn't want you to spend it all on the house." Cathy's fingers clasped the doorknob. "But I gotta get back to work. Any way you look at it, too much money is always better than not enough." She opened the door and paused. "I'm sorry I can't see the dilemma here. Money's a sore subject for me these days. Stan and I have two mortgages on our house. You don't know how lucky you are."

Ilene shrugged. "Maybe you're right. Call me later." She dashed out. If only she could talk to Philip in private.

The phone rang at 5:06 a.m. Sunday, January 20th. Her conscious mind clawed its way to the surface. Even in sleep she knew it must be him. When she answered her deep sluggish voice echoed into the receiver. "Hullo Philip."

"This is crazy. I have ten minutes to warn you that I don't know when I can call you again."

"Like prisoners of war." She rubbed her eyes vigorously as if that somehow massaged away her grogginess. The room was so dark. She sat up and switched on the television—no sound—just for light.

"We have to keep moving so we're not sitting ducks. There's no scuds out here. Just flies and scorpions."

"Are you headed toward Kuwait?"

"Can't answer that."

"Where are you now?"

"Not in Dhahran."

"Cmon Philip. Can't you even give me a general idea? What am I supposed to tell the girls."

"Tell them we're at a military outpost in the desert. Far from Baghdad. Like I said before, the phones over here have ears."

A lump rose in her throat, but she swallowed it. Ten minutes. There wasn't enough time to hash out their own bugs or the millions in the bank. And she dared not tip her hand to the ears that were listening on her end. "Let's try this one. Are you okay?"

She heard his breath of relief. "*That* I can answer. Yes. We're relatively safe here. No one knows where we are. That's the beauty of anonymity. As long as we keep moving and no one knows what we're up to, we're not a threat and therefore not a target. We just stay out of the way. It's pretty weird. Tell Hazy and Gladdy it's like a hectic camping trip. Now is everything else okay back there? I can't get over this feeling like there's something going on I should know about."

Ilene hesitated. She had never known such longing for the truth. Yet she lied. "Everything's fine. You must sense my worry. The war's on television constantly. It's nerve wracking for all of us. And we miss you like crazy."

"Me too. By the way, don't bother with letters. We can't send or receive mail. The twentieth century is *news* to these people."

"So I've heard. Did you know about the payroll glitch?"

"Yeah. Everyone's worried about money over here. But we'll be okay. Aren't you glad we got that loan now?"

She couldn't believe the irony sweeping through this conversation. It was as if their subconscious minds were jamming the lines of communication to let through some semblance of the truth, so what came out was a paradox she could not resist. "I'm not glad for any of this. The money.

The war. The ears that are listening. Or the danger it puts you in."

"It's out of our control. But it won't last forever. I love you."

The line went dead. At the abrupt termination she felt nauseous and dizzy.

"I love you too," she said sadly into the void.

3

"Who *are* you?" Through swollen eyes Ilene squinted at the wry grin in the dim TV light. His violet eyes examined her.

And the lips spoke, "It's Kevin. Remember me?" He adjusted the ice pack on her forehead.

"What are you doing here?" She pushed herself upright in bed then slumped backward feeling woozy.

"You're sick. Here let me help."

While Kevin arranged her pillows as props for her head and shoulders, memories trickled into her conscious mind of skiing with the girls on Sunday afternoon even though she felt lousy. At some point Philip had called. She remembered running into Kevin in the chalet. She had a headache from the wind on the chair lift. Unnerved by his presence, she accused him of spying on her. They argued and the rest was incredibly foggy. Scooting up against the pillows she gasped. "I'm soaking wet. What happened to me?"

"Fever." He explained steadying her shoulders. "You were reading me the riot act, when you keeled over in the chalet at Spirit Mountain.

Saving yourself from further embarrassment, I might add. Good thing I was there. Drove you all home. Fed the girls pizza. They crashed hours ago. You've been out of it pretty much ever since."

"God." Rubbing her face with clammy hands her tongue felt thick. "Must be the flu or something. What time is it?"

"Around one in the morning."

"Why are you still here?"

He rolled his eyes. "Good question."

Ilene crawled to the edge of the bed and pulled herself upright. "I'm going to change my clothes." She was still wearing a sweat shirt and her navy blue silk long johns from skiing, plus thick socks. He steadied her while she teetered to a stand. "I'm fine. Really."

"Yeah right."

She marched sloppily over to the bathroom and closed the door. Inside she pulled off the sweat shirt. Her chest felt like she'd slept on a patch of nettles, hot and itchy. Her armpits burned. In the lighted mirror she saw the huge red blotches. *Chicken pox.* She changed into a fresh, sleeveless white cotton night gown and pulled on her red plaid robe. Feeling light headed she brushed her hair into a ponytail. Back in the bedroom she found Kevin busy changing the bed linens.

He picked up the pile of sheets. "Where do you want these?"

"Put them in the washer. Thanks." She crawled into the clean crisp sheets and snuggled down gratefully. A nagging cough had begun. She was dozing when he came back with a glass of ice water. She opened her eyes and smiled.

"Heard you coughing. This might help." After he set the glass on the night stand, he sat down on the bed and touched the exposed flesh on her chest. "What's this rash?"

"Chicken pox. Got it from the Carrick kids. Thought I'd had it. Guess I was wrong. You had it?"

He nodded. "Contagious though. And you had a hell of a fever. The kids'll be next."

"Thanks for helping out." She glanced around, suddenly nervous about the bugs then reached for the tablet and pen on the night stand.

He tugged gently on her arm. "No need. I snipped the wire in here. Decided you could use some privacy. Basement's clean but the plumber's in and out."

"*You* decided." Sick as she was, the words came out less snappy, more whiny.

"You pretty much decided things for me when you passed out."

Ilene shuddered with sickness. "Will they notice this room is missing from the rest of the noise?"

"Maybe not." Staring out the window he said quietly, "I should probably stay the night. It'll attract attention if I leave at this hour."

She smoothed the wrinkles in the comforter. "What about your truck?"

"I parked it in the garage."

"All right. Go ahead and stay in the guest room. I could use some help with the girls in the morning anyway."

His cool eyes looked steadily back at her. "That room's wired. If I stay there, I'll be heard for sure."

She coughed and slapped the bedding. "I hate this. I'm a prisoner in my own house. Let's just disconnect everything."

"Not yet," he advised her.

On the edge of sleep she jabbered about her husband. "Philip called really, really early Sunday morning. It was so hard. I wanted to talk to him about the bugs and the money."

"The money," Kevin repeated.

Ilene couldn't remember if she'd told either of them about the money. "You know the Army hasn't even paid anyone in Philip's unit. And they can't get mail service." She knew she could tell him that.

"So what'd he say."

"We're okay. We have the money." Unable to keep her eyes open she thought she felt Kevin's fingertips on her cheek and around her eyes. She dreamed she was part of a tribal ceremony. She slept through most of the morning. When she awoke after ten, Kevin convinced her that he'd managed to feed the girls and send them off to school.

"I don't think Gladdy's gonna make it through the day," he warned. "She looked ragged. But wanted to go."

Ilene called Cathy at eleven. No answer. She tried the store. She was coughing when her friend picked up. "It's me," she wheezed. "Did you check your mail today?"

"What's wrong with you? Are you sick?"

"Come see for yourself. Bring your mail."

"I'm busy now," Cathy told her. "I'll go home and check later."

"Okay. But hurry."

Around 1:00 p.m., Kevin brought her fried rice and wonton soup from his favorite Chinese restaurant. "You need some healthy food."

She sat up in bed. "I feel like I've been hit by an Iraqi scud."

He nodded at the TV. "What's this?"

Ilene turned up the sound. CNN broadcast a news story about the ground troops. She sat cross legged in the center of the mattress and Kevin stretched out his long legs across the foot. While he helped her finish the food they watched the television report which mostly covered the tank units. No news of medical units.

Cathy peeked in. Her eyes widened as she spied the two of them. "This looks cozy." Then she waved an envelope and held up a pint of liquor. "Brought you some blackberry brandy for that nasty cough."

Kevin jumped up. "Catch you all later." With a twinkle in his eye he backed out the doorway.

Cathy stopped short inside the door. "What's going on here?"

Ilene felt the flush rising along her cheek bones. "Can you believe it?" She hopped out of bed. On her way across the room to close the door she paused next to Cathy and pulled open her nightgown, exposing the red blotches. "Chicken pox."

"Ohmygod."

"I didn't want to talk about it over the phone," Ilene continued, "Kevin disabled the system in here so we can talk."

Cathy sat down on the bed and handed her the envelope. "Maybe you should get a cellular phone."

"That's a good idea." Ilene tore open the envelope. "This is driving me crazy."

Cathy rolled her eyes. "Obviously."

Ilene nodded completely missing her friend's sarcasm. Skimming over the vehicle license request forms from the state of Illinois, she grabbed a pen and notebook from the bed table and began filling in the blanks. "Let me finish this right now and you can put it back in the mail. Overnight."

"Give me the ten bucks for express mail."

Ilene picked up her wallet from the table, pulled out a twenty and handed it over. "I really appreciate this."

Cathy took the bill. "I wish I could do more. But I'm working full time and taking care of two sick babies."

"Don't worry. I'll be fine by tomorrow. I never should've dragged you into this."

"That's not what I mean. Stan agrees that you should get rid of all the bugging devices." Cathy glanced over her shoulder. "And are you sure you should trust *him*?"

"I don't know." Ilene rubbed her forehead in exasperation. "So trust me. I'll get it taken care of."

"Don't do anything foolish."

Frowning, Ilene concentrated on the forms.

Cathy walked over to the other side of the room. "Who's sleeping on the futon?"

Ilene's heart skipped a beat. Her spotted flesh prickled. "Hazy. Was worried about me." She coughed and changed the subject. "Did I tell you Philip called?"

Her fever had mounted again when Gladdy crawled in bed with her after school. She turned down the sound on the television. "How was your day?"

"Something awful. I have a headache."

Ilene groaned. "See all these funny blotches on my skin. You're going to get them too. We'll be in the chicken pox club with Arnie and Sara."

"Kevin too," she said. "He already had chicken pox he said."

"That's good," Ilene replied. She looked up as Hazy appeared in the doorway wearing her backwards baseball cap.

"How do you feel?" she asked her mother.

Ilene coughed. "Pretty yucky right now. It comes and goes."

"Kevin said you didn't eat much today," Hazy informed her. "You better eat something."

"I will. I promise."

"What's the matter with the goonie?" Hazy referred to her sister under the covers.

Gladdy whimpered her disapproval.

"She's coming down with the chicken pox, too" Ilene told her. "You're next."

"Not." Hazy sauntered out of the room.

For supper she and Kevin brought in chicken noodle soup and toast squares. He disappeared. Hazy stayed. Ilene ate a little bit but the girls finished it off as they watched the news reports on TV. She grew concerned about their constant focus on war coverage.

"Let's see what else is on." She found *My Three Sons* on Nick and dozed off again.

Hours later Ilene awoke sweating. Nick at Nite was playing on the TV. She turned it to CNN with the sound low. Both Hazy and Gladdy were still clothed, asleep in her bed. She struggled to a stand and roused them. Grumbling, Hazy trudged up to the loft, while her mother wrestled to get sleepy Gladdy into her nightgown. By the time she climbed back in bed a coughing seizure had her gasping for air. She reached over, opened the pint of blackberry brandy that Cathy had left and took a few swigs. The warm brandy slid down her raspy throat. She drank more and closed her eyes as the berry liquor melted the tension in her chest. She watched television and sipped the brandy. Coming up was a playback of a pre-recorded live report from Dhahran.

"How compelling," she muttered. She drank more then carried the bottle downstairs to fetch a glass of ice water. Without thinking she turned on the TV in the dining area. Some guy reporting from Dhahran. Philip had been there once upon a time. Or maybe not. "Such a big goddamn secret," she grumbled. The picture seemed blurry.

Dropping ice cubes into her water glass, Ilene looked up to see Kevin standing under the living room divider beam scratching his lop-sided ponytail, T-shirt hanging out of his rumpled jeans. "What're you doing?"

Dulled by the liquor she wasn't even fazed. "Started coughing. Couldn't get back to sleep."

"Did you just guzzle all that brandy?" He pointed at the bottle, half empty.

Ilene hiccuped. "Its really helps. Try shum."

Shuffling over, he collapsed on the bench. "You're gonna be so sick. I'm not taking care of your kids again tomorrow."

Ilene turned up the sound on the TV to dilute her hoarse whisper. "What're you doing here?"

"Fell asleep on the couch," he muttered. Ilene slugged down more brandy. He took the bottle away from her. "That's enough."

She grabbed it. "Stop it. That's my cough medicine."

Walking around the island he herded her along, both hands seizing the bottle from her. "It worked. You're not coughing."

She said thickly, "I've shump-thing to shay to you."

He nodded. "Better go on upstairs before you *shay shump-thing stupid.*"

She punched his arm, but allowed him to spot her as she climbed the stairs. In the bedroom Ilene yanked him across the threshold and closed the door. Feeling emboldened by the alcohol she demanded, "I can't live like this. Let's tear it all out. Right now!"

Towering over her, hands on hips he said haughtily, "You're drunk."

She straightened up defiantly, legs wobbling. With a firm grip on her torso, Kevin steadied her. She shook her finger at him. "If you won't help me, I'll do it myself. Eventually."

He laughed and wrapped his arm around her shoulders, easing her toward the bed. "You're gonna hate yourself in the morning."

She stood still and gazed up at him in the flickering light of the television war. Her blackberry haze softened his rough edges. His sarcastic humor amused her. Full of inebriated curiosity, she kissed him. His mouth felt warm against hers. Then he pulled away. "No way. Not like this."

Feeling ashamed, Ilene took a deep breath. "Must be the brandy. Think I'll go to bed now." She turned and stumbled in that direction.

Kevin backed away. "Take it easy."

Tucking herself in she babbled, "One thing's for sure. I'm getting a phone like yours. Something private. Dammit."

"Whatever you say." He strolled over and kissed her hand.

"You think this is all so amusing," she complained. "Watching me go to hell like this."

"Yeah right." After her eyes were closed awhile he must have thought she was asleep. She heard him whisper, "What a fucking mess."

She didn't understand. Although she didn't think he was talking about her chicken pox.

4

The telephone awakened Ilene around 9:00 a.m. Tuesday, January 22nd. By the time she picked up, Kevin had answered downstairs. She listened.

"May I speak with Mrs. Singleton please." Ilene recognized the voice as Mrs. Westphal, Lakeside School counselor.

"I'll see if she's awake," Kevin replied.

"Hullo. This is Mrs. Singleton." The words spilled out like thick blackberry syrup. "I forgot to call in. We're all sick here."

"I'm sorry. Was that Mr. Singleton who answered?" she pried.

Even though it was none of the woman's business, Ilene cringed at her own lie. "No. That was my—brother." She couldn't think of anything else to say. He's the carpenter. He's the nurse. He's the nanny. It all sounded suspicious.

"I'm calling to find out why Hazel and Gladys aren't in school today." *Obviously*. She was about as chatty as voice mail.

"They came down with chicken pox. Actually we all did."

"Chicken pox," she repeated with alarm. "That's contagious. I don't know of any cases at school."

"We got it from a couple pre-schoolers. Friends of ours," she explained.

"The rule for contagious disease is that we cannot admit the children back in school without a note from the doctor stating they're no longer contagious. And don't forget to call in."

"You want me to call in every single day these girls are sick."

"We like to be kept informed," Mrs. Westphal stated.

"Okay. Since I have you on the phone, this is Tuesday. They won't be in school for the rest of the week. How about I call you Monday with an update."

"You'll need to pick up their assignments."

Ilene coughed. "I'm contagious too. Remember?"

"Perhaps your *brother* could then."

"I'll see what I can do." She hung up. "Bitch." She spat at the phone."

Kevin stirred up macaroni and cheese for the girls. She was in dire need of a grocery run. They ate at the dining table. She watched Gladdy count seven pox on her arms while Hazy turned up the television, ignoring everyone. Kevin fixed a couple bacon and egg sandwiches then set one on a plate in front of her at the center island.

She looked at the sandwich. "I don't eat bacon."

Raising his eyebrows he lifted the top piece of toast and peeled the bacon off the egg. He stuck it in his sandwich and gobbled it in four bites.

"Gotta go run some errands," he said, then left.

Hung over and sick that day, Ilene was no match for the girls. Chicken pox slowed them down but it didn't stop the chaos and clutter as they bounced from projects to playthings, ransacked cupboards, spilled juice for themselves, and watched God-knows-what on TV. She gave up and took an oatmeal bath to soothe the burning itches, then passed out in bed.

"Ilene. Are you okay?" Cathy awakened her as the afternoon sun faded past the windows. Wolf Blitzer's graveled voice murmured on TV in the background.

She sat up blinking. "What're the girls doing?"

Cathy rolled her eyes. "The place is a mess. But they've managed. When I called a bit ago Hazy answered and said she couldn't wake you."

Scratching her chest she shook her head. "I don't think she tried. I better get up."

Clutching her shoulder Cathy insisted, "Don't. Where's Kevin anyway?"

Ilene shrugged.

"You need to get a nurse in here. I'll make some calls," Cathy offered.

"No way," she muttered. "I just needed a little more rest. The worst is past. I can handle things now."

"Let me get you something to eat. I'll feed the girls." As she walked out the door, Cathy bumped into Kevin, holding a liter of Evian in his hand.

"By the way, I'm Cathy," she said to him.

"The friend with the blackberry brandy." He glanced over. "Did a number on her."

Ilene stuck out her tongue.

Cathy cocked her head at them. "I was just going to get her something to eat."

"Picked up a few groceries." He pulled an object out of his vest pocket and tossed it onto the quilt. "And something else."

"A phone!" Embarrassed at this scene in front of her friend, Ilene picked up the cell phone and started coughing. "I don't know what to say." She looked at him, then Cathy.

Her best friend clucked her tongue. "Generous."

Ambling over to set the bottle on the bedside table, Kevin smiled at them. "I work here. Remember? You'll get the bill." He left the room.

Cathy eyed her friend. "I'll get things under control here before I leave. If that's okay with you."

"Thanks." Alone with her new toy, Ilene found the cell phone number on a sticker. She dragged the phone book out of the drawer and looked up the number for US West customer service. She dialed then persevered through voice mail until she reached a representative. After giving her name and address she said, "I need to have a private line installed for my computer modem."

"We can send a service person sometime tomorrow."

"Hope he's had the chicken pox." Ilene hung up and staggered over to the bathroom to pull herself together. She put on a fresh T-shirt and cotton sweats.

Cathy returned with a tray of vegetable soup and bread. "He got this from the deli."

Sitting on the edge of the bed, Ilene tasted it. "Not bad." She ate a little then paused. "What are the girls doing?"

Cathy had seated herself in the arm chair beside the table. "He made them clean up their messes. Now they're eating soup."

"They listen to him better than me."

"He does have a way with them," she agreed. "Actually I went down there and threw my weight around a little. But he didn't seem to mind."

"What do you mean?"

Cathy pressed her lips together. "I figured if he's up to something, he'd try to get rid of me. But he seemed happy for the help. I even asked a couple nosy questions."

"Like what?"

"Like why he's doing all this for you. He said somebody has to." She cleared her throat. "Which is true enough. He said working here he's seen first hand all the pressure you've been under and he wasn't surprised that you collapsed. He said you try to handle too much on your own."

Ilene finished her soup in silence.

"He's very perceptive," Cathy added. "When it comes to you."

"He's been a big help." Setting the tray on the floor, Ilene drank from the Evian bottle.

Cathy leaned forward. "Have you considered that he might have a crush on you?"

Ilene spurted water. "That's absurd. We bicker constantly." She patted her friend's hand. "I appreciate your concern. He can be a nice guy. But he probably just wants more money."

"When I went out to the porch, he followed and sort of waited for me to ask the question."

Ilene blushed. "What question?"

"I asked him if he could take out the bugging equipment for you. He said as soon as you tell him to do it, he will."

She didn't tell her that Kevin had talked her out of it for the second time last night. She remembered that much. Besides the clumsy kiss. "You see? It's my decision."

"Then do it. You're way too stressed out." Cathy stood up. "I have to get home."

"Thanks for everything. I owe you. Big time."

She paused at the door. "Ilene. I know you think you can handle everything that's going on around here. But we plan to keep an eye on you anyway. Whether you like it or not."

"Hey!" Ilene laughed. "Join the club."

5

Ilene struggled through a rocky Wednesday morning, January 23rd. She made pancakes for the girls and choked down one herself. Her stomach was hungry enough, once she got the food past her mouth. A long steamy shower, followed by a clean pair of Levis and the pale blue cashmere sweater Philip had given her, all together worked miracles. After checking on Hazy and Gladdy playing video games in the loft, she moved slowly downstairs and turned on the TV in the dining area to CNN. A report on the first Marines killed by friendly fire nauseated her. Peering out the windows she spotted Kevin's truck and assumed he was back at work on the basement. She noticed the US West service van pull in the driveway. Ilene grabbed her jacket from the porch and ran outside to greet him.

"Hi. I'm Ilene Singleton." She held out her hand. "Never mind all these red spots. You ever had chicken pox?"

He shook her hand gingerly. "When I was a kid. Sure."

"I want you to install a private phone line in the den for me today." She told him as he unloaded the tools from the side of his van.

He gave her a queer look. "That's what my work order says."

"Once we get inside please don't say anything about this. My daughters are home from school with chicken pox and I don't want them to know about the new line. You know how it is with girls and phones." She led the bewildered man through the house to the den and silently showed him where to install the new line. She scribbled on a notepad, "*If you have any questions, write them down here.*"

The service man's eyes bulged as he read the message.

Hazy came to the door. "What's going on?"

Ilene glared at her. "Nothing. He's fixing my computer."

He worked hastily. Ilene figured he was anxious to get some distance between himself and her peculiar behavior. Of course Kevin showed up in the kitchen as the phone man was leaving. Ilene closed the porch door and turned around.

He winked at her. "Feeling better."

"I am. Thanks."

Approaching her, he bowed his head next to her ear. "You didn't call in the phone company to sweep this place."

"That wouldn't be very discreet." She kept up the charade. "I'll be in the den. I have a ton of work to do."

He let her pass without a word. She knew that was his way. If she didn't volunteer the information, he wouldn't confront her. Besides, the box for the Smart Bank program had been sitting on her desk in plain sight. He could figure it out for himself.

Ilene pulled the door closed and flicked on the little 13-inch black and white portable on the bookshelf. She plugged in the modem to the new line and fired up the hard drive. Loading Smart Bank seemed to drag on endlessly as did CNN's war analysis. Finally she released the last disc and the Smart Bank icon appeared on screen. Her hand trembled as she activated the program. Well trained in computers from her job at the chancellor's office, Ilene zipped through the tutorial file in no time. Under the cash management file, she called up the specific account bearing Philip's name. Scrolling through all the transactions she saw that every day of the week a nine thousand dollar deposit had been wire transferred from an account at the Bank of America in New York. She wrote down the account number. Paging through each numbered account file she found similar deposit activity. In every one of ten accounts, identical deposits across the board had originated from November 26, 1990. The Monday after Donald and Marie had visited. Two days after Philip left for McCoy.

As she stared at the account activity of DMS500204, the computer beeped and the cursor flashed, the signal to wait. The data scrolled up the current deposit record of that account and a brand new nine thousand dollar wire transfer appeared on screen. Ilene checked her watch—11:30 a.m. When the cursor returned to normal, she entered each account and found that ten deposits had just been wired from ten different accounts at Bank of America. Ninety thousand dollars. She wrote down every single account number.

Ilene glanced over at the bank statements on her desk. The only accounts listed were her own personal and their joint account, plus Hazy and Gladdy's savings accounts. Unlocking her bottom right desk drawer she pulled out her smoking supplies. She'd stashed a lighter, ashtray and two packs of Camel lights in the drawer. With its own private doorway to the deck for her to open and air out, the den was perfect for sneaking a smoke. She'd already bitten her nails down to ragged stumps from the war. But these finances were mind boggling. *Four million dollars.* She lit a cigarette and smoked the thing. Staring at the screen, she noticed the numbered accounts all began with the same prefix—DMS. *Short for Donald and Marie Singleton?* She wondered if she could coax any more information out of Ms. Cray. Putting out her cigarette, she took her cell phone out the sunny southwest deck and called the bank.

"Ilene Singleton," Esther Cray's enthusiastic phone voice bolstered her confidence. "What can I do for you today?"

"My bank statement doesn't include these numbered accounts."

"Let me take a look. Are you at the computer?"

Ilene coughed. "Not at the moment."

"Never mind. I've got it up now. When you go back to the main menu, you'll find a file labeled account management. Key that up and under report it designates that those account records are mailed quarterly to Donald Singleton at National Bank in Chicago."

This news did not surprise Ilene. "That's a mistake. From now on please have those statements sent to me."

Silence momentarily on the other end then, "Donald Singleton has power of attorney over your husband's financial assets."

"I see." Ilene clenched her teeth. "And what about the deed to our house? What happened to that?"

"As a matter of fact we transferred it to the National Bank of Chicago on December third."

Damn. Ilene bristled. She'd spent three years of her life in and out of court fighting for that piece of paper. "Looks like Mr. Singleton has everything under control."

"I'm sorry," Ms. Cray apologized. "I thought you were aware of those arrangements."

"I suppose he was informed that I switched to computer banking,"

"Why no. Did you want me to pass along that information?" Ms. Cray seemed to choose her words carefully. "That is confidential you know."

"Then I'd prefer to keep it that way," she said quickly.

"I understand."

Wondering just what it was she understood, Ilene sensed an opening. "Tell me something. Even though Philip's father has power of attorney, do I have the right to keep track of the financial transactions like this?"

"Of course. The accounts are in Philip Singleton's name. As his spouse you are eligible to review them. My job is to provide you with whatever information you ask for."

"I appreciate that."

"If I may be frank with you Mrs. Singleton. Ilene. It's obvious that you weren't aware of your husband's financial affairs until you came to me. That's not unusual. Happens all the time. Please don't be embarrassed."

"I'm just worried that we might be borrowing a lot of money." She slanted the truth.

"That's not the case," Ms. Cray assured her. "As I understand it, the funds are coming from an investment property that your father-in-law turned over to your husband before he left. It looks like a very secure investment. I'd say you needn't worry about a thing."

Due to her discovery of Donald Singleton's control over the fiscal big picture, Ilene put off her goal to exterminate the bugs. Now that she was monitoring the account activities she couldn't risk drawing attention to herself. Whatever Kevin's reasons were, he was right about keeping things in place for the time being. More than ever she needed to master the illusion of a normal life.

She and the girls recovered from their chicken pox by Friday. Much to her dismay Kevin disappeared on the weekend, leaving the sauna nearly finished when they could've used it the most. Although she knew that the true source of her irritation was that she had leaned on him while she was sick. That brief dependency spawned loneliness on Saturday and Sunday. Plus Philip didn't call.

Kevin's truck pulled in the driveway Monday morning January 28th, as she was turning the car around to drive the girls to the pediatrician. Ilene's heart thumped as she parked and walked over to greet him. Trying not to smile she felt ashamed of her relief at the sight of him.

Setting the brake he leaned out the window. "Go ahead. I'll park on the right."

She nodded, scowling. "Where were you?"

Raising his eyebrows he teased, "Did you miss me?"

Embarrassed by her obviousness, Ilene ambushed him. "You could've finished the sauna before you split for where ever. You knew we were all sick."

Rubbing his chin he eyed her. "Sorry. Something came up."

Her green eyes flashed. "Would it kill you to let me know what the hell's going on?"

He rolled up his window, pulled ahead and parked. She drove off in a huff.

Hazy and Gladdy had several faint clusters of pox on their backs and arms, but the contagious stage had passed, Dr. Street the familiar old pediatrician pronounced. They both assured him they felt much better.

Glancing over his spectacles, he frowned at their mother. "You on the other hand, still have spots. And you're looking rather flushed."

The nurse stuck the thermometer in her ear until it beeped. "One hundred degrees."

"I'm fine." Ilene scratched her neck. "It's just hot in here."

Dr. Street shone his penlite in her eyes.

"Are you eating well?"

"Not!" Hazy piped up.

"Drinking enough fluids?" he continued.

"No!" Gladdy added.

Ilene rolled her eyes.

Dr. Street shut off the light and manipulated the swollen glands in her neck. "Getting enough sleep?"

Coughing, she glared at the girls. "No!"

Grinning at their little game, he wrote on a prescription pad. "I don't normally prescribe antibiotics or cough medicine for chicken pox. But it looks like you've got a secondary infection brewing. Mrs. Singleton, I'm not your primary physician but I have to do something. I've never seen you so run down. I know these are tough times. With your husband away. You need to take better care of yourself." He glanced at them. "For these girls."

She took the prescriptions. "You're right. I know. Thanks for caring."

He handed her the girls' health clearances. "Now put Hazy and Gladdy back in school. Then go home and get some rest."

Precious notes in hand, Ilene went from the clinic out to Lakeside school. Once she dropped them off, she dialed Cathy's work number on her cell phone, hoping to lure her away for lunch.

"She's working up at the Spirit Mountain shop today," Sally told her.

"Could you give me that number?" Ilene dialed the satellite store. Cathy answered. "Hi. What are you doing? Mixing business with pleasure?"

Cathy groaned. "Hardly. We're so swamped. I worked up here all weekend."

"So that's where you were. I tried to call."

"Ohmygod. The day care thing really blew up in our faces. I mean chicken pox has raged through there like the plague. Not only are the kids sick but so are their parents. Who just so happen to be our employees. We've been short handed at both stores. Day care's closed until the epidemic passes. Some even want us to pay their child care expenses. Gees. Offer a service and suddenly it becomes a constitutional right."

Ilene sighed. "Sounds like a mess." She parked at Walgreen's to fill her prescriptions. Clearly Cathy was in a horrible mood and lunch was out of the question.

"Anyway. How are you feeling? Heard from Philip?"

"Not since the twentieth. I have to keep dreaming up stories to tell the girls. They have this *need* to know what he's doing every minute."

"Turn on the TV. The media blitz is sickening," Cathy complained. "Making war junkies out of everyone. Some of the kids who work for me. I swear to God they're addicted to CNN."

"Sounds like me," Ilene conceded.

"At least you have a stake in it. These kids think Desert Storm is so cool. They're so detached."

Ilene didn't really want to talk about the war. "Guess what I found out from the bank. Donald Singleton not only holds the deed to our house, but he also holds power of attorney over all our financial assets, while thousands of dollars are pouring into Philip's bank accounts daily. Allegedly from some investment property he turned over to Philip."

"That certainly goes a long way toward explaining the goings on around there. Did you get that taken care of?"

"I'm on my cell phone." Ilene let her know. "And I've decided to hold off on doing anything right now."

"Why?" Cathy cried.

"I told you. Power of attorney. The deed to the house. What if I do something to piss him off? He could literally put me and the girls out on the street."

"Ilene! Listen to yourself. This whole thing is making you so paranoid."

"With good reason," she snapped. "Besides, I just need a little more time."

"For what?"

"Cathy. I don't have any say in the big picture here. At the slightest provocation they could freeze Philip's accounts. What if they decide they don't like what I'm doing with the house? I think it would be a good idea for me to build up my own personal account with enough money to get me through this crisis. Don't you agree?"

"Maybe you should get some legal advice," Cathy suggested.

"Are you out of your mind? All I need is to add a lawyer to the mix. Trying to steal the money for himself."

"You need to talk to someone you can trust."

"That's why I call you."

Cathy exhaled deeply. "Then I need to point out another side of this."

"What do you mean?"

"Maybe Kevin is the reason they're keeping an eye on you. Maybe they think you're fooling around."

"Jesus Christ Cathy!" Closing her eyes, Ilene swallowed hard, thankful the car was parked. She might've hit the ditch otherwise.

"You said yourself they're eccentric. Paranoid. Whatever. Let's say they were worried about the house or the money at first. But now they think Kevin's hanging around there a lot. Maybe they think he's up to no good."

"That's absurd."

"No more absurd than your theories. You can't see the evidence. Last week he spent a lot of time there. He even slept over. Didn't he?"

"Nothing happened Cathy. I was sick." Ilene bit her lip to contain her outrage at this new twist.

"I'm talking specifically about appearances here," her friend said.

Ilene bristled. "And you're saying it looks like I'm fucking around? I don't have to take this shit from you."

"Don't be so defensive," Cathy scolded, then paused. "Ohmygod. Ilene. You're not. Are you?"

"I'm hanging up on you now," she growled.

Cathy chuckled with relief. "Just testing. I gotta get back to work. Think about what I said." She hung up.

Ilene shut off the phone. After retrieving the drugs she drove out to Highway 61 where she wound her way up the north shore. She wasn't eager to go straight home and deal with Kevin. Not after Cathy's unsolicited observations. But there was nothing going on. *Okay.* They kissed. Twice. So there was *something*. Tears clouded her vision as she pulled into a scenic wayside and stared out at the frozen lake shore in winter.

The temperature outside hovered around zero. A few cumulus puffs darted across the sky. This far north the sun hung low on the horizon. Even in the bitter cold, steam rose from the churning water because it was warmer than the air temperature. Repeated wave action had formed giant ice castles along the shoreline. She thought about him. The last thing she needed in her life was a relationship with another man. She pulled out the pack of Marlboro lights she'd stashed in the glove compartment and lit one. She hadn't made up her mind yet which brand to smoke. Cathy was right about how things might look to the almighty Singletons. She had to be more careful. The cigarette caused a coughing spell. She squashed it in the ashtray and drank some cough medicine. Turning the car around she headed home.

Kevin stayed late working on the sauna downstairs. After supper Ilene herded Hazy and Gladdy to their rooms for the evening. Alone in the kitchen she swallowed two antibiotic capsules, chasing them with a 7Up. She saw his reflection in the window above the sink. Watching her. She spun around.

Kevin stared at the pill bottle. "You okay?"

"Antibiotics. Just a precaution," she told him.

"Sauna's finished. Got those rocks fired up to a hundred seventy degrees. It's all yours."

Avoiding his eyes she wiped off the counter. "Maybe later."

He rocked backward on his heels. "So what was that tantrum all about this morning?"

Ilene filled the dishwasher. "I needed it on the weekend. I'm busy right now. I said I'll use it later."

"Shouldn't waste the heat," he cautioned. "Mind if I try it out?"

"Would it matter if I did?"

He stood there for a minute while she watched an NBC news break, ignoring him.

After he'd gone downstairs, the pungent odor of cedar wafted through the house. Staring at Arthur Kent, the one they called *Scud Stud* on the screen, she visualized Kevin down there dripping wet in the heat. Shutting off the TV, she went upstairs and immersed herself in mounds of bubble bath.

6

The bombing of Baghdad into the stone age continued through the end of January, and into the first week of February. Along with scuds and patriot missiles added to Hazy and Gladdy's vocabulary, their newest word was *sorties*—the polite word for bomber missions. Iraqi troop movements turned out to be sitting ducks for allied sorties. No ground war existed. The smidgen of retaliation from Saddam's army usually occurred in prime time. During the Super Bowl an Iraqi scud missile blasted into Riyadh, like military theater, making the most of hefty ratings. Now that she could talk to him freely on her cell phone, Philip didn't call. Not since January 20th. Without word, the TV coverage had become her only link to him. She worried less hearing reporters' repeated claims of sporadic and few American casualties.

Kevin and Mr. Christianson, the plumber worked on the spa and bathroom downstairs all week long. She utilized the time on the computer to beef up her personal account with transfers from their joint account. The problem was, by the time she finished paying invoices she'd depleted the build up and didn't want to attract attention with another large transfer.

With the boost from antibiotics she felt stronger. Her appetite was back. And while the cough medicine helped her sleep at night, it was Kevin who showed up in her dreams, contributing to her frustration. During the waking hours she heeded Cathy's warning and went out of her way to avoid any hint of a relationship with the carpenter. Unfortunately she sacrificed his friendship with her aloofness. Ilene was beginning to think she had her life under control until she collected the mail on Monday, February 4th.

Stopping outside the front door that damp gray morning she found the letter from the Deputy Secretary of the state of Illinois in the middle of the pile. She tore it open.

"Dear Mrs. Singleton,

"This office has received your request for the identity of an Illinois registered motor vehicle license holder. Upon initial notification of the owner, your request was denied. However this office has further investigated the matter and have since determined the death of your daughter's cat to be just cause for your request.

"You will find the identification of the driver on the enclosed form. Let me know if this office may be of any further assistance.

"Sincerely,

"Lawrence Albright, Deputy Secretary

"State of Illinois"

Ilene glanced upward. "Thank you Mr. Kitty. Wherever you are."

Studying the attached form, under identification she found "DMS & JDP Holding Company". Must be Donald's trust, she thought to herself. Then a cold wind blasted the back of her head. Kevin had said it was registered to Donald Singleton. If she didn't even know for sure, then how did he make the connection? She marched down to the basement.

Headphones stuck in his ears and backwards baseball cap on his head, Kevin knelt on the concrete, laying blue and yellow design ceramic tiles around the hot tub. Acknowledging her presence he cajoled,

"Don't be shy. Grab a tile. This adhesive dries fast."

"How 'bout I buy you a sandwich at the New London Deli?"

"Give me fifteen minutes to finish this row," he told her.

Kevin insisted on driving his pickup and started talking at once before she had the chance to speak. "Hot tub's looking good. Should be ready in another week."

Ilene nodded. "Do you like the tiles I picked out? Hand painted. Very south Florida. Don't you think?"

"You have exquisite taste," he teased. "But you didn't lure me out of there for decorating advice."

Ilene watched the Amity Creek flowing beside them as they wound down Seven Bridges Road. She hadn't quite figured out how to broach the subject of the Mercedes registration. Whether she should confront him. Or squeeze it out of him.

Kevin obliged her moodiness without question, driving patiently to the deli at the bottom of the hill on London Road. Parking the truck he asked, "Heard from Philip?"

"Not since the twentieth."

They walked inside and ordered sandwiches. Ilene asked for the vegetarian cheese melt and Kevin ordered a reuben. They sat at a corner table with a view overlooking the frozen sculptures along the lake shore. Beyond them cold steam hovered over the dark open water rolling up toward the layers of gray sky. Now that they were seated across from one another, Kevin's closeness distracted her. She had denied herself his company for so long she felt intimidated. Without a word she pulled the letter out of her bag and handed it to him.

Wiping his hands with napkin he read it over an examined the attached form. "DMS and JDP Holding Company," he repeated.

"How did you know that was Donald Singleton?" she interrogated him.

He didn't flinch.

"Simply a matter of public record. Thought we hashed this out already."

"I don't believe you."

He winced artificially. "I'm crushed."

Ilene put down her fork. This was getting her nowhere. Lunch had been reduced to an obligation.

Sliding the letter across the table Kevin declared, "I don't see what this has to do with me anyway."

"Just that you seem to know more about what's going on around me than I do."

"Then open your eyes," he admonished her. "Quit treating me like the enemy."

"How do I know the Singletons didn't set you up to make it look as if we're fooling around."

He laughed. "Really. That's the worst agenda you can think of to saddle me with." He held her hand. "And would that be so bad?"

"You dog." She jerked her hand away. "Maybe you get your kicks by humiliating lonely older women."

Violet eyes pierced the barrier she'd put between them. "And maybe you're pushing me away because you don't trust yourself alone with me anymore."

Sensitive to her own transparency she refused to look at him. "I'd slap you for that if we weren't in a public place."

Leaning back defensively he smiled at her. "Which makes this place that much more special for me."

"Look." She sighed. "You're the one who pointed out that I'm being watched. Listened to. Whatever. You knew who the Mercedes belonged to weeks before I did."

He waved his hand. "So. We're back to that."

"This letter proves my suspicions about the source of your information."

"If I'm sposed to be part of your in-laws little spy network, then why would I let you in on it."

Exhaling her frustration, she surmised, "Maybe you changed your mind."

"When I change my mind, you'll be the first to know." Kevin dabbed at his smirk with a napkin.

She watched his hand set it on the table to avoid looking at his lips. "There you go. Avoiding the truth with sarcasm."

"The truth is. You have nothing to fear from me, Mrs. Singleton. I can hold out as long as you can."

"What the hell is that supposed to mean!" Ilene stood up abruptly. "Take me home and get back to work."

7

The letter from the deputy secretary of Illinois piqued Ilene's curiosity in the bank accounts that week. Tuesday morning, February 5th, she sequestered herself on the deck outside the den and called the Bank of America in New York from her cell phone, setting in motion a reckless subterfuge.

"Hello. My name is Esther Cray from Northwest Bank in Duluth," she lied. "I need to verify a series of wire transfers."

"One moment please," the first woman responded.

Another woman with a heavy Brooklyn accent came on the line. "This is Penny. May I have the account numbers please?"

Ilene repeated her request and read off the Bank of America account numbers listed on the printout of deposits.

There was a pause, then Penny replied. "There are twenty numbered accounts in all depositing wire transfers to Northwest in Duluth. Do you need all of those?"

"That's right. Twenty." Compelled by the success of her bluff she demanded more information. "I need the original depositor on those accounts."

"No problem. They originated from the Banca Nationale de Lavoro in Atlanta. I'll fax those numbers to you."

Ilene groped for a professional response. Her computer had a fax modem. She gave Penny the number.

"That's some audit you've got going."

Ilene jumped on the suggestion. "My first one."

"Word of advice. Be cool. This kinda stuff happens all the time."

"Thanks for your help."

Back inside the den, the account records from Bank of America came up on screen in the fax program. The balances in those twenty accounts in New York were almost as healthy as the ones in Duluth. Ten additional nine thousand dollar deposits doubled the figures she already knew about. Ilene clicked back to the Smart Bank main menu and went into "file management". She inspected the options and chose "auxiliary files". Ten accounts labeled FAB2000 popped up on screen. Returning to the fax program she printed the account records and compared the ten additional deposit records to the FAB2000 records. Numbers and dates corresponded. Referring to the manual she learned that FAB2000 was an acronym for Financial Assets Beyond 2000—restricted access accounts. Philip had ten.

Reaching for her cigarette stash she lit up a Camel and loaded the figures into the calculator. Over eight million dollars had been transferred through the Bank of America from Banca Nationale de Lavoro since November.

She leaned back in her chair smoking the cigarette. Donald and Marie Singleton weren't keeping an eye on her because of Kevin. They didn't want her to find out about all the money floating around. If only Philip would call. If only she could be given the opportunity to ask the right questions.

Gerry Cusick phoned on Wednesday the 6th. "How are you Ilene? We missed you at our last meeting." She said that every time she called.

"I'm fine Gerry," Ilene always replied.

"We finally pinpointed how the paychecks got lost. They were mailed to Saudi Arabia. But the mail hasn't been delivered to the 477th over there. Makes sense when you stop to think about it."

"It does? Sounds like a colossal military screw up to me."

"If money gets tight, we've arranged for low interest loans for family members from Northwest Bank."

Ilene rolled her eyes at the irony. "Actually it looks like we'll be okay."

"That's good to hear. You're lucky."

Ilene knew that luck had nothing to do with the millions flowing through her husband's numbered accounts. "Philip hasn't called in weeks. Has anyone else heard from the unit?"

"Nothing. In fact Tanya Peterson had a baby boy. So the Red Cross has been combing the desert to give James the news. Judy Carlson saw a field reporter on CNN interviewing a soldier who said he was from the 477th. But she didn't recognize him."

"What'd he say?"

"Just that everyone was okay. He said they'd come upon some Iraqi POW's and had stopped for a couple days to give them medical attention."

"Maybe that means they're close to Kuwait."

"I'll let you know as soon as we hear something definite." Gerry wound up the conversation.

Ilene spent the rest of the week intermittently posing as Esther Cray on her cell phone, unraveling the chain of deposits. Dusting off her executive secretary skills from her years at the chancellor's office, she picked up the time zones and long distance codes like hopping on a bicycle in the middle of winter. First she contacted the Banca Nationale de Lavoro in Atlanta, using the name "Ms. Cray", plus the auditing rap that Penny at the Bank of America had laid on her. She learned there were only five accounts at the Atlanta BNL wiring funds into the twenty accounts at Bank of America. And the five BNL accounts were supplied by wire transfers from the Cayman Islands Bank of Credit and Commerce

International. A cryptic labyrinth emerged. Borrowing the name Karen from the Atlanta bank, she called the Cayman BCCI and found out there was only one account that wired deposits into the BNL accounts. And deposits in that account originated with the Bank of Credit and Commerce International in Luxembourg. She looked up the time zone and discovered they were seven hours ahead. In order to phone them during banking hours and before the girls woke up, she had to plan for the wee hours. Her next opportunity came on Friday the 8th.

The alarm awakened her at 6:00 a.m. Bundling up she tiptoed quietly down to the darkened study then out on the frigid deck with her cell phone. The time in Luxembourg was just after 1:00 p.m. But the overseas call turned out to be her shortest yet. By then she'd forgotten the name of the account handler at the Cayman Islands BCCI. She used the name Mary.

A gentleman with a thick Middle Eastern accent responded to her inquiry. "Excuse me. But I do not recall anyone by that name at our Cayman Islands Bank. Tell me Miz Mary, what is your last name?"

Ilene punched the *end* button instantly, crossing her fingers that there had not been sufficient time to trace the call. Shivering, she ducked indoors as though covering up her actions somehow. Obviously she had stumbled into sensitive territory with the Luxembourg Bank of Credit and Commerce International. Her fingers trembled as she reached for the cigarettes in the drawer. She smoked one which only stimulated her sleeping bowels and bladder. Back upstairs in her bathroom with the door closed, she assumed that in all likelihood Luxembourg was the bank of origin. Especially since the account activity had narrowed down to one account at two branches of the BCCI.

Wide awake, Ilene curled up in the warm bedclothes to watch the dawn creep through the lake fog. She thought through the maze of funds, wondering how many millions of dollars were being zapped around the world. Even though the National Bank of Chicago was not on the list of depositors, she assumed it was all somehow connected to Donald Singleton. Beyond the shadow of a doubt she was convinced the money did not belong to Philip. Or some phantom investment property.

Gail called after the girls had left for school. "Hey stranger. What's the word from your desert fox? Is this war about over?"

"Haven't heard from Philip since January 20th." She spoke the tired phrase automatically. "All we know is their unit's out in the desert somewhere steering clear of flies and scorpions."

"What?"

"That's what he said," Ilene explained. "Their phone calls are monitored so he couldn't say much. I think the flies are bombers. And scorpions are tanks."

"Ah. Friendly fire," Gail mused.

"Stop it. Gives me the creeps." Ilene shuddered. "So. How's life in the big city?"

"Sandy and I had a huge fight. She moved out."

Ilene thought about the wiretap. It wasn't fair for Gail to confide in her without knowing. "Someone's at the door. Are you home? I'll call you back."

"Whatever." Gail hung up.

Grabbing her cell phone, Ilene drove off in the Camry. She dialed Gail's number right away. "It's me. Sorry about that. I'm on a cell phone now. Let me give you my number." She repeated it.

"Very cool. I've been thinking of getting one. Do you like it?"

"It's been a god send. Believe me," Ilene said. "Now what's with you and Sandy?"

"She invited her friend Holly from Boston to come stay at my place last weekend. Can you believe that?"

"I thought she was living there too," Ilene stated. "She's not allowed visitors?"

"Ilene! They slept in the same goddamn bed," her sister fumed. "Then she accused me of being an anal retentive bitch who doesn't understand lesbian relationships. And I said 'why because I don't fuck around'."

"So you threw her out."

"She moved out on her own. Good fucking riddance."

"You don't sound too brokenhearted."

"I'm devastated!" Gail cried.

"Then why don't you drive up north for the weekend. Get away from the situation."

"Are you kidding? We're swamped down here. War is great for the bar business. We're up over a hundred percent," Gail boasted. "They come in to watch the war on CNN and drink to oblivion."

"How depressing."

"Besides, Betty said you and the kids had chicken pox. You must be exhausted. I was hoping to convince you to bring them down here. Let Grandma baby sit so we can spend some quality sister time."

"Both Hazy and Gladdy have birthday parties and ski spree. I'm on my way to pick up wallpaper books, paint and fabric samples. Since I fired Marie's decorator I haven't done a thing about that part. I'm meeting with the window covering lady on Monday and I haven't even decided between shades or blinds. I could use your help."

"Private party here tomorrow night. I can't leave town."

"Can't you get someone else to cover for you? There's so much shit going on here right now. I really need to talk to you."

"So talk."

"Not on the phone."

"Ilene I have to handle this party. It's Norm Costello's sixtieth."

"Good customer."

"The best. Get your hired man to handle things. What's his name—Kevin."

"He's part of the problem."

"What problem?"

"He's just around. All the time," Ilene explained awkwardly. "At first I thought maybe Philip's parents hired him to spy on me."

"Whoa. Wait a minute," Gail interjected. "What's that about?"

"They've been keeping very close tabs on me. But I can't get into that on the phone," she cautioned. "Anyway I don't think he's involved with them."

"What makes you think they're spying on you?"

"The phones in the house are wiretapped."

"Jesus Christ Ilene. That's fucking illegal."

"I realize that. But the problem is that Kevin's planning to work on the basement project. He'll be here all weekend. I'm trying to avoid certain appearances. If you know what I mean."

There was a long pause on the other end before Gail said, "Are you trying to tell me something?"

"I'm telling you that I'd like you to be here for me this weekend. So it doesn't look like there's something going on between me and the hired man."

"And is there?"

"Oh Christ. Gimme a break."

"That's not an answer. Is he coming on to you?"

Their conversation was so completely deranged at that point her only option was brutal honesty. "We're friends. Sort of. But there's tension. Look Gail. You wouldn't believe how much he's done to help me. With the house. The girls."

"Gratitude can be a tricky thing. Betty noticed the sparks between you two last month. Putting myself in your shoes. Philip's gone. Haven't even heard his voice in weeks. Kevin's right there. He's a nice guy. Young. Oh god sister."

"Nothing's happened," Ilene assured her. "We kissed. A couple times."

"You want me to come and hose down the fire."

"It's not that out of control. After the basement's finished he'll probably be gone. I could use a buffer right now. That's all. I'm lonely." She dabbed moisture from her eyelids like sweat.

"Listen to me," Gail ordered. "Leave the kids with Cathy or someone. Get your sweet ass down here. We'll talk it out of you."

"Cathy's swamped with the new store. It's the middle of ski season. Stan's coaching. They've got two babies." She sighed. "Never mind. I'll manage."

"Go shopping tomorrow," Gail suggested. "I'll try to get out of here after the party gets going. Hang in there. I'll call you."

"Use this number. We'll talk Saturday night."

At home later around 6:30 p.m., Ilene sat on the third step of the spiral staircase studying a big book of wallpaper samples for the foyer. She half listened to the *MacNeil Lehrer News Hour* broadcasting from the television in the dining room. Munching a turkey avocado sandwich she saw him out of the corner of her eye as he appeared in the lighted foyer. He strolled over and plopped down beside her. She felt his denim shirt sleeve touching her sweater. He smelled earthy like sawdust and glue.

Peering over her shoulder, his breath touching her hair Kevin said, "Hate to disappoint you but those samples all look the same."

She smiled and elbowed his left side. "I requested antique white. I'm looking at the textures in the wallpaper." Although they both knew from the diagram there were no mikes in the foyer, they spontaneously spoke in hushed tones.

"If you ask me, this foyer could use some color," he assessed.

"I didn't ask you," Ilene replied. "I plan to hang paintings on the walls. Splashy landscapes like Raul Diego. Or something like that."

"What? No duck prints. This *is* northern Minnesota." Plucking the other half of the sandwich off the plate he took a bite then asked, "So where are those two young lovelies tonight?"

She watched him devour her supper. "Hazy went on a sleep over. Gladdy's out for pizza and a movie."

He swallowed. "Did I mention I'll be working this weekend?"

Ilene nodded, fingering the embossed designs propped on her knees. "By the way, feel free to eat my sandwich."

He reached his arm around her shoulders. "Thanks. Couldn't resist. Good sandwich."

She stiffened at his embrace.

"The plumber's ready to finish the hot tub next week. But I'm not," he explained. "Got way behind when you all were sick."

"Whatever. Suit yourself."

His hand, still attached to the arm around her, patted her shoulder. "What are you up to this weekend?"

Struck by the question Ilene sat upright and stared at the wall. "Think my sister's coming tomorrow night."

"Why not take the girls down there for the weekend? See their Grandma. Spend some time with your family. You've had a lotta shit thrown at you lately." He squeezed her affectionately.

Feeling the lump rising in her throat, she swallowed. *Damn. He was good.* "Actually I think I'm handling things much better now, thank you."

"Okay. So now you're feeling better. You should get away from this place awhile."

She turned to face him. "Are you trying to get rid of me?" That was her mistake.

His eyes locked onto hers. "No." He surprised her with a small kiss. Then his mouth drew hers in with more light kisses, testing for deeper ones. She let him. His gentle determination paralyzed her while he tasted her neck. In that moment she censored her ardor with thoughts of Philip.

Wiping her mouth with the back of her hand she whispered, "Is this the part where the lonely housewife gets fucked by the horny carpenter?"

Dropping his hands he stomped to his feet. "Damn! You can be nasty."

Ilene rose to a stand. "Good night Kevin."

She climbed the stairs to her bedroom and closed the door. Hearing the porch door slam she listened for his truck engine starting. Her left hand massaged her lips as she leaned against the door reliving the incident. Heart beating through her nostrils, she stumbled over to the bed and sprawled backward. His kisses felt so delicious. Raw desire hammered away at her allegiance to Philip. His kiss was out of reach. Kevin was becoming as comfortable as the furniture. Picking up the remote, Ilene switched on CNN. She watched the war until Gladdy burst through her bedroom door.

"Oh wow! *Beauty and the Beast* was so good." Her youngest bounced on the bed. "You and Hazy hafta see it. The Beast was so cool."

Ilene listened to her enthusiastic little silhouette chatter in the pale light from the TV screen. Her father's daughter. The eyes and chin carved from the same tree. Tears welled up in her eyes. She reached out as Gladdy fell into her arms. They hugged and kissed. Ilene gently smoothed her hair and cooed, "I love you Cookie Monster."

Gladdy pulled herself up by her hands. "What's the matter Mommy? Do you miss Daddy?"

Ilene nodded wiping tears that spilled. "Really a lot."

"Me too." Gladdy patted her arm. "I won't leave you alone anymore. You get too sad."

"No. No. That's not it," Ilene assured her. "I'm glad you went to the movie. That was lots of fun. Then you came home and cheered me up."

"But you're crying," Gladdy protested.

"I'm okay now." Ilene smiled. "See."

"You shouldn't watch too much war on TV," Gladdy scolded. She grabbed the remote and switched the channel to Nick. "It makes you worry about Daddy."

"Tonight I *needed* to worry about your daddy," Ilene said, even though she wouldn't understand.

8

"Today the UN begins closed-door sessions to review the war and examine Saddam Hussein's offer to withdraw from Kuwait." Katie Couric's voice awakened Ilene. *"This is Today, Thursday—Valentine's Day—February fourteenth, nineteen ninety-one."*

She'd fallen asleep with the TV on. Getting to be a bad habit. Stretching out spread eagle in bed, she dared to fantasize about Philip's return and the problems it would solve.

Buoyed by hopes of an impending surrender, her morning slipped by. Temperatures quickly melted into the mid-thirties. Ilene used the warmth as an opportunity to clean the slush off the decks with a shovel. It also gave her an excuse to avoid Kevin which she'd managed to do most of the week. Gail never showed up last weekend but it hadn't been difficult to hold up Hazy and Gladdy as barriers between them. After her rebuff he kept his distance, intent on finishing the spa, which was fine with her. Mr. Christianson the plumber was costing her a bundle.

Even though Cathy phoned to check in she had no time to get together. Ilene built up her account balance to one hundred thousand

and tried to put those mysterious accounts out of her mind. She grew increasingly uneasy about the phone fax trail she'd laid using Esther Cray and other names while contacting those four banks she knew nothing about. None of it made sense. Ordering window shades and picking out wallpaper simplified her life. Aside from the fact that she was always conscious of listening ears, her life was as normal as she could make it seem.

Her afternoon was spent with Gladdy's first grade class. Mrs. Westphal had encouraged her to volunteer to help Mrs. Swanson with the Valentine's Day party. Ilene was in charge of games. With sunshine and temperatures in the forties she sent the six-year olds on a scavenger hunt.

"Find Minnesota winter things," she instructed. "Each team who brings back the most wins." She read off the list. "Chunk of ice. Broken branch. One mitten." The kids laughed. "Bird seed. Dried leaves. Stray hockey puck."

The kids hooted louder as they grew restless wearing their winter jackets at their desks.

An elderly teacher around sixty years old, Mrs. Swanson clapped her hands. "All right class. Let's form a nice straight line and file out to the playground quickly," she barked. "And quietly. We don't want to disturb the other classes."

Ilene trotted after them. "I have extra lists!"

"We generally play indoor games in winter," Mrs. Swanson commented as they rushed out to the playground, making it clear she wasn't thrilled with Ilene's idea of a game. "I guess I missed the connection with Valentine's Day."

Ilene smiled. "Maybe it'll do their little hearts good to run around in the fresh air."

Teachers in-service day meant no school on Friday, leaving Thursday night open for kids' activities. After their respective Valentine's Day parties, Ilene drove Hazy to Jessie's house in Lakeside and Gladdy to Kirsten's house nearby for sleepovers. Alone again, she despised the notion of going home to that big empty house. Philip hadn't called in nearly a month. She hated not hearing his voice. The absurdity of it went beyond her own loneliness, it was as if he no longer existed. She phoned Carricks from the car.

Stan answered. "Hello Ilene."

"I'm surprised *you're* home," she gibed.

"I'm watching Arnie and Sara till Cath gets back from the shop. She thinks I'm heading out to Spirit to coach but I've actually got a sitter coming. Gonna take her out to the Lakeview Castle for dinner and dancing."

"Oh Stan," Ilene gushed. "That's so sweet. You guys've had a rough winter."

"Tell me about it." He groaned. "We haven't opened up the day care since the quarantine. Five employees submitted over three thousand dollars in child care expenses. Turned it over to our attorney. We'll probably pay half since everyone paid in for about half the day care expenses originally. Everyone wants it back but we're in negotiations." He took a deep breath. "Anyway. That was a long story. How's Philip?"

"I'm so tired of that question," she whined.

"What's wrong?" he sounded alarmed.

"It's been a month since he called."

"Aren't they on the move constantly?"

"Yes. And there's reason to believe he's in no danger," she added. "But it's so weird. He's just not here. Or there. Not anywhere."

Stan sighed. "I'm sorry. You guys are going through hell. And I'm all pumped up about day care. Christ."

"Life goes on," she said. "So. You two have fun tonight. I envy you."

"Aw. Happy Valentine's Day, Ilene," he offered. "This mess in the Gulf will be over soon. You heard the news today."

"Yeah. Bye Stan." Ilene pressed *end*.

She'd driven the five miles down Park Point toward the lake while yakking it up with Stan. As long as she was there, she parked the car and hiked onto the frozen dunes. The air was almost balmy for February. The watery surface of Lake Superior absorbed the blueberry color of the sky in the fading light. Clouds had gathered to the west, blocking out all but the pink stripe of sunset. She perched on a bench in front of the beach house and listened to the cold water lap against the ice castles, rounding the sharp edges, wearing them down. Darkness outweighed the daylight. By the time she steered the car up the hill again traffic had thinned.

Kevin's truck was still parked in the driveway at home. Ilene drove her own car into the garage and entered through the basement. Inside the spa room she found the hot tub full of warm, not yet hot water, the jets bubbling. The design on the tiles danced in the mirror's reflection under the soft track lighting. She peeked in the dressing room and switched on the light in the new bathroom—a sink, a toilet, and separate shower, in a tongue and groove cedar on sand-colored slate with a floor drain. Still looking institutional, it would need some decorating.

"You ruined my surprise." Kevin came up behind her.

She jumped half a foot and backed away.

He laughed. "Sorry."

"You've done a great job," she said with awe. "You and Mr. Christianson that is."

They walked by the churning hot tub. Ilene sniffed the air. Her nostrils ached from an exotic aroma. "It smells wonderful in here."

"Scented chlorine," he said.

She followed him upstairs. "You must be rather proud of yourself."

He turned with a wistful look. "I am."

"You do nice work."

On the center island she discovered a vase filled with two dozen red and white long-stemmed roses, plus Mumm's chilling in a bucket. Candle light bathed the dining table.

Kevin leaned against the counter, arms folded across his chest. "Afraid I'm not so creative with food. I picked up Chinese again. Hope you don't mind." Dressed in clean faded jeans, a plain black sweater, his long hair tied back and shining he cast a striking profile.

"What is all this?" she asked finally.

"This is for you. Happy Valentine's Day." Hands innocently tucked behind his back, he leaned forward and kissed her cheek.

Ilene did not respond. The house remained silent. She reached for the TV remote.

He grabbed it from her. "Don't. There's nothing new. I checked. Let the war go for just one night."

"No surrender yet?" she asked fretfully.

Shaking his head calmly he said, "Here. Have some champagne."

"All right."

He opened the bottle out on the deck like he'd done New Year's Eve. Ilene joined him out in the thirty degree night air, carrying two flutes. He poured the vintage and offered a toast. "Roses are red. Violets are blue. Your husband's at war. So you're stuck with me on Valentine's Day. Too."

Ilene giggled helplessly. They drank champagne. Her first glass slid down too easily. "You make me laugh."

He stole a kiss.

"I think I'd better eat something," she decided.

He moved away and poured more champagne. "I'll get the food. It's in the oven." Kevin's ease in the midst of her kitchen unnerved her. She started to get in his way. "Let me handle this," he said firmly.

Taking a deep breath she wandered over to the gorgeous bouquet of red and white roses tied together with a lace ribbon that flowed down the crystal vase. "These roses smell so good."

"I like the white ones," he said. "Let's eat."

They finished one bottle of champagne in the middle of Szechuan lobster, shrimp fried rice and egg rolls. Kevin popped open another.

Ilene sipped from her glass then set it down, glancing around nervously. "It's too quiet in here. Aren't you curious about the news?"

"You're addicted." He stood up. "How about some music." He strolled over to the CD player in the living room and slipped in a disc.

Ilene listened to the twang of the guitar as it filled the air, followed by the familiar complaint in Chris Isaak's voice. Kevin adjusted the volume. "*Heart Shaped World.*" Music she and Philip had made love to. She stood up and cleared the table, no longer hungry. Perching his butt on the kitchen counter he cleaned up the last of the fried rice from the carton. He reached for her flute and filled it with more champagne. Chris Isaak wailed in the background.

"Hot tub should be warm by now," he said. "I was hoping we could try it out."

"After hanging with first graders all afternoon I'm pretty tired."

He cocked his head. "Please. I worked my ass off to get that done."

"Go ahead. Use it. Don't let me stop you. I'll use it later."

Holding up his left arm he sniffed. "Do I smell bad or something?"

His antics amused her. "Maybe I don't trust you."

He emptied his glass. "We've already established that."

Ilene stood in front of him, pointed to her ears and murmured, "This conversation is not happening."

He mimicked her. "Seriously now." Then leaning forward he whispered, "We need to talk. Meet me downstairs." He jumped down and sauntered out.

Ilene released her exasperation with a sputtering breath. Upstairs in her own bathroom, she stepped into her low cut leopard one piece. She barely filled it out anymore, having lost weight. Her other suit was a floral two piece. Too sexy. She checked her hair and eyes in the mirror. High from champagne she told herself that she'd find out what he had to say out of listening range then be done with it. She'd be free to go to bed and watch the news. Throwing on her robe she headed out.

"*Wicked Game*" played like an omen on the stereo as she descended the stairs. Ilene stood in the dining room, robed in darkness listening to the husky refrain.

"*And I never dreamed that I'd find somebody like you. No I want to fall in love. With you.*"

After the song ended, she picked up a stack of towels from the bathroom linen closet and drifted downstairs to the spa humming "*Blue Spanish Sky.*" Immersed in hot water, Kevin looked cozy with the champagne bucket and glasses next to him. He watched her set the towels down. Her robe dropped to the floor. She climbed in and sat in the jets directly across from him. He offered her more champagne. She put up her hand and shook her head. He chugged it instead never taking his eyes off her.

"The water temperature is perfect," she commented, unnerved by his stare.

"One hundred and one degrees," he reported setting down the glass.

Ilene cleared her throat. "Was there something you wanted to talk to me about?"

"I wanted to get you in this tub."

She groaned. "You are such a pain."

He grinned and poured more champagne. "Just want you to relax. You've been real uptight lately."

She accepted the glass this time and continued drinking. "Actually. This feels terrific." She curled her toes.

He stretched his leg and tickled them with his own. She grabbed his foot and yanked him under water. He came up between her legs. Realizing he was naked she clamored to a stand. He shadowed her movements with persistence. Face to face he kissed her like he did last Friday night, many little kisses sucking her in. This time his powerful hands massaged her torso. Animal instinct rippled through her body.

Wide eyed she put her hand between their lips. "Now we do need to talk."

He pushed her hand away. "No we don't."

"I love my husband," she insisted.

"He's not here. I am." He kissed her. "You're unhappy." He cupped her cheek in his hand. "We can make each other happy. Right now."

She rubbed her face against his wet palm, then kissed it. Taking her by the hand he pulled her out of the jets. Luring her with his kisses, he inched her toward the sauna. She felt like a cat needing to rub against this human flesh, touch male muscle again. He snatched a fistful of towels and opened the door. Her head swimming with desire, Ilene crumpled onto the bench. With the heat turned low, the sound proof room was comfortable without clothing. He laid out a towel and coaxed her upright. Slipping the straps from her shoulders he slowly eased the suit off her body, his lips caressing places that had not been caressed for a very long time. She moaned and they collapsed together on the towel laden bench.

Ilene surprised herself. So hungry was she for a man—*this man*—that she went down on him and swallowed him up. Then she opened her legs and let him slide in and out of her until they exploded into one another. Lying there trembling in his arms, she felt a grateful sense of release.

"Thank you," she murmured.

Kevin rolled over and laughed. "You're welcome." Brushing strands of her hair he kissed her again and again.

Stripped bare Ilene admitted to herself that she found those kisses irresistible. She closed her eyes and breathed in his scent so as not to forget. "It feels so good to be touched."

"By the way, I parked my truck in the garage while you were upstairs," he advised.

Her eyes popped open. "You planned this whole thing."

He rolled his eyes. "Like I can plan anything when it comes to you."

Closing hers, she didn't want to talk about it. She only wanted to lie quietly and feel the man beside her. The sex on top of the champagne had set her adrift in an unknown sea. He allowed her voyage.

Before she passed out, he spoke up. "It's getting too hot in here. I'll help you upstairs to bed."

"Okay." Groggy, Ilene sat up and pulled a towel around herself.

Kevin smiled at her belated modesty as he headed out the sauna door still dangling nude. She pulled her robe on in the bathroom and splashed cold water on her face. Disheveled hair and smeared mascara stared back at her in the mirror. Toilet paper and fingertips worked wonders.

Kevin was dressed and waiting for her on the other side of the door. He handed over her suit. Silently they walked her upstairs to her bedroom.

Hugging her he asked. "Do you want me to stay?"

Overwhelmed by the embrace she couldn't bring herself to say no. They kissed again. His mouth felt so good against her lips. Confused and blurred from alcohol, Ilene withdrew and shuffled to her bed. She crawled into a ball and pulled the covers over her head. Kevin laughed at her antics.

"Good night Ilene." He patted her butt sticking up under the comforter.

"Good night Kevin," she muttered.

Then he left.

9

Sobriety gave birth to guilt. Even though Ilene enjoyed the luxury of a peaceful night's sleep for the first time in weeks, she opened her eyes at dawn to a sky full of gray clouds. The clocked flashed 6:38 a.m. She could still taste and smell the man on her body. Tears threatened. She had betrayed Hazy and Gladdy's father. At the thought of them she sat up in bed, then remembered they were with friends. Knowing he wouldn't ordinarily be there this early, she listened for Kevin in case he'd spent the night. She couldn't face him yet. She felt like such a fool. A tired old middle-aged cliché.

"Shit." Tears streaming freely, she turned on the TV. CNN was pumping out footage of a bombing raid that killed hundreds of Iraqi children and old people inside what the Allies thought was Saddam's headquarters. What a blunder. She knew the feeling. *How embarrassing.* They hadn't even used a condom.

She knew of only one other person who could help her get through this painful remorse. Gail would never judge her. Ilene showered and packed a weekend bag. She jotted down the phone numbers where the girls were staying and headed out the door by 8:00 a.m. On the deck in the early morning fog she paused. She'd forgotten to leave a note for Kevin. Before last night she wouldn't have hesitated. But it happened. And it changed everything. She kept going.

A half an hour out of Duluth on the freeway, Ilene's cell phone rang. She grabbed it before it woke the girls who were both laid out in the back seat, wiped out from their sleepovers.

"It's me." Kevin said. "Where are you?"

She panicked. "Where are you calling from?"

"My truck."

"I'm going to see my sister."

"You okay?"

She blinked away tears and sniffed. "Yes."

"No you're not."

She grabbed a wad of tissues from the small box on the dashboard and mopped up some of the spill. "Last night was a mistake. It never should've happened."

Kevin was silent.

"I can't do this to Philip," she said.

"Should I leave?"

Her heart ached at the thought. No matter how confused or ashamed she felt, she needed him. "Just give me some space. Please. "

He hung up.

About sixty miles north of St. Paul, Ilene called Gail to make sure she was home. "It's me."

"Ilene! You'll never guess who showed up here last night with white roses," Gail cried.

"Busy little Cupid," she cracked.

Her sister laughed. "Sandy's back from Boston. She's here with me now."

"Don't tell me. You kissed and made up. Or whatever lesbians do."

"I'm really happy about this," her sister pouted.

"That's good. Hope you don't get hurt again."

"I won't. We're keeping separate bedrooms," Gail explained. "Where are you anyway?"

"Just past Pine City. We'll stay at Betty's."

"Rather sudden. Is everything okay?"

"Sure." Ilene paused to swallow the lump in her throat. "Just lonesome."

"Oh god," Gail groaned. "Let me guess. Valentine's. You and the carpenter. You caved in. Didn't you."

Ilene started to cry.

"Good thinking to chill out awhile," Gail said. "See you soon." They hung up.

Ilene worked the bar that night so her sister could spend time with Sandy. After the dinner crowd thinned, Betty deserted the hostess station. "I'm going upstairs now and watch movies with my grand babies."

Ilene waved. "Good night. I'll stick around and help out Julian." The bartender.

She walked around the end of the bar and perched on a stool nearest the television. CNN was focused that night on plans for a ground war offensive should negotiations with Saddam break down. Ilene sipped a beer and smoked a cigarette. Julian played R.E.M. on the CD player. *"It's the end of the world as we know it."* Diplomatic signs indicated that the shelter bombing in Baghdad had vanquished all hope of Iraqi cooperation. It was before ten and only a dozen or so people still hung out. She barely noticed the man until he sat down beside her. She glanced into the mirror behind the bar.

"Kevin." Her face flushed. "What are you doing here?"

He peered back at her reflection. "Might've known I'd find you glued to a TV."

She smiled at his image in the mirror. He looked both handsome and worried. She looked orphaned and sad. What an odd couple they made, conversing with each other's reflections.

"Can we talk about it?" he asked.

Ilene glanced around. "Not here. We're not anonymous enough."

He stood up. "Where's your car parked?"

She led him through the kitchen where she grabbed her coat. They walked out the back door to the Camry waiting in the alley lot. Ilene quietly dug for the keys.

"Let me drive," he said.

She was amazed to feel comfortable with him after such intense intimacy. He drove confidently through the streets of St. Paul.

"Where are you going?"

"Some place anonymous," he teased.

Eventually he turned into the ramp of the Radisson overlooking Harriet Island on the Mississippi. He parked the car. "I have a room here." Escorting her through the hotel and up to his room, he unlocked the door. Inside the narrow entryway, he used her body to close the door, then kissed her delicately yet insistently.

She'd drank one other glass of beer earlier to chase down a chicken taco. Even without much liquor she felt the intoxication of him. He kissed her longer, deeper and more often. Her passion surged like a tidal wave. She let him handle her. Half naked, they fell onto the bed when Ilene pushed him away breathlessly.

"Wait a minute." She still had on her green sweater, but the rest of her clothes were in a heap on the floor. She rolled over and dialed Betty's number. "I'm at Gail's." Her voice sounded tipsy which suited her plan. "Drank too much wine. I'll spend the night here. Take care of the girls."

"I saw you leave with him." Betty stunned her. "You don't know what you're doing. Get your head straightened out. Of course I'll watch the kids." She hung up.

Ilene covered her eyes. "Oh God."

"What's wrong?"

"She saw us."

"Your mother." He moved toward her.

Ilene nodded. "She said I don't know what I'm doing."

With his right index finger, he traced her eyebrows and nose. "You know exactly what you're doing here."

"This won't last. It's a fling. Sexual gratification." She looked him in the eye. He kissed her. She closed hers. His right hand wandered along her soft skin. Her body quaked enjoying his delicate touch. "What's going to happen when Philip's parents find out?"

"They won't. We've been careful." Kevin played with her left nipple until it was extremely hard, on the edge of painful.

"That's very distracting."

"It's meant to be."

She continued talking, "You're not being very realistic. These things are never secret. Even Betty figured it out already."

Swiftly he maneuvered his hand between her legs until she gasped. His lips retreated south. She thrust into his mouth fulfilling one long orgasm. His large hands manipulated her on top of him and carried on the dance they had begun. They spent the rest of the night making love as much with their imaginations as their bodies.

Near dawn she dozed in and out of sleep, wrapped in a single bed sheet lying in his naked arms. She sensed his sleeplessness. "What do we do now?"

"I'm hungry." He smoothed her hair. "For food."

"You go get breakfast. I'll pick up the girls and take them home. Then maybe you and I should resume a normal friendship without all that ugly sexual tension."

Kevin scratched his head. "Can I hitch a ride?"

"How did you get down here last night?"

"Took a plane," he said sheepishly. "Didn't want to be followed."

"You're pretty good at covering your tracks."

They helped one another dress, laughing like drunkards from too much sex and not enough sleep.

Back at the Silver Dollar the girls didn't even blink when she showed up with him for breakfast Saturday morning. He was no stranger to them. However Betty acted cold and indifferent. And that night Hazy proved the girls' oblivion when her mother tucked her into bed.

"I'm really glad you're letting Kevin do fun things with us. I don't think he has very many friends."

Cathy telephoned Monday night, February 18th.
"Heard about your Valentine from Stan," Ilene razzed. "Did you have a romantic night?"
"Actually we got into a hell of a fight," Cathy confessed. "Over you."
"What?"
"Stan told me to back off on my obsession about you and Kevin. That I shouldn't jump to conclusions. He said you're stronger than that."
Ilene winced at his misplaced vote of confidence. "You guys shouldn't worry about me so much."
"Have you heard from Philip?"
"Nothing yet."
"Hang in there. You sound better. More like your old self again."
"That's good." Ilene pondered how that could be true when her old self seemed long gone and his new self emerging seemed so detached from her best friend.
Arnie and Sara demanded her attention in the background. "Call me tomorrow." They hung up.
During the ensuing week she discovered she was right about one thing. With the sexual tension finally released, she and Kevin relaxed into friendship again. He threw himself into the basement project and never pushed himself on her. In fact, she found herself disappointed by the amount of restraint he displayed in front of the girls. Of course she was careful to avoid even the possibility of an intimate moment with him near the microphones. He ate most of his meals with the three of them, becoming like part of the family. After so much intensity between them, just having him there felt like enough for the time being.
The war escalated through the week as Saddam's soldiers set fire to hundreds of oil wells in Kuwait. The Allies threatened ground assaults and the bombings increased. On Friday night, February 22nd, Ilene assumed Kevin had gone back to his apartment. Exhausted she made up

her mind to get some sleep for once and not watch TV all night. She settled the girls in the their rooms, then wandered through the darkened hallway. As she stopped at her bedroom door to view a breaking news report, she pulled off her sweater and unhooked her bra.

"Need some help?" Kevin's voice at the top of the stairs startled her.

She dropped her hands but the hooks snapped open anyway. "You're such a comedian."

He moseyed in the room and shut the door. Tugging the sweater back on she continued to fish for her bra then tossed it on the chair. Intent on the report of an imminent ground war she perched on the edge of the bed. Kevin peeled her bra off the chair and sat down, fingering the lace as it slid to the floor. She gaped in disbelief at the satellite feed of tanks rolling through the black night toward a horizon in flames.

He leaned forward. "That looks like hell."

"Christ! Why hasn't he called?" Humbled by the outburst she buried her face in her hands.

He moved over to the bed and massaged her shoulders. "He's okay."

"I don't know that," she sobbed. "Do you have any idea what this is like?"

"I do now."

"What am I sposed to tell my kids? I can't keep lying to them."

He lifted her tear streaked chin. "They know more than you think. You're just not paying attention. When they see the war on TV they pretend they're watching their dad. He's there every night. You're the one they worry about."

He rocked her back and forth while she cried it out. Once her grief was spent she looked at him as though struck by a revelation. "It's the uncertainty that's so unbearable."

He raked his fingers through his own hair. "I know."

10

From the weekend's bleak onset of the ground war through the triumphant takeover of Kuwait City by Allied units, Kevin stayed through her ordeal. Ilene felt grateful for his comings and goings during her preoccupation with massive tank movements and surrendering Iraqi soldiers. General Norman Schwarzkopf had become the newest man in her life, as she clung to his every word at the televised press briefings. Gladdy called him General "S-ward Cough".

The wallpaper crew finished the hallway. Kevin put up sheet rock in the basement then drove off to his own apartment in the evening after supper. Sometimes he stayed for a beer while she ranted about the war and how it had changed everything. Consumed by politics, the bombings, the surrendering multitudes, chemical weapons, oil fires, she confessed her fears, "The world will never be the same. Think of the peoples' lives. Ended or changed forever. The property damage. The destruction of the planet. Can never be undone." Her speeches were cathartic, as she recognized the metaphor in her own life. These were not discussions however. Ilene unleashed her angst. Kevin listened.

Wednesday morning, February 27th, the phone rang.

"Ilene it's Gerry. I have news. The Red Cross reports they've located the 477th in King Khalid City. That's an Allied military hospital compound in the desert north of Dhahran."

"Is that all?" This morsel did not satisfy her.

"It appears they'll be sent into Kuwait behind the occupational forces. As soon as a cease fire is called."

The girls were delighted with the news of their dad. They repeated "King Ka-leed City" all the way out to the bus that morning so they could share it with everyone at school. Even though nothing but good news about Allied successes came across CNN the rest of the day Ilene felt cheated. Pinpointing his whereabouts on a map was not enough for her after all these weeks.

Kevin stayed to watch George Bush declare a cease fire at 8:00 p.m. that evening. She hugged the girls while they cheered. He stared out at the frosty drizzle falling on the deck. She left him alone as she tucked the girls in bed.

"Will Daddy come home now?" Gladdy asked.

"From the sounds of things that won't happen right away," Ilene told her.

She stayed with her until she drifted off. With Gladdy she felt closer to Philip. Downstairs she found Kevin drinking beer and watching TV. Grabbing one from the fridge she sat down at the table across from him.

"Thanks for staying." She touched his hand. "You've been a good friend to me through all this. I'm glad we salvaged that much. I honestly don't know what I would've done without you."

His soulful eyes glanced away from her. "Should be getting a call from Philip soon."

"God. I hope so. I need to hear in his own words he's all right." Shuffling to his feet he paced the room. Ilene walked over and stepped in his path. "Come with me," she whispered.

In her bedroom she closed the door behind him. "When Philip comes home things will change."

"That's unavoidable."

"Have to admit I'm surprised at your reaction."

"You think I don't want him to come back."

She searched his face. "Is something else bothering you?"

He looked away.

"Hey. You're the one who convinced me everything's cool." He looked so forlorn she couldn't help embracing him.

He held her head in the palms of his hands. "This isn't easy for me." He kissed her as if her lips might break.

As he laid her down on the bed in darkness she warned, "Maybe we shouldn't keep doing this."

No reply. Just his kisses everywhere. The strength of his mouth and hands manipulating her overwhelmed the unspoken pain with pleasure. They rolled together teasing and smiling, sucking and squeezing in and out until they slipped into savory unconsciousness.

Hours later when she opened her eyes, he was gone. She lifted her head and looked around. The clock glowed 2:17 a.m. She saw his shirt on the floor. He must still be in the house somewhere. Curious, Ilene climbed out of bed and pulled on her robe. She crept down the padded stairs. Her awareness sharpening, she sensed foreboding as she tiptoed toward the faint beep coming from her office den.

The only light came from the computer screen—a green hue like the night vision TV cameras. She saw his silhouette at her desk, hard drive humming. Her heart skipped a beat. *What was he doing?* Dizzy from holding her breath, she exhaled without a sound. The Smart Bank manual sat open. He'd broken into her drawer. *Kevin!* That manual provided him with access to the password, codes, every instruction. She checked the screen. *Oh shit.* He was there all right. All those accounts right in his lap. Not to mention the ability to wire transfer out of her accessible accounts. He still hadn't noticed her shadow in the doorway, intent as he was on the riveting data. She watched his skillful fingers play across the keyboard. Obviously he'd been with a computer before. Shock dissolved into outrage. *The bastard.*

She stepped into the room and walked deliberately toward him. He turned abruptly. Their eyes met in the gleam of the computer screen. He didn't look the least bit guilty. Ilene reached the desk and scribbled on a note pad. *"What the HELL do you think you're doing??"*

He read as she wrote and stood up. Moving quickly around the desk, he clasped her arm behind her back and marshaled her out of the room. She allowed the wordless manhandling until they were out of listening range.

When they reached the basement she shoved him aside. "You sonofabitch."

He opened the sauna door and ushered her inside. The moment the door closed, she lunged and kneed his groin.

"Dammit Ilene." He grasped her arms gruffly. "Settle down. Listen to me."

"Fuck you." She went for the door. "I give the orders around here."

"Fraid not. You know as well as I do Donald Singleton's running this show." She slapped his face. He yanked her wrist. "That's enough."

"Who the hell are you?"

"Kevin Wyland."

"Who are you working for?" she demanded.

"FBI."

She collapsed on the bench. Because of the bank accounts she knew he might be telling the truth. "Do you have a badge or something to prove that?"

Bewildered and barefoot, Kevin clutched his naked chest and patted the empty pockets of his baggy jeans. "Christ. You want me to get official now?" He looked ridiculous.

"Oh forget it." Ilene wiped her face with both hands. The sauna was off, but she was starting to sweat. "So. Am I under arrest or what?"

Hands on hips, he took a deep breath. "This could take awhile."

"Start talking or I'll call the police."

He rolled his eyes. "Ilene. I am the police."

She gritted her teeth. "And I can walk upstairs right now and make one phone call that could blow this thing wide open."

He exhaled. "I don't think so. You know about the bank accounts. All of them. The information I have on your husband right now could put him away for quite awhile. If the Bureau wanted to, in forty-eight hours they could have him on an aircraft carrier on his way home to face charges of money laundering."

"Oh I get it." Ilene swallowed. "Sleep with the bitch first. Then arrest the old man. Damn. That's sleazy. Even for you."

His violet eyes pierced through her. "You don't have a clue who these people are. Do you?"

"What are you talking about?"

"Jesus Christ. How do I put this?" He tossed up his hands in frustration. "You don't fucking know who Donald and Marie Singleton really are."

She glared at him. "I'm getting very impatient."

"Marie Singleton is Marie Lansky. Meyer Lansky's daughter. He was Al Capone's bookkeeper for the Syndicate in those days. When Capone went up the river for tax evasion, Meyer moved to Florida and into the banking business. Opening up National Bank put him back in Chicago and heavy into money laundering. When he died, Donald and Marie Singleton took over the family business. Such as it is. The Bureau's been onto them for decades. And now finally you and your computer files contain the information the Feds need to link National with a global bank scam."

Stunned she asked, "Does Philip know about any of this?"

"What do you think? He'll have to answer those questions. But I'm pretty sure I can get you off the hook. You cooperated with the investigation."

"Why because I slept with you? That makes me sick," Ilene snarled.

"For whatever it's worth, that wasn't part of the plan."

"You really blow my mind. Your sole purpose in coming here last summer was to find out if we were involved with money laundering for Donald's bank."

"Actually I arrived in November. Advance men clued in our friend, Terry Wilson ahead of time. That's what the free rein was all about. Obviously I do have carpentry skills. That's how I got assigned to this particular case."

"You used me. I hate that."

"Look. I walked onto this case with the assumption that you all were in on the business. Couple of new age criminals. Whatever. Gradually it became clear that Philip never told you they were an OC family."

"OC," she repeated the letters.

"Organized crime."

A nagging anxiety surfaced as she rose to her feet. "I suppose I was on my way to finding that out. Once I discovered those accounts it was just a matter of time before I found out what it all meant. In fact, here you are with all the answers." Tears stung her eyelids. "I don't understand. Why didn't you talk to me about this months ago? Instead of leading me on."

He gingerly put his arms around her. "Please don't slap me again."

She turned away in anguish. "I didn't trust you at first. I should've followed my instincts. But I set my suspicions aside for the sake of this—this friendship. I was so lonely I wanted to believe you. And you betrayed that."

"No." He kissed her temple, then his lips hesitated by her ear. "Listen to me. When this started out you were named in the investigation. You're cleared now. It's in my report that you had no knowledge of the scope of their financial dealings."

"What's going to happen now?"

"The information I have on disk will be turned over to DOJ. A Senate Committee ordered the investigation so they'll have to take a look at it. Then I imagine indictments will start falling out of the sky. I don't know."

Repulsed by his cold professionalism Ilene backed away panting. "That phrase—how could you do this to me—keeps popping up in my head. But it sounds so trite. I hate trite." She flailed her arms. "Oh fuck it! How could you do this to me!"

"Ilene. The wheels were set in motion for this train wreck years before I came on board. The damage was already done. I promise you I'm not at the controls here. This thing is much bigger than you or me. I did my job because I had to. And I did what I could to protect you from indictment."

"So what!" She sneered. "You want me to pat you on the back? Excellent covert activity Mr. Special Agent. You really had me snowed."

Wiping her eyes with the sleeve of her robe the front fell open exposing her breasts. She reached down as Kevin gently tugged on the fleece to cover her naked flesh, then tied the waist sash.

He smoothed away the tears and kissed her. "What happened between us wasn't part of the investigation."

With a bitter glance she accused, "I spose you bugged my cell phone. And my car."

His face flushed. "I'm sorry about everything. And I can't say anymore until I get the information to Washington. I've told you way too much already."

"How do you know I won't go to Philip's family with this?"

He shook his head. "You won't."

Utterly defeated Ilene crumpled onto the bench. The answers she'd been searching for turned out to be so incredibly shocking. Yet there was a keen awareness building within her that it was the only true picture that accommodated all the pieces of the puzzle. Kevin opened the sauna door. She'd lost the will to continue their battle.

"Where are you going?"

"Gotta deliver the disk. Get a sitter for later. We'll need to get out of here and talk. I'll have more news by then."

"Go to hell," she grumbled.

"I'd have to take you all with me." He winked at her and left.

Alone, Ilene curled up on the smooth cedar bench. The truth was as clear as the bare bulb illuminating the sauna room. Her darling Philip had been lying to her since the beginning of time. His straight wealthy family had been involved with international organized crime for generations. Gladdy's great-grandfather was Meyer Lansky of the old Chicago mob. Now his own father was using bank accounts in Philip's name to launder huge sums of money from some bank called BCCI. And Philip wasn't the only man in her life who betrayed her. She must've been blind not to catch on that Kevin was FBI. It's the only explanation that made sense. That's how he knew about the Mercedes. The bugs. Everything. She felt humiliated for slithering into his trap. Her whole body ached as she buried her face in her hands and wept.

By the time she stumbled upstairs Kevin had dressed, covered his tracks and left. At the dining room table she sucked down cups of coffee, chain smoked and stared through reddened eyes as the night gave up the dawn. Everything about her life with Philip was a lie.

The phone rang shortly after 5:00 a.m. Before she answered she knew it was him. At long last. "Philip."

"I'm okay."

"Thank God," she cried. "Are you coming home?"

"Don't know that yet. We leave for Kuwait City tomorrow. Going to set up a MASH unit. Don't look forward to heading into those oil fires. We can see that raging hell from out here."

"Where are you?"

"King Khalid City they call it. It's a military hospital and medical supply center. A radio station in Duluth paid for satellite time for us to call home. I only have a few more minutes."

"This is the hardest part." She spoke the words like a poem to a lost love. "You never call. And when you do we never speak."

"I know. And it doesn't sound like that's going to change. Our mail never did catch up with us. Communications are bad enough and we're headed for no man's land. I can't even promise anything."

Trying not to scream she said, "Philip. I don't know how much longer we can go on like this. We need to talk."

"Something's wrong. Isn't it?"

"Actually if you sit down and think about it, you could probably figure out most of it on your own."

"You're not making any sense. Just tell me what the hell's going on."

Ilene feigned cheerfulness. "Me and the girls had chicken pox. But we're fine now. The basement's almost finished. Looks really great."

"Ilene," he interrupted. "I'm out of time."

She winced. "Of course you are."

"I want you to listen to me," he instructed. "You sound exhausted. I know this has been hard on you. Take the girls and fly to Disneyworld in Florida. We've got the money. You need a break."

"Sure Philip. Disneyworld." She rolled her eyes at the absurdity of his simplistic advice. Like Mickey Mouse could straighten out this mess.

"Good girl," he said. "Gotta go. I love you."

The series of electronic clicks disconnecting his voice ripped through her like an invisible blade. She turned off the phone without another word. Burying her head in her arms on the tabletop, she sat motionless. The girls reacted to her emotional state when they came downstairs for breakfast.

Hazy frowned. "You don't look so good."

"I'm just tired. Didn't sleep too good." She yawned. "Daddy called really early this morning."

"Mommy. You said you were gonna wake us up this time," Gladdy whined.

"I'm sorry. He only had a few minutes to talk. There wasn't time to wake you."

"What'd he say?" Hazy asked.

"He's in King Khalid City like the Red Cross said. And they're going to Kuwait City and set up a temporary hospital."

"You mean he's not coming home right now?" Gladdy cried.

"I thought that stupid war was over," Hazy protested.

"Not yet I'm afraid. They still need doctors and nurses over there," Ilene explained as best she could.

"Is that why you're crying?" Gladdy observed.

Unconscious of her tears, Ilene splashed them away. "Guess I'm a little weepy. I miss him."

Hazy eyed the ashtray full of cigarette butts. "You've been smoking." Then to her sister, "See! I told you I smelled it in the car."

"Mommy that's really bad," Gladdy scolded.

Confronted by their looks of scorn, even in her state of mind she could sense that her condition frightened them. She definitely needed to change their scenery until she could pull herself together. *Damn. Why did Kevin have to be right all the time?* Composing herself she called the Carricks.

"I tried to call you last night," Cathy informed her. "Was your phone off the hook?"

"Not that I know of."

"Your line was busy all evening. I finally gave up."

"Maybe one of the girls left the phone off the hook in her room," Ilene suggested, though she assumed the mischief was Kevin's doing.

"Anyway have you heard from Philip since the cease fire?"

"Yeah. Five o'clock this morning. He 's fine. They're on the way to Kuwait City to set up a MASH unit."

"So he's not coming home yet."

"Doesn't sound like it."

"That's a bummer."

"I really need some space today. I don't know. Clear my head. These past few weeks have been intense. Could you take the girls for me? Just for a couple hours after school."

"I'll do better than that. I'll keep them over night," Cathy offered.

"Thanks." Ilene bit her lip to keep from crying.

"You sound so sad. Let me get Stan to watch the kids tonight. Then you and I can go out. Just the two of us."

"Not tonight Cath."

"I get it. This is about you and Kevin."

Ilene stifled her irritation. "Please don't start with me."

"I'm just trying to understand your relationship. That's all."

"There is no relationship," she insisted more for the benefit of the wiretap. "Eventually I'll explain everything. Trust me."

"Okay. But I want to see you. Bring the girls over here after school and I'll take them home in the morning."

"It's a deal. I love you for this."

11

"Ilene," the voice whispered. Hands shook her. "Wake up." *Philip.* She opened her eyes. Kevin. He looked worried. "Did you take something?"

She struggled to sit up in bed. Her mind flooded with reality. She had finally succumbed to exhaustion after she dropped the girls off at the Carrick's and received a reprimand from Cathy for "looking like shit". She looked at the clock—6:47 p.m.—the longest day. "What are you talking about?"

"Drugs. Sleeping pills. Don't sneak out on me."

She curled up her nose. "Don't flatter yourself."

"You're depressed. It's not unusual."

"I'm not insane," she spat. "Or suicidal."

"Pissed off though."

She snorted. "Like you haven't pulled the rug out from under my life."

Hands on hips he sized up her physical state. "Pull yourself together. We need to get out of here for awhile."

"Stop bossing me around."

"You're not exactly a functional human being at the moment," he rebuked her. "Someone has to get you through this. And since you think this is all my fault it might as well be me. So get moving."

She stuck her tongue out at him and ambled into the bathroom. He waited patiently watching TV while she showered and dressed.

Then he knocked on the door. "We're going to dinner. Wear something besides sweats."

She flipped him off from behind the door. But she chose a black suit with a black and white striped vest underneath, a suitable dig. She used the blow dryer to fluff her long auburn hair and brought her face back from the dead with make up. When she stepped out of the dressing room to put on her shoes, Kevin stood. He cocked his head then walked toward her. His hands caressed her shoulders as he leaned forward and kissed her playfully. "You look much better."

She stared back at him woodenly, her lips in a slight pout. "I fail to see the point of this."

"Let's go." Half agent, half decent human being he escorted her down to the garage where he instructed her to drive to the Blackwoods Grille in Two Harbors, a small shipping village on the north shore. "I'll meet you there."

She didn't argue. When she arrived and the hostess seated her, she ordered a brandy and water because she imagined it was the only combination that could hit her empty aching stomach and stay there. Kevin walked in the door and noticed her immediately. "Make that a double," she added.

As if sensing the electricity between the two of them, the hostess waited while he sat down. "I'll have a beer." When she left he smiled at Ilene. "I promise. No public displays of affection. We'll keep it anonymous."

Ignoring his mocking reference to her previous demands for secrecy Ilene lit a cigarette. "I forgot to mention earlier. Philip called today. But you probably already know that."

"The FBI didn't bug your house," Kevin reiterated. "How is he?"

"Good. We couldn't talk long. Some satellite deal. And I kind of went to pieces. He told me to take the girls to Disneyworld." She chuckled. "How zany is that?"

He smiled. "No doubt he's worried about you."

Their drinks arrived. She took a long slow swig.

"So am I," he added.

She put the glass down half empty. "I'm confused about something. You said the Singletons are an organized crime family. And yet I've seen no sign of that over the years. No gangsters. Or hit men. They've always presented themselves like aristocracy. Old money. Respectable Catholics. I mean upper crust all the way."

He shook his head. "You watch way too much TV. It's the nineties. Think about it. Every other family you know is dysfunctional somehow. Nobody's as straight as that family pretends to be. That's because they're hiding something. Now days OC families spend millions of dollars for the appearance of class and respectability. Why kill off their enemies when buying them is so much easier? Lobbyists. Congressmen. Senators. Meyer Lansky built a banking empire on that new philosophy. A global Fort Knox. Marie Singleton was his only child. Before he died, he pulled Donald Singleton—aka Sonny Disher—out of Chicago's south side, sent him to Northwestern for that business degree. Literally bought him a new identity."

"Why him?"

Kevin shrugged. "Obviously Lansky needed an accomplice to carry on the system. Sonny Disher was exceptionally intelligent and dirt poor. Rumor has it he was Capone's illegitimate son. Nobody knows for sure. But Donald played the game, married Marie and inherited the empire."

Ilene shook her head slowly. "I still don't understand how Philip could hide that from me and the girls."

"Easy. He thinks he's protecting you all. Philip doesn't have any choice in this life. He's a Singleton. My guess is he joined the military to rebel against the family business. OC sons serve family not country. He can't help his own wealth so he hides it. Even from you. I've read his profile. He's never been part of their criminal activity before. My guess is the family's using him."

"Profile," Ilene repeated.

"The FBI's been tracking this family since the fifties."

The waitress brought more drinks. Since they'd barely glanced at the menu, Kevin ordered two dinner specials—poached salmon with au gratin potatoes and Caesar salad. Then waited patiently for her reaction.

"Whatever," she approved.

After she walked away Ilene looked at Kevin. "Then why didn't they bust them for money laundering a long time ago?"

"Money laundering's just a cover up. The Bureau wants to know where the money's coming from."

"And do they know?"

"Weapons sales," Kevin whispered. "The real war."

A shiver traveled up and down her spine. "I don't get it."

He leaned forward. "Do the letters BCCI mean anything to you?"

"Cayman Islands. Luxembourg is where the deposits originated from."

"They're known overseas for handling enormous cash sales for weapons. They move the money around to look like investments. Out of sheer necessity they've had to transfer funds through US banks. Besides the respectable appearance, banks owned by OC families have been eager to oblige."

"So why would they be floating millions through numbered accounts in my husband's name?"

"Since last fall BCCI and National have been aware of an inquiry by the Federal Reserve into any connection between the two banks. Evidently Singleton needed to divert the money quickly."

"Hasn't he succeeded? How can you make any connection?"

"You." He drank from his glass. "And Philip. Those aren't your accounts. Even though they're in Philip Singleton's name at his bank, you can testify to the fact that Donald used your situation with the house and the war to coerce his son into breaking the law. Donald Singleton is National Bank. He can't prove otherwise."

"But if they're aware of an investigation, they might be on to you."

With a sly smiled he said, "I'm the carpenter who's fucking the wife. Remember?"

"Hope you're thirsty. Cuz I'm about to throw this drink in your face."

"Don't do that," he warned.

"You wanted it to look that way to keep them off track."

"I told you that wasn't the plan," he countered. "Besides my tracks were pretty well covered. When they ran a check they found out I'm Kevin Wyland. Carpenter. The Bureau made it look like I leased that apartment almost a year ago." He sat back. "While I'm thinking of it, that black Mercedes is now a green van. Looks suspiciously like a Forest Service vehicle with no insignia."

"I haven't seen it."

"That's the idea."

"Who's driving?"

"Not sure. Couple goons for Singleton I suspect. They have an apartment down in Lakeside where they sort through all the recorded conversations in your house looking for suspicious information."

"How do you know?"

"Scoped it out. You were right about appearances. They do think we're getting it on."

"You're kidding! Why didn't you tell me about this before?"

"Dammit Ilene. Every time I tried to gain your confidence you went off on me with all sorts of accusations. So I'm telling you now."

"If you had explained you were FBI right from the beginning I might have believed the rest of it."

"I didn't know you back then."

"Now I'm in even deeper shit. If Marie Singleton knows I've been fooling around with the likes of you."

"I said appearances," he interrupted. "They don't know anything for sure. Once I'm gone, they'll forget about it."

"You're leaving." She was stunned. "Of course."

The waitress served their dinners. Ilene picked at hers. Kevin ate hungrily.

Eventually he explained, "I need to chill out. Someone's on my tail. The bugs. The goons. I'm not sure anymore that it's just the Singletons. There's something else. My apartment got ransacked when I disappeared to St. Paul." He paused and winked. "By the way I flew down there on an F15. What a rush."

"I see. You were supposed to keep tabs on me," she stated. "And I split."

"Something like that." He cleared his throat. "Anyway if I want to lose these monkeys on my back I gotta get out of town."

"Don't get me wrong." She held up her hand. "I think you should go. But what am I supposed to do about the house?"

"I can pull together a crew from Wilson's to finish downstairs. Everything's in good shape. I'll be gone by tomorrow night."

Ilene nodded. Sipping the brandy water she didn't trust her fragile emotions enough to speak. *Alone.* Better that way. He grabbed her hand. Glancing around she pulled away.

"Be careful," he cautioned. "I can't be sure anymore whether you're safe."

Her eyes grew wide. "Jesus Christ Kevin. That's a real nice thing to be telling me on your way out of town. *Oh by the way. You might be in danger.*"

"The danger's been there for a long time. You're just now seeing it for the first time. Don't do anything rash. Don't set off any alarms."

She smoked a cigarette. "Appearances."

"You're good at it," he said. "Listen. I told you. Nothing's set in stone. Once I get some answers I'll be back."

"Why bother."

After dinner, Ilene drove Kevin to the bar across town where he'd parked his truck then walked to the restaurant.

She kept the Camry idling. "Anybody follow?"

He peered around. "Doesn't look like it."

She slapped the steering wheel. "I don't get it. If everyone but the Pope's following me then how the hell did the Jeep get stolen?"

Kevin laughed. "That was a minor catastrophe. You and your sister got drunk. Nobody could find you. I almost got reassigned over the whole incident. You saved me with that call for help. The boss decided you finally trusted me."

"Lucky you."

Kevin looked long and hard at her. "I think so."

She glanced away, trembling. "Whatever happened between us back then. It's over now."

"Not yet." Clasping her hand, he pressed a business card into her palm. She looked down and saw the familiar Wilson's logo. "On the back is a phone number. It's an answering machine. Don't use any names. Just say, *it's me*. Leave a number. I'll call you back as soon as I can."

Ilene sniffed. "I can't think of any reason why I would need to call you."

"Neither of us can predict what's going to happen."

"Good night Kevin." She drove home alone to a dark, deserted house. What had once been the ultimate challenge and pride of her life had become a tower of captivity.

As promised Kevin brought four men to the house on Friday, March 1st, and introduced them to Ilene. Hearing him instruct them about the job she realized that he must have lined up that crew days, maybe even weeks ago. He'd planned this exit for some time. Around 3:00 p.m., he found her doing laundry.

"Can I see you outside?" he whispered in her ear.

Shuddering as she followed him out to his truck, she waited for the signal that he wasn't coming back this time.

What he did say as he lingered by her side against a brisk lake breeze was, "Listen to me. The pressure's on. Shit is just beginning to hit the fan over that disk. Don't make any waves."

"What about the bugs?" she asked.

"Leave them alone. Don't draw attention to yourself." He reached up and rubbed between her shoulder blades "Say good-bye to the girls for me. Tell them I'll be back."

"I need to know one thing. Is Donald Singleton going to be arrested?"

"Watch CNN. You'll see."

"Why can't you tell me?"

He exhaled. "I'm just a foot soldier. I leave the big decisions to the generals."

After everything they'd shared, a part of her longed to embrace Kevin. Even beg him to stay. Except her desire was buried under the mountain of turmoil he'd dumped in her lap. She had to bite down and sever the tie.

As if he could read her thoughts, Kevin embraced her instead. His eyes full of concern. "Please be careful."

Refusing his warmth she withdrew before any kiss. "Good-bye then."

He departed hastily. As she walked alone up the exterior deck stairs, tears streamed down her face. She clutched the top railing and allowed the harsh wind to whip against her raw skin. *Appearances.* It was all a game with him. He didn't know the difference anymore. But she could see it plainly. His embrace. The good-bye in the driveway. It was all for show. To let anyone watching see that he was indeed leaving. To protect the charade.

12

On Monday March 4th, as fate would have it Ilene happened to be watching CNN when she heard the news report.

"Today the Federal Reserve ordered the Bank of Credit and Commerce International to sell its secret holdings in the National Bank of Chicago. The BCCI will also close down operations in the United States through its agency and representative offices. Bank owners have complied with the order at the same time submitting a press release that denies any wrong doing. In a separate statement, National Bank management said, 'BCCI has never directly or indirectly controlled the actual management or operations of National'."

"Jesus Christ," she muttered. Fumbling for a cigarette from the center island she staggered into the dining area and smoked it at the table. She wondered if that was a result of the information Kevin downloaded from her computer. Had she unwittingly brought the Singletons to their knees? She had no clue whether Donald and Marie could trace this thing back to her.

Sprinting into the den she turned on the computer and called up Smart Bank. To her surprise, she discovered new account activities. In addition to the regular deposits, huge sums were being wired out of selected accounts to other institutions. She requested a printout of the transaction report. Their joint account and her personal account had not been disturbed. Whatever Kevin turned over on disk, these accounts had not been frozen. Rather they had accelerated to another level. She let out a breath of relief. Perhaps there wasn't any connection with the CNN story. Maybe the information didn't come from her after all. She could tell there was a hell of a lot more to the investigation than what he revealed. Certainly other incriminating evidence could've been uncovered which had nothing to do with her.

Shortly after noon the phone rang.

"May I please speak with Mrs. Philip Singleton?" a man's voice requested.

"This is." A salesman, she thought.

"Mrs. Singleton. I'm a freelance journalist. I'd like to talk to yall about your husband's role in Desert Storm."

In a panic, Ilene hung up on him. *Like hell* he wanted to talk about Philip's role in the war. More like Philip's role in the National-BCCI investigation. *Journalist*. She didn't even want to think about publicity. For him to be on her trail already meant secrets might be on the verge of explosion. News reports of the bank scandal on CNN were sketchy and repetitious, indicating they had little information. The networks weren't even airing the story thus far.

Cathy called before the girls came home from school. "Stan's gone to State Alpine Championships with the team. Come over for supper."

Ilene sighed. "I'd love to."

That evening she relaxed in the safe haven of Cathy's comfortable home. No listening ears. She'd made veggie lasagna. While they fixed salads in the kitchen, Hazy and Gladdy played Barney videos with the two little ones in the living room.

"Feels like old times. You and me," Ilene tested the water.

"Do you think so?" Cathy asked. "I've never felt so out of sync with you. You seem depressed."

"I'm getting better. The war's over," Ilene said.

"I see." Opening the refrigerator Cathy searched inside.

"Dressing's right here. What are you looking for?" Ilene asked automatically.

She closed the door deliberately and turned to her. "The truth."

Her eyes darted away. "This war has been a lot harder than I thought. We never expected this—this black hole—in communication. I went for a month without so much as the sound of his voice. Talking to him was impossible. Seeing him was out of the question. Nobody prepared me for this kind of emptiness."

Cathy studied her. "Are you explaining your relationship with Kevin?"

"What? He's gone."

"So that's what you're so bummed about."

"I don't want to talk about it." Ilene shut her down. "Let's feed the kids before we eat."

With the children fed and busy in the play room, Cathy opened a bottle of Zinfandel while they ate lasagna at the kitchen table. Ilene discovered the wine went down easier than food.

"I don't understand why they're not sending Philip's unit home," Cathy brought up. "They're just Reservists for God's sake."

"Hey. Nothing surprises me anymore. I will never understand why they were sent over in the first place."

"You must miss him desperately."

"I'm way past desperate."

Cathy fingered her wine glass. "Is that because of Kevin?"

Ilene chugged hers. "Not gonna let go of it. Are you?" She refilled the glass.

"Ilene. It's written all over your face."

"What is."

"The guilt."

"I don't have anything to feel guilty about."

"You didn't sleep with Kevin."

"Are you saying I should feel guilty about that?"

Their eyes locked into a staring contest, like when they were girls.

Cathy blinked. "Okay. Now that's out in the open. Like pulling teeth."

Ilene pushed her plate away and smoked a cigarette. "Don't you judge me."

Cathy shuffled over to the refrigerator and opened another bottle of wine—Chardonnay this time. She filled Ilene's glass. "Whatever happened between you and Kevin these past couple weeks has taken it's toll."

"That obvious. Huh." She bowed her head and struggled not to shed any more tears.

Cathy squinted at her. "Ohmygod. Are you in love with him?"

Ilene winced. "No. I'm not in love with him." She pounded her fist on the table for strength. "It's not Kevin. He is not the reason I'm such a wreck." She squeezed the fist with her other hand.

"Ilene. You're scaring me. What's going on?"

"I can't talk about it."

"Did Philip's parents find out about you and him?" she fished for answers.

"Even if they suspect something they don't have any proof," Ilene repeated Kevin's assurance.

"So that's what you're so freaked out about."

"It's not that either." Shaking her head Ilene asked, "Did you hear anything on the news lately about National Bank?"

Cathy gulped wine. "Ohmygod. Was that Donald Singleton's bank?"

Ilene nodded solemnly. "He downloaded bank records off my computer and turned them over the FBI."

"Who? Kevin?" Clutching her chest she gasped, "Oh. My. God. He's an agent!"

"Bingo," Ilene exhaled.

Rubbing her hand over her mouth, Cathy jumped to her feet. "So this was all about an FBI investigation! No wonder you're—oh god

Ilene." She hugged her neck. "I'm so sorry."

Ilene smoked a cigarette. "I just pray it's over now. And they never find out how the Feds got the information."

Cathy patted her head. "Get rid of those bugging devices now."

"Kevin said I shouldn't draw attention to myself."

"God. He really is a spy. Isn't he?"

"Yeah."

"I can't believe this! I'm in shock. You must be—" Cathy wrung her hands. "I can't even imagine how you must feel."

"Used up." Ilene rose to her feet. "I better get the kids home. School tomorrow."

"Are you sure you're safe in that house anymore?"

Her fears verbalized, Ilene's heart sank. "I don't care. It's all I have left of Philip. It's our—home."

On Tuesday morning Ilene drove Hazy and Gladdy to school. As she pulled out of the parking lot, she suspected the white sedan in her rearview mirror was following her. She stopped at the grocery store. The white car parked one row away in the lot. She'd come to despise tinted windshields.

Inside the store a tall, husky man about Philip's age with wavy strawberry blond hair approached her by the dairy case. "Mrs. Singleton. I'm JD Casadero. I called yesterday."

Ignoring him, Ilene dodged to get at the milk containers.

"Please. If I could just have a word with you," he spoke quietly. "Your husband and I were classmates at Northwestern."

"May I see some identification?" Ilene demanded without making eye contact.

He glanced around nervously. "This is a real public place. Can we talk somewhere private?" His southern accent was similar to Kevin's, only deeper.

She observed his smiling face, from his receding hair line to his boyish blue eyes and ruddy complexion. "We don't have anything to talk about."

"Then could you *not* talk about it someplace else so a person can get at the milk?" An elderly woman pushed her aside to reach the cooler. Their encounter was beginning to attract other customers' attention around them.

"I have information," he spoke quickly. "Meet me at the library downtown. It opens in less than an hour. Genealogy Room. Second floor." He walked away.

The library. Who was this guy? At first she didn't even consider it. His whole approach was far too dubious. She did not need another mysterious man in her life. What if he was a hit man sent by the family? Except she'd never heard of anyone getting wasted in the library. What if he was another agent? She could not forget his face, open and friendly, yet concerned. More like a journalist. Plus he said he had information. That carried it's own weight with her these days. Strip away the paranoia and he could simply be a reporter with news about the 477th. Maybe he really was a college buddy of Philip's looking for a war story.

The architecture of the Duluth Public Library suggested a Great Lakes shipping vessel of the future. Ilene parked at the meter on the street below. Unfortunately, the library's interior didn't follow through with the anticipated bridges, decks, or portals. Not even one spiral staircase. Inside was just another gray building. She climbed the lackluster metal stairway.

He was waiting for her in the Genealogy Room as promised. Strolling past her he whispered, "Gold Room. Basement." Then he walked out.

Another fucking spy, she seethed. Would a college buddy of Philip's act so surreptitiously? Or a journalist? Certainly this was no way to conduct a magazine interview. *I should sneak out of here*, Ilene told herself on the elevator to the basement. But her insatiable curiosity gnawed. She stayed the course. Stepping off the elevator, she followed the narrow passageway to the Gold Room. He sat at the table in the farthest corner of the small room with his back to her, nose buried in a book.

Leaving the door ajar, she stepped inside and complained, "This is silly."

He turned around with an innocent demeanor. "Wanted to make sure you weren't followed."

"You're not a college buddy of Philip's. You don't even know my husband."

"Easy on the eyes. And quick-witted." He grinned. "I'm an investigative reporter looking into the National-BCCI story."

"Dammit!" Heart racing, Ilene went for the door.

"In the middle of the journey of our life, I found myself in a dark wood, having lost the straight path," he read aloud.

She spun around to face him.

Holding up the book he said, "Dante's *Inferno*." He offered her his wallet full of identification. "Please. Sit down."

His engaging nature intrigued her. Ilene almost liked the guy, though not enough to sit down. "First of all, I don't know anything about National Bank."

Wearing a goofy smile, he walked over and shut the door. "Then it's about time you did."

"Whatever happened with that bank has nothing to do with me or my family," she assured him, still standing.

"Is that so?" JD gripped his knuckles then cracked them. "Quite a remarkable coincidence that your husband was called to active duty in the Persian Gulf during a federal investigation into his father's international banking connections. Don't you think?"

He struck a nerve. She held her breath. "I don't know what you're talking about."

He sat down at the reading table. "I hear tell the 477th hasn't been activated in nearly forty years. Matter of fact they were one of the last units deployed. Sort of like an afterthought. I'm sure you're aware they've never had an assigned station over there. Whole unit's gone nomad. Just wanderin' from one oasis to the next."

Fascinated with this version of reality, Ilene slid into the chair across from him. "Are you insinuating that the 477th was called to active duty specifically to get my husband out of the country?"

"You tell me," JD replied. "Mrs. Singleton. There is a war going on. But it ain't the Persian Gulf. That over there's military theatrics in its finest hour. Remember April Glaspie and the July warning? The CIA let the Kuwait invasion happen to keep us media hounds trailing the wrong scent. And they succeeded. Today only a handful of people know and even fewer care about the BCCI story."

"Wait a minute." She held up her hands. "You're blowing this way out of proportion. You're talking about the lives of everyone in the 477th disrupted just to get one man out of the country. In a war to cover up a petty little money laundering scam."

"The kind of master puppeteering it takes to manipulate investigations into people's lives happens on a regular basis in Washington D.C.," he revealed. "And believe me. This ain't no petty little money laundering scam. The current sweeping investigation involves National Bank, the BCCI, the Federal Reserve, DOJ, a Senate committee, FBI. Are you aware of how intimately the FBI knows your family? And now throw in the CIA for some real fire power."

She rolled her eyes. "Are you an agent?"

"No. But I'm writing a book about one. Character's name is Kevin."

Blushing she whispered, "He sent you." She flailed her arms. "Why didn't you say so in the first place? What was all that *classmate of Philip* bullshit about?"

With a twinkle in his eye he wiped the smile off his face. "He seemed to think you wouldn't talk to me if I used his name."

Ilene considered that. "He's probably right." She ran her fingers through her hair. "God. He's such a snake. He told you to mention *Philip* and *information* because he knows that's what pushes my buttons."

"It worked. Obviously he knows you quite well."

"He's good at his job," Ilene sassed.

"Known him a lotta years. Never seen him so wrapped up in a case. He worries about yall," JD confided. "I can see why. You're quite a—

interesting woman."

Ilene stood up. "He also told you to try flattery. Didn't he? He relies on that when the conversation's going nowhere."

With a harried glance, JD coaxed, "Wait. Let's get back to the novel I'm working on. Please. Sit down."

"I don't see the point." But she perched reluctantly on the edge of the table.

"You will," he said. "Now. Forget about Kevin. Let's call the main character Arnold Schwarzneggar. For the sake of the movie version."

Ilene rolled her eyes.

"When Arnold last saw his leading lady, he was leaving town in a big hurry. His cover was blown with somebody. He knew it wasn't the Singletons. He laid a trail on the way back to headquarters to turn over the disk. He's pretty sure they're spooks."

She raised her eyebrows. "Excuse me?"

"Spooks," he repeated. "CIA's shadowing him."

Ilene froze. "And does he think they're shadowing the leading lady?"

He nodded. "By the way, I see her as Cher."

"Arnold Schwarzneggar and Cher?" She sneered folding her arms across her chest. "Is this a novel or a sideshow?"

Ignoring her sarcasm he continued. "Got the idea for the plot when I dug up a story about a little ol' software company. They created one hell of an information network. To make a long story short the CIA pirated it. While checking into government software sales I traced one through the BCCI. So I researched it. Found out at DOJ they snidely refer to it as the 'Bank of Crooks and Criminals'. They won't even grant them a charter to do business in the US because of hard evidence they finance illegal Mideast weapons sales. Yet the government's doing business with them."

"Excuse me. What does this have to do with me?" Ilene quipped. "I do have a life to get back to."

He pointed at her. "Exactly the reason you need to hang in here with me. You're an intelligent woman. You can see where I'm going with this."

"Sounds like a conspiracy theory to me," she scoffed. "I don't buy into that."

"Of course not. They say you never see the octopus once you're caught up in its tentacles," he warned. "My investigation turned up several government accounts with BCCI not linked to software sales. I traced those accounts to banks with CIA accounts. Do you see where this is headed?"

"Sure. The CIA deals weapons. So what."

"And BCCI handles the sale and launders the money through a chain of US banks. Until it winds up in banks owned by crime families."

"Oh I get it. You think the CIA is spying on the Singletons."

He shook his head. "Think of their relationship as more like hand in glove."

"That's preposterous!"

He slapped the table. "A-ha! That's the very nature of conspiracy. No one is supposed to believe it. Especially not you."

"Assuming what you say is true. And I'm not admitting or denying anything. One way or the other." She chose her words carefully. "Then the disk from the leading lady's computer possibly contained information to link the two."

"Excellent. You're really getting into the whole plot thing. You should write a book."

"I need a cigarette." Ilene checked her watch. 11:32 a.m. "You hungry? Let's run over to the Bread Board. They make great soup."

He frowned. "We can't be seen together."

"There you go with that silly spy act again. You really think the CIA's watching me?"

"Worse. They're manipulating your lives."

"Join the club." She laughed nervously. "I mean isn't that what Kevin was doing for the FBI?"

"He's not capable of having you or members of your family activated, incarcerated. Or eliminated."

She rubbed her temples with her fingertips. "Then Philip's in danger over there."

"They've pretty much got him where they want him. Wandering through the desert. Out of reach. Overwhelmed with Iraqi casualties," he assessed. "You're the easy target. You and your kids."

"No one can prove I know anything."

He frowned. "These guys don't act on proof. Anyway the information's traceable to you. Eventually."

"So what would Arnold advise Cher to do?"

"He hasn't made up his mind. He thinks she should sit tight through the initial fallout. Await further instructions. All that bullshit."

She tilted her head. "You don't agree."

"While stumbling *my* way through the middle of this *dark wood* I've come across no less than fifty casualties in this dirty little money war."

"Seriously?"

"Couldn't make this stuff up if I tried," he declared. "You or your husband might be subpoenaed about the bank records."

She exhaled. "So if the Singletons don't get to me first, the CIA will."

"Listen. Call him. Use the number he gave you," JD instructed. "Demand the government's witness security program. He can set it up so US Marshals fly yall out of the country. Tell them you want your husband flown directly from the Gulf to join you. No contact with his family."

She considered that. "If I make those kinds of demands, they'll expect something in return. I'd have to tell them what I know. Philip would have to testify against his father."

"Once you're out of the crossfire, you can hire a lawyer. Give them a vague deposition. The point is you and the kids'll be safe."

"Well." Taking a deep breath she stood up and brushed at the wrinkles on her jeans. "I'll certainly take everything you've said under consideration."

He sighed. "The leading lady needs to take some defensive action at this point in order to ensure a happy ending."

She backed away. "Good-bye Mister. Uh. JD."

Queasy from her voyage on the "conspira-sea" with the disarming stranger, she steered her car toward home. Smoking a cigarette she sorted through the circumstances. She had no way to convince Philip to agree to window shades, much less testify against his family. Hell. She hadn't even told him about the Jeep. They were already separated. So if he didn't go along with the plan, the government could use the separation to coerce their cooperation. As devastated as she was by his family's secrets, she deserved the chance to hear his side of it. If she did what Kevin said—pretend everything is normal—then she could buy some time to work out a plan before Philip's homecoming.

Wilson's crew returned to work on the basement family room Wednesday morning, March 6th. Far Side mug in hand, Ilene slipped into the den and faced the computer. When she entered the Smart Bank program, a dialog box popped up indicating that the bank's main system was down. The clock said 10:13 a.m. Stepping onto the deck she phoned the bank.

"The main system is on the fritz." Esther Cray's secretary told her. "Go ahead and press OK. All incoming transactions will be stored on disk for retroactive processing once we're back on line. Just go about your business as usual. It'll catch up later."

Turning off the phone she saw a fog bank rolling in off the lake, now that the air temperature was warmer than the frigid waters. Watching the vapor cloud camouflage the shoreline, an idea took shape. Collecting her jacket and purse she raced down to the garage and backed the car out. First she swung by her own bank and picked up a thousand dollar cashier's check in the name of Julie Sweeney, a classmate who had died in a car wreck back in high school. Then she drove north to Two Harbors where she stopped at the post office and purchased a box in the new name. She walked over to the North Shore Bank and opened an account in Julie's name, explaining that she'd forgotten her purse at home. Not one of the friendly employees insisted on ID. She lied about everything, from working as a hairdresser to her social security number.

Driving down Highway 61, she devised a plan to transfer money from numbered accounts to their joint account. Past work experience taught her that after a computer glitch like the one happening at Northwest Bank that particular day, recovery would take a few days. And sometimes little things slipped through that might ordinarily raise eyebrows. She intended on taking full advantage of this down time, counting heavily on the computer malfunction to cover her tracks.

The fog was thickening back in Duluth as she pulled into a car dealership and traded the Camry for a new white Mitsubishi Montero right on the spot. The salesman was so flabbergasted by her boldness, she sold him her cell phone for twenty bucks. She dropped by Cellular One on the way home and bought a new one. Assuming Kevin had wired them both, since he hadn't denied it, she figured that took care of the FBI's intrusion in her life.

At home in front of her own PC once again, she ordered disbursements of five hundred thousand dollars each from two of Philip's numbered accounts over to their joint account using the DMS code name. She followed that up with a 30-day transfer order of twenty-five thousand dollars a day from that same joint account to her brand new Two Harbors account in the same code. She calculated a simple forty business days, or about eight weeks to accrue one million dollars. From CNN she'd learned that the Pentagon had already announced all medical units would be held over for at least thirty days. Iraqi POWs and Kuwaitis were in bad shape, needing medical attention. That gave Philip plenty of time to get back home. JD—if that was even his name—was right about one thing, they would have to leave the country. But not in the custody of US Marshals. She decided they should head north as soon after Philip's homecoming as possible. The Canadian border was only three hours north. A million seemed like a small ransom to pay for their sacrifice.

The pea soup shrouded the hillside by the time the girls got off the bus and Hazy caught her mother smoking a cigarette on the deck. "You better quit that before Dad comes home."

She squashed it under her foot. "I will. Don't worry."

"Will he make it home for my birthday?"

"That's a couple weeks away. I'm sure he won't."

"Did I tell you I want a puppy for my birthday?"

"Only like once a day." Ilene tousled her daughter's hair. "Sorry. That'll have to wait until Daddy gets home."

"But you said he won't be home by then," Hazy argued. "You make me so mad."

"I know," her mom conceded.

"So what happened to Kevin anyway?"

"He had another job to go to." Not really a lie.

"Darn. I've got a math test this week."

"What does that have to do with him?"

"He helps me with math."

"He does?" Looking at her daughter, she was taken aback. She hadn't paid any attention to his impact on *their* lives.

"So is he coming back for my birthday?" Hazy persisted.

"I don't think so."

She frowned. "He didn't even say good-bye. Or anything."

"He told me to say good-bye for him. I just forgot."

Hazy kicked the cigarette butt off the deck. "I miss him. Don't you?"

The foghorn bellowed from the harbor. A light drizzle started to fall around them. Without waiting for an answer, Hazy shivered and ran indoors. Running her fingers through her hair, Ilene remembered the first morning he appeared in the driveway. If only she'd sent him packing that day. She never would've learned the awful truth. And she'd be able to plan Philip's homecoming without his memory haunting her.

She smoked another cigarette. Her heart thumped as a pickup like Kevin's passed on the road. In the mist she couldn't tell what color. She squinted—maybe charcoal gray. She knew he would never approve of what she'd accomplished that day. A speck of rain blew into her eye. Wiping away the moisture she confessed, "I'm not over you—yet."

13

The first time it happened during Hazy's birthday party on Saturday, March 16th.

Ilene farmed Gladdy out to Carrick's for the night with the explanation, "You don't want to put up with a bunch of obnoxious fifth graders all night."

Gladdy shrugged it off. "Cathy lets me babysit Arnie and Sara."

She and Hazy met her five friends at the Pizza Wheels roller rink at 4:30 p.m. They devoured two large sausage and pepperoni pizzas while Hazy opened presents. While skating afterward, all of a sudden Ilene felt as if she was riding a roller coaster. When her stomach dipped, she lurched forward onto one knee. Hazy skated to her side and helped her up. Feeling nauseous she scrambled to the women's room with her hand over her mouth.

Ilene vomited three times then sprawled onto the cold bathroom floor. Mopping her face with a soggy brown paper towel she refused to consider the possibility.

Hazy wandered through the door wearing a backwards baseball cap, reminding her of Kevin. "Mom are you okay?"

"Of course." Ilene crawled to a stand. "I'm sorry honey. Didn't mean to ruin your party."

"You look sick. Maybe we should go home."

She shook her head. "I'm not sick. That pizza just didn't agree with me."

At Hazy's insistence Ilene piled six girls and presents into the Montero and traveled back home. They acted more excited about the hot tub awaiting them at the house anyway. Feeling more or less recovered, Ilene didn't eat the rest of the evening. She served them birthday cake and mercifully they disappeared upstairs to the loft to watch *Beetlejuice*.

After cleaning up their mess in the hot tub room, Ilene stripped down and soaked in the jets awhile. She closed her eyes. The memory of that night with him seeped through her meditation. The deeper she sank in the bubbles the more the possibility floated to the surface. Pizza made her sick with Gladdy. Philip had a vasectomy after she was born. She hadn't thought about birth control in seven years. Her period was two weeks overdue. She couldn't deny what might be happening inside her—a pregnancy.

On Sunday afternoon Ilene dropped off the party girls and picked up Gladdy. She sneaked off to the drugstore next to the grocery stop, and bought a home pregnancy kit. She was upstairs in her bathroom waiting for the test result when the phone rang.

"It's Daddy!" Hazy's squeal echoed through the house. Abandoning the vials and paper strips she picked up the phone in her room. She listened to the girls chatter excitedly to their father.

"Philip how are you?" she broke in finally.

"Good. I'm calling from Kuwait City. This place is in ruins. Trying to help these people put body and soul back together. Unbelievable."

"Any word on coming home?" Ilene asked.

"Not yet." He paused. "Listen. Before they cut me off. I thought about what you said last time. I want you to leave things alone. Don't do anything about anything until I come home."

She heard Hazy and Gladdy whisper battling over the extensions.

"Is there any way I can call you back?" She walked in the bathroom.

"Impossible."

"Mom-mee," Gladdy whined. "It's my turn."

The strip was blue. Positive. She couldn't speak.

"Ilene I love you," Philip vowed. "More than ever. Remember that."

Staring at the result she replied, "I will." Feeling woozy she leaned against the vanity. One of the girls made kissing noises. Ilene shut off the phone and slid to the floor.

The abortion was scheduled for Monday March 25th, at a clinic in St. Paul. The only doctor in Duluth who could do it was a friend of Philip's. She planned to fly down and back while the girls were in school. Ashamed of her recklessness she confided in no one. Throughout the early week, the evening sickness was the worst. She failed to keep down any supper.

Spring weather erupted on Thursday the 21st. Cathy phoned and coaxed her out for a jog in Chester Park. Enjoying the warm sun and mild temps they sprint tested one another the first mile until Ilene cramped up and clutched her abdomen. She limped to the next bench and stretched out on her back.

"What's wrong?" Cathy asked.

"Just a stitch. I'm out of shape."

"Me too. We should slow down."

The pain vanished and they resumed a relaxed pace. Passing the two mile mark they headed downhill. Ilene felt a sharp jab deep inside. The trail fell away and she landed on one knee.

"Ohmygod. Did you trip?" Cathy cried.

The next wave sent her rolling in the dirt.

Cathy knelt down. "Where does it hurt?"

"My stomach." She curled around the pain.

"Ohmygod," her friend gasped. "You're bleeding!"

Ilene struggled to sit up. "Jogging must've triggered my period. Not too embarrassing. I just need to get home." Her vision blurred.

"I don't think so. Don't move. Is your cell phone in the car?"

She nodded weakly.

"Wait here. I'll go call 911." Cathy dashed for help.

Crawling over to wrap her aching body around a tree stump she closed her eyes and shuddered. *So this is how it will end.*

A couple hours later she opened them as Cathy entered the hospital room.

"You had an emergency D and C," she said with cool dismay.

Ilene sat up. "What about the girls?"

"I just picked them up at school and dropped them off at home with Stan."

"Thanks." She smoothed the scratchy white blanket covering her bed sheet. "I should be out of here by tonight."

Cathy shook her head. "You lost a lot of blood on the way in. They're keeping you on IV overnight.

"Damn. Can the kids stay with you?"

"That's the plan."

"I owe you big time," she pledged. "I'll take Arnie and Sara for a whole weekend so you and Stan can get away."

"Ilene. You were pregnant. You had a miscarriage."

"Guess I should cancel that appointment at the clinic."

Cathy sniffed. "So you knew."

Ilene groaned. "Spare me the sermon, church lady. I got all the hell money can buy."

"Then let me warn you. The hospital grape vine is out of control at the moment." She glanced around. "See any nurses around here?"

"I'm sure they're all busy spreading the word."

"Your little secret with Kevin just blew up in your face, Ilene. You're not going to be able to keep this one from Philip. Or his family."

"I'll deal with that when it happens."

"For God's sake Ilene. Talk to me," Cathy pleaded.

"What do you want me to say?" Ilene sassed. "I fucked up. This just makes it that much more over and done with."

"Philip doesn't deserve to come back to this."

"I can't exactly call and tell him ahead of time," she deadpanned. "Besides, nothing's changed. I still love him."

"Who are you talking about?" she probed. "Philip. Or Kevin."

"Philip!" Ilene fumed. "I'm begging you Cathy. Don't put me through this third degree. I appreciate everything you and Stan are doing for me and the kids. But I can't handle your righteous indignation right now."

"Fine. Then I'll just let you wallow in it awhile." She stomped out.

Cathy was right. After she left, the head nurse informed Ilene that she'd be spending the night. As she rested alone in her hospital room that evening, propped up on pillows watching CNN, the phone rang.

"It's me. Don't use any names."

Kevin. Her heart raced at the sound of his voice. How did he find her? She hung up and sat there in silence a few minutes. It rang four more times before she picked it up again.

"Don't hang up," he demanded. "I know what happened." He paused. "I'm sorry."

Frantically wiping away tears she said, "Don't be. I should've been more careful."

"You're pretty sure it was me then."

Ilene smiled. "Very funny."

"You okay?"

"Fine. How did you find out?"

"Wasn't easy. You got rid of the car. And the phone."

"That's right. I need some privacy."

"How am I sposed to look out for you all?"

"I'm a big girl. I can take care of my own family."

"No you can't. This isn't over yet."

She hung up. His phone call served as a harsh reminder that she was being watched from too many angles. Before they discharged her the next morning, Ilene phoned the North Shore Bank from her room.

"My name is Julie Sweeney," she told Mr. Johnson, the account representative. "I opened a new account there this month. I was recently separated from my husband and I don't want him to know where I am. So I was wondering if there have been any inquiries about me or my new account with you."

"No Mrs. Sweeney," Mr. Johnson replied. "I certainly would've paid attention to that type of inquiry."

"If anyone does contact you, would you please let me know?" she requested.

"Of course," he assured her. "That's our policy."

"Thank you so much."

Next she phoned the Two Harbors Post Office and asked the same questions using the same explanation and final instructions. She hung up the phone the second time with great relief. Apparently her financial arrangements had gone undetected so far.

14

Ilene felt as though she was living from one phone call to the next. When the phone rang Friday evening, April 5th, she picked it up in the den sensing it was Philip. "Hello Philip?"

"Excellent radar you've got there."

"When are you coming home? I'm anxious for you to see the house. So much is done." Out of habit she switched on the computer while seated at the desk.

"Still no official word. It's like they forgot about us out here. We've probably got a couple more weeks worth of clean up in KC but no longer."

"That means you'll miss Gladdy's birthday." She watched the hard drive boot up on screen.

"Yeah. We'll never make it home by the twenty-sixth."

"I don't understand why you're still there." In the Program Manager, the fax icon blinked indicating that a memo had come in. *But no one knows my fax number*, she realized.

"Will you and the girls be okay awhile longer?"

"Of course. It's pretty much routine by now. We just go about our normal boring lives." *Unless it was one of the banks I called back in February*, she wondered.

"I still think it would be a good idea for you and the girls to get away for awhile. Take a little trip like I suggested."

"Philip, there's so much left to do with the house. I'm really focused on that right now." *Or Kevin*, she thought.

"Can't Kevin handle the rest?"

Taken aback at the coincidental mention of his name, she cleared her throat. "He had to leave for another job. I got Wilson's crew back in here. They finished up the basement."

"So what's left?"

"Wallpaper. Furnishings. All that expensive stuff."

"I have to go soon," he warned. "Better get the girls or you'll be in trouble."

"By the way, no matter what they say about getting a puppy, they both got bikes for their birthdays," she informed him.

Calling out their names she let them talk. Once she was off the phone, Ilene called up the fax program and found a cover page with a handwritten comment, *"Look what happened to one of the men who hired KW. JDC"*

JD Casadero. He must have weaseled her fax number out of Kevin who got it from listening in on her old mobile phone. As if her life was being broadcast on National Public Radio. Following his scrawl was an article clipped from today's Washington Post about the death of Senator John Hunt of Pennsylvania, on April 4th. Yesterday. His private plane was involved in a mid-air collision outside Philadelphia, with a corporate owned helicopter. The copter hit the Senator's plane which then burst into flames, killing him and his two pilots. The burning helicopter crashed onto an elementary school ground killing those two pilots, and two first grade girls. The article also mentioned Hunt was a Republican member of the Senate Banking and Finance Committee. Ilene stared at the photos of Senator Hunt and the crash site. Unable to catch her breath she walked outside along the deck. After all these months a frayed rope still hung from the railing where Kevin had pulled up the Christmas tree. She inhaled a breath of crisp spring air.

She'd heard about Senator Hunt's plane crash on CNN last night. A piece of bad news that at the time didn't seem relevant. Now she remembered that Kevin and JD both had said the investigation was ordered by a Senate Committee. The Banking and Finance Committee. Was the dead Senator involved in this somehow? No wonder Kevin had left in such a hurry when he thought he was being followed. Of course there was always the possibility that the Senator's death was nothing more than a terrible accident and JD was sucking wind.

Over the next week the twenty-five thousand dollar deposits accumulated rapidly in the Two Harbors bank account. In order to get it over with, Ilene entered into Smart Bank memory the final ten wire transfers needed to total one million by May 1st. She wanted the money in cash by the time Philip came home.

Oddly enough it was Mrs. Westphal's phone call on Monday the 8th, that planted the seed of a plan for withdrawal of funds. "Mrs. Singleton, I'm hoping you can help me out of a jam here."

"Is there a problem with one of the girls?"

"Oh no. I can assure you Hazel and Gladys are getting along very well. I think it's safe to say they've weathered Desert Storm. You must be so relieved it's over."

"It isn't exactly over for us yet," Ilene replied coldly.

"Any word yet on their father's homecoming?"

"None."

"That must be very difficult after all this time. Especially with so many other units returning already."

"Yes it is."

"I called to let you know that Mrs. Swanson's class is taking a field trip this Friday," Mrs. Westphal said. "They'll be taking a ride on the Scenic North Shore Railroad up to Two Harbors for a tour of the *Edna G* tugboat and back home again. I was hoping you'd agree to chaperone for us. Two mothers have said yes but district regulations require one for every ten children. I need one more volunteer."

As soon as she said Two Harbors, Ilene recognized the opportunity to collect on her accounts. "I'd be happy to go along." A completely harmless excursion train up the shore and a boring tugboat tour with first graders offered the perfect cover to go to the bank undetected and make the first withdrawal.

That Friday the 12th, Ilene parked the Montero in the front lot at Lakeside School. Dressed in a brown leather jacket over a long sleeve white T-shirt and black jeans tucked into boots, carrying a black leather day pack, she departed through the back door of the building and climbed onto a yellow school bus with twenty-six first graders, Mrs. Swanson, and two other mothers. As they pulled out of the school yard, Ilene's eyes carefully scanned the panorama through the bus windows. No one followed.

The train ride to Two Harbors was noisy and long with thirteen boys and thirteen girls. Gladdy sat next to her mom.

"You should go sit with your friends," Ilene recommended.

"Everybody's mad at me," Gladdy pouted. "Cuz I can't invite them all to my hot tub party."

Ilene groaned. "Maybe you shouldn't talk about it so much."

Gladdy sighed. "Maybe I should just forget the whole thing."

When they stepped off the train in Two Harbors, their tugboat guide was waiting at the station to walk the two blocks down to the *Edna G*'s pier.

Ilene took Mrs. Swanson aside. "I'm not feeling very well. Cramps. If you don't mind, I'm going to stay on the train and take a little nap. Maybe this headache will go away too."

Mrs. Swanson frowned but patted her hand. "We'll get along just fine. You rest dear."

Ilene watched from the train window. As soon as the group reached the pier, she grabbed her leather day pack and dashed up the hill to the bank. When she requested a $250,000 withdrawal, the teller said she would have to get approval from Mr. Johnson, the account representative.

"How can I help you, Mrs. Sweeney?"

"I need to make a withdrawal."

He reached for a pad on his cluttered metal desk. "And the amount you'll be needing today?"

"Two hundred fifty thousand." She swallowed. "In cash."

He raised his eyebrows. "That's a rather large sum of money." He turned to his computer and called up her account.

"I've always wanted to buy my very own beauty salon," she lied "Now's my chance."

"I see. Then good luck to you." He handed her the white slip of paper. "Take this over to Helen, our head cashier. She'll take care of you."

"One more thing." She took the paper. "Have there been any inquiries about my account?"

"Not that I'm aware of," he replied. "Why do you ask?"

"It's just that I don't want my husband to know anything about this money. I won it at the casino. So it belongs to me. If you know what I mean."

"I understand. Your money's safe with our bank," he assured her.

"Thank you sir." She backed out of his office and walked toward the teller windows.

Ilene stared at the cash as Helen stacked it on the counter. Two hundred fifty thousand dollars came in five bundles, each containing fifty one thousand dollar bills.

"If I give you any smaller denominations you'll need a suitcase."

She blinked at the woman. "No This is fine. I guess."

As though she did this kind of thing on a daily basis, Helen tossed the bundles in a large manila envelope and wound a string around the two cardboard circles. She looked at Ilene. "You want me to seal this with tape?"

Feeling a little anxious about the attention she seemed to be attracting, Ilene wanted nothing more than to grab the packet and run. But she remained calm and obliged Helen so as not to appear reckless. "That's a very good idea. Thank you."

When she finally had her hands on the envelope, Ilene stuffed it in her day pack.

"Sign here," Helen said.

She almost wrote her own name, remembering just in the nick of time. Luckily the letter *I* was easily drawn into a *J*, for Julie Sweeney. Stepping out of the bank she felt giddy. Her keen awareness of the tremendous risk she'd taken was overshadowed by her stronger conviction that Donald and Marie should have to pay for what they'd done to their lives.

Ilene traveled the North Shore Scenic Railroad on her own once more before Gladdy's birthday. At the Two Harbors bank, Mr. Johnson was out of the office that day. Luckily Helen the head cashier remembered her but objected to authorizing another withdrawal.

Ilene offered no lengthy explanations for the money this time, only whiny demands. "I can't believe I don't have better access to my money than this! It's not like I'm asking for any more than I did last time."

"Well I suppose. Since you made a special trip and all." Helen relented. "Next time call ahead."

Acting indignant, Ilene tucked the gold envelope inside the long raincoat she wore. Outside the bank she ducked into the women's bathroom at the Food n Fuel gas station on the corner. There she stuffed the fifty thousand dollar bundles into the lining. On the train ride back to Duluth, Ilene felt certain she'd passed through Two Harbors undetected. But she felt uneasy that she hadn't been able to find out whether anyone was checking up on her account.

15

A strong familiar scent met Ilene's nose as she unlocked the porch door on Friday, April 26th. Gladdy's birthday. Her party was scheduled for Saturday afternoon. She'd been out shopping for balloons and decorations, napkins, favors, ice cream, cake and enough hamburger and French fries to feed thirteen girls. She glanced at her watch. The girls would be home soon. *Perfume.* That's the smell, she thought. Arms loaded down with packages, Ilene didn't see her right away.

"My you certainly are a busy gal these days."

Marie. Startled, Ilene spilled her sacks across the kitchen counter. "How did you get in here?"

Dressed in a blue tailored suit and long, smoky gray scarf Marie posed on the bottom of the great staircase, her nose held high in the air. "You seem surprised, *Elaine.* You gave me a key."

Her mind busy fretting over the computer files, Ilene neglected to correct her. At least the hard drive was turned off and the Smart Bank manual was locked up in the desk drawer. After Kevin, she'd become more careful about leaving a trace. "What are you doing here?"

Marie hunched her shoulders mockingly. "It's nice to see you too."

"Look. You appear out of nowhere in my house. It's the middle of the afternoon. I didn't see a car in the driveway," Ilene observed.

"If you must know, I came here to personally deliver little Gladys Marie's birthday present."

She glanced around. "So where is it?"

"It has not yet arrived."

"All right. Fine. But if you don't mind I have things to do for Gladdy's party tomorrow." Ilene started putting away the supplies.

Marie walked toward her authoritatively. "Not so fast. The two of us have some business to discuss."

"I seriously doubt that."

"I believe his name is Kevin Wyland." Marie paused dramatically.

Ilene's mouth went dry. So that's what this was all about. How much did she know? "He's been gone for months."

She nodded pompously. "Eight weeks to be exact. Shall I get right to the point then?"

Ilene sensed that Marie had become the cat, leaving her in the dubious position of the mouse to be toyed with.

"I know about your disgusting little tryst with Mr. Wyland at the St. Paul Radisson on February fifteenth. And your abortion on March twenty-first."

Ilene's mind reeled from the shock of her words. She wondered whether that was all she knew. "What the hell kind of people are you? It just so happens I know you had this place bugged."

"Don't you dare get huffy with me!" Marie pulled a videocassette out of her blue purse and set it on the counter. "I have the filthy details right here on video."

"That's impossible."

"I always knew you were nothing but a stupid whore," she spat. "Kevin Wyland is a federal agent. He played you for the biggest fool on the face of this earth."

Marie didn't think she knew. Ilene played dumb. "I don't believe this!

What would a federal agent want with me?"

Frowning at her Marie said haughtily, "Trust me. The financial world is clearly out of your league. However it is a fact of life that bankers are constantly hounded by investigations."

"What does that have to do with me?"

"That agent was using you to get to us. You should blame him for *bugging* this house, as you say. I wouldn't know anything about that."

"Now I know you're bluffing." Ilene swallowed. Her mouth felt parched from the audacious risks she was taking in front of this barracuda. Evidently she didn't know about her Smart Bank program.

Her mother-in-law leaned forward across the counter. "I guarantee you Philip will indeed be told about your sleazy little affair."

Ilene closed her eyes to block out the woman's twisted expression. "Stay out of it Marie. This is none of your business."

When she stuck her hand in her purse this time, Marie pulled out a check. "This is a cashier's check for one million dollars with your name on it. Take Hazel and get out of Philip and Gladys' lives."

Ilene laughed out loud at the coincidental sum of money. "Is this your idea of a joke?"

Picking up the video cassette, Marie stalked across the room. "Imagine for one moment a custody hearing. After Philip has filed for divorce, naturally. My presence will not be required. But yours will." She put the cassette in the VCR and turned on the TV. "My attorney will be instructed to show this tape to the judge." She pressed play.

Two writhing naked bodies exploded onto the screen. Heart throbbing, Ilene looked at the clock. Marie turned up the sound of her own voice moaning with passion. Her face flushed with embarrassment. Hazy and Gladdy would be coming through that front door any minute. Dizzy with fury she cried, "Stop the damn tape!"

Marie sat perched on the arm of the couch wearing an ugly grin. The front door opened. Lunging for the VCR, Ilene turned off the power.

With rosy cheeks and hair all wind blown, Hazy's eyes were wild with excitement as she ran through the foyer. "Hi Grandma Singleton. The zoo was fun."

Eyes wide, Ilene stared from one to the other. "What are you talking about? Where's your sister?"

"She's out in the car." Hazy pointed over her shoulder. "Wait till you see what she got for her birthday."

"What car?" Brushing past her daughter, she tore out the front door.

The black Mercedes was parked along the road in front of the house. A beefy man wearing a long, black leather coat over a T-shirt, black jeans and boots stood beside the car with his hands folded in front of him looking like the Terminator. Even though the clouds had begun to spit rain, he kept his wire-rimmed sunglasses on.

"Gladdy!" Ilene pounded on the car. The Terminator held a remote control device and the rear passenger window rolled down. Her daughter's head popped out, all smiles.

"Look what I got for my birthday!" she shrieked. A chunky little golden retriever puppy wearing a huge red bow stumbled across Gladdy's lap. She tried to lift him. He licked her fingers and she started giggling.

Ilene rubbed her face in frustration. "Gladdy. Get out of that car. Right now."

"Okay. But can I keep my puppy?"

"Of course you can." Ilene felt like her head would burst from the anxiety. "Why don't you bring him out here so I can see him."

The Terminator rolled up the window and locked the doors with two clicks on his remote. Gladdy disappeared behind the tinted glass. "Mrs. Singleton's granddaughter will accompany her back to Highgate."

"Like hell she will!" she snarled at him.

Feeling the strength of five women, Ilene lashed out at the brute. She got her hands on the remote immediately. Powerfully he clutched her arm and pushed her backward behind the car. Everything happened so quickly. He glanced around and with his free hand punched her. Taking the force of it in the lower right jaw she stumbled backward, releasing the remote. Stars flashed in front of her eyes as she landed on her butt. The Terminator picked up the remote and wiped it off with a clean handkerchief, never once looking at her. Her vision blurred, Ilene put her hand to her mouth.

As she sat there motionless, mouth burning, lower lip dripping blood, Marie sauntered past offering one last bit of advice. "By the way. I would refrain from calling the police if I were you. I have several copies of that video cassette. I would assume the Duluth police frown on local women producing pornographic movies for profit." She shuddered. "Makes my skin crawl."

Ilene scrambled to her feet. Moving quickly for an old woman Marie ducked into the back seat. Lunging for the passenger door she screamed, "Run, Gladdy! Run!" As the Mercedes sped off she lost her balance, falling forward on her knees into the mud.

Hazy raced to her side. "Mom. It's okay." She patted her shoulder.

Ilene was inconsolable. She wept into her muddy hands. "Oh God. Please. Not Gladdy."

"Cmon. It's raining. Come back in the house. You're all full of mud."

Speechless with grief, Ilene looked up at her oldest daughter standing there in her backwards baseball cap reminding her of Kevin. Huge raindrops smashed against her tear-soaked face.

"Your mouth is bleeding!" Hazy cried. "Cmon. Please."

Ilene struggled to her feet sobbing, "I tried to stop them. But that asshole slugged me."

Hazy led her mom through the front door. "Why did Grandma take off with Gladdy anyway?"

"You tell me." Soaking wet she ducked into the bathroom and wrapped herself in a towel. "What the hell happened today?"

"Grandma Singleton got a puppy for Gladdy. I bet you said she couldn't keep it. Didn't you?" Hazy accused. "She said you'd be mad about the puppy."

Ilene wanted to slap Hazy for that. Gritting her teeth she grasped her by the shoulders. "I told her she could keep the damn puppy. What I want to know is how that bit—how Grandma—got you two out of school."

Hazy backed away. "Mom. You're a mess."

Ilene wiped her muddy hands. "Just tell me what happened."

Hazy shrugged. "She just showed up in the lunchroom and said we could go with her to the zoo. She bought us McDonald's and everything. Then at the zoo, Mr. Smith—that big dude that hit you—came over and said we had to go look at some puppies. He drove us some place past the mall and Gladdy picked out a puppy." She hung her head. "I don't understand why you got so mad. It was fun."

"Grandma never got my permission for the puppy. Or the zoo. Or anything. You better believe I'm mad." Ilene wiped the rain, sweat and grit from her face. "Now go pack a bag. I'm taking you over to Cathy's."

"What for? Where are you going?"

"Chicago. Gladdy's coming home with me." Ilene headed for the den.

Hazy marched in step behind her. "Why? She's just going there for the weekend. Grandma said she okayed it with you."

"She did not okay it with me." Ilene noticed the light blinking on her answering machine. *Philip?* She pressed the button.

"Mrs. Singleton. This is Mrs. Westphal at Lakeside School. Hazy and Gladdy's grandmother is here. I'm just calling to confirm that she has your permission to take the girls out of school for the afternoon because of Gladdy's birthday. Please give me a call."

"See? I told you," Hazy blurted.

Running her fingers through her damp hair she sighed. "She must've flown up in the jet. But there's no time to catch up with them at the airport. I'll check on flights."

"I'm going with you."

Ilene shook her head. "Out of the question."

Hazy stamped her foot. "Look at yourself. You act like you're crazy or something. I can't let you go alone."

Lighting a cigarette, Ilene sat down at the desk. Her mud stained fingers shook as she looked up the number of the airline. She caught a glimpse of her reflection in the computer screen. The matted hair and bloody swollen lip had probably frightened Hazy.

"I'm fine. I'll take a shower. Now go pack your bag."

Folding her arms across her chest Hazy declared, "I'm not going to Cathy's. She'll just make me babysit her kids."

Too frazzled to deal with her bullheadedness Ilene relented. "All right. Okay. Depends on how many seats are available. Just do what I said."

Hazy dashed out as Ilene dialed the airline on her cell phone. There was one more flight to O'Hare at 6:55 p.m. And Hazy lucked out. There were a half dozen seats left. She booked the reservations. Since it was already 5:15, they didn't have much time. She showered and changed quickly, then tossed underwear and toiletries into an overnight bag. In case they couldn't get a flight back tonight.

On her way through the kitchen Ilene found the check from Marie on the center island. Taking a quick detour she locked it and the videotape away in her desk drawer. For evidence. In case she ever needed it.

Hustling Hazy out the door and into the Montero, she headed for the airport. On the way she called Cathy. "Hi. It's me. Listen. Marie paid me a little visit today. We had it out. Big time. And she took Gladdy to Chicago without my permission. I'm flying down tonight to get her back."

"Ilene! My God!" Cathy cried. "Why'd she do that?"

"I can't get into it," she warned. "Hazy's with me. We'll talk later."

"Bring her over here."

"She insisted on going with me. Marie bought the girls a puppy."

"God. She's so manipulative. Where is it?"

"With Marie and Gladdy."

"I see." Cathy paused. "Ilene. Does this have anything to do with Kevin? Did they find out?"

"Oh yeah."

"How much does she know?"

"She has a video from the Radisson. X-rated. If you know what I mean."

She gasped. "You and Kevin."

"And she knows about the hospital."

"Ohmygod. What about the accounts on your computer?"

"She never mentioned them. But she knows who he is."

"You mean that he's an FBI agent."

"That's right. Look. I denied everything. Acted like it was all news to me."

"Are you sure it's such a good idea to go down there? Maybe it's a trap."

"She offered me a million bucks to give up Gladdy, take Hazy and get out of Philip's life."

"She's brutal. I think you better go there with a police escort."

"No way. There's things I've found out. But I can't tell you right now. Except to say the police can't help me."

"Then call Kevin. At least let him know what's going on. Please. You could be in trouble."

Ilene sighed. "There's nothing he can do. I got myself into this. It's up to me now."

"Ilene. If you don't call him, I'll call the FBI myself. This is a kidnapping."

"All right. Okay. I'll call him."

"Let me know as soon as you get back."

At the Duluth airport, Ilene checked in and paid for the tickets. The flight was delayed until 7:15 p.m. She settled Hazy in the waiting area and strolled down the walkway to make the call. She fished the card with his number out of her purse and dialed. "It's me. Call back 218-333-0600. Right now. Dammit." She hated giving him her cell phone number. For all she knew the FBI had some way to tap it without her knowledge. The phone rang once. "Yes."

"It's okay to talk." Kevin's voice. "I already know that Marie took Gladdy to Chicago. What's going on?"

Ilene rolled her eyes. Where did he get his information? "I'm at the airport. I'm flying down to bring her home."

"Don't do that. Let me check things out first."

"Check this out. Marie knows you're FBI. She knows about my little hospital visit." She couldn't bring herself to say the words "miscarriage" or "pregnancy" to him. "And she has a video of you and me at the Radisson to prove it."

"Jesus Christ," he muttered.

"I don't think she knows about the account records on my computer."

"You don't know anything for sure. Just sit tight. Wait this out. She's toying with you right now. She'll bring her back."

"Forget it. I'm going."

"You have no idea what you're getting into. You don't even know where they live."

"I have an address in Evanston. I think it's a townhouse or something."

"Listen to me. I can get federal agents to detain you at O'Hare," he warned.

"Go right ahead you sonofabitch!" Ilene turned off the power so he couldn't call back. She knew it was a mistake to contact him.

16

Ilene and Hazy scooted into the back seat of the yellow taxi at around 9:20 p.m. outside O'Hare.

"Can you take us to Evanston?" she asked.

"I know street. What is street?" the little brown man in the front seat replied.

Ilene noticed a metropolitan map mounted on a clipboard, hanging over the dashboard. She also noted the name on his driver's license, Saiid Jafari. Which she recognized from her university days as a common Iranian name. Pointing to the north shore she asked, "Do you know how to get there?" She handed him the slip of paper with the address, 12 B Court, Highgate written on it.

He drove off enthusiastically. "I get there."

Ilene looked at Hazy in frustration. She shrugged. Sitting back she kept her eyes on the road. They had breezed through both airports. Kevin hadn't sicced the Feds on her after all. She noticed Hazy glancing furtively out the back window.

"Something back there?" Ilene asked casually.

"I kinda think we're being followed."

Peering out at the lighted freeway spreading behind them, she couldn't mistake the black Mercedes. Outside her window in the lane beside them was also a blue Chrysler. Both cars had tinted windows.

"They've been with us since we left the airport." Hazy informed her.

"Interesting." Ilene stared at the two cars. Saiid Jafari wasn't breaking any speed limits. Either car could easily leave this Ford in its exhaust. The Mercedes was obviously family. She assumed the tenacious Chrysler was FBI, courtesy of Kevin.

"Why are they following us?"

"Maybe Grandma and Grandpa Singleton sent someone to the airport to meet us but we caught a cab first."

"Two cars? Duh. I'm not *that* stupid." Hazy waved at the vehicles.

The Chrysler backed off. With two escorts trailing them Ilene figured they'd steer Saiid in the direction of Evanston eventually. Turning her attention to her curious daughter she challenged. "Why don't you tell me what you think that's all about?"

"All's I know is you did something that made Grandma Singleton really mad."

"Did she tell you why she's mad at me?"

She shook her head. "I saw the check. I heard what you told Cathy. She tried to give you money to go away with me. I always knew she hated me. She treats me different."

"Hazy. This doesn't have anything to do with you."

"But why do they want us to go away?"

Ilene grimaced. She preferred not to answer that question. "It's just too complicated. It's not you your grandma hates. It's me."

"She's not my real grandma anyway. Not like Grandma Betty. And I never liked *her* either."

Saiid Jafari exited the freeway into Evanston and wound the taxi through the immaculate, tree-lined residential areas. He turned down a private road. Ilene wished she'd been watching the street signs. She leaned over the front seat as they rounded a curve. The headlights shone on a security gate in the middle of the road.

"This can't be right," she objected.

"Dis right. Yes." He nodded insistently as the cab came to a stop.

Floodlights snapped on blinding them momentarily. A burly man with a pistol strapped to his black uniform stepped out of the pale brick gate house. "Halt."

They had already come to a stop. Ilene jumped out of the cab. The guard pulled his gun on her. She threw her hands in the air. "No. Wait. We're lost."

Then everything started happening really fast again. A black Mercedes pulled up and screeched to a dead stop. Marie's kidnapping accomplice strode hurriedly from the driver's side.

Fearing another kidnapping Ilene shrieked, "Hazy! Run!"

The brute in uniform grabbed Ilene by her arms. Dragging the day pack along with her mom's purse, Hazy hobbled to her side.

"Well if it isn't our buddy, Mr. Terminator Smith," Ilene wisecracked.

The Terminator, still wearing his trademark sunglasses at night, leaned into the taxi and handed something to the driver. Almost immediately Saiid Jafari backed up the cab, turned around and peeled out, back doors open and flapping in the wind. Mr. Smith shook his head disapprovingly at the ornery gatekeeper who shoved her forward. Ilene took advantage of the opportunity to slug him in the shoulder. Without even flinching he strutted away.

She turned and challenged Mr. Smith. "Where's my daughter?"

"Come with me," he ordered.

"Hell of a welcoming committee," Ilene sassed. "Forget it. Just tell me where the Singletons live. We'll walk from here."

He frowned. "This is Highgate."

"So where's Twelve B Court."

"You're standing on it," he replied sarcastically. "This is the only residence on B Court. Number Twelve. Highgate. Number Ten, Shorewood is on A Court and Number Fourteen, Cherry Hill is on C Court. Any of this getting through yet?"

Ilene made a face at him. "Yeah. I get it. They don't live in a goddamn townhouse like Philip said." She tossed her hair. "Guards with guns. That's why he never brought us here."

He glanced at his watch. "Marie Singleton is waiting." He picked up the day pack. "Let's go."

Reluctantly she followed with Hazy at her side. "Just how is it that Marie knew I was coming? I can't for the life of me figure out how that woman gets all her information. Do you know?"

"You ask too many questions." He held the rear passenger door open for them. When Ilene bent forward to get in, they passed extremely close to one another. "That mouth of yours looks pretty sore."

"You sonofabitch," she swore.

"Watch your language around the young lady, Mrs. Singleton."

Ilene fell against the plush back seat and pounded the cushion. Hazy patted her mom's shoulder. She only had a couple minutes to pull herself together. She sat up and braced herself for the ordeal in front of her. Wide-eyed Hazy gazed through the tinted windows at the spectacle unfolding along the lighted driveway. Highgate was a compound. Spread out like a resort were bungalows around a sprawling rambler, built in that fifties style with sandstone bricks. Mr. Smith stopped the Mercedes in front of the main house. Ilene and Hazy hopped out before he could get to them. They marched up to the door and tried the knob. It was locked. Hazy found a button and pressed it. They didn't hear a sound. Ilene turned around in time to see two armed guards approach across the manicured lawn. The door opened to reveal two more security guards.

"Don't look now. But I think we're surrounded," Hazy observed aloud.

Ilene glared at Mr. Smith who stood stoically beside the Mercedes, hands folded in front of him. He nodded politely. "You could have avoided this little scene by simply following my orders."

She sneered at him. "Go to hell."

He promptly climbed back in the car and drove off. Ilene turned around. The soldiers were still standing there ready for action.

"Hey guys. We're unarmed." She waved her hands at the four of them. "Is this any way to treat members of the family? My name happens to be Ilene Singleton. And this is my daughter, Hazy Singleton."

The guard on the inside spoke their names into his walkie talkie. "Follow me," he said finally.

The front of the home was a maze of corridors leading back to the living quarters. It was difficult to judge the square footage because the wings seemed to go on forever, reminiscent of her old high school building. In the center courtyard was a lighted pool, visible from the walkway leading to what looked like a huge family room.

"Wait here in the Great Room," the guard said, then left.

"Can you believe this place?" Ilene paced the floor in front of the wall of windows overlooking the pool area. "Highgate," she said aloud. "This must be where Philip grew up."

Hazy had found candies and cookies on the coffee table. She filled her face and pockets.

"Hazel Lee Singleton."

"What'd you say?"

"I said, Daddy grew up here. This was his home." But the thought of his childhood here in this cold compound made her sad.

"Wow. Man. I could live here easy."

Ilene groaned. "I'm *so* sure."

The double doors burst open and Marie swaggered through with Gladdy in tow followed by a short, fat Oriental woman wearing a maid's uniform.

"It's very late *Elaine!*" her voice resounded through the Great Room.

"Ilene!" Hazy barked.

"Hi Mommy. Hi Hazy." Gladdy trotted forth pulling her chubby puppy in a brand new red wagon with wood sides. "You should see my room here. It's got a big screen TV."

Ilene rushed forward and fell to her knees hugging her youngest child. "Sweetie I'm glad you had fun. Now it's time to go home."

Gladdy yawned. "Okay."

"Remember Gladys. If you go with them, you must leave the puppy here," Marie instructed.

"But Grandma!" Gladdy wailed. "That's not fair!"

Ilene stood up to face the woman. "How can you be so cruel! Gladdy's not a puppet you can use to pull my strings."

Marie ignored her. "Gladys I explained the rules. Did I not?"

She nodded tearfully. "You promised I could come back and see him wherever I want."

"Of course you may stay here with your puppy if you like," Marie offered softly.

Ilene shuddered. "Leave her out of this Marie. This is between you and me."

"Mylee. Take the puppy away," Marie ordered.

Clinging to the wagon, Gladdy whimpered and stamped her feet.

"Gladys. I am very disappointed in you," Marie scolded.

Ilene bent down to comfort her. "It's all right Cookie Monster. I'll get you another puppy that can live with us at home."

"Honest?"

Ilene nodded, rising to her feet. She'd promise her a litter of puppies if it would get her out of there. Mylee whisked the puppy away in the wagon. While Gladdy sobbed, Hazy comforted her. They heard muffled voices from the hallway.

"What's going on in here?" Donald Singleton strolled through the doorway. Though short in stature, dressed in gray wool slacks and a yellow cotton sweater, his presence filled the room. Noticing her he reacted. "Ah. Good evening Ilene." He hugged her.

She backed away. "Marie has been torturing these kids over that puppy. It's insane!"

"Please. Calm down. Marie see to the grandchildren. I'd like to have a word with our daughter-in-law. In private."

"I'm taking Gladdy home with me tonight," Ilene insisted.

Marie ushered the girls out of the room and shut the door.

"She had no right to take off with Gladdy like that!" Ilene assailed him.

"You'll have to forgive Marie. I'm afraid she overreacted." He cleared his throat. "The news about your—relationship with Mr. Wyland upset her deeply. Mothers and sons. You know how it is." He walked over to the cabinet. "You look like you could use a brandy."

Ilene shook her head. "No thanks. I just want to collect my kids and go home."

He poured it anyway and handed it to her. "It's late. You've come all this way. Stay the night. Let the girls enjoy the pool in the morning."

She accepted the glass and drank the brandy. "Gladdy has a birthday party tomorrow. We have to get back."

"I see." He stared at her.

Ilene glanced around. "Philip never told me you lived like this. In a palace. On a compound. With armed guards. I had no idea."

"Banking is a formidable business. Security is a fact of life. One can never be too careful these days. As you found out with your friend. The FBI agent."

"Is that what this is about?"

He raised his eyebrows and sipped his drink. "Maybe you should tell me."

She laughed. "I don't have anything to say. Except he disappeared months ago. Now I know why. It's really none of your business. I made a big mistake."

"A mistake," he repeated. "Everyone makes mistakes. Marie made a mistake. Even I make mistakes. I've been messing around with that damn computer. Boy do I make mistakes. But an old man like me needs to keep up with these things." He paused. "People can do their banking by computer these days. Did you know that?"

"I've heard of it." Ilene studied his stony expression. Was he mocking her? Their conversation seemed more like a game. She sensed two distinct sides to this man. At the moment he was the concerned father-in-law. Under different circumstances perhaps someone far more ruthless. Taking a drink her fingers played with the cold surface of the glass. "Look. No matter what you or Marie think happened it's between me and Philip."

"I'm afraid it's not that simple." He drank his brandy. "The man is a federal agent."

Feeling trapped she abandoned her drink on the end table and walked toward the windows. "Well that's news to me."

After a long silence he said, "We've taken very good care of you and the grandchildren while Philip's away. Don't you agree?"

Turning sharply, she raised her eyebrows. "Let's see. Bugging my house. Spying on me. Kidnapping my daughter. That's what you call taking care of us?"

He laughed. "I always liked your spunk." He finished his drink and set the glass on the cabinet. "I'm glad we had this talk. I think you understand this family a little better now. I realize that over the years Philip has been—shall we say—somewhat embarrassed by his family's—prosperity. But he's learned to accept certain things for what they are."

"Is that so?" she retorted. "It almost sounds like you've been in touch with him."

Taking her by the arm, he moved toward the door. "I know where he is. We've spoken. Yes." He hesitated. "I can't promise you that Marie won't tell him about your—mistake."

Ilene stopped in her tracks. "What're you saying? That I should just drop this on Philip next time he calls. Should I tell him his mother kidnapped his daughter too?"

He patted her shoulder. "Whatever you think is best."

She rolled her eyes. "I don't really give a damn what Marie does. Philip knows what bag of wind she is. He trusts me."

"Of course he does. Philip is a smart man. You're an intelligent woman. The two of you can work this out." He opened the door. "Are you sure I can't convince you and the girls to spend the night?"

"Gladdy's birthday party."

"You're a devoted mother," he stated. "In that case, Smith will arrange for the jet to fly you home."

"See this?" She pointed to her swollen, cut lip. "He did this to me."

He eyed her wound. "Doesn't look too serious. A minor misunderstanding. He's very protective of Marie. I promise he'll behave himself."

He escorted her down the corridor to the foyer where Smith—still in sunglasses—was waiting with Hazy and Gladdy. As much as she disliked the big goon, she figured a safe trip home was the least these people could do for turning her life inside out. Adding insult to injury Smith accompanied them on the flight. The girls slept while Ilene ignored the brute in sunglasses.

They stumbled through the back door after 1:00 a.m. Hazy and Gladdy sleepwalked up to their rooms. Ilene found the message light blinking on the answering machine. She lit a cigarette and listened.

"Ilene. Gladdy. Hazy." It was Philip. *"Where are you guys? I called to wish Gladdy happy birthday. I love you. Ilene. Listen. You're not gonna believe this. They're flying us up to the Turkish border to give medical assistance to the Kurds. We must be the last ones left. Nobody knows what the hell's"*—Beep.

The machine interrupted. The next message played.

"It's Cathy. Call me as soon as you get back. I'm worried sick."

The machine beeped again. Then silence. Ilene smoked her cigarette and replayed Philip's message. JD believed the government was maneuvering the 477th to keep Philip out of the country. As incredible as that seemed his message only offered more ammunition to back it up. The sound of his voice brought all the emotions she'd kept in control during the previous ten hours crashing down around her. She wept quietly in the darkness.

17

On Tuesday, April 30th, Ilene brought in a local security company to sweep the house of all listening devices.

"Don't ask me any questions," she told the technician as she pointed out the extent of the problem. "Just get it all out of here."

With that out of the way, the rest of the week she endured the torment of having promised the girls a puppy in the heat of battle with Marie. They'd latched onto that like leeches. At breakfast every morning Hazy read aloud the puppy ads from the newspaper.

"Remember what I said. Daddy made me promise not to get the puppy until he gets home." The truth was, they'd never discussed the subject. But she had to resort to a fib to avoid the issue. A puppy would only complicate things.

"I sure wish he'd hurry up and come home," Gladdy complained.

Ilene's visit to Highgate had opened her eyes to the immensity of the family's power. The conversation with Donald haunted her. She called the Two Harbors bank on Thursday to ask if there were any inquiries about her account.

"As a matter of fact," Mr. Johnson began. "A federal agent called to verify your account."

Kevin, Ilene thought. "I'll be closing out my account tomorrow anyway. That's why I called."

He cleared his throat. "Mrs. Sweeney, I'm required by law to verify accounts for government agents."

"I just don't need the hassle. That's all," she said abruptly.

"The agent assured me there was no cause for concern," he explained. "And your money's safe with us."

"All the same. I need the cash right now."

She pulled off the withdrawal and closed the account on Friday, May 3rd, feeling certain she wasn't followed. Having parked the Montero outside the Super One grocery store, she'd walked to the bank. When she returned there was a pickup parked next to her advertising *FRee PuPPeeS*. Peeking in the truck bed she counted five gorgeous fat mutt puppies. Two black and white ones, two brown speckled and a red one. Summoning all of her strength she resisted snatching one. A lump rose in her throat as she turned away and climbed in the driver's seat. She longed to go on with their lives as if nothing had changed. After all, she had lived in the shadow of organized crime for nine years without even knowing. And no harm had come to them. The Singletons were pillars of respectability. But the investigation had changed everything. She recalled a news magazine show she'd seen on TV last Sunday night exposing US weapons sales to Iraq allegedly financed through the Atlanta Banca Nationale de Lavoro. She couldn't deny the scope of this any longer. She could not ignore JD's warnings.

In the middle of a rain storm late Saturday afternoon, Stan appeared at the back door. She turned down the TV volume and let him in. "Hi. Where's Cathy and the kids?"

He shook off the water as he removed his pullover. "They're home. Just got done shooting hoops at the Sports Garden. Thought I'd stop by and check up on you."

"Want a beer?" She fetched two Molsons from the fridge and opened them.

"Thanks. Where's the girls?"

"Upstairs. Playing video games." She leaned against the center island.

Glancing around nervously he drank his beer. "Is there somewhere we can talk?"

Ilene waved her arm. "Right here. I had the place swept clean. Or whatever you call it."

Stan exhaled. "If you ask me you should've done it months ago. I don't know how you put up with that."

Ilene shrugged. "Surprisingly I sorta got used to it. Besides my bedroom and the basement were free zones." She drank beer from the bottle. "So what'd you want to talk to me about?"

He paced into the dining area. "Cathy's been keeping me up on what's going on with you. She's pretty worried." He finished his beer.

"I don't want you guys to worry about me." She got him another beer, trading him for the empty bottle. "Philip will be home soon and everything will get straightened out."

Stan eyed her. Then as if he'd been trying to find the courage to say the words he blurted, "Ilene. You're not the type of woman who has a one night stand and walks away. You were pregnant for god's sake."

She turned away. "Bugs or no bugs. There are some things you and me ought not speak about."

"Don't give me that. I've known you longer than Philip. Kevin meant something to you."

"Kevin!" Ilene shouted, then softened her voice. "Was an FBI agent. Investigating Philip's family."

He peered at her. "So you feel betrayed by that."

"Leave it alone Stan," she pleaded. "It's over and done with."

The only sound was the muffled voices from the TV.

"Are you in some kind of trouble because of that investigation?" he asked.

Ilene shook her head adamantly. "Look. There's things I can't talk about. I'm sorry but it has to be this way."

Stan gulped the rest of his beer and set it on the counter. He walked over and kissed her forehead. "I'm sorry too. Look. Kevin called our place. He insists you call his number. So if you're not in any trouble, then this isn't as *over with* as you say it is."

Dumbfounded by Stan's last minute message, she watched him grab his pullover and walk out the door.

Waiting until long after the girls had gone to bed that night she poured straight brandy into a snifter and carried it upstairs where she propped herself on bed pillows with the cell phone. She dialed the number. "It's me. You have the number."

She pressed *end* and leaned back. Sipping brandy she closed her eyes and prepared herself. The phone rang. "Yes."

"What the hell's going on with that phony bank account in Two Harbors? Are you out of your mind?"

No matter how calm she intended to be, her heart always thumped at the sound of his voice. "When Marie came here last Friday she left me a check for a million bucks to take Hazy and get the hell out of Philip and Gladdy's lives. I never cashed it. The way I see it this way we get the money and the chance to start over somewhere together. When Philip gets home. Instead of paying me to split our family apart, they're paying me to keep it together."

"That's embezzlement! That money doesn't belong to them either. You're gonna get caught."

"We should be long gone by then."

"You can't hide from these people."

Ilene snickered. "Just watch us."

"For chrissake! This isn't a game. Stop messing with those accounts. You're gonna get yourself killed."

"I already closed the account."

"Put the money back."

"That's impossible."

"Goddammit. How the hell am I sposed to swear you weren't

involved when you go and do something so stupid?"

"How did you find out anyway?"

"The computer files. I have the access codes. For your information those accounts are still being monitored."

Unwittingly he'd just given her the excuse she could use if ever confronted about the unusual account activities. Blame it on FBI monitoring. "Did you know I had this place swept clean of bugs?" She changed the subject.

"So I heard."

"How do you find out all this shit?"

"You're under surveillance by the local field office."

"So the blue Chrysler in Chicago was FBI. Call me stupid—and you did. But don't you think the Singletons knew the Feds were trailing me that night?"

"For your protection. It would've been even more suspicious if you weren't being tailed. Which is exactly why you should've kept those bugs in place."

"But I told both Marie and Donald that I knew about them. I had to follow through."

"They already knew you were aware of their surveillance. It looked like you didn't care. You played the obedient wife. Until now. You took matters into your own hands. You attracted attention to yourself."

"As if going face to face with the old man at Highgate didn't attract attention to myself," Ilene reminded him. "After my major melt down, it would be totally out of character for me *not* to do something drastic. I was pissed off. To come home and do nothing, believe me *that* would look suspicious."

"You are so naïve."

"Fuck you."

He sighed. "Can't you see what they're doing? Letting out all the rope you need to hang yourself. You just keep tightening the noose. You mean nothing to them."

She felt the hair rising up the back of her neck. Her breathing turned shallow. Her mouth was dry. She licked her lips. "You listen to me now. If I turn out to be the scapegoat in this then so be it. But I mean to do everything in my power to protect my own family. Even Philip. We didn't deserve this. These actions are all I have to keep me going. To free us from this fucking mess. I'm on my own now. There's nothing you can do."

"You're wrong." He was silent for a moment then, "I wish you would trust me to get you all out of this."

"I can't." Tears threatened. "You're part of the problem." Unable to speak anymore she turned off the phone. Wiping away the moisture, she inhaled deeply. The future was unfathomable at this point. Stealing the money and shutting down the family's surveillance were undoubtedly dangerous moves to make. They were all spying on her now. The FBI. The Singletons. Maybe even the CIA. As long as they continued to keep their distance maybe she and Philip could disappear with the girls right under their noses.

However she deleted all the account records from her computer on Sunday the 5th. She considered buying a new machine and getting rid of the old one, then realized that would definitely attract attention. She figured Kevin was probably right that she do her best from now on to keep a low profile. Monday morning she phoned Esther Cray at the bank to find out how to purge Smart Bank from her system.

"I'm sorry. Esther Cray no longer works here," her secretary explained. "May I ask who's calling?"

"This is Ilene Singleton. She was my account representative," she replied breathlessly, feeling alarmed.

"Mrs. Singleton, I can refer your account to David Mahoney."

"No. No. I don't understand," Ilene cried in panic. "What happened to her?"

"She was dismissed suddenly last week," the secretary lowered her voice. "No one here seems to know anything about it."

"I see. Thank you." Ilene hung up the phone in a cold sweat. Unable to catch her breath she rushed out to the deck. Maybe Ms. Cray worked for the FBI too and she'd done her job, so she moved on. Clutching the railing she felt the morning sun filtering through the new lime green aspen leaves above. But if she was an agent she could've monitored the accounts from the bank's computer system. The more she tried to talk herself out of any connection to the woman's dismissal, the more irrefutable it became. She was running out of time.

18

"Mommy. What if I fall asleep before Daddy's plane comes?" Gladdy fretted from the back seat of the Montero late Wednesday afternoon, May 22nd, Ilene's thirty-seventh birthday.

"Don't worry I'll wake you up," her mother assured her.

"But sometimes even when you wake me up, I don't remember," she whined.

Gerry Cusick had called Monday night to inform Ilene that the 477th would be arriving at Fort McCoy the night of the 22nd, sometime after 11:00 p.m. "We're handling things the same as we did back in January. Officers and wives can reserve up to two adjoining pool side rooms in your name at the Holiday Inn."

"Put us down for two," Ilene had told her.

Gerry also explained the procedure once their unit arrived. "Reservists can spend one night at the hotel with family. However they will be required to return to Fort McCoy by o-eight hundred hours Thursday morning to start the debriefing process, which should last at least forty-eight hours. Once that's complete they'll be bused back to

Duluth."

"So you're saying we can't bring Philip home with us."

"That's correct. Army regulations," Gerry had declared.

Gladdy continued complaining in the back seat. "I probably won't even get to see him."

"Shut up, you little goonie!" Hazy snapped. "You won't remember anyway. I don't remember hardly anything from when I was six."

"Seven!" Gladdy shouted. "I'm seven."

"You sure don't act like it," Hazy grumbled.

"Mom-mee. Hazy's being mean," Gladdy whined.

"Stop bickering you two. Or I'll light a cigarette and smoke you out," she threatened.

Both girls gagged.

As disappointed as she was by the strict re-entry procedure she'd grown callous to the manipulation. It was coming from too many sides to even stay on top of, much less do battle with. Since 90% of the troops had already returned home by the first of May, the satellite phone system in Saudi was dismantled and members of the 477th could no longer call home. The last time she'd heard his voice was on the recorded message. At least she felt certain he hadn't talked to his parents either.

At the Tomah Holiday Inn, Ilene checked in to learn more bad news.

"You're with the Army Reserve group," the woman at the front desk said. "I'm sorry to say the plane was grounded in Saudi Arabia due to a sand storm."

"Oh no!" Ilene, Hazy, and Gladdy cried in unison.

"We've been in contact with Officer McClellan at Fort McCoy. He'll let us know as soon as there's word of a new timetable. You're welcome to stay here. We'll extend your booking."

"Great. Thanks," she replied unenthusiastically. Another hoop for them to jump through.

Hazy and Gladdy hit the pool immediately. Ilene looked at her watch and wondered what kind of marathon they were in for this time. Hazy had mentioned twice on the drive south that they were being followed.

But she'd been saying that so much since the Chicago trip, Ilene had become desensitized. Nonetheless she ventured outside and searched the parking lot for any suspicious vehicle. As if she possessed some sort of radar, her gaze locked on the blue Chrysler across the parking lot at the Motel 6. Walking along the sidewalk she spotted the black Mercedes in the Perkins lot on the other side of the highway. Turning toward the lobby entrance her heart raced when she saw the green van idling in the alley behind Perkins. *The bozos were so damn obvious*, she thought.

Word came via telephone in her motel room later that evening. "This is Officer McClellan over at McCoy. Just wanted to let the officers' wives know personally that the plane is in the air and on it's way here. It is a twenty-two hour flight. So they should land sometime around 1900 hours Thursday evening."

"Thanks for calling." Since the girls were already asleep, she decided to tell them in the morning.

Thursday the 23rd was an unbearably long day. A rumor spread through the restaurant at breakfast that it could be as late as Sunday the 26th, before the unit would be released and on buses home. Ilene realized that she would have very little time to explain things to Philip before he would be sent back to base. Army personnel circulated a flyer that insisted family members return home on Friday and *"wait for word from their loved ones about final homecoming plans."* She crumpled the blue paper. Trapped in the hurry up and wait of this military madness her aggravation grew intense.

Chain smoking, she stared out the window. The blue Chrysler was still parked at Motel 6. Ilene decided to have a little fun with her trackers. Hustling the girls out to the Montero, she drove the long way over to the mall where they wandered through the stores buying books, toys and food enough to keep them entertained during this latest siege. Taking their sweet time they shopped for clothes. Ilene picked out some things for Philip. She doubted he had any clothing with him other than Army issue. As she wound her way through the streets of Tomah, the parade of vehicles in the rear view mirror amused her.

Back at the hotel around 5:00 p.m., another rumor flashed through the crowd by the pool. Hazy trotted over to give her the news. "Somebody said the plane's going to land sooner."

She and the girls joined in the slow mass exodus creating a stream of traffic en route, ending up in a multitude at the landing field. At 7:30 p.m., the Pan Am 747 skidded along the pavement. Finally. The crowd around her was delirious. Simultaneous crying, laughing, cheering, and screaming swirled around her. Because of the throngs of people, the soldiers spilled out onto the runway haphazardly as families hungrily searched for one another. The media people were eating it up, lights and cameras focused in on joyful faces. Ilene kept her eyes peeled to the jet's exit ramp but she couldn't pick him out.

"There he is!" Hazy cried out and dashed off.

Ilene called after her, "No. Wait! Stay together." She grasped Gladdy's hand.

As soldiers and families found one another the pandemonium increased to a mob scene. She glanced over at the plane. The ramp stood empty. *Where was Philip?*

Digging in her heels Hazy stopped short. "That's not him."

Someone tapped Ilene's shoulder. She twirled around. The man standing before her dressed in desert camouflage was tall and thin, with shoulder length gray hair and a scruffy gray beard. "Philip?"

A shaky hand removed his wire-rimmed sunglasses. The eyes gave him away. Then his voice, "You don't recognize me."

"Daddy!" Gladdy squealed, attacking him.

Ilene blushed and threw her arms around him. Hazy jumped into the group and the four of them held on tight to one another crying, unable to speak.

Like exiting a rock concert they moved with the masses toward the parking lot. Ilene hung back and studied Philip as he ambled along, both girls hanging off his arms and shoulders, chattering happily. He must have lost fifty pounds, not to mention the gray hair. It seemed incredible to her that his appearance could have changed so radically in such a short amount of time. She looked around at the other Reservists. Philip wasn't alone. Everyone in uniform looked thin and ragged around the edges, like tan ghosts. The stress showed on their gaunt, prisoner of war faces. She wondered what horrors had scarred their souls over there.

Philip stopped and waited for her. Putting his free arm around her, he kissed her deeply. "I forgot to do that." She scratched her nose from his whiskers and smiled. "You're awfully quiet," he ventured. "Everything okay?"

"Sure. I'm sorry," she apologized tearfully. "This is harder than I expected."

"I know." Looking like the absent minded college professor, he peered into her eyes. "You look incredible."

Eyes wide she stared back at him.

"You guys! Come on!" Hazy called impatiently.

Gladdy pulled on his arm. He restrained her gently, still staring at his wife. "I know what you're thinking. You can say it out loud."

"What?"

"I've changed."

She glanced away. "You look different. That's all. I spose I'll get used to it."

They stopped at the Montero.

He scratched his beard. "So this is the new *Jeep* the girls were just telling me about. Mind if I drive?"

She tossed him the keys. "It's all yours. I got rid of the Camry."

"That's what Hazy said. What about the Jeep?" he asked.

"Oh God. I never told you. The Jeep was stolen back in January. Right after you left for Saudi." The girls helped her relate the unfortunate incident on the short trip back to the hotel. So much had changed since then.

Philip took his time that night tucking the girls into bed in the next room. They were pretty wound up. As Ilene changed into a new green negligee she felt uneasy, like someone might be watching. Or listening.

She figured there'd been plenty of time for any one of those nosy spies to bug their room. Remembering the Radisson with Kevin, she felt they couldn't risk talking freely in here.

When Philip came back he latched the door and turned to eye her standing in front of the mirror. He had already showered and changed into the sweat pants she'd bought for him the day before. They were too big so he'd tied the drawstring waist tighter. Gliding over to her, he gently wrapped his body around hers and hugged. They kissed over and over eventually collapsing onto the bed. The negligee didn't stay on long. There was little time for foreplay, after more than four months they needed one another too desperately. Ilene helped him out of his sweats and he eagerly pulled her on top of him. They moved together very slowly at first like the intro to a favorite old song, then the familiar tune struck home and they danced feverishly until passion made the two become one again. Sensing something different about the sex she let go and enjoyed his sweetness. In the past he could be hungry and demanding. As she melted forward onto his chest, Philip clutched her torso and wept into her hair. For the moment she lay there and felt his tears, knowing this too was part of the release he needed. Then she rolled over and cried beside him.

"I can't even begin to tell you how much I love you," he whispered.

"I love you too Philip." She struggled to a stand and put on the blue tunic and leggings she'd worn that day. "But you have to be back at the base in less than ten hours. And we still have so much to talk about."

Scooting up on the stacked pillows he reached out for her. "But I just want to touch you and kiss you."

"We can't talk in here. This room is probably bugged."

"What?"

"Please don't make me get into it here. We can't take any chances. Let's go sit by the pool." She walked out the door knowing he would follow. Having rehearsed this conversation a thousand times over the past weeks, now she couldn't decide how to tell him. She surveyed the pool area which was mostly deserted except for one table of four still drinking and talking. There was no sign of any agents or Terminator types.

Exasperated Philip trotted over and sat down next to her on a chaise. "I ordered some drinks. They'll be here in a minute. Would you please tell me what's going on?"

"I don't even know where to begin." Ilene tossed up her hands. "Remember the black Mercedes and how I thought it was your parents?"

He nodded. "It *was* them."

"You knew all along."

"Of course. I'm not going to lie to you anymore."

"Even about the bank accounts?"

"I gathered from our phone conversations you found out about those. But how?"

"Computer banking."

He rolled his eyes. "I told you not to do that."

"You should know by now I never do what I'm told."

"That information wasn't supposed to be made available to you," Philip explained.

"I have a feeling Esther Cray was trying to be a good feminist account representative by teaching me how to handle our finances in your absence," Ilene surmised. "Anyway she doesn't work there anymore."

He eyed her. "What else do you know?"

She squinted at him. "I know everything about your family. I know about the federal investigation. I've even been to Highgate. I know your mom is Meyer Lansky's daughter. And your dad could be Capone's son."

"Who told you all this?"

"Kevin. The carpenter. He's FBI." She left it at that for the time being. "The point is I *know*. Your parents bugged our house. Tapped our phones. They've been trailing me for months. Even here. Keep your eyes open for a black Mercedes."

He glanced around the pool area. "So that's why we're out here."

A waiter arrived with a quart of brandy, a pitcher of ice water and two glasses full of ice. "Would you like me to pour?"

"I'll get it." Philip signed the tab. Then he poured the drinks. He took a slow sip of strong brandy water. "Okay. So Kevin was investigating us. Did he find out about the bank accounts?"

The two of them sat facing one another on the edges of their seats. Ilene drank from her glass. "He hacked into my computer and downloaded the account records."

Philip's rocked backward at the news. "Jesus Christ. Ilene. What have you done?"

"Don't lay this on me. If I'd known the truth I never would've had those records on my computer. I don't understand why you never told me about your family years ago."

"Cmon Ilene." He shook his head. "You never would've married me. I'm not exactly proud of my heritage. Isn't it obvious? I've devoted myself to building a separate life away from them. I actually believed I could keep that corruption out of our lives by helping others."

"Until you needed their money."

"Dammit Ilene! I lost my income when I was activated," he replied defensively. "That in combination with the payroll delay, we would've lost the house for sure."

"But you must have a trust fund."

He lowered his eyes. "I do. But it's all tied up with investments. I couldn't get at it soon enough. Because I resented that money, I never made it accessible."

"I see." He was only telling her what she'd already surmised. "I could've gone back to work."

"The girls needed you."

"Philip. We've been over this before. You can't make those choices for me," Ilene insisted. "Believe me. I understand you were raised by the ultimate control freaks. But we have to make the big decisions together. From now on."

"That's hard for me to do," he responded. "I'd convinced myself that I couldn't tell you everything last fall. You were already pissed off about the house loan. I was afraid if you found out that I was allowing my father to launder money through bank accounts in my name because of an investigation, you might bail out with the kids."

Ilene looked at him sorrowfully. "How can you say that to me?"

"We were so frazzled back then. Don't you remember? That land battle took forever. The damn dog died. The house construction was a fucking hassle. We ran out of money. Then I got called up." He poured more brandy and fished ice cubes out of the pitcher.

She shook her head. "And I found out on my own anyway."

Leaning forward he kissed her. "It doesn't really matter anymore."

They were definitely not on the same wave length. Ilene slammed her glass down on the table and stood up. He wasn't getting this at all. "It sure as hell matters to me. This has turned my life inside out." She stalked off.

He caught up to her and wrapped himself around her in a body block reminiscent of Kevin. For one split second she drifted on a memory. But she came back to Philip as he began coughing and wheezing.

Turning around she comforted his spasms. "What's wrong?"

Stumbling over to a chair he sat down, still hacking. When he could speak he said, "Feels like there's something down there and I need to get it out." Ilene poured him a glass of ice water. He drank it and held up the empty glass. "Water. It's just amazing to have water."

She frowned at him. "What are you talking about?"

"The little things we take for granted. A glass of water. A chair to sit on," he said. "It's nebulous."

"You haven't had much alcohol these past few months, have you."

"Not a drop."

"Oh boy." Ilene laughed. "You're done for. I'll help you to bed."

He tugged her arm and coaxed her onto his lap. Burying his face in her neck he murmured, "I'm sorry about everything you've been through."

She fingered his frosty hair. "Oh Philip. I have plenty to be sorry for too. We've both been through the ringer. But you more than me I'm afraid."

Lifting his head he persisted, "My father came to me at

Thanksgiving. He told me that National was under investigation for money laundering. Shit. That's what the damn bank was all about. His plan was to set up accounts in my name to divert the wire transfers. Dammit. He'd just bailed us out with the money for our house. Enough to support you and the kids while I was gone. And there he was. In need of help. The kind of help that could mean the difference between having the money for the house or not. If I got in any trouble I figured—what the hell—the bank owns a law firm. They'd get me off." He sighed. "What the fuck am I saying? I didn't have any choice."

"You might have to testify," she warned. "I think we should disappear for awhile. Leave the country."

"Cmon Ilene. It's not like I was arrested when I got off the plane. I'm sure we can salvage the situation. We'll deal with it when I get home."

"Trust me Philip. It's bad."

"Nothing compares to what I've just been through. Nothing's *that* bad."

Ilene gazed into his sallow eyes. "What happened to you over there?"

He reached for her hands and kissed her palms. "We're not sposed to talk about the war right away."

She glanced around. "It's just you, Philip. Lose the unit. You get your own life back now."

He laughed. "I missed your sarcasm."

She cuffed him playfully. He kissed her.

They went back to bed. Within an hour, Philip's coughing spasms awakened her. He was out of bed and stumbling toward the bathroom, coughing and gagging. She shuffled over to him. He stood retching in the bathroom with a wet towel pressed against his mouth. She watched in horror as he pulled the towel away from his mouth to reveal a dark stain.

"Oh God. Philip. That's blood," she cried.

He shook his head and replied hoarsely, "Not blood. Oil soot. From the fires."

"Didn't you wear masks?"

He nodded. "We would've had to change them every hour to be effective. We didn't have that kind of time. Much less supply. The air was always thick with hot acrid soot. Saddam's black death, the Kuwaitis called it. We breathed that shit for weeks on end."

Ilene shuddered. "Sounds horrible. You need to see a doctor."

"I will tomorrow." He started in coughing again.

Reaching for a fresh towel she filled the sink with cold water. She wrung it out quickly, Philip still hacking behind her. His spasms brought him down on one knee. They slumped together on the cool tile floor.

"Maybe I should call an ambulance."

Shaking his head adamantly, Philip inhaled the wet terry cloth and calmed down. "It's some kind of pollution induced asthma. I'll be fine once my lungs clear out."

"But you're dripping wet. Feels like you have a fever."

"Maybe low grade. Nothing serious."

"How can you say that? You're a health care professional."

He exhaled. "If you only knew what happened over there. Like hell on earth. The Allies massacred the Iraqis. Then we came along and picked up the pieces. And I do mean pieces. On the road to Basra one day we saw this man on his knees hitchhiking. We stopped. He was obviously an Iraqi solider. He asked for a ride, complaining that his feet hurt too badly to walk. But my god Ilene," Philip groaned. "The man had no feet. They'd been blown off. By some ugly twist of fate he was still alive. Delirious from shock and pain. We brought him in the ambulance. While I set up an IV, he said his name was Faribe Rahman. He was a student at Northwestern last year. With a wife and son back in Evanston. He'd returned home last August for the funeral of his brother, a soldier killed in Kuwait. When he tried to leave Iraq, Saddam's Army drafted him into the military. I was horrified!" he cried out. "Anyway at some point he must've realized his own condition. When we're out on patrol inside enemy lines like that, as an officer I'm required to pack a pistol." He spoke as if he was still there. "I left it on the tray behind me while I tried to make Faribe comfortable. Then the damn driver hit something on the road and the ambulance lurched. When I grabbed for the supplies, Faribe grabbed my pistol and shot himself in the head."

Ilene gasped. "He could have killed you."

Philip shook his head and wiped his tears. "Don't you see? That was the furthest thing from his mind. We were comrades. Not enemies. Alumni. He was gonna die anyway. He knew it. We had no way to save his life out there."

Huddled on the bathroom floor, Ilene held her wounded soldier in her arms. "Now I know why they don't want you to talk about the war."

19

"*The 477th Army Reserve medical unit is expected to return to the Twin Ports on Memorial Day. That's tomorrow morning at approximately eleven thirty. A parade is planned through the city of Superior as well as food and festivities at Bayfront Park,*" a local woman TV newscaster reported on Sunday, May 26th.

Did the politicians plan it that way or what, Ilene wondered. Philip had not called since Friday night. Assuming that as an officer he was caught up in sensitive debriefing meetings and medical exams, she made up her mind not to worry. All that mattered was that he was coming home at last.

The morning of the 27th, she let the Carricks take the girls with them to the parade in Superior. Which consisted once again of Army vehicles, two coach buses transporting Reservists from Fort McCoy, a couple of local marching bands and of course Senators, Congressmen and State Legislators riding in cars, cashing in on the patriotism of war.

"Sorry. But I've had it up to here with the big lie. It's all bullshit," Ilene begged off the festivities. "I'll pick up Philip at Bayfront Park. You guys meet us at home after the parade."

She arrived at the park as the buses rolled in. This time she found Philip right away and rushed through the small crowd as he stepped off the bus. His hair had been cut short again. But the beard stayed, in trimmed form.

"Got my discharge papers right here." He waved the envelope. "I'm a free man."

She hugged him. "Thank God that's over with."

"Where's my girls?" He searched past her.

Ilene sensed something was wrong immediately. "They're with the Carricks. Didn't you see them along the parade route?"

He shook his head. "I was hoping they'd be here."

"They'll catch up with us at home." As though guiding a disoriented old man, she led him toward the parking lot.

A male reporter stuck a microphone in his face, a cameraman aimed behind him. "How does it feel to be back in Duluth after all those months in the desert?"

Philip's expression was pained. "It's home," was all he said.

"Your name sir?" he asked.

Philip walked away coughing and wheezing. Ilene glared at the reporter. "You need to back off. Give these people some space."

"Sorry ma'am." He retreated in search of a more congenial target.

She stopped at a booth selling cold drinks and bought a lemonade. Catching up with him she handed over the cup and showed him to their vehicle. "Want me to drive?"

He nodded.

As she persevered through the traffic jam she wanted to ask him if there was something wrong. But it seemed like such a stupid question. Of course there was something wrong. The war. The debriefing. This manic media driven re-entry into the civilian world. All taking its toll on his fragile nervous system. He seemed more exhausted than the night the plane landed. And he was still coughing. "What did the Army doctor say?"

"My white count was high. Gave me a shot and a prescription. It's probably just an infection. Once my lungs clear out, I'll feel better."

The Carricks had already arrived at Hawk Ridge with the kids and a picnic lunch. Eager to see his friends and play with the girls, Philip perked up anyway.

"This is incredible," he said repeatedly as they toured the house.

"Ilene's done a great job with the place," Stan agreed.

Philip was especially pleased with Kevin's work in the spa downstairs, describing for them the makeshift hot tubs their unit dug in the desert sand, using garbage bags and old inner tubes. "Wasn't exactly private. But the water was always warm because of the hot sand."

"Sounds like everyone made the best of a bad situation," Cathy assessed.

"We tried." He shrugged. "Couldn't dig tubs in Kuwait City though. Beach sand was full of land mines." Shuddering he added, "Had daily pickups out there. Body Parts Beach we called it."

"Philip," Ilene scolded. "Don't get gory in front of the kids."

"They're not paying any attention," he retorted angrily.

Behind them Hazy and Gladdy were running through the empty family room with Sara and Arnie.

Upstairs in the kitchen Stan remarked, "Noticed the sod finally came for your yard."

Philip peered out the porch windows. "What's the deal with that anyway?"

Ilene tossed up her hands. "They were here when I came back from Fort McCoy. I'll call the landscaper tomorrow and find out what they plan to do."

The success of the Sportstalker shops was the other major topic of conversation. The four of them managed to avoid any mention of the explosive secrets that would soon be triggered by this homecoming. For one precious afternoon Ilene allowed herself to slip into blissful ignorance and pretend they were a normal family again.

In the evening after Cathy and Stan had surrendered homeward with their cranky, over stimulated toddlers and the girls had passed out in their beds, Ilene smoked a cigarette on the deck. The wind switched sending in clouds and a breeze that chilled the air. She closed doors and turned out the lights, then padded barefoot upstairs to a mine field of her own making.

Philip had propped himself against the pillows and stared out the windows at the lake view. Hopping onto the bed she crawled toward him and planted a sexy kiss on his lips. No response. *That did it.*

She finally asked the question. "Is something wrong?"

He sniffed. "You started smoking again."

Her face flushed. "Bad habit. I've cut way back. Don't worry. I'll quit."

Philip pulled a video cassette out from under the pillows and threw it down on the comforter. Speechless, Ilene sat up rigidly. He didn't look at her. So that's what his moodiness was all about. Marie had gotten to him. She'd done her dirty work.

"My debriefing turned out to be a bit more extensive than everyone else."

"Goddammit!" Ilene climbed off the bed and paced the floor. "It's just like that bitch to pull a power trip like this. She didn't even give me the chance to explain. Don't you see what she's done?"

"What *she's* done?" he asked incredulously. "Ilene. Trust me. My mother's not in that video."

"Dammit! I am so pissed off right now I can't even think straight."

"You're pissed," he repeated with aloofness.

"I don't know what to say." She tossed up her hands. "I'm sorry Philip. I'm sorry it happened. And I'm even sorrier you found out this way. She did this to turn you against me. How the hell did they get to you anyway?"

"Both Donald and Marie arrived at McCoy Saturday night. Under the circumstances, they were allowed to spend a few hours with me."

Ilene fled to his side and smoothed his hair. "You didn't deserve to be put through that. What did they tell you?"

Slapping her hand away, he sneered. "What a coincidence. They asked the same thing about you. *Christ.* I can't believe I walked into a fucking mess like this."

"Philip. I mean it. What did they say about me?"

"I'll ask the fucking questions now," he snapped.

Sitting on the edge of the bed, Ilene hung her head. She guessed he was entitled to his wrath. "Go ahead."

"How could you fuck that guy when you knew he was an agent!"

She winced at his crudeness. "I didn't find out until I caught him going through my computer files. That was after—the video."

"And was that before or after your abortion?"

"It was a miscarriage." She exhaled. "They certainly didn't spare you the details."

"Minor little details you conveniently left out of your version last Thursday night," he grumbled.

"You need to understand that for me all that shit with Kevin was months ago. It's in the past. I'm focused on putting our lives back together now."

"I don't see how that's possible."

It was her turn to look incredulous. "How can you say that? We bonded all over again that night."

"Are you still in contact with him?"

Ilene's own hesitation betrayed her. "I talked to him three weeks ago."

"So they were right then. Are you cooperating with the investigation?"

"How dare you ask me that!" she wailed. "Kevin used me. Dammit! I was a fool. I'm sure Marie told you that. I'm into this just as deep as you are. And the rest of your goddamn family."

"With those account records the FBI has enough information to shut down National Bank."

"That's not what they want. National's just a stepping stone. They want the BCCI."

He looked quizzically at her. "So you do know what's going on."

"That's what I've been trying to tell you."

"Then their suspicions aren't too far off base."

"Okay. Maybe I cooperated with the investigation without knowing. But I never told Kevin about those accounts. He found out completely on his own. I'm caught in the middle here. Everyone's been spying on me. FBI. Your family." She glared at him. "Tell me something. Did Marie happen to mention that she kidnapped Gladdy on her birthday? And did she tell you she offered me a million bucks to take Hazy and disappear?"

"What?"

"I didn't think so." She fired back. "That's how I discovered Highgate. I went there to get Gladdy back."

"Has everyone gone mad here?" he raged.

She crawled toward him once more. "I have a plan Philip. We can take the girls and disappear in the middle of the night until this whole thing blows over."

Shaking his head he started coughing. "No way. I'm staying right here."

"But what if the Feds subpoena you to testify about the accounts?"

"I told you. That's what the bank's lawyers are for. To quash subpoenas."

"What if it's not that simple?" Ilene cleared her throat. "Kevin thinks the CIA's involved. Between them and the banks we could be in more danger than you think."

"Then we might as well leave the planet." His breathing was labored. "Look. I've been running from my family since Nam. I realize how bad things seem to you right now. But nothing compares to these past five months. I've seen hundreds of men buried alive in trenches. I'm through running for my life. I'm home now. I'll stand and fight." He hacked furiously.

Sitting up cross-legged on the bed Ilene stared at the wind spattered raindrops on the windowpanes. Philip was too battle scarred to face another so soon. She had to hope there was still time for him to take the antibiotics and get strong. Once he realized the extent of the investigation, he would understand the urgency of their predicament. She grasped his clammy hand and pledged, "The most important thing right now is that you know I love you. I admit I made some terrible mistakes. But I have always loved you."

Philip remained silent, although he accepted her hand holding.

She squeezed his fingers. "Do you want me to get on my knees? And beg your forgiveness."

"Have you seen that videotape?" He closed his eyes. "I didn't notice a gun pointed to your head."

Arching her back, she withdrew her touch. "My—relationship—with Kevin began Valentine's Day. He was gone March first."

"You were pregnant."

"That only proves how careless I was." He had no idea how painful it was for her to rehash their affair.

"You can say that again."

"Philip. How do we get past this?"

"Why are you still in contact with him?"

"I told you. He wanted to warn me about the CIA's connection in all this." She dared not bring up the money. In his present frame of mind he wasn't capable of comprehending why she took it.

"I need time to think," he said. "I won't move out. Spent too damn long getting back here. But you might want to get away from the tension."

Shaking her head adamantly she vowed, "I'll stand my ground. You see. I'm light years ahead of you. I already know where I belong."

"Then I'll move into the guest room," he stated flatly.

Ilene groaned. "Oh stop it Philip. You're just exhausted. Get some sleep."

"It's going to take some time to repair the damage."

"As long as it takes, I'll be here for you. There's enough pain to go around." She leaned forward and kissed his lips. "I love you."

He nodded with resignation.

20

On Tuesday, May 28th, Ilene let Hazy and Gladdy skip school to be with their dad. She believed the buffer of those two chatty clowns would ease the tension between them and bring him around to the important things in life—his home and family. With Philip too wasted from coughing to argue and Ilene too stubborn to move, they shared the same bed overnight while maintaining a safe distance.

He slept in, then after a late breakfast the girls coaxed him onto the deck for some fresh air. When Ilene checked on them after while they were out in the yard.

"Mom-mee!" Gladdy ran screaming into the house before noon. "Daddy fell down. He can't breathe!"

His lungs. Ilene rushed toward the door then stopped to grab the remote phone. She dialed 911, and ordered an ambulance. When she reached his side on the burlap next to a pile of sod, Hazy was flapping her hands, nearly in shock.

"It's okay honey. I called an ambulance." Ilene put her arms around her reassuringly.

Philip's lips were blue and his eyes were closed. His pale yellow face breathed in tiny wisps of air, barely enough oxygen for a butterfly it seemed. Ilene loosened all of his clothing, praying silently that he would be all right. "What happened Hazy?"

"I don't know. He told us to help him roll the grass." She pointed at the lush green strips already laid out in the yard. "He was bending over. And he just fell down."

Gladdy burst into tears.

Their dad opened his eyes and mouthed the words, "I'm okay."

"Don't speak." Ilene smoothed his gray hair. "Just breathe."

Reaching up she squeezed Hazy's hand. "I know it's scary. But he'll be all right."

The ambulance careened onto the driveway in what seemed like record time.

"Looks like a collapsed lung," the paramedic told her as he set up the IV. "Once we get the oxygen flowing he should feel better. Which hospital?"

"St. Mary's," she instructed. "I'll meet you there." By the time Ilene piled the girls in the Montero and opened the garage door, Philip was loaded in the ambulance.

On the way to the hospital, Gladdy spilled the beans. "Daddy said we could get a puppy. I told him all about the puppy Grandma gave me for my birthday. Except that I could only really have it if I stayed at her house."

Gripping the steering wheel Ilene slowly exhaled, containing her fury. No wonder Philip collapsed. It must've been devastating for him to hear about his mother's conniving cruelty from his own daughter's lips. Another nasty secret revealed.

"There's an ad for golden retrievers in the paper," Hazy spoke up.

"I think we should probably wait until Daddy feels better."

"That's not fair!" Gladdy wailed. "I wanna go to my grandma's. I already have a puppy there."

Ilene bit her lip. "You don't mean that sweetie."

At the hospital the girls watched TV while Ilene paced the hall outside the waiting room, feeling frustrated at how Philip's illness changed everything. She'd made no provisions for an obstacle like this. The awful reality was that he wasn't strong enough to go anywhere. Perhaps for quite some time.

Finally after more than an hour, Dr. Andersen approached her and explained, "His right lung partially collapsed on him earlier. He's doing much better now. Although his lungs are essentially polluted. We'll set him up with a respiratory therapist tomorrow, on a daily basis to start."

"Can we take him home?" Ilene pleaded. "He just got back."

"I know. And I gave him that option. Come back tomorrow for tests," the doctor replied. "But he seemed perfectly satisfied to get them done today while he's here. Therefore I prefer he spend the night in case there's any minor complications."

"He's the boss," Ilene relented. She knew exactly why Philip would consent to a hospital stay right now. Like he said, anything was better than the war and apparently he felt uncomfortable around her now that he knew about Kevin.

The girls dashed ahead to their dad's room on their own.

"Ilene," Dr. Andersen detained her. A co-worker of Philip's before the war, he knew them both by name. "Philip's in pretty tough shape. What the hell happened to him over there?"

"From the few things he's told me it was some kind of living hell."

When she caught up with the girls in his room, so as not to upset them, she didn't let on that there was any problem other than his silly old cough. "Hear you're spending the night."

Conscious and sitting upright in bed he mentioned, "Might as well get the damn tests done right away."

"Whatever," Ilene said. "Only you know how you feel."

An orderly came to deliver him to x-ray.

"I'll come back later, after your tests are finished." She kissed him gently.

"Bring the girls," he said without kissing her back.

At home the landscapers had arrived and were busy spreading out the rolls of sod along the terraced lawn. She stopped to chew out the foreman.

"Sorry we didn't get up here sooner," he apologized. "We got backlogged. Finally got caught up."

"That may be. But my husband wound up in the hospital after he tried to deal with this himself." Ilene unleashed her anger at the man in overalls. "He just got home from the Gulf. He's a very sick man. You never should've dumped this sod here in the first place."

"Gees. I'm really sorry ma'am." He scratched his head. "Must be why nobody was home when we tried to call last week."

"Well I expect a credit on my account for this hassle."

"Whole bid was paid for last November."

"What?" Then she remembered that Marie had hired the landscaping firm after Thanksgiving. Flustered she snapped, "Just get the job done and clear out of here."

Marching up the stairs to the house, she thought about those innocent days last fall when it was only this house standing between herself and Marie Singleton. At the time she thought that was unbearable. Little did she know those would become the good old days.

Hazy and Gladdy remained outdoors harassing the three workmen. Still fuming over the situation, Ilene let them do their stuff. She mulled over the million in cash locked away in the desk drawer. She had to find a way to tell Philip. But in his fragile condition she didn't know how much more he could take. A very real possibility existed that the Singletons already knew. Especially since Kevin found out and Esther Cray had presumably been fired. Maybe in a week—maybe six months, eventually the account irregularities would catch up with her. Philip would know what to do.

Trudging upstairs to the bedroom she reconciled that if he was so annoyed with her that he chose the hospital over sleeping in the same bed, she needed to move temporarily to the guest room rather than stress him out anymore than he already was.

She noticed his Army duffel bag on the floor at the end of the bed. He hadn't even had time to unpack. Sitting on the bed she opened the bag and scooped out the wad of gritty T-shirts, underwear and socks. As she carried them to the laundry chute, a thick envelope dropped to the floor. She picked it up. Stiff and heavy, it obviously contained photos. But Philip had taken the video camera. Someone else must've taken pictures for him. She sniffed the air, detecting a sweet fragrance. She smelled the envelope. *Perfume.* Opening it she pulled out the color prints and stumbled over to the bed. She could hardly believe her eyes.

One after another she shuffled through the images. Philip and a young, dark-skinned brunette walking on a hazy beach under a yellow sky. The two of them embracing. Their naked backs entering the water. Chocolate and vanilla. Them kissing. Them walking hand in hand. Philip lifting her into the surf. Frolicking. The two of them cuddled under a blanket in the sand. Twelve photos in all that completely blew her mind. Wiping her parched lips with one hand she scrambled for her cigarettes with the other. Lighting one, she could not take her eyes off the petite woman with no name. One of the prints was a close up of her exotic face with a sprinkle of freckles on a cappuccino complexion. Huge soulful brown eyes stared back at Ilene. *Did you make love with my husband?* The next photo answered her question. The two of them embraced in a lip lock. A closer examination placed her hands inside the front of his shorts. She wondered who shot their little romp on the beach that day. *And when?*

Clutching the stack of photos Ilene smoked the cigarette. On the one hand these surely provided the ammunition she needed to get Philip past her affair with Kevin. She held up a frontal nude shot of the woman displaying pert round bosoms. Obviously the pose was meant to photograph the tattoo above her left breast—a heart flanked by two scrolls with two arrows above. On the other hand this exquisite nymph's sinewy body made her feel like a foolish old shrew. Squashing the cigarette in the planter she glanced at the clock. The hospital would be calling soon to let her know Philip had finished his tests. She decided to wait until he came home to show him the pictures.

A mixture of emotions smoldered inside her. She fell back on the bed quilt. All the tragic secrets of the past six months came crashing down around her. The whole thing struck her as incredibly funny. She laughed until the tears came. Then she wept.

21

Philip came home from the hospital on Wednesday, May 29th, more exhausted and grouchy than when he went in.

Ilene phoned Dr. Andersen's office and demanded to speak with him. "What's going on with Philip?" she asked him. "He won't tell me anything. What did the tests show?"

"His lungs are definitely coated with some sort of residue. He claims that's from breathing the polluted air during the fires in Kuwait. No matter the cause, it's created an asthmatic condition where his lungs constrict and he loses air pressure. Plus all of this is complicated with an infection. Like walking pneumonia. He's on medication for that. We need to keep an eye on that condition so it doesn't get any worse. And he needs to get in here every day with the RT."

Philip insisted on driving himself to see the respiratory therapist. Otherwise that was the extent of his independence.

"My lungs ache from that damn bronchoscopy," he complained. Most of the time he made his way around the house from bed to chair to couch, back to bed again. He watched CNN for hours on end usually wearing sweats and a T-shirt. He also put away a good share of brandy. "For the cough," he claimed.

Only Hazy and Gladdy could coax him to put down the remote control. Ilene catered to him in every way imaginable. She cooked his favorite foods—fettucini alfredo, walleye in almond butter, wild rice soup with Swedish rye bread. She prepared the sauna for him and helped him into it twice a day. Yet nothing satisfied him. Her only consolation was that his illness served as a good cover explanation for the girls once she started sleeping in the guest room.

Thursday evening, Hazy and Gladdy dished up a colossal banana split, surprising him in his bedroom throne. Without turning down the sound on *Cheers*, he attacked the ice cream and toppings hungrily. Then he nodded off to sleep.

"Uh-oh." Gladdy cringed. "Daddy's watching TV with his eyes closed again."

"I'm going to my room." Hazy headed out the door. "I wish he wasn't so sick all the time."

His spoiled, boy-invalid behavior finally got on Ilene's nerves. After the girls drifted away, she picked up the glass ice cream dish and metal spoon from the comforter, clattering the two together loudly.

"What's that?" He sat up, eyes wide.

"Your daughters gave up on you." She perched on the edge of the bed. "Are you really that sick. Or is this some kind of punishment for my sins."

"Maybe a little bit of both," he replied.

Rubbing her face with her hand she longed to shove those photos in his face like he'd done to her Monday night with that video cassette. Instead she hinted, "I cleaned out your duffel bag and washed all the dirty stuff."

He waved his hand. "I'll go through that some other time."

She stared at him so pale and thin, leaning on the pillows. In the lamp light she saw a patch of skin on the side of his head. "Is that a sore?" She touched his scalp.

He pushed her fingers away. "Leave it alone."

"Get some rest now." She kissed his forehead. No response. "Tomorrow is the girls' last day. They're having an all school picnic down at Park Point. Parents are invited. You should come down for an hour or so. The fresh air might do you some good."

"I'll be fine here alone," he said.

Ilene sighed. "I was afraid you'd say that." What she neglected to tell him was that she'd arranged for Hazy to sleep over at Jessie's and Gladdy to sleep over at Kirsten's, so they could have one night alone to hash out their sordid sexual misdeeds.

However when Ilene came through the porch door after the picnic late Friday afternoon, she was met with a chilling twist of circumstances. Setting the grocery bags down on the counter she turned to see Philip standing in the sun's lengthy shadows of the dining area, dressed for once in his old baggy jeans and a favorite green shirt.

"Hi. You're dressed. You must be feeling better." She unpacked the bags cheerfully. "I've got everything here to make chicken dijon. With angel hair pasta. And Caesar salad. You love my Caesars."

"Kevin called," he informed her. "He told me about the money."

Clutching a bottle of Riesling in midair Ilene froze. "What are you talking about? He would never call here."

"He said you embezzled a million bucks so you could run off with him."

"That's ridiculous." She set the bottle on the counter. "Did you find the money? Is that what this is all about?"

"Locked in the desk drawer."

"Listen to me. I withdrew some cash. I told you. My plan was for you and me to take the girls away for awhile."

"Or was that your payment for giving the Feds what they wanted."

"Philip. If that was true, why would I still be here! I could've run away with him weeks ago."

"Cmon Ilene. It's so obvious what's going on here. He's got it bad for you. And I want you out."

Enraged she smashed the wine bottle to the floor. "Wait just a goddamn minute. I don't have to take this shit from you. I found those pictures of you and your little brown sugar. So get the hell off your high and mighty pedestal."

Dumbfounded he stared at the green shards of glass in the pool of wine. "It's not the same. We spent a weekend together. Months ago. Giselle was a nurse. Not an FBI agent. And I wasn't exactly surrounded by all the comforts of home."

"So! Her name is Giselle. How French!" Ilene spat. Heaving a sigh she declared, "Can't you see how crazy this is? We both screwed around. So what! Let's stop torturing each other like this. We need to get on with our lives."

He refused to look at her. "You heard what I said. Pack your things and get the hell out."

"Fuck you!" Ilene screamed. "I'm not leaving this house!"

"Go upstairs and pack or I'll do it for you," he said coldly. "Take the Montero. You bought it."

"Fuck it. You can have it." she sobbed. "You can have the goddamn money too. I don't understand why you're putting me through this."

He walked out the north atrium door onto the deck.

Ilene fled upstairs and called Cathy. "Can I stay with you tonight?"

"Of course. What's wrong? Did something happen to Philip?"

"Only that he's gone completely berserk on me," Ilene cried. "He thinks Kevin and I are still seeing each other. He kicked me out."

"Ohmygod. Would it help if I come over there and tell him it's not true?"

"Maybe. I don't know."

By the time Ilene finished packing, Cathy had arrived downstairs. No matter what happened, she decided to spend the night at Carricks. Philip needed to cool down. Shuffling downstairs she found her best friend striking out in the living room.

"So. Basically you're telling me that you knew about them," Philip accused.

"I don't want to interfere. But you guys can work this out. She loves you, Philip."

"Bullshit!" he roared. "She went after the money. Stayed long enough to grab her share."

Ilene stepped forward. "I told you I don't want the money. Give it back. Do whatever you want with it."

He walked away again, this time toward the south atrium door.

"Cmon Cathy. Philip is acting like a spoiled child. He'll get over it. Let's just give him some space right now." Ilene hoisted her purse and day pack on her shoulder at the same time. Picking up the small suitcase she called after him, "I love you Philip." She thought she saw him flinch.

Stan was back at their house watching Sara and Arnie. He and Cathy sat spellbound at the kitchen table as Ilene explained why she withdrew the money. Then she described the photos she found. "Don't get me wrong. I don't hold it against him. I just expected him to be more understanding about what happened to me. With Kevin. That's all."

"Looking at this strictly from Philip's point of view, the money makes you look bad," Stan commented.

Ilene chain smoked. "I figured the Feds were going to put the squeeze on him about those accounts as soon as he got home. And I sure as hell didn't plan on him being so sick."

"He's had a ton of shit thrown at him this past week," he reminded her. "It would take me awhile to sort it all out."

"I realize that," she agreed defensively. "Look. You understand what I've been going through. Maybe you could talk to him. Reason with him."

He patted her hand. "I'll try."

"Wait a minute," Cathy interjected. "I already tried to talk to him. What he said about Kevin. Calling your house. Talking about running off with you. It's not rational. That time Kevin called here he refused to call your house."

"What are you getting at?" Stan asked.

She looked at Ilene. "I think you should call Kevin. Find out if he knows what's going on."

A noise like thunder interrupted their conversation.

"Must be a storm coming in," Ilene remarked. "Why don't you guys go out and get some dinner. I'll watch the kids."

"Call Kevin first," Cathy insisted. "I want to hear his side of the story."

"All right. The phone number's in my purse out in your car. I'll get it." As Ilene walked out the back door to the driveway, she looked up into a pale blue evening sky. No storm in sight. She heard the woeful wail of a siren in the distance. Another joined in. Reaching into her purse for the card she clutched a band of currency. She fumbled with the familiar bundles by the handful. "Dammit," she cursed. *Philip must have stuffed the money in there.* What the hell kind of game was he playing? A distressing chorus of sirens echoed across the hillside. Ilene dashed into the kitchen.

"Cathy. I need to borrow your car. Philip put the money in my purse. I'm taking it back. I have to make him understand it's not about that."

Ilene backed out the driveway and raced through the residential streets. The fray of howling sirens sounded closer. Turning onto Skyline Parkway she saw smoke billowing from Hawk Ridge. She followed the deafening noise. Heart racing she recognized the break in the treetops. She drove madly up the hill, blinded by an enormous dread engulfing her. Barely breathing she rounded the final curve. Smoke swirled around the fire trucks littering the roadway. Two police squad cars formed a blockade. As she jumped out of Cathy's station wagon, she saw the flames leaping from her beloved house. Their home. Firefighters shot hoses of water in an effort to control the blaze.

Her mind reeling she screamed, "Oh God! Philip!"

22

Ilene didn't see the blue van pull up behind Cathy's station wagon as she scrambled toward the female police officer. "Please!" she cried. "This is my house!"

A badge flashed in front of her eyes. Then a large firm hand grasped her arm. "FBI," a man's voice uttered. "I'll handle this."

The officer nodded and turned away. Ilene found herself face to face with Kevin, his hair cut short. His bossy demeanor still intact.

"You did this!" she shrieked.

He strong-armed her backward away from the road block muttering, "Nice to see you too again, Mrs. Singleton. Where's your husband?"

"He threw me out!" She stared in shock at the blazing house. "Oh God. Kevin. My house. What the hell happened?"

Opening the rear door on the van he pushed her inside. "Someone tried to kill you all. We gotta get out of here. Now. Where's the kids?"

She sat down on the cushion. "Sleepovers with friends."

"Damn. Let's round them up first."

"What about Philip?"

Kevin jumped into the driver's seat and sped off. "He's sposed to meet us at Carrick's."

"What are you talking about?" She climbed into the front seat.

"I just found out today there was a hit going down at your house tonight. I flew in as soon as I could to try and stop it. But I was too late."

"Did you talk to him on the phone?" she rebuked him.

"I called to warn him. The plan was to get you and the kids out of the house as quickly as possible. Then wait for me at Carrick's."

"He didn't say anything about a warning. He said you told him about the money," Ilene argued. "That's why he threw me out. He was pissed off. He thought we were gonna run off together."

Kevin pulled in the driveway and stopped the van. "Ilene, you're not making any sense. I never said anything about any money."

Cathy rushed out to meet them. "Ohmygod. Ilene. It's all over the TV. Your house! They're looking everywhere for you. Should I call the police?"

"No way!" Kevin hopped out.

Cathy frowned at him. "You don't know what they said." She looked at Ilene. "They found a body."

Ilene fled into her best friend's arms. "Oh God. Not Philip. Oh God. No."

"All right. Listen up," Kevin commanded. "Someone wants this family dead. Carrick! Take your wife over to the road block and get your wagon out of there. Don't talk to anyone. Find those kids and bring them back here. I need to move these people out. Now!"

Stan stepped forward. "Wait a damn minute here. What about Philip?"

Kevin glared at him. "I don't know what happened. I told him to meet me here. Now I intend to do everything in my power to save Ilene and the kids. Don't you all stand in my way."

Stan looked to Ilene. "What do you want me to do?"

"Get the kids," she sobbed.

Cathy and Stan exchanged fearful glances.

"Dammit man!" Kevin shouted. "This is a fucking war zone. They could be closing in on us any minute. Help me get them out of here."

"Let's go Stan." Cathy hugged Ilene. "Watch my kids. We'll be right back."

The two of them drove away in Carricks' mini-van. Traumatized, Ilene wandered through the back door into the living room. Sara and Arnie were watching *The Little Mermaid* on the VCR. She curled up on the sofa and stared at the colorful cartoon characters dancing across the TV screen. Kevin stayed behind with the kitchen portable watching the local news updates of *"the residential explosion and fire"*, as the reporters were calling it. The phone rang. He didn't answer. The machine picked up. It was a woman from the police department looking for her.

Kevin leaned against the door frame until the message ended. "The firemen are saying there was an explosion. Could've been a bomb. Maybe he didn't get out in time. They haven't identified the body."

Her mind was so numb she could barely understand a word he said. "He was sick."

"I know." He clenched his fists. "Where the hell are those two."

Within fifteen minutes Hazy and Gladdy burst in the back door through the kitchen to Ilene.

"Mom-mee!" they squealed.

"There was a fire," Hazy cried.

"Where's Daddy?" Gladdy wailed.

Ilene looked helplessly at the frightened faces of her two daughters.

"He's dead isn't he?" Hazy decreed.

"He's not!" Gladdy shrieked.

"Grow up you little goonie!" Hazy snapped.

"Ilene. We don't have time for this," Kevin's voice thundered. "Let's go. Now!"

Stan and Kevin tossed the handful of overnight bags into the back of the blue van. Cathy handed over Ilene's purse while she settled the girls in back with sleeping bags donated by Stan.

"Ohmygod. I can't believe this is happening," Cathy sobbed.

The three friends hugged quickly. Ilene climbed in the front seat as the van rolled backward down the drive. Kevin steered north under a darkening sky through Two Harbors. Past Silver Bay. Stunned and confused, Hazy and Gladdy drifted in and out of sleep. Overcome by her own grief, more than an hour passed before Ilene found words.

Glancing in back at her children she conceded, "It's going to be so hard on them. Thank God they didn't see fire." She lit a cigarette. "Christ. What a nightmare! I'll never forget that day I came home from school and saw our house in flames. I was thirteen. Malibu, my tabby cat died from the smoke. I was devastated. Not about the house. I figured we'd get a new house. And new stuff." She sniffled. "But we never got a new house. We moved into an ugly little apartment. I couldn't even have another cat there. Then my dad left."

"Must be why you had such a fit about that cat back in December," he commented.

She looked at him, his eyes focused on the road ahead. Reaching over she touched his short brown hair that was combed straight back. "You cut your hair. Now you really look like a Fed. Did you come back to put us all in the witness protection program?"

"I'm not a US Marshal," he stated. "And you're not a government witness."

"Okay. So we're headed for Canada. What then?"

"Once we cross the border we'll head west for BC."

"How do we get through border patrol? They'll be looking for us."

"I don't plan to let them see you all. I'll just flash my badge and tell them it's official government business."

"You sound awfully sure of yourself."

"That's because I am."

"What if it doesn't work?"

"Then I'll have to start shootin' up the place."

Ilene sneered. "How can you be so sarcastic at a time like this."

"You're going to have to trust me now," he told her. "Like it or not, I'm all you got."

She sighed. "Haven't been to BC in years. Spent a couple months in Vancouver back in the seventies." She and Bill had explored the Pacific Coast searching for jobs and a place to live. "Maybe I should look up Hazy's father."

"Australia's one of the first places they'll look for you."

"How do you know about Bill?"

"It's in your file."

"Is there anything you don't know about me?"

"Plenty."

"Well here's a news flash for you. I found photos of Philip with a beautiful, mostly naked little French nurse. Giselle—he said her name was."

"Didn't know there were pictures."

"Christ. You knew about Philip's little weekend fling?"

"You and your husband were under investigation. Of course I knew."

"Was she a spy?"

He shrugged. "I don't know who she was. But she wasn't hired by the Bureau. Doesn't mean she wasn't an operative for someone else."

Clutching her temples Ilene groaned. "God. You knew about her. I spose you even knew where Philip's unit was before I did. Every time I turn around I remember something you said or did. And I realize there was always a double meaning. Christ. You listened to my phone calls. You probably knew how I felt about you before I did."

His eyes glanced toward the side mirror.

She shook her head. "I'm right. Aren't I? Everything you ever said or did had some hidden agenda."

"Not everything."

Disgusted, Ilene stared silently out the window. Her tears flowed like water until she slept.

She awakened in complete darkness to the sound of the driver's door closing. Rubbing her eyes, the horrible reality seeped through her consciousness like an oil slick. Peering through the windshield she watched Kevin walk to the edge of the wayside. Ilene could tell by the headlights, they were on a point along the lake shore. She saw him hurl something over the bluff. He walked deliberately back to the van and stepped behind the wheel..

"What was that?" she asked.

"My badge." Starting the engine he drove off.

"I thought you needed it to get across the border."

"I did. You slept through it. We crossed over a mile back. Said it would be easy." He pulled into the next gas station. "By the way. Don't use any credit cards or ID. Strictly cash."

"I'm not stupid," she sassed. While the girls remained in the merciful arms of slumber she used the restroom. Back on the road she asked him, "If we're going to Vancouver, why are you headed for Thunder Bay?"

"We'll turn off soon," he explained. "I wanted the Highway 61 border crossing. I knew they'd let me through with the badge. Not so easy at International Falls. This may be the long way round. But our trail's ice cold."

"So why did you toss it?"

"The badge? I'm through with the Bureau. They took me off the case. Not because I didn't do my job. Because I *couldn't* do my job. Gladdy's kidnapping. The fire. Philip. None of that should've happened. After I left in March, I found out how deep this goes. I tried to get you all under protection. But they turned down my recommendation."

"What did you find out?"

He stretched and rubbed the back of his neck. "Last year the Federal Reserve notified the Senate Finance Committee that they suspected the BCCI was in this country illegally doing business with National Bank. The Committee ordered an FBI investigation on National and the Singletons. Once I got those access codes, the Director ordered my supervisor and me to back off. The case was closed. Found out the order came from DOJ."

"Department of Justice."

"Convinced something was screwed, I took it to one of the Senators on the Committee. He went ballistic. Obtained a court order to proceed with the investigation."

"Senator Hunt," she guessed. "Now he's dead."

Nodding he continued, "Whenever I smell a rat, it's usually spelled CIA. I suspected they were using the BCCI to finance illegal weapons deals abroad. The BCCI made sure the funds could never be traced. And where do you turn when you need to make money or anything else disappear?"

"Organized crime," Ilene replied.

"No doubt the Federal Reserve and the Senate Committee pulled some strings to get Philip out of the country. That certainly paved the way for me breezing into the picture."

"But who destroyed our house?" Ilene lowered her voice. "Who killed him?"

"CIA," Kevin declared. "Looks like a classic mop up. Destruction of evidence. Termination of potential witnesses. That's how they operate."

"You said you knew something was going to happen. How'd you find out?"

"Process of elimination. I was tailed for weeks. The Senator died in a copter crash. The supervisor on the case was killed in a car wreck. My pickup exploded. All of a sudden the tail stopped. I went underground about forty-eight hours ago. Got a buddy back at Quantico who's an old timer. He covered for me and kept his ears open. Early this morning he contacted me about an explosives technician on his way to Duluth. Looks like they did this to keep the Singletons in line."

"Then you think the CIA gave Marie the videotape from the Radisson."

"If they did, they achieved two goals. Got me off the case. And got the Singletons on yours."

"Maybe they're the ones trying to kill me."

"No offense Ilene. They wouldn't waste the hit on a daughter-in-law they think is a slut," he said snidely. "Besides they already got the goods on you for extortion. Or embezzlement. Take your pick."

"So you think everyone knows about the money."

"That's absolutely certain."

"And what about the investigation?"

Kevin shook his head. "Dead in the water."

"So it was all for nothing. Just like the Gulf War. Saddam is bloodied but still in power. The CIA is jittery but still in control."

"You're catching on."

"Then I have to go back and testify. I have to make this mean something."

"Not a good idea."

"Why not?" she demanded. "Why should Philip's death be in vain? His own family did this to him! Why should they get away with murder?"

"Because they can," he insisted.

"No!" she objected stubbornly. "When we get to Winnipeg, I'll fly to Washington and give my testimony to the Senate Committee. Then I'll get protection."

"Forget it, Ilene. You're in shock."

"Call your buddy at the FBI and make the arrangements."

"No way."

"Listen to me. I have to make some sense of this. For Philip's sake."

He withdrew into a frustrated silence. Clinging to her newfound convictions Ilene smoked a cigarette, then dozed off.

Kevin pulled into the Red Oak Inn of Winnipeg shortly after 1:00 p.m. Saturday, June 1st. He turned to Ilene. She looked into his bloodshot eyes.

"Gotta get some sleep. I'll get us a couple rooms."

"Remember what I said," she badgered him. "I'm going back."

He rolled his eyes and slammed the driver's door behind him.

In the adjoining rooms, Ilene naturally teamed up with Hazy and Gladdy. After ordering room service for them she marched into Kevin's room unannounced. CNN was playing on the TV.

Standing in the bathroom doorway, stripped down to his briefs Kevin said, "Look. It's a lot less suspicious if we stay together. In one room."

She stared at him, remembering his body. "I don't think so."

He scratched his head. "Ilene. There's two double beds in here."

"I'll stay put."

"Cmon. We're way past this," he complained. "We can time share the damn room if you want."

She turned down the audio on the TV. "Before you fall asleep, call your buddy at Quantico. Get me a hearing. Or I'll do it myself."

"Listen to me," he argued. "It's not that simple."

Putting her hands over her ears she recoiled. "I don't want to hear it. Just do what I said." She stalked off to buy swimsuits for her and the girls at the hotel boutique.

When they returned to their room to change, Ilene saw Kevin dressed and walking the other way. He found her a little while later stretched out on a chaise by the outdoor pool, watching the girls from behind sunglasses in the shade of the courtyard trees.

He set an open newspaper on her lap. "Read the article."

The newspaper was today's *Chicago Sun-Times*. The headline of the article circled in blue ink on page two said, "Explosion Kills Gulf Vet." Ilene shivered as she read on.

"*In a peculiar twist of fate, an explosion occurred Friday evening in Duluth, Minnesota, at a property owned by Donald Singleton, President of National Bank of Chicago. When called to the scene of the burning home last night, Singleton and his wife, Marie of Evanston, positively identified the body of their youngest son, Philip Singleton of Duluth, who had coincidentally returned home from Army Reserve duty in Desert Storm last week. The younger Singleton and his wife Ilene, and their two daughters were living in the new home at the time of the explosion. The whereabouts of his wife and two children are unknown.*

"*Although the Duluth Fire Marshall initially indicated the blast was accidental, caused by a leak in the home's gas furnace, in a further twist, Marie*

Singleton, mother of the deceased, has publicly implicated the daughter-in-law in her son's death. In a hastily called press conference late last night in Duluth, Mrs. Donald Singleton claimed to have proof that Ilene Rosenthal Singleton used her husband's war absence to embezzle her share of the family fortune in cash withdrawals from his bank accounts. When he came home and found out, Mrs. Singleton alleges, the daughter-in-law then killed him in order to run off with another man. The wife's lover has not yet been identified, nor is it known whether he is alleged to have taken part in any embezzlement or murder scheme."

"Shit." Nauseated, Ilene set the paper down and buried her face in her hands.

Kevin sat on the edge of the chair next to hers and massaged her back. "Sorry. Heard it on CNN in the room. But you had to read it for yourself."

"It's incredible how they can manufacture a grain of truth into a pack of lies. If I didn't know any better I'd think I was guilty as sin."

"That's the idea," he uttered. "The point is you can't go back now. If they filed charges against you, the Committee can't hear your testimony until you answer those charges."

"What about immunity?"

He gritted his teeth. "You were never subpoenaed."

"That's it then." She tossed up her hands. "I've lost everything. For no good reason." Mopping her tears with a guest towel she snapped, "Fuck. I hate motels!"

Looking thoroughly exhausted, Kevin rubbed his reddened eyes. "Look. You're still alive." He glanced at the pool. "Got both your kids."

"But Philip's dead," she cried. "God! He was so mad at me. He threw me out."

"Maybe he was trying to protect you."

She hung her head. "And now we'll never know."

"He loved you," Kevin assured her. "That much I know."

"Thank you for that." She touched his kind but weary face. "You better get some sleep."

"I'm afraid you won't be here when I wake up," he confessed. "You're gonna go do something stupid."

She smiled weakly. "That's very funny, Kevin."

"It wasn't meant to be."

"It'll be easier if we split up here. I'll buy a car and head west with the girls."

He held her hands in his, so exhausted he looked to be on the verge of tears. "Let me take you all to Vancouver. Get you settled in."

"We shouldn't stay together."

"I'll move on from there." Tugging on the bridge of her sunglasses he looked in her eyes. "It's gonna be a long time before you stop blaming me for everything that's happened."

23

"From now on your name is Emily Matheson." Kevin handed Ilene a Canadian driver's license on Monday, June 10th. "Gladdy, your name is Greta Matheson and Hazy, you're Heidi."

She groaned. "I *hate* that name."

"Of course you do," he replied. "So get used to it."

"How'd you pull this off so fast?" Ilene asked.

He smirked. "Used to be my line of work. I know where to look. The money helped."

She studied the picture on her new driver's license. "Who is this?"

"You," Kevin told her. "I used the photo from your Minnesota license."

"But this person has short blond hair," she argued.

"The guy doctored it up on the computer. Looks good on you."

"No way, Kevin. I'm not messing with my hair."

Ilene let it go at that. She had no choice but to trust him now anyway. He'd driven them safely across Highway 1 to Vancouver without incident. Seemed like no one followed them. He'd only let her drive once for five hours so he could sleep again. Awake Hazy and Gladdy were whiny and quarrelsome. No doubt their sorrow and uncertainty caused some depression. At least they didn't ask a lot of questions. She hardly knew herself what questions to ask, so how could they. Luckily they slept a lot.

In the Canadian Rockies at Banff Sunday evening, Kevin had stopped and coaxed the girls to join him in a walk down a meadow trail. Ilene had helped Hazy and Gladdy pick an assortment of mountain wildflowers which they braided into a heart-shaped wreath. On the shore of Lake Louise at sunset they'd set it adrift "for Daddy." Standing there in all that mountain splendor, feeling as if she had just stepped off the edge of the earth, Ilene was thankful for Kevin's momentum propelling her forward. Tempted to succumb to her own grief she needed the time to regain her strength.

They'd arrived in Vancouver late Monday night, June 4th and stayed at the St. Regis Hotel only two days before Kevin helped them find a tiny, fourth floor, two bedroom furnished apartment on Keefer over by McLean Park. Each step forward for Ilene was easier than the last.

"This is temporary. Too many transients here. You need to blend in," Kevin advised her. "Find a house as soon as possible. Something with privacy."

The four of them had spent the week reconstructing their lives. They'd brought little else with them but the clothes off their backs. The adventure of shopping for new stuff revived Hazy and Gladdy.

By the time Ilene forked over twenty-thousand for a Volvo wagon she fretted, "The money's gonna go fast." The dealer was happy to take US currency at the going exchange rate of twenty-two percent.

Fearing the Duluth police or border patrol could've ID'd his van, Kevin unloaded that also. But he kept the Canadian currency without mentioning his plans.

In the new apartment kitchen that Monday afternoon, Ilene sifted through the phony birth certificates and documents that comprised their new identities. Picking up a travel packet she read aloud, "Passage for one on the Alaskan Ferry Line." Swallowing the lump rising in her throat she said, "You really are leaving."

"There's a safe house up in Whitehorse. I can chill out there for a good long while."

"When?"

"Wednesday. Tomorrow's my birthday," he revealed.

"Your birthday!" Ilene cried with delight. "June eleventh. Let me guess. The big three-o."

He smiled.

Later that evening Ilene left Hazy and Gladdy watching their new TV while she and Kevin walked over to Canada Place.

"I prefer they don't hear these warnings and instructions all the time," Ilene explained on the way. "They're still so fragile."

"Make sure they understand that everything's changed. Do whatever's necessary. Make it a game. They have to play along."

"They will. Gradually."

"Don't spend a lot on a house. Once you buy it, make it secure," he coached. "Never do anything to attract attention to yourself or the kids. Keep your distance from people. Be suspicious of everyone. Don't contact anyone from your past."

"What about Betty and Gail?" she asked.

"Then use letters. No return addresses. No phone contact. Tell them to burn your letters. In fact buy a house with a fireplace and burn all your mail. And be careful what you put in your garbage."

"Can we have a phone?"

He nodded.

"Buy a house with the jacks installed. Don't let the phone company or any other repairmen into your home. If something breaks, buy a new one."

"What about school? The girls don't have any records."

"Private schools ask fewer questions, as long as you pay the tuition."

"Can I get a job?"

He considered that. "Not at the University. Too predictable.

Develop some new career interest. Preferably not in banking."

Ilene slugged him. "So what should I do about the money?"

"Good question. I don't know. Stuff it under your mattress," he quipped. "You'll need cash anyway. Never use checks or credit cards. Especially ATM cards."

"Why?"

"They're traceable. A new account holder with no credit history stands out like a sore thumb." He glanced across the street and smiled mischievously. "Come with me." He escorted her over to the Hair Affair Salon.

The sign on the marquee said, *"Open Evenings."*

"Forget it. We don't have an appointment," Ilene objected.

Kevin sat her down in the reception area. "Wait here." He consulted with the receptionist, handing her a few Canadian bills. She summoned a male hairdresser and the three of them discussed Ilene from afar.

Momentarily the hairdresser called to her, "Come with me Ms. Matheson."

Glaring at Kevin she balked. "Is this really necessary?"

"Humor me. For my birthday." He winked at her and added, "Always wanted to see you as a blond."

Stiffly she perched in the chair and surrendered her thick auburn locks to the silver shears. Not all the tears that slipped down her cheeks during the treatment were from the chemicals in the hair coloring. An hour later she was transformed into a short-haired blond, close cut along the neck and lots of long wavy locks around the crown.

"Very sexy," Kevin whispered in her ear as they sauntered out the door. On their way back to the apartment, they picked up Chinese food and champagne. "For old time's sake," he said.

Ilene peeked in the girls' room to find they'd both fallen asleep in Hazy's bed with the TV blaring. Kevin glanced in over her shoulder.

"They've never shared a bedroom before," she confided. Turning off the set she closed the door to find her vision filled with Kevin. They stared into each other's eyes for one long moment. Then she gestured over her shoulder. "The room. Really slumming it for those two."

He blinked and backed away. "Hazy can take over the sofa bed after I'm gone."

Feeling the first breath of isolation looming on the horizon, her fingers searched for her new hairline. "I was just getting used to you again. Guess I wasn't expecting you'd leave so soon."

"That was the plan. It's not safe for us to stay together," he stated without betraying any emotion.

"I wish you'd stop making sense," she grumbled.

Leaning against the concrete block railing of the narrow lanai, the two of them shared the Chinese food out of the cartons and drank champagne from clear glass mugs she bought at the mall. From that vantage point, Ilene could see the ship traffic out on Burrard Inlet. Harbor lights twinkled in the darkening sky.

She sighed as the champagne gradually dulled the ache inside. "I suppose there's a lot worse places than this to start over."

"Don't get complacent. If you're uncovered. For any reason. You'll have to move on," Kevin warned.

She held up her hand. "Can we close up the Guide to Living in Exile for tonight?"

He frowned. "You need to take precautions."

"I'm going to miss you," she blurted as if it just dawned on her.

Almost like a reflex he tousled the soft blond locks spilling onto her forehead. His hand rested on her cheek. Leaning forward he kissed her lips. Touching those lips again a flood of memories washed over her. There in the last crimson rays of sunset over Vancouver Island, she let go of her despair and melted into his mouth and arms. They followed their passion into her bedroom. Behind the closed door, their bodies explored new boundaries with one another and tasted the bitter sweetness of what they might have had together.

Tangled around him afterward Ilene murmured, "Well if nothing else, we have great sex."

"Nothing else?" He sat up abruptly. "You actually think I've gone through all this just to get laid? Christ!" Pulling on a pair of shorts he stalked out of the room.

Surprised by his outburst, Ilene put on shorts and a T-shirt and padded after him. Standing on the lanai he breathed in the cool night air in deep sighs. She'd never seen him so raw with emotion. "It was a joke Kevin. I'm sorry," she apologized. "You must know how I feel. How grateful I am for everything you've done. You saved our lives. I don't know how we can ever repay you."

Turning his head slightly he said, "I didn't stay on this case because of some lofty notion about government corruption. Or organized crime. Or dirty banks. It's not about some noble principle. And it sure as hell isn't about sex."

Reaching out she grasped his arm. "Fine. Then would you please tell me what this is all about?"

"I don't believe this." Irritated, Kevin jammed his hands in his pockets. "I love you." He said the words with such exasperation.

Her hand fell limp at her side. "Then why are you leaving?"

"I'm like a signal beacon. They can track me down here too easily. When I left you back in March, it took the pressure off. You were safe. Until Philip came home anyway."

Ilene stared at the boats passing through the harbor. "Sometimes it feels like Philip died back in January. And it's actually his ghost I've been living with all these months."

"Gonna take awhile to sort it all out." The night breeze ruffled his hair. He ran his hand over it. "You'll be okay."

For Kevin's birthday Ilene and the girls took him to the zoo at Stanley Park. They presented him with a collection of comical snapshots they made of themselves at the corner drugstore photo ID machine. Ilene saw to it there was a set of her alone.

Even though they were together every minute, she had plenty of time to think about what he'd said to her the night before. His leaving now was like a prison sentence, a punishment for her crimes. That night after the girls fell asleep, he organized a duffel bag with his few belongings on the couch in the living room.

"What time is your flight? Or voyage. Whatever you call it."

"Seven a.m. Centennial Pier. About five blocks from here."

Ilene knelt down on the carpet beside him and laid her head on his lap. "I wish this night would never end."

Stroking her new hairdo he kissed the top of her head. She lifted her face and their lips met. Enticing him into her bedroom, she removed her clothes and seduced him with her mouth and tongue. The two of them made love together savoring the touch and taste and smell forever.

In the afterglow this time she said, "I can't believe how right this feels. Even though it's not supposed to be."

He kissed her. And they drifted off to sleep in each other's arms.

She awoke suddenly in the half light of dawn to the vacuum sound of a door closing. She looked at the clock. 6:30 a.m. Kevin was gone. Flying out of bed she pulled on a pair of jeans and a sweater. Fumbling with her tennis shoes, she raced out the apartment door. A cold drizzle was falling as she jogged down the sidewalk. Not knowing which direction to turn, she ran blindly tears streaming down her face. She stopped at the next corner looking frantically for sight of him. She noticed a male figure in a parka stepping out of a café more than a block ahead.

Sprinting madly she caught up to him and clutched his sleeve. "I forgot to tell you." The styrofoam cup splashed onto the sidewalk. "I love you. Too."

He looked sadly at the spilled coffee, then smiled and wrapped himself around her. They held onto one another in the foggy mist. Having run out of words to describe their feelings Ilene walked silently arm in arm with Kevin. The rain mixed with her tears.

At the pier the ship was loading passengers. Kevin turned to her. Holding her face in his hands he said, "Go back and take care of those girls. I'll be okay. And so will you. This isn't the worst thing that's ever happened."

"God. I wish it didn't have to be this way."

"I promise I'll come back."

He kissed her deeply for the last time. They embraced. The ship's horn blasted. He backed away. Standing alone she watched him board the vessel until he disappeared in a cluster of tourists. Another blast. Quickly the deck hands released the giant cables from their moorings and the boat floated away from the dock. Drenched and weeping, Ilene still mourned the loss of Philip. Numb with grief she shuffled along as the ship steamed toward the inlet. *And now Kevin.* Stopping at the end of the pier she relived every moment she had ever shared with him. And anguished over all they had left undone.